Burgstyle Publishing, LLC
Presents

GHETTO RÉSUMÉ

FREDDIE SIMMONS

Ghetto Résumé by Freddie Simmons

This is a work of fiction. The author has invented these characters. Any resemblances to actual persons, living or dead, are purely coincidental.

If you have purchased this book with a "dull" or "missing" cover, you may have purchased an unauthorized or stolen book. Please immediately contact the publisher advising where, when, and how you purchased the book.

Published by Burgstyle Publishing, LLC
Edit and layout by Carla Dean of U Can Mark My Word
Cover Design by Marion Designs

Library of Congress Control Number: 2008901438

ISBN-10: 0-9801864-0-4
ISBN-13: 978-0-9801864-0-6

Sales inquiries should be forwarded to:
Burgstyle Publishing, LLC
P.O. Box 13047
St. Petersburg, FL 33733-3047

Email: burgstylepublishing@verizon.net

GHETTO RÉSUMÉ

FREDDIE SIMMONS

GHETTO RÉSUMÉ

BY

FREDDIE SIMMONS

FREDDIE SIMMONS

ACKNOWLEDGEMENTS

First, I gotta give thanks to the Almighty Creator, because through him all things are possible. Second, I gotta thank my parents for coming up with the brilliant idea of bringing me into this word thirty-three years ago. I gotta tell you that you two have always been my role models. Dad, I plan to pay my debt to my sons and be the father figure to them that you are to me. Mom, I gotta praise you for always believing in me, because nobody knows your son like you! I take full responsibility for some of those grey hairs. Don't worry, though. This book is the fruits of your labor.

I gotta send love to my two baby mommas, Tanika and Sheniqua, for conceiving my two lil' men. To my handsome lil' boys, Lil' Fred and Dequan, you are my heart; every day I look at the picture of you both it breathes life into me and gives me the strength to make it through the day. I know that Daddy has been gone for awhile, but don't worry. When I touch, it's all good.

To my three beautiful sisters, Michelle, Adrienne, and Sonya. First, I gotta let ya'll know how much I appreciated having a key to all of ya'll cribs. It always came in handy. You three have always been there for me. Family means everything to me, and I just wanted to let ya'll know how much I appreciate the sacrifices you made to accommodate me during the bid. To my lil' brother Jason, you know I ain't got nothing but love for you. I just wanna let you know that all of the times you thought I was being hard on you, I was only trying to be a big brother and save you from coming to this place.

To my lil' nephew Dontrel, words can't express the love I have for you for looking after Lil' Fred. To my nephew Damien, you a man now. Man, how the years fly! To my lil' nephew Deontae, I know the lil' girls in school sweating you hard, but stay in them books. Don't neglect the females, but do your schoolwork first, and then attend to them. To my other lil' nephews, Deon, Dijon, Devon, and Lil' Jason, stick to that football, and I look forward to sitting up in them stands and watching. To my two beautiful nieces, Yafarah and Trai, I'm so proud of the women you have become. Keep doing your thang!

I gotta send shout outs to my uncle Harry Simmons, aka Dirty Harry. Keep your head up, Unc. You've been holding it down for twenty-five years now, living proof that the bloodline is pure. To my cousins on lockdown, E-Love and Deondre, keep your heads up, do the bid, and don't let it do you. To all of my other cousins, it's entirely too many of you to name. So, if somebody don't believe you, I'll verify that I'm your cousin.

I gotta send my love out to my partner _____. I know you shy and all, but I couldn't leave you out. You've been holding me down since as long as I remember. You are the true definition of a strong, black woman, and I cherish our friendship. Don't worry; you got your trip to the Bahamas that I owe you coming when I jump!

To my other lady friends, Reca, Adriana, Nichola, and Alice, good looking out!

To my nigga Cornelius Clark, hold your head up, my nigga. I just want you to know I dedicate this book to you, homie, and I feel your pain. I got nothing but love for you, my nigga. In me, you forever have a friend.

I gotta send shout outs to the Luciano Family: Mike, Clay, Clack, Greg, Von, D-Boy, Lee, Mr. Hughes, D.C., Steve, and Tomeka. L2K for life, niggas!

I gotta send a special shout out to my lil' prodigy Ryan Moore aka Crack, "Young Goldie". Damn, dawg, words can't express the love I have for you, lil' homie. Since day one, you've been *Ghetto Résumé*'s number one fan. Day after day, you were right by my side in the library, proofreading all the pages I typed, like a faithful employee. It's on and popping now! I'm a man of my word. So, just keep waiting at mail call for them hundred book of 37's I promised you and 50 mackerels.

I gotta send shout outs to the streets of St. Pete, from Play Lot 3, to James Town and James Park, Bethel Heights, 9th Street, Childs Park, and Pinellas Point for making me the man that I am today. I am my city; the Burg is in my veins!

I gotta give thanks to the people who made my work industry standard. My homeboy Keith of Marion Designs for designing the banging cover, magazine ad, and flyers. Your creativity runs wild! I gotta thank Shana Anderson for transferring my thick manuscript into a PDF file. I gotta thank the beautiful Carla M. Dean from U Can Mark My Word Editorial for polishing up my manuscript and putting the finishing touches on it.

During this bid, I've had the chance to run into some real niggas. This is the segment of my book when I give a soldier salute to all of the real niggas who, just like me, fell victim to a nigga that didn't wanna do no time. My nigga "Tampa's finest" Marlon Wright, Terry, Dave Brown, John Hudson, Drake, Griff, Black, Bobby Ingram, Frank, Upshaw, Leroy "46" Tillie, Vern, Digit, Pauldo, D-Reed, Alonzo Lee, Curt, Wayne "Pimp" Bennett, Wink, Ike Lane, Stanley "Tookie" Seabrooks, Taz, Gary, Curt, Sugarfoot, Cornbread, Black Jack, Juice, Slate, Jarvis Walters, Jerry King, The Kinloch's, Lil' John, Varsheen Smith, Big White, Fats, Cooley, Earl, Rodney, Mack, Fudge, Big "E", Demetrius, Glenn Williams, Torrie Hood, Fresh, Bullet, K.J., Kake, Murder, Carlos, Shiz-Mac, T.C., Coup, Friday, Sidney, Charlie, D.C. Ray, and Ronald Holly.

I gotta send a special shout out to my lil' homie Leon Collins for holding me down during the bid. You were the only nigga that came and visited me during the bid, and that meant a lot. Shout outs to my other homeboys Rick, Amp, and Marlo.

To my partner, bestselling author Mike Sanders, *Hustlin' Backwards* and *Snitch*. Good looking out on all of the insight. It's on and popping when we touch! If the streets only knew what we had in store for them! To my home girl, bestselling author Wahida Clark, *Thug Matrimony*, *Payback Is a Mutha*, *Thugs and the Women Who Love Them*, and *Every Thug Needs a Lady*, one love and thanks for the advice.

I gotta give special thanks to the best unit manager in the B.O.P., Mrs. Simmons, and one of the best secretaries I know, Mrs. Keel, for all of the photocopies.

To the two cowards that put me in here. You niggas tried your hardest to pronounce me dead, but you niggas didn't know that I'm like Morris the Cat and have nine lives! You niggas' punishment is not being able to look in the mirror because you know you crossed a good nigga. The funny thing is the crack law changed. So, I'm gonna be home sooner than you niggas thought!

Last but not least, this book is dedicated to all the dreamers. From the little girl in the projects, sitting on her porch doing her baby doll's hair, who says she wants to be a hairstylist, to the little boy on the basketball court shooting free-throws, who says he wants to be a NBA star. This book is inspiration to all of the convicted felons out there and everybody on lockdown. Determination is the key ingredient to turning dreams into reality. No matter what your situation may be, never give up on your dreams!

In conclusion, to all of my fans and future fans, as long as there is a demand, I'm your supplier. I'm gonna keep giving you that fire! I'm a hustler; it's all about supply and demand.

Freddie Simmons

PROLOGUE

The day was January 27, 1975.

"Yes, sir!" the little boy joyously shouted, restlessly laying in the fetal position.

With today being his scheduled release date, his body filled with bliss. Regardless of the fact that his parents were to blame for his current incarceration, his only concern now was his freedom. For nine long months, he had lived in total darkness and tight quarters, which were extremely uncomfortable to him. Ever since the first day of his sentencing, he had longed for this day to come. Now, it was finally here.

"We're almost ready!" the little boy heard a mysterious voice say.

The little boy's face lit up with an ecstatic smile. All he could do was visualize what waited for him on the other side. His body craved for a decent meal. Although during his stay he hadn't been fed much, it served as just enough for him to get by.

"This calls for a celebration!" the little boy said to himself. "As soon as I get up out of here, I definitely gotta get me a bottle of some of that top-shelf shit! I think I'm just gonna take things slow and peep everything out. Yeah, that's what I'll do; just chill in the crib until I'm able to get on my feet."

The little boy then examined his body. "Damn, your yellow ass ashy as hell! You look pale, too. You definitely gonna need some sun," he said to himself.

The little boy thought about his family. "I wonder what their first impression will be when they see me. All they've ever seen were some pictures of me during my confinement. I wonder if I resemble them."

The little boy sighed. "Man, I'm just ready to go home."

The little boy prepared himself for all the visitors that he knew were soon to come. He could hear their dreadful voices now...

"Ahh, gurl, he's so cute!"

"Ahh, don't he got the cutest little baby face!"

"Man, that lil' joker's yellow!"

The little boy grew impatient. "Damn, I wonder what time it is. That damn voice said they were almost ready for me over an hour ago! Okay, calm down, champ. Get yourself together. Have patience. Hell, you've waited nine long months. What's a couple extra hours gonna hurt you?"

The little boy turned over on his side and made himself comfortable. "In the meantime, I'll just get a little rest." He smiled, as he arrogantly thought, *I don't think the world is ready for me. Wait until they get a load of me!*

Meanwhile, an edgy woman was in a delivery room, pushing with all of her might. Balls of sweat dropped from her forehead, as she experienced excruciating pain that seemed as though it would never end. All she wanted was for it all to be over. Even though she had been down this road several times before, something seemed uncanny about this time.

During her pregnancy, she read several pamphlets that were scattered on the table in the waiting area of the OB/GYN office. One particular pamphlet in general had caught her attention: EDUCATE YOUR BABY WHILE IN THE WOMB. Curious, she picked the pamphlet up and immediately started reading it. The article was interesting. She never knew that reading while pregnant, as well as several other activities, could have a direct effect on a fetus.

So, from that day on, she began reading every night aloud. Every morning after waking up, she would prepare breakfast, and then position herself in front of the television for hours, watching educational programs for children while rubbing on her belly. Determined to raise a young Einstein, she recited arithmetic as she vacuumed the house, followed by repeating the alphabet backwards and forward, repeatedly.

For relaxation, she often played soulful music, like The Temptations, The Isley Brothers, Teddy Pendergrass, and a vast variety of The Motown Family. It always tickled her the way the baby always seemed to kick whenever the music played. This unprecedented approach was something she had not tried with any of her other kids. She just wanted to see for herself if in fact this theory was true.

"I see something!" the doctor shouted. "Push...push... we're almost there!"

The woman was perspiring heavily, showering herself in her own sweat. She tightened the vice grip she already had on her husband's hand, and made faces she would never want anyone to see her make.

"Feisty lil' fella!" the doctor said.

"Oh God...can you...please...please just get it out!" she shouted, while she violently swung her hair.

* * * * *

"Can't...seem...to get...this door open," the little boy uttered.

* * * * *

"Push...push...push!" the doctor screamed, as the baby's head appeared, displaying a head full of hair.

The woman braced herself, took a deep breath, and then bit her bottom lip. With a grimace on her face, she pushed with all the strength left in her.

"WHAA...WHAAA!" the little boy cried.

"Congratulations, ma'am! You're the mother of a healthy baby boy. And I do mean healthy!" the doctor said, amazed at the unusual size of the baby boy's penis. "Black folks!" the doctor said, shaking his head while still in disbelief at how hung the little boy was for a baby.

"Ahhhhh!" the little boy said, as he arrogantly stretched out his arms. "DAMN IT FEELS GOOD TO BE ON THE BLOCK!"

CHAPTER ONE

Born into this world Dequan Walker, son of Albert and Loretta Walker, he remembered his first ride home like it was yesterday. That was when he first saw her. The minute he laid eyes on her, he felt an immediate attraction. He thought about formally introducing himself to her, but he knew he was only a baby in her eyes.

In due time...in due time, he told himself.

From that day on, Dequan knew he would not have to look any further. It was imminent she was the one he would one day grow up and marry...THE STREETS.

When he arrived at what he assumed was his residence, Dequan had to admit he was not particularly enthused. As he stared out of the window, he saw little kids running around barefoot, while soggy Pampers hung off their butts. Alcoholics were sitting on their porches with their shoes off and cheap bottles of liquor turned up. The unfamiliar faces seemed to be content with their current living conditions. It was as though they lived by the "It is what it is" philosophy.

Today was not an ordinary day. It was a holiday, celebrated fifty-two times a year in ghettos all over the world. It was Friday, the day people in the ghetto rewarded themselves for a week's worth of hard work. Women would dress in their tightest fitting dress, fix up their hair, and throw on a little make-up, hoping to reel in a working man at the local bar who would be generous with his cash.

Dequan, he was just finally glad to get some light! And although he could not speak for the rest of them, he had already made up his mind to make his stay there as short as possible.

* * * * *

Over the years, Dequan picked up on things quicker than the other kids. By the time he turned seven months, he had kicked his walker to the side and started walking on his own. A month later, he inherited the name Goldie from his mother because of his high-yellow complexion. Not only did he inherit a nickname when he turned eight months, he also started talking around this time. Both of his parents stood around his crib, then looked at each other dumbfound when they heard his first word. "MoooNNNeeeYY."

All his parents could do was look at each other and laugh. Dequan's mother thought for sure his first word would be Ma Ma; whereas, his father thought it would be Da Da. Needless to say, he fooled them.

Throughout Dequan's entire childhood, he was more diverse than the other little kids. By the age of three, he was doing what some five-year-olds could not do, like riding bicycles, reciting the alphabet, and most of all, counting money.

Immediately after starting kindergarten, Dequan's teacher called his mother to inform her that he was functioning on a third-grade level. She went on boasting to his mother how in her twenty years of teaching, she had never seen a kindergartener as bright as Dequan. She felt confident he needed to skip kindergarten and go straight to the second grade. However, Dequan's mother felt a little uneasy about the whole situation, and wanted to take things slow and not jump the gun. Finally, after numerous debates and a couple of phone calls, the two of them reached an agreement, and after only spending three weeks in kindergarten, he was moved up to the first grade.

An education was something his mother demanded out of her five kids. With Dequan being the second youngest, he had three older sisters, Melissa, Adriana, and Ciera, and a younger brother, Jeff. Dequan led his younger brother by thirty-five months. His sisters were all five or more years older than he was and a year apart.

A month before Dequan's tenth birthday, there was an addition to their family. That year, his sister Adriana gave birth to a newborn baby boy. Although their living conditions were tight, being the strong woman that she was, Dequan's mother made the adjustments needed to accommodate her first grandchild. These conditions were only temporary until Adriana and her boyfriend's apartment was ready. Since Adriana was eighteen now and a mother, it was time for her and her boyfriend to get a taste of what the family life was like.

Although they did not have much, the house was always kept immaculate. Each child was assigned weekly chores, as well as the daily maintenance of their room. As a result, Dequan learned a lot at a young age. By five years of age, he knew how to iron, wash, and fold his own clothes.

"Baby, one day you gonna grow up and thank me for everything I'm teaching you now," his mother once told him. "None of my boys are gonna have to depend on a woman to cook or clean for them. They gonna be able to take care of themselves."

The only downside to living in the projects was they came furnished with unwanted pets. Even though they kept their place immaculate, there was no way to control the roaches or the rats. It was like their names were on the lease, also. There were nights Dequan would wake up thirsty, march downstairs, flick on the kitchen lights, and see a hundred roaches staring at him as if he had interrupted something. Raid didn't help! They drank that shit like they were thirsty camels in a desert. It seemed like the more they were sprayed, the bigger they got! Even the roach motels didn't help. To them, it was just that; ten of them would go in and thirty would come out.

The rats were no different. They were geniuses. It was as though they would peep around the corner and watch you while you put cheese in the trap, as if they were saying, "Look at this stupid motherfucker!" It was like they would take the cheese and dare you to put down some more tomorrow. Over time, Dequan's family just became content with the roaches, said fuck the rats, and started eating the damn cheese themselves.

For the first six years of Dequan's life, he and his father were inseparable. Being that Dequan was his first son, his father would showcase him to the whole world like he was a priceless jewel. Then things changed. Dequan's entire life made a 360 degree turn when his father started having an affair. With this ultimate change, things started crumbling in their household. Although he maintained a decent paying job, he used the excuse of petty hustling on the side as an alibi for his late-night rendezvous. Being that Dequan's mother was a CNA who worked the night shift, his oldest sister acted as his guardian.

Over the years, Goldie began developing a sense of emptiness. Although he remained a top student at his school, he felt alienated because he was not receiving the proper praise he deserved at home. He never faulted his mother. She did her best to show him and his siblings love and affection. Whenever she was off, Goldie received special attention. Not only did his mother set aside time to help him with his homework, but she was all ears to whatever he wanted to talk about.

It was his father he had grown to hate. He never understood how someone who once was so close could become so distant. Even though his mother tried her best to compensate for his father's absence, she could never give him the connection that only a father and son shared.

One day, Goldie asked his mother, "Ma, why Daddy don't love me?"

"Ahhh...baby," his mother said, taking him into her arms and cradling him in her bosom. She looked him in the eyes. "Why you say a thing like that?"

"'Cause we don't never do nothing!" Goldie pouted.

Goldie's mother could see the anger in her son's eyes. It was true that lately her husband had been neglecting the entire family. He wasn't the same man she had married. Lately, she was beginning to feel like the two of them were only roommates. For some strange reason, Albert always appeared anxious to leave the house, like he was living a double life.

One day, Loretta's curiosity got the best of her. Her inquisitive side decided she would do a little investigating of her own. It baffled her why it always took her husband several hours to arrive home from work when his job was only located a couple of blocks from their apartment. On this particular day, Loretta had a trick up her sleeve. She had been planning this for weeks. She lied to her boss, telling him that one of her kids was sick, so she could have the rest of the evening off. Since they had enough staff on hand to manage, her boss said yes.

"Dear Lord, please forgive me! I hope I didn't wish anything bad on my kids," she mumbled to herself.

Loretta had borrowed her best friend Sharon's car for the mission. As she headed towards her husband's job, she wasn't quite sure why she was doing what she was doing, but something inside of her felt the need to know if her husband was cheating. Their sex life had become non-existent. Lately, he complained about everything, such as her weight, what she wore, her hair, etc. For years, he had loved her cooking, but lately, the food no longer tasted the same to him.

"This man is tripping!" she used to say to herself.

Loretta wondered if she had competition. Was Albert having an affair? Part of her wanted to know the truth. Yet, another part of her was scared. The part of her that was scared knew all the visible signs were there, but she just didn't want to face the facts.

Loretta pulled into the apartment complex across the street from her husband's job and parked in a parking space. She checked her watch. It was 4:55 p.m. She had made it in perfect timing. As she tapped her fingers on the steering wheel, she sat back and staked-out the parking lot of her husband's job, like she was plotting on a major lick. Her mind was racing a hundred miles per hour. All she kept hearing was her best friend's last words...

"Girl, are you sure you're really ready for what you may find out?"

"I gotta know, Sharon. I mean, he just ain't been himself lately. I remember when we use to be a family. Now, it just seems like everybody's got their own agendas."

"Okay, girl," she remembered Sharon saying, before dropping her keys in Loretta's hand.

"Thank you, girl," she said, giving Sharon a sisterly hug.

Loretta snapped out of her daze. She repositioned herself and reclined the seat all the way back. She was camouflaged behind Sharon's dark tint, impatiently waiting on Albert to get off. After five long, nerve-wrecking minutes, Albert appeared in full view. Instinctively, she sat up in her seat.

"What's he so damn happy about? I haven't seen him that happy in years," she said to herself.

Albert waved goodbye to a couple of his fellow workers, and then jumped into the car. As Loretta cranked up Sharon's car,

Albert backed out of his parking space and circled the parking lot before exiting. He was in another world and never even noticed Loretta cunningly ease behind him. Loretta trailed him all the way down 16th Street. He made a left on 22nd Avenue, drove for a couple of minutes, and then made a right at the light on 9th Street. Loretta stayed three-car lengths behind, trying not to be detected. She almost lost him at the light on 9th Street and had to run a red light. Fear raced through her heart, but she felt relieved when she looked in her rearview mirror and there weren't any screaming police sirens behind her.

When Albert came to 50th Avenue, he made a left, drove for five blocks, then made a right and pulled behind a blue Chevy Corsica in front of a red brick house. Loretta circled the block. When she returned, her world would never be the same.

Albert was standing on the front porch with a beautiful, young woman. She was struggling to keep her housecoat closed with her right hand, while she affectionately rubbed the side of Albert's face with her left. The woman threw her hands around Albert's neck, and then the two of them shared an intimate kiss. They giggled after their kiss, then Albert was escorted inside of the house.

"Why...why...why!" was all she could manage to get out, as she violently beat her hands on the steering wheel. Tears rapidly showered her pants, like she was trapped inside of a thunderstorm.

A million things raced through her head. Where had she gone wrong? She evaluated herself in the rearview mirror. She saw a beautiful, light-skinned woman. Although she had gained a measly twenty pounds since the two of them first met, those additional pounds were from carrying HIS children. Loretta stood at about 5'5" and had a high-yellow complexion. She weighed 165 pounds, but carried most of her weight in her butt and thighs. She wasn't fat; she was just a little chunky. Was that what it was? Did Albert like petite women?

"FUCK HIM!"

The drive to the nursing home was a bumpy one. During the ride, Loretta started feeling like she was about to black out. She had stopped by a payphone and briefed Sharon on everything that had happened.

Sharon could hear in Loretta's voice that she was in no condition to drive. Although Sharon's car was brand new, Loretta by far was her main concern.

When Loretta pulled up in front of the nursing home, Sharon was already standing outside waiting on her.

"Girl, are you okay?" Sharon asked, as she walked over to the driver's side of the car.

"I'll manage," Loretta mumbled, reaching over and opening the door for Sharon, then slid over to the passenger seat.

Sharon could look at her friend and tell she was experiencing a nervous breakdown. She desperately wanted to help, but she didn't think it would be a good idea to pressure her.

"Cheating son-of-a-bitch!" Sharon said, observing the pain in Loretta's face. She knew when the timing was right, Loretta would eventually open up to her.

Besides the radio, the car was silent during the entire ride to Loretta's apartment. As Sharon turned into her apartment complex, Loretta wiped away her tears, preparing to enter her apartment. Sharon pulled in front of Loretta's apartment and parked.

"Are you okay?" Sharon asked, looking over at Loretta and placing her hand on hers.

Loretta looked over at Sharon and smiled. "I'll be fine." She grabbed her purse, then stepped out of the car and closed the door. "Thank you, Sharon," she said.

"Anytime," Sharon said, then threw her car in reverse and backed out.

Loretta paused on the sidewalk to retrieve her keys from out of her purse. Her nerves were so bad that her hands were still shaking. When she arrived at the front door, she paused and took a deep breath.

"Get yourself together, Loretta. You've gotta be strong for your kids' sake," she mumbled to herself. She stuck her key into the lock and fiddled with it. "Damnit, wrong damn key!" she yelled, frustrated.

Her hands couldn't seem to stop shaking, as she fumbled with her key ring, searching for the house key. When she finally found the right key and stuck it in the lock, the door opened.

Goldie instantaneously frowned when he noticed his mother had been crying. He studied her face. "What's wrong with you, Momma?" he asked.

Loretta kneeled down to Goldie's height, gave him a hug, and kissed him on the forehead. "Momma's alright, baby."

"Why you look like that then?" Goldie asked.

"Momma just had a bad day, that's all," she said.

"At work?" Goldie questioned.

His mother smiled. "Yeah, something like that."

Goldie poked out his chest. "Don't worry, Momma. When I get big, I'm gonna buy you a big ole' house, and you ain't gonna have to work no more either," he said, all in one breath.

Loretta smiled. Goldie's comments instantly brightened her day. She held the back of his head, and then smiled. "I'm gonna hold you to that," she said, pointing her finger at him.

"I promise!" Goldie said with authority.

"I'm gonna see. In the meantime, go run upstairs and wash up so you can help me out in the kitchen," Loretta said.

"Okay," Goldie said, and then stormed up the stairs.

Loretta headed towards her room. When she made it there, she closed the door behind her and started undressing.

"Maybe I'll feel better after a nice hot shower," she said to herself.

She walked into the bathroom and turned on the shower. While waiting for the water to get hot, she walked over to the bathroom mirror and studied herself.

"You are a strong black woman! You're gonna make it through this! You're not gonna let a man bring you down, you hear me? You have five kids out there that need you. Now get yourself together!" she ordered the woman in the mirror.

When the steam from the running, hot shower made her face no longer visible in the mirror, she walked over to the shower, pulled back the curtains, and stepped in. She received instant gratification, as the hot water seemed to serve as a temporary antidote for the day's disaster.

Fifteen minutes later, a rejuvenated Loretta emerged from the shower. As she reached for a towel, she heard the bedroom door open. It was Albert.

"Stay calm, and just handle this like a woman," she said to herself.

After taking a deep breath, she calmly walked into the bedroom. Albert was sitting on the edge of the bed taking off his shoes when she entered.

Loretta walked over and stood in front of him, then crossed her arms and said in a calm voice, "We need to talk."

"Look, Loretta! I've had a hard day at work today. I just wanna take me a hot shower and rest!" Albert said, while standing and removing his work clothes.

"I'll join you in the shower then!" Loretta challenged, with her hands on her hips.

Albert slid out of his pants. "Like I just told you, I'm tired. All I wanna do is take me a hot shower by MYSELF...and lay down!"

Loretta sucked her teeth. She remembered the days when Albert wouldn't have thought twice about taking her up on her offer. Somewhere, somehow, he had lost interest in her. He was no longer attracted to her. She had lost him to another woman. But why? Was it just because the woman she had seen him with was beautiful? What about her? What about their family? Was she really worth leaving behind his family? Had he ever loved them?

Loretta dressed quickly, and the minute Albert disappeared inside of the bathroom, she rushed over to where his boxers were laying. She stared down at them, took a deep breath, and then picked them up. She instantly became delirious the moment her eyes spotted the cum stains inside of his boxers.

Furious, she stormed out of the bedroom and into the kitchen. She was in a frenzy, searching for the first knife she could put her hands on. Recklessly, she opened the kitchen drawer. Once she found a butcher knife, she slammed the kitchen drawer shut and stormed back into the bedroom. Albert was just stepping out of the shower and returning into the bedroom when she entered.

"How could you?" Loretta said, sniffling. "After all of these years!"

"What are you talking about?" Albert asked, baffled as he dried off.

Loretta charged over to Albert's boxers and lifted them up with the knife. "This is what I'm talking about!" she shouted.

Albert looked like a deer caught in headlights, as she charged over in front of him.

"I followed you today, Albert! Followed you to your lil' skeezer's house!"

Damn, I'm busted, Albert thought as he walked off.

"I'm talking to you, Albert!" Loretta said, spinning him around.

Albert gave her one of those "do that shit again" looks, before attempting to walk off again.

"All I want to know is why, Albert? After all we've been through over the years. Where did I go wrong? What did I do? Do you still love me, Albert? Do you love us? Damn it, I need answers!" Loretta said, violently charging towards him with the knife in her hand.

Effortlessly, Albert sidestepped her and snatched the butcher knife from out of her hand.

"Why...why...why, Albert?" was all she kept repeating, as she ferociously beat her hands on his chest and sobbed.

Albert was empathetic. He just stood there, taking every single lick, while wondering to himself just what he had gotten himself into.

When Goldie heard his mother's cries, he heroically stormed into his mother's bedroom and into her arms. "What's wrong, Momma?" he asked.

"Momma's okay, baby. Daddy's just leaving, that's all," she said, eyeing Albert.

Goldie shot his father a look that was equivalent to ten rounds of 9mm shells. Albert studied his son and saw the fire inside of his pupils. That startled him. He had never seen that much evil in a man's eyes, let alone a kid. Goldie's eyes were locked in on his father's, like they were two cowboys facing off in a duel.

Goldie's eyes were bloodshot red. His mouth was tight, and his fists were balled up. "I hate you! I hate you! If you ever try and hurt my momma again...I'll kill you!" he lashed out.

Loretta and Albert both looked at each other in shock.

"Goldie!" his mother yelled. "Tell your father that you don't mean that!"

Goldie looked at his father and gritted his teeth with a grimace on his face. "Yes, I do!" he retorted with a straight face.

"Go to your room!" his mother ordered. Loretta was puzzled, wondering what could have provoked Goldie to say such a thing.

Goldie did not budge. He was still courageously staring his father down. It was a standoff.

"Goldie, I said go to your room!" his mother repeated, wiping away the tears that had just recently fell.

Goldie kept a visual on his father, as he slowly headed towards the bedroom door. Albert was speechless. Goldie opened the bedroom door, but not before spinning around and making an animated hand gesture at his father, as if he had just shot him with an imaginary gun. Goldie blew his finger, then smirked at his father and exited the room.

Albert's mouth dropped to the ground. Although he stood 6'5" and weighed a whopping 230 pounds, a 100-pound ten-year-old had just scared the living shit out of him.

Loretta was worried about her son. He had been through so much emotionally over the years. It was sad to say that even though his father lived under the same roof as him, he had still pretty much grown up fatherless. Loretta knew she had to make a critical decision, and she wondered if it would affect Goldie's future if she were to kick Albert out.

Shit, he ain't been doing nothing but taking care of him financially anyway, she reasoned with herself.

Although Goldie had yet to hit puberty, she felt like he was a twenty-year-old man trapped inside of a ten-year-old body. For some strange reason, it seemed like there was something supernatural about him, like he had been here before. He was extraordinary in every way imaginable, and was way ahead of any of the kids his age. Not only was his IQ higher than some of the project people's beacon scores, but his grades were impeccable, and it hurt Loretta that everybody except his own father saw it.

"Get out, Albert!" Loretta ordered, pointing towards the door.

Albert grabbed his keys from off of the dresser and walked to the door. Before leaving, he paused and asked, "Are you sure this is what you want, Loretta?"

Loretta lifted her head up from out of her hands. "No, Albert...this is what you wanted!"

"Can't we just...?"

Loretta jumped up off the edge of the bed. "Go, Albert!"

Albert just nodded his head. "Okay, if that's how you want it," he said, and then disappeared out of the door.

When he got to the front door, he paused for a minute. How did he ever become the enemy in his own house? Or was it still his house? There was no one to blame but himself. He took a deep breath. He had made his own bed, and now it was time to lie in it. Albert exited the apartment.

Loretta's daughters were just coming down the stairs when they witnessed their father walking out of the door, looking like he had lost his best friend.

"Momma, where's Daddy going looking all sad?" Ciera asked.

"Daddy's just leaving us for awhile, that's all. Everything's gonna be fine," Loretta said, managing a fake smile. "Just as long as I got my babies, that's all that matters," she added, reaching out her arms as the four of them shared in a group hug.

Meanwhile, Goldie was upstairs furious, his blood boiling. "I hate his motherfucking ass!" he yelled, with venom in his voice.

"Who you hate, Goldie?" Goldie's younger brother, Jeff, asked.

Goldie eyed him with a frightening look on his face, appearing to be possessed. Jeff looked at Goldie and was scared to death.

"Momma!" Jeff screamed, as he shot out of the room, looking like he had seen a ghost.

Goldie's tantrum escalated. At the moment, he wanted to hurt something. So, he charged over towards the wall and violently started punching it until he started crying. Ironically, these tears were coming from all of the pain he had built up inside, not from the pain that seemed non-existent from his now bleeding knuckles.

Breathing heavily, Goldie plopped down on the edge of his bed, but not able to sit still, he jumped back up and started kicking his dresser.

"Fuck this shit!" he said, pacing the room. "I don't need to have no stupid daddy to throw no damn football with! I don't need no stupid daddy to be proud of my grades! From now on, I'm gonna be my own damn man! I don't need no stupid daddy for nothing!"

Goldie walked over and stared into his bedroom mirror. "From now on, I'm gonna take care of myself!"

CHAPTER TWO

For as long as Goldie could remember, he had been a hustler. Every morning before going to school, he would stop by the corner store and buy fourteen packs of Now & Laters with the $1.40 his mother would give him for lunch. He had the white kids at school on lock! Unfortunately, for them, they didn't have the luxury of a corner store in their bourgeois neighborhoods. And even if they did, their uppity parents weren't going to stop for any candy on their way to dropping them off at school. That's were Goldie, The Candy Man, came in. Since they were little rich kids, he charged them 25 cents a pack. He would take orders for the next day, while taxing the shit out of them. Even at a young age, it was all about supply and demand for Goldie. The more he made the more inventory he stocked.

He was an independent and persevering ten-year-old going on twenty. See, in the projects you matured at a younger age. In all actuality, you could say he was a man trapped inside of a young boy's body. Goldie's parents furnished him with all of the basic necessities the best that they could, while he hustled on the side for all of the material things he desired.

At the time, they resided in a Jamestown apartment complex. When the Laurel Park Projects were torn down, the government moved many of the tenants into Jamestown. That was over three years ago. Jamestown was the neighbor to James Park, a lower income apartment complex that mostly housed single parents. To

Goldie, both were pretty much the same, with only a fence separating the two complexes. Although Goldie's family was borderline poor, they were surviving off both his parents' income and weren't receiving any government assistance at the time.

After one week at Goldie's grandmother's house and another staying at a roach-infested hotel, his father returned home. Although Loretta had kicked him out, for the children's sakes, she both overlooked and forgave him for cheating. Being a strong, smart black woman, she knew she had to look at the big picture because she didn't want her kids growing up without a father in their household. So, after numerous lonely nights of sitting around and listening to Betty Wright, she took Betty's advice and decided having a piece of a man was better than having none at all. After all, being that the two of them were married, she had vowed to tough it out for better or for worse. She hoped Goldie and his father could see eye to eye and preserve their relationship, but little did she know, Goldie was already far gone!

* * * * *

SUMMER OF '85

Knock...knock...knock.

"Who is it?" Goldie asked, already knowing the answer to his question.

"It's me!" D said.

"What's up, nigga?" Goldie said after opening the door and leading the way into the living room.

D and Goldie had been friends ever since Goldie's family moved to Jamestown. They shared a lot of the same likes and dislikes. However, D was not as smart as Goldie.

While D waited in the living room, Goldie ran upstairs to grab his Chuck Taylor's. When he came back downstairs, they were just about to leave, when Goldie's oldest sister, Melissa, stopped him at the door.

"Don't be where you ain't supposed to be. And don't make me have to come looking for you either!"

"Whatever," Goldie said, waving her off, as he and D bounced up out of the apartment.

It was 9:30 a.m. and a sunny day outside. Goldie and D were en route to get their hustle on. Their first stop was across the street from Goldie's apartment complex. In front of the building stood three newspaper machines, which also served as Goldie's slot machines. See, he had this technique where he would insert the coins into the machine, and then open the machine while simultaneously hitting the coin return. As a result, the machine would open and the coins would drop back out. Depending on the time of day, there would usually be anywhere between twenty to thirty newspapers in the machine. Not wanting to look obvious, Goldie would only grab five to seven newspapers per machine, and average hitting anywhere from five to six machines, until he and D had accumulated thirty newspapers. Next, they would grab one of the shopping carts from out of the parking lot, and load it with the newspapers. Afterwards, it was off to the mango tree.

Once at the mango tree, Goldie would climb to the top of the tree and pick about ten to fifteen of the ripest mangos, before they moved on to the pecan tree. Goldie and D then went to work to fill the sandwich bags that Goldie had taken from out of the kitchen cabinet. Those plastic bags were the ones Loretta used to pack Albert's sandwiches, and if she knew Goldie was pinching off them, she would have had a fit.

Fuck him! He can put his damn sandwiches in his pockets for all I care, Goldie thought.

After filling ten bags with pecans, they headed downtown to catch the twelve o'clock afternoon rush. Stocked with thirty newspapers, ten mangos, and ten bags of pecans, which they would sell for 50 cents apiece, they stood to walk away with twenty-five dollars if all went well.

They posted up in between McCory's and Walgreen's, where the majority of the lunchtime traffic came through. Goldie was indeed one helluva salesman. Using the good ole' "I don't got any change" tactic, he persuaded every customer that presented a dollar bill to purchase a mango or a bag of pecans with the newspaper. By 12:15 p.m., they had sold out of everything.

"That's a rap!" Goldie told D, as he handed their last customer a newspaper and a mango in exchange for a dollar.

With their mission complete, just as planned, they were walking away with twenty-five dollars. Goldie paid D ten dollars, and by being the brains of the operation, he kept fifteen for himself.

"Dang, Goldie! Why you always gotta get the most money?" D pouted.

"Cause, nigga, I'm the boss!"

D just bit his tongue and gave him a stupid look.

When they made it back to the park located in the center of the projects, Goldie noticed all of the older cats were out. The park was the center stage were all of the older dope boys with rank would post-up. Since the park was located in the center of the projects, it is where the majority of the traffic flowed. Crack was in popular demand, and people from all over the city, both white and black, came through itching for a fix. While some auctioned off their food stamps, others sold their jewelry, televisions, and even their bodies. It was routine to find used needles, empty baggies, and used condoms on the ground from the night before.

Goldie was fascinated with the type of attention the dope boys received, especially from the girls who would get all dressed up just to stroll down the sidewalk hoping to be noticed. You should've seen them with their hair all done and lipstick on, wearing bicycle shorts tight enough to catch a yeast infection. And as always, the nigga with the most money got the finest female.

That was Snake. Snake was well known throughout the projects, as well as feared in the streets. At nineteen years old, Snake was sitting fat. He showcased the type of expensive jewelry the rappers wear on *Yo! MTV RAPS*. He owned two tricked-out vehicles, a Fleetwood Cadillac and an Audi 5000, as well as a street-bike, which gave him the rights as a GHETTO CELEBRITY.

Snake had moved out of the projects and into his own crib when he was only seventeen years old. That was rule number one of the streets: NEVER LAY YOUR HEAD WHERE YOU WORK. Besides his workers in the projects, he had a couple of lil' niggas in traps who he fronted work, not to mention all of the other niggas in the city he sold work to. His rocks were so big that even if you didn't like the nigga, you still had to do business with him just for money's sake.

Snake had lost both of his parents to the streets when he was ten years old. It was then that his pop caught a FED case. His father was a local street hustler named Bo, who slipped up and got caught in a pool hall with 200 bags of heroin. When the FEDS started pressuring him and told him that he was facing thirty years, he cracked under pressure. When word got back to the streets that Bo was snitching, his connect felt like he needed to send him and the streets a powerful message.

One night, when Snake and his mom were home all alone, they heard mysterious noises. Donna protectively instructed her son to go inside of her room and hide, as she frantically reached inside her purse and pulled out a .22 semi-automatic. Gun in hand, she searched the house for intruders, her .22 leading the way. Once in the living room, she noticed one of the windows was open. Fear raced through her entire body, leaving her motionless for a couple of seconds. She terrifyingly turned around, and when she did, it was already too late. One of Donna's assailants grabbed her by the mouth and lifted her off the ground, while his accomplice removed the gun from out of her hand.

When Snake heard the cries of his mother and the physical struggling coming from the living room, he panicked. Tears began racing down his eyes and his body started to tremble. Snake was furious! He felt defenseless. His mother was in the living room being strangled, and his father was nowhere around to protect them. Why were they there? What did they want? Did his father owe them money or something?

Snake made a decision. He heroically rushed into the closet and grabbed his father's .38 special from out of the shoebox he had seen him put it in on numerous occasions.

"Somebody's in the room!" Rodney told his partner Ray.

Cautiously, Ray walked towards the bedroom. Upon reaching it, he pulled out his gun and kicked in the door, only to find Snake standing in front of him with a .38 special pointed straight at him. Snake closed his eyes, and then let off two shots.

BANG...BANG

Both shots hit Ray square in the upper torso, as his body lifelessly fell to the floor. When Rodney heard the discharge, he dropped Donna's body to the ground, then pulled out his .45 and headed towards the bedroom.

Snake was in the room hysterical. He heard footsteps rapidly approaching. The minute the door cracked and a dark shadow appeared, he unloaded the rest of the bullets remaining in the gun.

The house instantly became quiet. Snake stood frozen, smoking gun in hand, wondering if there were others. After waiting a few minutes, he stepped over the dead bodies and rushed into the living room. He heard sirens approaching, and saw his mother lying on the floor.

"Momma...Momma...get up!" Snake frantically yelled.

The living room curtains ruffled, and the room instantly became frigid. Snake held his mother's body as he called her name, but there was no use. She couldn't hear him. Donna was dead.

After his mother's funeral, Snake was never the same. When word got back to him that his father was the reason for his mother's death, he hated his guts. Snake wished his father were the one dead. Bo had made a crucial decision that had jeopardized his entire family.

Meanwhile, in jail, Bo was catching hell. When word got back to him about Donna's death, he was crushed. What hurt him even more was when he found out Snake was being placed in foster care. The funny thing was Bo only ended up catching five years. The thirty-year sentence the FEDS had threatened him with was all a bluff. Bo had cracked under pressure, and it had cost him dearly. Bo found himself sitting in his cell, deliberating and trying to figure out how he would make things right with his son, but if only he knew; it wasn't possible.

Word on the street was that Snake waited patiently until his father got out and killed him. Bo's death was ruled drug related due to the amount of drugs found scattered around his body. Plus, the fact of the matter was that the police knew Bo was one of theirs.

Snake resented a snitch. A snitch had caused his mother her life. And, in return, revenge had caused his father's his. Snake's aunt had rescued him out of foster care when he was eleven years old. She was a family-oriented woman and felt that family needed to be raised around family. Therefore, she moved him in. As Snake grew up in the projects, he learned the ropes of the street. His promise to his aunt as a kid was that as soon as he got a hold of some money, he was gonna move her out of the ghetto. And he did just that.

Over the years, Snake climbed to the top of the ladder. He initially started off as a runner, and then moved up to serving on the block until he graduated to his current status, THE MAN, who Goldie idolized because of all his respect, money, jewelry, clothes, and dime pieces at his disposal. Goldie was familiar with the entire operation, and at the time, he was taking in every aspect of the game.

Today was the first of the month, and traffic in the projects was ridiculous. Everybody and their momma had been impatiently waiting on the mailman all day. The minute he finally came, you would've thought an evacuation had been ordered the way people anxiously stormed out of their apartments, rushing to go and cash their check. Goldie loved that shit and stood in a daze, daydreaming about the day he would become THE MAN.

"Yo, shorty, come here!"

Goldie pointed at himself. "Who me?"

Snake nodded his head. "Yeah, let me holla at you!"

Goldie walked over, and then asked him, "Yeah, what's up?"

"Wanna make a lil' change?" Snake asked.

Goldie's eyes lit up. "Yeah!"

Snake peeled off a dub. "Won't you and your lil' partner go grab me a Nehi peach soda from the store. Ya'll can keep the change," he said, handing Goldie the dub.

Thinking about the extra nineteen dollars and some change he knew would be leftover, Goldie's eyes lit up brighter than Christmas lights. He stuck the twenty in his pocket, and he and D were on their way.

Fifteen minutes later, the boys arrived back at the park and wondered why an unusual crowd of people was gathered at the park. Nosey, Goldie made his way towards the crowd. He had Snake's Nehi soda in a brown paper bag, and wanted to give it to him while it was still cold. When the two got a little closer, they noticed one of Snake's soldiers had a man pinned face down on the ground. D stopped dead in his tracks, while Goldie boldly proceeded to walk closer to get a front row view of the action. Goldie saw Snake go into his trunk and return with a Louisville slugger bat in his hand. Goldie smiled because knew some action was about to jump off.

"So you wanna be muthafuckin' friends with the police, huh? Tell me what the fuck you're doing talking to Detective Ross?" Snake asked in a persuasive tone.

"I wasn't talking to no cop, Snake! I swear!" the man cried.

"So you calling me a muthafuckin' liar? Huh?" Snake challenged.

"No, Snake…I'm just —"

"Shut the fuck up!" Snake said, issuing Pookie a vicious body shot with the bat.

"Ahh shit!" Pookie cried. "I swear..I swear!" he pleaded.

"Come here, Gina," Snake ordered.

Gina, a crackhead from the projects, made her way through the crowd. Everybody knew Gina was one of those people who always mysteriously seemed to see you, even when you never see her.

Snake placed his hand on Gina's shoulder. "Tell me what you saw?"

"Well, the other day, I saw Pookie hopping out of Detective Ross' car. When he stepped out of the car, I saw him stuffing something inside his pocket. I knew he was up to no good, because he was looking around all paranoid, trying to see if anybody saw him. He didn't see me, though!" Gina said, showing off her gold tooth. "I was turning a trick, giving some smoking head! When I looked up, that was when I saw the whole scene unfold."

"Thank you, baby," Snake said, patting Gina on the shoulder and handing her a couple of rocks.

"Stankin' bitch," Pookie mumbled under his breath. "Muthafucker will do anything for a damn hit."

Then Pookie thought to himself, who was he to talk? The truth had been exposed, and now, he had to face his consequence. He felt uneasy knowing how much Snake resented snitches. He took a deep swallow over the lump in his throat. He knew for a fact he had fucked up. Pookie spent his last seconds getting right with God.

Snake was fuming. He hated a lying motherfucker, let alone one that lied to his face. He walked around Pookie's body, and then violently kicked him in the ass. "Muthafucker, don't you know I got eyes everywhere? And then you got the audacity to sit here and muthafuckin' lie to my face? Muthafucker!" Snake yelled, issuing numerous horrendous blows to wherever his bat landed on Pookie's body.

With each blow, blood splattered everywhere. Snake's crew couldn't let him have all of the fun, though. So, they all joined in and commenced to stomping the shit out of Pookie.

Goldie just stood there and observantly watched everything. For the most part, he wished he had some popcorn. To him, this was better than the movies. He was enjoying every minute.

"Let this be a lesson to any and every muthafucker!" Snake said, looking around and holding his bloodstained bat in the air like Joe Clark to all of the observers. "This is what happens to snitches!" Snake said, issuing yet another blow to Pookie's already lifeless body, which lay in a river of blood.

"Get this hot muthafucker outta here before he makes my muthafuckin' block hot!" Snake ordered, breathing heavily.

Pookie was placed into the trunk of a hooptie and driven off the premises.

Snake looked over at Goldie and motioned for him. "Hey, Shorty, bring me my soda! I'm thirsty!" he humorously said, as he wiped the beads of sweat off his forehead, and him and the remainder of his crew started laughing.

CHAPTER THREE

"Man, it's boring!" D said, throwing rocks across the field.

It was three o'clock in the afternoon, and the boys were just sitting at the ditch, throwing rocks.

"I got an idea. You got your library card on you?" Goldie asked.

"Yeah, why?" D replied.

Goldie walked over and picked up his bike. "Let's go to the library," he suggested.

D shrugged his shoulders, then walked over and picked up his bike. When he hopped on his bike, Goldie took that as a yes. So, in turn, he hopped on his bike and led the way.

The library was a place they visited at least once a week. Goldie enjoyed pulling up old newspaper slides and viewing the city's history.

Fifteen minutes later, the boys arrived at the public library, chained up their bikes, and walked inside. For a summer, the library was empty. To Goldie, the library served as an adventure for him. Truthfully, the bulk of the knowledge he had obtained over the years was credited to his frequent visits to the library. A speed-reader, Goldie had this system where he would spend an hour per book thumbing through the pages.

"Hey Goldie, I'm going upstairs to the kids' section!" D yelled, heading towards the stairs.

"Alright," Goldie said, heading the opposite direction toward the Black History section.

He saluted all of the early pioneers who lived in such an harsh era, but still managed to persevere for what they believed in. Such people like Harriet Tubman, Martin Luther King Jr., Malcolm X, Sojourner Truth, W.E. Dubois, and Rosa Parks were all prominent leaders to him. After reading several sentimental books on slavery, he was immediately able to derive where blacks obtained their strength. It made him think that maybe he did not have it so bad after all. He had to respect his ancestors. After putting himself in their shoes, it was then he realized that life was what you made of it. His theory on life was that every generation made sacrifices so that the next generation could live a more affluent life.

Goldie was seated at a table in the Black History section, engaged in challenging his mind by reading a couple of high-school level books. A librarian walked over and studied him with an imaginary question mark floating above her head.

"Can I help you with something?" she asked.

Goldie glanced up at her, then smiled. "I'm fine."

"Looking at pictures?" she probed.

Goldie laughed and decided to give the librarian an earful. "Actually, I'm reading."

Baffled, she sat down next to Goldie. "Do you mean you can actually read these types of books?" she asked in disbelief.

"About ninety-five percent of it," Goldie arrogantly boasted. "I usually have to look up some of the big words, though, and break them down into syllables."

"Mind reading me a chapter?" the librarian asked.

Goldie decided to entertain her. "Sure!"

For the next fifteen minutes, Goldie flawlessly read to the librarian non-stop. In her twenty years of working at the library, she had never seen a kid so gifted. Kids like Goldie made her love her job.

"Brilliant, simply brilliant!" the librarian cheered, while extending her hand for him to shake. "I'm Mrs. Bryant. If there's anything you need, don't hesitate to ask."

"Okay," Goldie replied.

The librarian patted Goldie on the back, then walked off to attend to her duties. When Goldie looked up, he saw D heading over towards him. D pulled up a chair, then leaned over and looked at the book Goldie was reading. "

"How you read them big ole' words in them books?" he asked.

"Because...I'm really a man trapped inside of a boy's body," Goldie joked.

"Funny!" D said.

Goldie closed the book, then stood up. "You ready to go?"

"Yeah, let's dip!" D said.

Goldie gathered all the books, then walked over and placed them back on the shelves where he had gotten them. Before leaving, Goldie waved when he passed Mrs. Bryant's desk. Mrs. Bryant smiled, then waved back. Three-fourths of the way to the front door, D stopped dead in his tracks, then reached into his pockets.

"Man, what you doing?" Goldie asked.

D did not answer him. His eyes were closed, and it looked like he was about to flick the dime he had pulled out of his pocket into the wishing well.

Goldie just shook his head. *I know he don't think that this shit really work.*

After D made his wish, he flicked his dime into the wishing well, and then opened his eyes to watch his dime descend to the bottom of the well.

"Come on, Goldie, try it!"

Goldie walked over to the well, reached into his pocket, and pulled out a quarter. He then closed his eyes, made a wish, and flicked the quarter into the wishing well. Goldie opened his eyes, then looked over at D.

"Happy?"

"Why did you toss a quarter instead of tossing a dime like me?" D asked.

Goldie smiled. "Since my wish was probably bigger than yours, I figured I needed to toss a bigger coin," he said, grabbing his stomach and laughing.

"You always gotta do something better than somebody!" D said.

On their way out of the door, Goldie accidentally bumped into a girl who was coming inside. Kneeling down, he helped her pick up the VCR tapes he knocked out of her hands.

"Sorry!" he said, while handing them to her.

"That's alright!" the girl said, blushing.

It was not until Goldie really took a good look at her that he realized how beautiful she was. The two stood motionless for a couple of seconds, speechless, lost in each other's eyes. It was love at first sight.

"Come on here, girl! You know I gotta be to work!" the girl's mother screamed, interrupting the two.

The little girl took one last look at Goldie, but not before saying, "Bye."

Before he walked out of the door, something told him to turn around. Coincidentally, when he turned around, he was surprised to see the girl had done the same thing.

Who is she, he said to himself.

"Come on, Goldie!" D said, snapping him out of his daze.

Goldie watched the little girl and her mother disappear around the corner, then he exited the library. D was at the bicycle rack, and had already unlocked both bikes. During the entire ride back to the projects, Goldie's mind was distant. For some strange reason, no matter how hard he tried, he could not seem to get the girl's face out of his mind.

The girl's mother impatiently checked her watch, as her daughter browsed through the list of movie rentals. After obtaining two of the newer movies, the girl and her mother headed towards the front door.

Her mother irritably spun around when she noticed she was walking by herself. "Girl, what's wrong with you?" she asked in an aggravated voice.

"Let me get a quarter," the little girl asked, standing at the wishing well.

Agitated, her mother took a deep breath, then opened up her wallet and handed her daughter a quarter. "You know, you working my nerves!"

"Thank you, Ma," the little girl said, then closed her eyes, made a wish, and flicked her quarter into the wishing well.

"Come on here, girl!" her mother impatiently yelled, standing at the exit.

During the entire ride home, all she kept thinking about was the boy from the library. She smiled as she looked out of the window, wondering if one day her dream would ever come true.

CHAPTER FOUR

After getting permission from Goldie's mother and Mrs. Love, D's mother, for Goldie to spend the night, the two boys left out so Goldie could go to his house to grab some clothes.

As the boys headed towards Goldie's apartment, they discussed plans of staying up late, playing video games, and eating pizzas. Well, maybe those were D's plans. It was true Goldie loved playing video games and eating pizza, but he loved nothing more than seeing Mrs. Love prancing around the house in a skimpy outfit. It was 8:30 p.m., and he was in a hurry to get back to D's apartment to catch Mrs. Love walk across the hallway to take her routine nine o'clock bath. Whenever in D's living room, Goldie always made sure he sat in the recliner that gave him the best view of the hallway. Out of habit, Mrs. Love always traveled topless from her bedroom into the bathroom. Seeing Mrs. Love's 36-DD's bouncing up and down as she walked down the hallway was always the milestone of Goldie's visit.

As the boys walked, Goldie just had to ask why D always took his football everywhere he went. "Hey, D! Why you always gotta take that football with you everywhere you go?"

"Because I'm gonna be a football player when I grow up!" D replied, tossing his football in the air and catching it. "What you gonna be, Goldie?" D asked.

"Rich!" Goldie said, laughing.

D giggled. "Me, too!"

When the boys finally reached the park, they found it bizarre that it was empty. This was unusual, especially for a Friday night. Usually around this time, all of the hustlers were out and posted up on the corner slanging dope. Then it hit Goldie. He remembered the flyer he saw earlier on one of the telephone poles on their way to the store.

"Dang, ain't nobody out here," D said, as the boys strolled through the lifeless park.

"They probably all at home getting dressed for that party," Goldie replied.

"What party?" D asked.

"Nigga, you too young to know!" Goldie said.

"You are, too, Goldie!"

Goldie laughed. D was his homeboy, but Goldie had way more game than him. D didn't know anything about the streets. He was a momma's boy. The difference between the two was that Goldie was independent. He didn't depend on any allowance, unlike D. Anything Goldie wanted, he went out and got it for himself.

All of a sudden, the boys heard footsteps rapidly approaching. Paranoid, they both turned around and noticed a man with a frightened look on his face running for dear life. As a reaction, Goldie pushed a now nervous D out of the way while the runner ran right past them. Hearing another set of footsteps approaching, Goldie spun back around. That was when a man wearing a grey hoodie came into full view. He stood motionless, making eye contact with the man in the hoodie, as he watched him militantly pull out a gun. The minute D saw the gun, he stormed towards the church's basement. However, Goldie boldly did not budge.

"Motherfucker!" the man with the hoodie yelled, as he let off five shots at the runner.

"Ahhhh!" was all the runner could manage, as his body jerked with each bullet that entered his body. After staggering for approximately ten feet, the runner's body fell to the ground lifeless.

Meanwhile, D was hiding at the bottom of the stairs that led to the church's basement, hysterical. He had run for cover the minute the first shot sounded off.

Goldie had not budged. He just stood there. Believe it or not, he was actually enjoying himself. Him and the shooter locked eyes with each other. It was a stare-off. The shooter tried to study Goldie's face, as Goldie studied the shooter's face and then gave a sideways smile.

"This lil' nigga is sick!" the shooter said to himself. The shooter didn't realize until then that he was standing in the light, and shorty had seen his face.

When the shooter heard the screaming sirens approaching, he took one last look at Goldie and then ran off. As the shooter fled, people began coming from out of everywhere. A man who ran over to check on the boys found D shaking as if he was naked in Alaska. D was in shock. While the man ran over to help assist D, Goldie walked over to where the runner's body was laying to investigate. Several nosey people ran over to join him where he was standing.

"Yep, he dead!" Goldie said to all of the onlookers. Where most kids his age would have been scared to death, Goldie just calmly stood there with his hands in his pockets, and felt absolutely nothing.

Within fifteen minutes, the projects were lit up like there was a carnival going on. Police were everywhere. There had to be at least ten police cars, three unmarked cars, and a K-9 unit. Channel Ten News was even on the scene. Both of the boys' mothers had arrived and were comforting their kids. D's eyes were still big as quarters, as one of the paramedics sympathetically threw a blanket around him.

"Baby, are you alright?" Goldie's mom asked, kneeling down to his height.

"Awww, Ma, all that happened was that somebody died," Goldie said nonchalantly, while looking over at the dead body in awe.

Loretta studied her son's face. Nothing. He was acting as if nothing had happened, when here it was he had been right slap in the middle of a deadly shooting.

The head detective on the case walked over to where both boys and their mothers were standing. "How are you ladies doing? I'm Detective Ross," the detective said, handing each boys' parent his card. "I understand these two fellas might have seen the shooter's face?"

"Goldie saw him!" D blurted out, pointing at Goldie while he clung to his mother's leg.

Goldie cut his eyes at D. "Damn sissy! How he gonna put everything on me," he mumbled to himself.

Detective Ross kneeled down in front of Goldie. "Hey there, lil' man. Do you like ice cream?"

"Yeah," Goldie answered casually.

"How about pizza?" the detective asked.

"Yeah," Goldie replied, showing more interest.

Detective Ross smiled; he had found his weakness. "I'll tell you what," the detective said in a tone that Goldie immediately recognized as game. "How about I order you a nice big pizza, and you can come down to the station and take a look at a couple pictures of some bad people. If you see the shooter who shot this guy, you just point him out to me. How about it, pal?" the detective asked, placing his hand on Goldie's shoulder.

Goldie disturbingly looked down at the detective's hand on his shoulder, then looked over at his mother. His mother made eye contact with him and shook her head. Goldie looked over at D and wanted to strangle him. Goldie hated police!

"How about it lil' guy?" the detective repeated.

Goldie looked back over at his mother, who was giving him one of them "it's the right thing to do" looks.

Goldie then looked at the detective and said, "Yeah," in a not too enthusiastic tone.

* * * * *

The shooter was in the living room of one of the apartments with the curtains drawn back, watching Detective Ross talking to shorty.

"Damn! Shorty saw my face. I wonder if he'll talk. Shit, I don't know what made that crackhead motherfucker try to steal from me of all damn people. Damn...that shit must make them think they invincible. Oh well, I guess I done caught another body tonight," the shooter said.

The shooter counted his fingers on his left hand, then went to his right. "Damn, I guess that makes six. Fuck it! Better them than me. I ain't even gonna sweat this shit," the shooter said, stepping away from the window. "Tonight, I'm just gonna enjoy myself and party like it's 1999." He plopped down on the sofa and sparked up a fat joint. "Damn, Detective Ross heading the investigation of all the detectives on the force," he said, as he shook his head and took a puff of his joint.

The shooter knew how long his record was. Not only that, he knew how badly Ross had wanted him every since he was young. "I can't believe the rest of my life is in the damn hands of a little kid!"

Meanwhile, Goldie and his mother had arrived at the police station and were sitting in the lobby, waiting patiently on Detective Ross to arrive. The officer at the front desk informed them that Detective Ross was still on the scene and due to arrive in a couple of minutes. Goldie's eyes lit up when the Pizza Hut delivery guy showed up at the front desk. Since Detective Ross was footing the bill, Goldie made it his business to order a meat lover's with the works. He smiled as he thought about what he had in store for Detective Ross.

"Here you go, lil' fella," the officer at the front desk said to Goldie, who rushed up and grabbed his pizza. When he felt how hot the bottom of the pizza box was, he rushed back to his seat and sat down.

Goldie observed the crazy look on his mother's face. "Boy! What do you say?"

"Thank you," Goldie told the officer at the front desk, with a mouthful of pizza.

"Now what I done told you about talking with your mouth full?" his mother said.

Dang, I wish she would make up her mind, Goldie thought.

Two slices of pizza, and five minutes later, Detective Ross arrived at the station and escorted Goldie and his mother down a long hallway that led to a small room. Once inside, they took a seat at the small table positioned in the center of the room. Goldie and his mother surveyed the room, which looked like a room used for interrogations. Goldie observed the books of photos sitting on the table that he assumed were for him.

"Ewwwee, it's a lil' chilly in here," Goldie's mom commented.

"Can I get you some tea, coffee, or hot chocolate?" Detective Ross asked.

"No, thanks," Goldie's mom said, adjusting her shawl.

"I'll take a Mellow Yellow!" Goldie blurted.

Detective Ross just smiled at Goldie's bluntness, and then patted him on the back before exiting the room. "Okay, I'll be right back, pal," he said.

Goldie proceeded to go through the pages of photos, while holding a slice of pizza in his left hand and flipping the pages with the right. He was halfway through the photo book when Detective Ross returned.

"I see you already got started," Detective Ross said with a smile. "Anything yet?" he asked, handing Goldie his soda.

Goldie shook his head, then reached for his soda. After popping open the can, he continued to flip through the pages and soon came across the shooter's photo. Cool-headed, he continued to turn the pages. He knew there was a possibility that the room was being monitored, and he did not want to show any change in behavior or facial expressions.

"That's the last book of photos," the detective who had recently entered the room said, as they watched Goldie view the final pages.

Goldie turned the last page of the book, and then closed it. "Nope! Not in here either," he said, pushing the book away.

Goldie thought about the shooter. Although he could have easily indentified him, he was not a snitch. It was not his job to make the police's job easy. Besides, "You didn't see nothing and you didn't hear nothing" was the ghetto anthem. Unlike D, he wasn't telling. Besides, he was just about to tell the detective that he had not seen anything before D opened his big mouth. So, Goldie just decided to take advantage of the opportunity to eat some free pizza and ice cream, while having a little fun spinning the detective at the same time. He knew he was destined to become a big-time hustler, and he could never allow anything degrading like that on his GHETTO RESUME. For Goldie, it was both an honor and a pleasure for him to exercise his faith of GHETTO SILENCE.

Meanwhile, on the other side of town, the shooter was busy at the party, drowning himself in shots of Hennessy, while smoking joints back to back like they were cigarettes. His nerves were bad. All he kept thinking about was the stare-off he had with shorty.

Back at the station, Detective Ross was growing agitated. Things were not going as smoothly as he had expected. Confused, he calmly walked over to the table, then kneeled down in front of Goldie.

"Goldie, do you mind describing this guy?"

"Well, he had a big ole' nose...a thick mustache...and some real thick sideburns." Goldie paused for a minute. "And he was kind of tall and had a big ole' gun."

"Well, Goldie...I'm not trying to be racist or anything," Detective Ross said, eyeing Goldie's mother, "but can you tell us what color the shooter was?"

"He was white!" Goldie blurted.

The two white detectives looked at each other like it had just been announced there was a black president.

"Are you sure?" Detective Ross turned and asked Goldie.

"Yep! I saw him with my own two eyes!" Goldie lied.

Goldie's mother read the expression on the two detectives' faces and was furious. It seemed to her like they wanted the shooter to be black. It was like they weren't going to pursue the case anymore now that they learned the shooter was white.

"Prejudice motherfuckers!" Goldie's mother shouted with an attitude, as she stood up and adjusted her purse over her shoulder. "Are we finished here?" she asked.

Detective Ross studied Goldie's mother's face. She was fuming. He rubbed the top of his receding hairline, and then pathetically said, "I guess we are, ma'am."

"Let's go, Goldie!" his mother instructed, swiftly grabbing him by the hand and storming out of the office.

Goldie knew his mother was pissed. He could see it in her eyes. Not to mention, she was walking down the hallway so fast that he damn near had to run to keep up with her. It was not until they reached the front of the station that Goldie realized he had left something. He stopped dead in his tracks.

His mother stopped and threw her hand on her hips. "Boy, what's wrong with you?"

"I left something. I'll be right back!" Goldie said, and then took off back down the hallway.

"A white guy?" Ross said, still in disbelief and finding it hard to believe the shooter was not a black man.

"Yeah.... I know," Mitch added, massaging his forehead.

Both detectives were drowning in their sorrows with their heads down, but when Goldie stormed into the room, they attentively sat up, hoping he had come back because he remembered a clue or something.

"Sorry! I forgot something," Goldie said, walking over to the table and picking up the pizza box. He then reached into his pocket and pulled out the twenty that Detective Ross had given him. With a sinister grin on his face, he twirled it in his hand like a priceless jewel.

"Thank you, Detective Ross, for everything. I'm sorry I couldn't help!" Goldie said, shrugging his shoulders. "I tried!" He then exited the room with his pizza, closing the door behind him, and let out a spooky laugh as he walked down the hallway.

The two detectives were left sitting and staring at each other. Had they been played?

Mitch buried his head back inside of his hands. "What are we gonna do, Ross?"

"I don't know, Mitch. I don't know," Detective Ross replied, as he stared off into nowhere. He just shook his head. "That fuckin' little kid is too damn smart!"

* * * * *

Snake was up early the next morning, in efforts of arriving at the projects at the crack of dawn. He knew today was going to be a big day. Last night, the block had been shut down as a precaution. He had gotten an inside scoop that the "green team" (task force) had plans of ambushing them yesterday. That was why everyone had switched things up last night and attended the party. Snake had obtained this information from Butter, a crackhead.

Butter had earned a position on the police department's payroll as a registered confidential informant, or a C.I., and was reaping the rewards from being on both Snake and Detective Ross's payrolls. Once a week, Snake met Butter at a secluded restaurant on the outskirts of the city for his weekly update. The meeting generally consisted of who was snitching, if any of Snake's crack houses were under surveillance, and how much information the police had on Snake. Once Snake felt pleased with the information Butter had given him, he would pay him the agreed upon amount of dope, give him the dummy information to relay back to Detective Ross, and then they would go their separate ways.

To remain on Detective Ross's payroll, Butter made several busts on other small-time drug dealers. He knew he had to be productive to remain on the police's payroll. Still, he knew the clock was ticking. It was only a matter of time before Ross started pressing him again. Although the several other busts had managed to buy him a little time, Snake was the one who Ross ultimately wanted. Basically, Butter was stuck in between a rock and a hard spot. Aware that Snake was known for making people mysteriously disappear, Butter always made sure he was never being followed whenever he drove to meet Snake for his weekly visit.

As Snake made his rounds around the city, he wondered to himself just how long could Butter continued to be trusted. After all, a crackhead is going to be a crackhead. Butter was a snitch, and just thinking about the fact that he was a snitch reminded Snake of his mother's death, and made him want to kill Butter just for being a snitch, but he needed him.

Unlike ordinary crackheads, Butter was what the streets labeled as a "weekend smoker". Snake had to give it to him, Butter kept himself up. From Monday to Thursday, Butter was a family man, and then when Friday evening rolled around, he got buck wild, tricking and smoking.

Snake pulled into the restaurant, which was the meeting place for him and Butter, and parked. He noticed Butter had not arrived yet. He checked himself in the rearview mirror, grabbed the envelope from off the passenger's seat, and hopped out of his Honda. He scanned the parking lot for any suspicious vehicles and then disappeared inside of the restaurant. Snake positioned himself at a booth in the back of the restaurant, where he always sat to give him the best view of both sides of the parking lot. He ordered a Cherry Coke, then waited patiently for Butter to arrive. Five minutes later, Butter strolled in.

"Sorry I'm late!" were the first words Butter uttered out of his mouth before joining Snake at the booth.

Snake finished taking a sip of his soda, then retorted, "Make it your last time," in a serious tone that said next time the penalty would be harsh.

"So, what's up, Snake?" Butter asked, trying to ease the tension in the air.

"What's up with ya?" Snake asked.

"You know...the usual," Butter said, motioning for the waitress.

The waitress walked over to their table, then looked at Butter and asked, "May I help you?"

"Yes...give me a hamburger, fries, and a Cherry Coke, please," Butter ordered with a smile.

The waitress turned toward Snake and stood with her pad in her hand, rolling her eyes, while she waited on Snake to order. When Snake noticed she was waiting on him, he arrogantly raised his right hand, indicating he was fine.

The waitress sucked her teeth, then turned towards Butter and smiled. "I'll be back in ten minutes with your order," she said, then sashayed off.

"Nice ass!" Butter said, admiring the attractive, young waitress's backside.

"A'ight! One of these days you gonna stick that dick of yours somewhere that you wished you didn't!" Snake warned.

"Oh well! I'ma use it while it still works!" Butter chuckled.

When Butter's lunch arrived, he grabbed his eating utensils, said a quick grace, and then dug in. Snake studied his body language as he ate. Butter was so caught up in his meal that he didn't even notice Snake hawking him.

Ten minutes later, Butter's plate was spotless and he was wiping the side of his mouth with his napkin. When Snake noticed he was finished with his meal, he slid him the envelope across the table. Curious, Butter opened the envelope and pulled out all of the contents. His heart started beating a hundred miles an hour, and he felt like he was about to black out. He looked up at Snake to see if this was some sort of prank. Snake, who was wearing a poker face, looked as serious as a heart attack. He stared Butter in the eyes and then nodded his head that this was real. Butter swallowed hard. Tears rolled down his eyes, as he now realized he was in deeper than he had ever imagined.

The envelope contained pictures of everyone in Butter's family dear to his heart. Each picture had little bubbles with sayings next to them, like the ones you saw inside of comic books. His wife's picture had "Help, honey" next to it, his kid's pictures said, "Help, Daddy," and his siblings' pictures each had "Help, bro" next to it. There were even pictures of Butter's parents inside with "Help, Son" next to each of their pictures. Snake didn't go through the trouble of photographing Butter's grandparents. They were up in age and he knew they could go any day now. Snake even went as far as enclosing various coupons inside of the envelope. Some of the coupons were for suits, and the others were for various funeral home services. Butter looked up at Snake with a petrified look on his face.

"Understand?" Snake asked in a spooky voice.

Butter massaged the sides of his temples. "I understand," he said in a pitiful voice.

"Good!" Snake said, then stood up and patted Butter on the back. "Cheer up! If you don't have any plans of crossing me, then you have nothing to worry about. I just wanna let you know that I play for keeps, and I'll do ANYTHING to protect my investment!" Snake eyed Butter and raised his eyebrow. Once he saw his point had been made, he said, "Alright then, I'ma holla at you later!" Snake then strolled off and headed towards the front door.

Left at the table with his head buried in his hands, Butter knew he would rather be dead before he allowed anything to happen to his family. He contemplated on suicide. That way, neither party would benefit.

Snake got halfway to the door before he turned around and walked back over to the table. "Hey, Butter...I almost forgot. You know that's a nice family you got there, especially your daughter, which brings me to the reason why I came back. You know...your daughter has a nice rack and a badass body! Tell her I wanna holla, and I'll see if I can throw you a lil' something extra, father-in-law," Snake taunted, while licking his lips.

Butter leaped up out of his seat, pointing his finger at Snake. "You leave her out of this, Snake!" he shouted, then calmed down and sat back in his seat when he noticed the customers staring at him.

"She's grown! We'll let her decide!" Snake said sarcastically. Then, once again, he headed towards the front door, while laughing and making a mental note to put Butter's daughter on his hit list.

* * * * *

Snake was beginning to grow agitated as he toured the projects searching for shorty. "I wonder where shorty's lil' ass at?" he said, hitting the steering wheel on his Cadillac.

When he turned the corner, he observed a group of shorties standing on the curb. He slowed down, pulled over to the curb, and let his window down. The three boys approached the car.

"Hey, yo, ya'll seen that lil' red shorty that stay on the corner apartment over there?" Snake asked, pointing to the apartments.

"Who? Goldie?" one of the boys dry-snitched.

Snake shrugged his shoulders. "I guess that's his name."

"He just walked to the store about five minutes ago," one answered.

Snake reached into his pocket, peeled off three twenty dollar bills, and handed one to each of the boys through the window.

"Good looking out!" he said, then drove off and continued his quest.

When he got to the next block, what he saw made him immediately want to make a U-turn, but it was too late.

"Damn! How the hell I run into her of all people?"

Snake's baby's mother, Lisa, was standing in the middle of the road with her arms folded, waiting on him. Getting her pregnant was the worst mistake he ever made in his life. He had buzzard luck. Lisa was a girl who him and his crew had ran a train on, and after a blood test, he ended up being the father of her child.

Snake stuck his head out of the window. "Move, girl! I ain't got time for yo' shit!"

"This is business!" Lisa shouted, making her way over to the driver's side of Snake's Cadillac. Lisa stuck her head inside of the car. "When you gonna give me some money for Lil Snake?" she asked.

Lisa was an airhead who was so stupid that the dumb motherfucker named Snake's son after his nickname and not his real name.

"Didn't I just give you some money?" Snake asked. "Ain't no way you could have spent two hundred that quick! That was just two days ago. I know what it is. Your ass thinks you slick. You tryna go to that damn concert, with your slick ass!"

Lisa nervously rubbed the side of her neck, a habit she had whenever she was lying. Snake's hunch was right. She had guilt written all over her face.

"Listen, man...I got some shit I gotta go take care of. I'll be back!" Snake said.

"You always say that!" Lisa said, displaying an agitated pout.

Becoming impatient, he let up the window, and Lisa jumped back to avoid her arms from being caught in the window. That was when Snake mashed the gas and pulled off.

"Sissy!" Lisa yelled, kicking the bumper on Snake's Cadillac as he pulled off.

Snake knew Lisa was only seeking attention. Therefore, he left it alone. She knew how much he valued his car, and kicking his bumper was her way of trying to get under his skin. Snake observed her through his rearview mirror, as she stood in the middle of the road and shot him a bird, while shouting something he couldn't hear. Snake just shook his head at the disgrace he had for Lisa. How could he ever have cheated on Mesha for something like that?

"It's a damn shame! Fifteen minutes of pleasure can cost a nigga eighteen years of hell," he mumbled to himself, as he came to a stop sign.

After making a left at the four-way stop sign, he laid eyes on Goldie, who was just about to walk inside the corner store. Snake blew his horn, stopping him.

Snake let down his window and called out, "What's up, Shorty?"

Goldie smiled. "What's up, nigga?" he said, making his way towards Snake's Caddy. When Goldie reached the car, he noticed Snake was riding solo.

Snake unlocked the door. "Get in, Shorty!" he said in an inviting tone.

Goldie opened the door and hopped in the passenger seat. He had never been privileged enough to ride in a luxury automobile. By far, Snake's Cadillac was the sharpest in town. Preachers had nothing on his Caddy, which was painted a high-gloss, factory brown, with Gucci interior and a matching Gucci top. His accessories were what breathed life into his Caddy. His music was so loud that it could be heard four blocks away, and when he turned the corner, his gold-plated house grille was always the first thing you saw. Whenever he cruised down the streets, it was always all eyes on him. On a sunny day, the sun's rays would beam down and illuminate every single gold-plated emblem and his gold-plated thirty's and vogues. Being that people often called his Caddy a panty-puller, the name stuck, and he always kept a pair of expensive, lace panties dangling from his rearview mirror.

As they cruised down the street, Goldie sat back, relaxed, and enjoyed the ride. He felt honored to be reclining on Gucci interior. As he examined the interior, he nodded his head, while admiring the consistency of the oak trimming throughout the car. He sneaked a feel, running his hand along the door panel. *One day, I'ma have me something just like this,* Goldie thought.

For the next ten minutes, Snake cruised the streets, periodically observing Goldie out of the corner of his eye. Shorty did not seem like someone who just fingered a killer; he was too relaxed. It was strange. As Snake further observed shorty, he smiled. He saw a reflection of a younger him sitting in the passenger seat. Although he could not quite put his finger on it, something was uncanny about shorty. Snake had been around a lot of different people, and he knew a thoroughbred when he saw one. His next series of questions would confirm if his hunch was right. If so, shorty had a bright future ahead of him.

Snake looked over and asked, "Yo, Shorty, what's your name?" already knowing the answer to his own question.

"Goldie!"

"What's up, Goldie? I'm--"

"Snake," Goldie said, cutting him off in mid-sentence.

Snake just stared at him and smiled. "How you know me, Shorty?"

"I ain't stupid! Everyone knows who you is!" Goldie proclaimed.

Snake shook his head. "How old are you, Shorty?"

"Ten," Goldie replied, with his chest poked out.

"You like my car, Shorty?" Snake asked.

Goldie scanned the interior and nodded his head. "Yeah, it's tight!" Tired of playing games, Goldie turned around in his seat and made eye contact with Snake. "Look, man...I know what all of this is about," he said courageously.

Caught off guard by Goldie's statement, Snake displayed a puzzled look on his face.

"What are you talking about, Shorty?" Snake asked.

"Look, man...you know I saw your face last night, and I know you were the one who shot that man. You had just better be glad it was me, and not D. He's real scared. Matter of fact, he the reason why I had to go down to the station. Right when I was about to tell that damn detective that I didn't see nothing, D opened his big mouth and told him I saw your face."

"So, what did you tell them?" Snake nervously asked.

"They just made me look at a bunch of pictures. How about all the pictures they gave me were of nothing but black people. Not one single picture in there was of a white man. That shit made me mad! I saw your picture, though," Goldie said in a soft poised tone, while staring out of the window.

Snake raised his eyebrows, looking like he had seen a ghost. "What!"

Goldie shook his head and continued staring out of the window. "Boy, you take some ugly pictures."

"Huh!" Snake said, sounding like Scooby Doo.

Goldie swung around in his seat, tickled blue, pointing at Snake while he laughed. "Sike! I gotcha!" he said, laughing his heart out. "Man, I ain't no snitch!" he said with pride.

Snake let out a sigh of relief. His troubles were over, and all because of a little ten-year-old boy. Snake looked over at Goldie and displayed a smile. His instincts were right. Shorty was a thoroughbred. Snake reached over and rubbed him on the head, while Goldie continued to squirm in his seat with laughter.

"What?" Snake asked.

"You should've seen your face. You was scared!" Goldie taunted.

Snake just smiled. Was he that transparent? Goldie had hit it dead on the head. His nerves had been bad all last night, thinking about all he stood to lose. Shit, in reality, his future was in Goldie's hands. Fortunately, for him, Goldie had spared him.

"And guess what?" Goldie added, grabbing his stomach.

"What?" Snake asked, curious.

"I told them the shooter was a white man!" Goldie bragged.

Snake joined him in laughter. "You...you...you told them what?" he asked, barely able to get his words out.

"Yep! And I slapped they head for twenty dollars and a pizza!" Goldie boasted. "You should've seen the look on they faces when I told them the shooter was a white man," Goldie said.

Snake just looked over at him and shook his head. He was laughing so hard that tears were coming out of his eyes.

"Hey, Shorty, you hungry?" Snake asked, reaching over and rubbing him on the head again.

"Yeah! Why, what's up?" Goldie asked.

"Let's go get us something to eat," Snake said, feeling relieved, and then turned the volume up on the tape player.

From that day on, a bond was formed.

CHAPTER FIVE

As the summer of '85 winded down and Goldie prepared for junior high, D and Mrs. Love prepared to move out of the projects and to Atlanta. Turns out the ole' dude who Mrs. Love had been dating proposed to her. Eager to secure a brighter future for D, Mrs. Love said yes. Ever since the night of the shooting, D remained traumatized. Mrs. Love figured a change of scenery would aid his recovery. Truthfully, Goldie would miss Mrs. Love more than he would miss D.

Goldie was on his way to catch the bus to the mall, when he stopped to see him off. The apartment was already bare, and Robert, Mrs. Love's fiancé, was loading their bags into the trunk of his Benz by the time Goldie showed up a little before nine o'clock that morning.

"Ten minutes, baby," Mrs. Love yelled to D, as she climbed in Robert's car and planted a kiss on his lips.

D and Goldie stepped off to the side away from the car and said their last goodbyes. Ten minutes later, Mrs. Love stuck her head out of the window, and said, "It's time, baby," as if she had on a stopwatch.

While D and Goldie hugged, D got teary-eyed and choked up. Goldie, however, sucked up his emotions, refusing to look soft. During their hug, Mrs. Love stepped out of the car to comfort D, who quickly wiped the tears from his face.

After opening the back door for him to get in, Mrs. Love walked over and gave Goldie a hug. During the hug, Goldie's thing hardened while brushing up against her.

"Remember, whenever you wanna come visit, it's fine with me," she said after releasing Goldie. Then, she kissed him on the forehead, gave him a quick hug, and hopped back into the car.

Mrs. Love left Goldie standing looking like he had a cucumber in the front of his pants, as Robert honked his horn and the soon-to-be family pulled off. D and Goldie kept eye contact with each other, as Goldie watched the tears run down his face, until Robert's Benz disappeared out of sight. When they disappeared, Goldie looked down at his erection.

"Damn, Mrs. Love!"

After gathering his thoughts, Goldie headed to the bus stop and waited for the 36 Express to take him to Tyrone Square Mall. He had three hundred dollars in his pocket that was burning a hole through his pants. Two hundred of those dollars was from his parents, and the other hundred was from Snake.

By the time he returned back home from the mall, Goldie was carrying a couple of bags full of clothes and still had fifty dollars to spare in his pocket, all thanks to his clever ability to switch price tags on the designer wear he wanted with the discounted tags of less expensive clothing. He was more than prepared for his first day of middle school as a sixth grader.

JUNIOR HIGH

At 5:30 A.M., Goldie's alarm clock sounded. He reached over and hit the snooze button, then rolled back over. A couple of minutes later, the alarm sounded again. When he turned the alarm off this time, a shadow appeared and the face became visible.

"Boy, get your butt up!" his mother ordered, pulling back the sheets.

"Aw, Ma!" Goldie cried.

"Breakfast will be ready in a few minutes!" his mother shouted on her way down the stairs.

Sluggishly, Goldie sat up on the edge of the bed and eased into his slippers. Ten minutes later, he was stepping out of the shower and drying off, feeling refreshed. It was not until he began drying off that he realized he had forgotten to remove his wave cap before hopping into the shower. Really, it was his mother's old stocking he converted into a wave cap. He removed the stocking from off of his head and checked his waves in the bathroom mirror.

"Tight!" he said in admiration.

The only thing he wasn't impressed with was the ring around his forehead the stocking had left behind.

After examining his forehead, he walked back into his room and started getting dressed.

Since today was the first day of school, he had to throw on his best outfit. The first day of school was always like a fashion show. Goldie was decked out in a pair of blue stonewashed Levi's, a blue and white stripped polo shirt, and a pair of all white Nike's. He squirted on two sprays of Obsession cologne before heading down the stairs.

At the bottom of the stairs, his mother was awaiting him with a warm smile. "Look at my baby!" she said, handing him a bacon, egg, and cheese sandwich, and then kissing him on the forehead. She stepped back to observe him again. "My baby looks handsome!"

"Thank you, Ma," Goldie said, blushing.

"Alright now, don't be getting caught up with them hot little girls," his mother joked.

Goldie smiled, threw his bookbag over his shoulder, and headed out the front door.

The first thing Goldie did when he arrived at the bus stop was scan all of the other boys to make sure none of them was wearing the same outfit as him. Seeing that none of them was, he relaxed. From the minute he arrived, he noticed a group of girls; out of the corner of his eye, he saw them huddled up and pointing at him and giggling.

Goldie decided to let the girls know he noticed them. "How ya'll ladies doin'?" he asked when he walked over.

"Fine, just like you," one of the girls said, then started snickering.

Goldie just rubbed on his chin and smiled.

The bus pulled up and all of the kids anxiously boarded the bus. Goldie was the last one to board, and by then, all of the seats in the front were taken. The only available seat was at the back of the bus. To his surprise, he ended up sharing a seat with one of the girls who had been admiring him.

"Ewwwwwweeee!" all of the girls teased, as Goldie sat down.

Goldie extended his hand. "Hi, I'm--"

"I know who you are," the girl said, blushing with her head lowered.

Goldie smiled. "So what's your name?"

"Tina."

"Nice to know you, Tina," Goldie said, while staring into her eyes. "So, tell me a little bit more about yourself."

Thirty minutes later, the bus pulled into the bus circle, and all of the kids began unloading the bus. Goldie and Tina were the last two to step off the bus.

"I'll see you around!" Goldie yelled to Tina, while stretching out his arms, amazed at how many more students there were in junior high compared to elementary.

To his surprise, not only did he and Tina share the same school bus, they also shared the same homeroom, lunch, and fifth and seventh period classes. To Goldie, it seemed like the more they came face to face, the more beautiful she looked each time. For an eleven-year-old, Tina's hair was extremely long, unlike a lot of the other girls her age. Her light-skinned complexion and silky smooth hair made it look like she could have easily been one of those black hair care models. In Goldie's eyes, Tina was the prettiest girl in school. He made up his mind and was determined to make Tina his girl.

During the thirty-minute bus ride home, the two sat together, as if they had assigned seats, and conversed non-stop. Although Goldie had accumulated more than three girls' phone numbers inside of his folder, Tina's was the number he ultimately wanted. By the time the bus driver stopped in front of their bus stop, Tina was busy writing down her phone number on a piece of paper. Her only stipulation was that Goldie agreed to call whenever her mother was at work. After Goldie gave her his phone number, they grabbed their belongings and hopped off the bus.

Later that evening, the two conversed for several hours, all the way up until 11:30 p.m., talking about everything under the sun, including their likes and dislikes, favorite food, colors, songs, etc. Tina even went into detail explaining why her and her mother had moved down to St. Pete. Goldie could not believe how one day her mother just up and left her wealthy father. Not only had her mother given up a lavish lifestyle, she also gave up a good paying job, all to escape an abusive husband.

After three weeks of continuous conversation, the two knew everything there was to know about each other. Eager to make Tina his girl, one night, Goldie asked her to go with him. Naturally, since the feeling was mutual, Tina said yes.

From that day on, everyday, the two of them routinely sat together on the bus, ate lunch together, and rushed home every afternoon after school to talk on the phone for hours. Goldie was so much of a gentleman that he would meet Tina in the hallway after fourth and sixth period class to carry her books to their fifth and seventh period class.

The two were like each other's shadow, and everyone knew they were going together. A lot of girls grew envious of Tina. Even a few of her friends started acting funny, and were jealous of how she rarely spent any time with them. Tina didn't care, though. Goldie was the only friend in the whole world she needed.

REPORT CARDS

Mrs. Miller was busy calling each of her homeroom students up to her desk, in alphabetical order, to hand them their report cards.

"DeQuan Walker," Mrs. Miller called out.

Goldie confidently walked up to Mrs. Miller's desk.

"Congratulations, Walker!" Mrs. Miller said, while smiling and handing Goldie his report card, along with a certificate.

"Dean's list!" Goldie cheerfully shouted in disbelief, observing the certificate in his hand. Then he looked up at Mrs. Miller for conformation.

Mrs. Miller nodded her head. "You're very special!"

"Thank you, Mrs. Miller," Goldie said with a smile, then strutted like George Jefferson off *The Jefferson's* back towards his seat.

Goldie was impressed. He was only expecting to make the honor roll. He thought for sure he had made B's in English and

World History. *I guess that extra studying helped,* he said to himself.

When the school bell rang to end the day, everyone stormed out of their homeroom class and headed towards the bus circle. It was easy to determine who had made what just by reading everybody's facial expressions. Mainly, all of the kids who received good grades were perky and viewing each other's report cards. While on the other hand, the kids who were not as fortunate were quiet, staring out of the window and debating on whether they should just enjoy themselves over the weekend and show their parents their report cards on Monday.

During the entire ride home, Goldie was excited and anxious to get home to show off his report card. Today was Friday and the timing could not have been any better, because it was also payday for both of his parents. He knew it had to be at least a thirty-dollar incentive in it for him. And even though him and his father were not on the best of terms, deep down inside, his father's praise was what he really wanted. Lately, his father had barely been around.

After walking Tina to her door, Goldie cut across the park while heading home, hoping to bump into Snake. He was successful. Snake was posted up on the corner, leaning up against his Caddy, spitting game in some big-booty red-bone's ear.

"What's up, lil' man?" Snake asked, acknowledging Goldie's presence.

"This is what's up!" Goldie boasted, handing him his report card.

Snake studied the report card, then nodded his head and reached into his pocket.

"Damn, lil' man, that's what I'm talking about!" Snake said, peeling off five twenty-dollar bills and handing them to him. "Here you go, lil' man. You deserve it!"

"Good looking out!" Goldie exclaimed, giving him a closed fist pound, and then stuffed the hundred dollars into his pocket.

"Come back through and holla at me a lil' later, lil' man!" Snake said.

"Alright," Goldie replied, as he headed home a hundred dollars richer.

When Goldie walked into his apartment, he threw his bookbag on the sofa and stormed into the kitchen to make a peanut butter and jelly sandwich.

His oldest sister, Melissa, stormed down the stairs. "Boy, why you home so late? Your bus dropped you off forty-five minutes ago!" she shouted.

Goldie ignored his sister's comments, as he walked over and sat on the sofa to watch television.

"Goldie, you hear me talking to you?" his sister shouted, standing in front of the television and blocking his view.

"Move!" Goldie ordered, trying to look around her body.

"I'ma tell Daddy that you came home late!" Melissa threatened.

Goldie laughed. "Yeah...whenever you see him!"

"You know what? You a stupid lil' boy!" Melissa said.

Reaching into his bookbag, Goldie pulled out his certificate and handed it to her. Melissa studied the certificate in disbelief, then looked up at him and was humiliated.

"Yeah!" Goldie said arrogantly, observing the look on her face. "Now get your stupid self from in front of the TV!"

* * * * *

When five o'clock rolled around, all the city's workers poured into the employee parking lot. Not only was today a Friday, but it was payday.

"I'll see you guys later," Albert said to his crew before hopping in his car and pulling off.

Albert was en route to World Liquors to cash his check. He was surprised with the unexpected $150 bonus he received on this paycheck, an extra $150 he had to go into his pockets that Loretta would never know about. Being that he was the man of the house, she never questioned his pay. For some strange reason, the extra $150 on his check had him feeling lucky. Not only that, his left palm had been itching all day.

Albert pulled into the parking lot of World Liquors, parked, and went inside, walking immediately back to the cooler and grabbing a six pack of Colt 45 before going to the counter. When it was his turn in line, he placed his beer on the counter, used the pen on the counter to sign his check, and handed his license and check to the clerk.

"A lil' extra this week, huh, Albert?" the observant clerk asked, stamping the back of the check, then retrieving various bills out of the cash register.

"Yeah, we got a bonus," Albert retorted.

"Here we go," the cashier said, as he counted the bills out on the counter in front of Albert.

"Thank you, John!" Albert said, while stuffing the money inside of his pocket and grabbing his beer to exit the liquor store.

* * * * *

As soon as Goldie heard the sound of a car pulling in front of the apartment, he immediately rushed downstairs to the front door with his report card and certificate behind his back. He opened the door, then stood at the screen door and waited on his father. Goldie read his facial expression and his body language. He seemed like he was in a good mood. Goldie saw that he was carrying a six-pack of beer in his left hand and his lunch sack in his right. So, he opened the screen door for him.

Albert noticed the Kool-Aid smile on Goldie's face when he walked inside of the apartment. "What's all that about?" he asked, heading towards the kitchen.

"What?" Goldie asked, following behind him.

"Boy, you know what I'm talking about...all of that grinning from ear to ear," his father said, throwing his six-pack in the refrigerator.

"Nothing, we just got report cards today, that's all," Goldie replied, while still hiding his report card and certificate behind his back.

Albert walked into his room and immediately began stripping out of his work clothes.

"Don't you wanna see what I made?" Goldie asked cheerfully.

"Not right now! I'll see it later," Albert said, rushing into the bathroom and hopping into the shower.

Dropping his head, Goldie dishearteningly walked out of his parents' bedroom. He was crushed. For a minute, he thought about crumbling up his report card and flushing it down the toilet, but his father was not worth it.

"Fuck him! I hate his ass! I don't even know why I even waste my time when I know he doesn't care!" Goldie said, fuming as he stormed upstairs to his bedroom.

* * * * *

Albert stepped out of the shower and dried off. He rushed to try to make it out of the house before Loretta came home from the hairdresser and started asking him one hundred and one questions about where he was going.

It was six o'clock, and he knew that now was when all of the real money was at the gambling house. Friday was payday. Albert knew everybody and their momma would be present tonight, all sharing the same dreams as him...trying to come up.

Albert threw on a pair of white slacks, a black silk shirt, and slid into a pair of black and white Stacy Adams. As he straightened himself out in the mirror, he tipped things off by putting on his white Panama Jack fedora, with the black band. After two conservative squirts of Grey Flannel cologne, he left the bill money for Loretta on the dresser, grabbed his keys, and bounced out of the door.

CHAPTER SIX

When Sharon pulled up in front of her apartment, Loretta instantly caught an attitude when she noticed Albert was gone. "He better be done left the money for the house." Loretta hopped out of the car, closing the door behind her. "Thank you, Sharon!"

"Anytime, girl!" Sharon said, then honked the horn and pulled off.

When Loretta made it to the front door, Goldie opened it and ambushed her with his report card in his hand.

"Look what I made, Ma!" he boasted.

Loretta took the report card and examined it. "Oh Lord, my baby's a genius! Come here!" she said.

She took Goldie into her arms and squeezed him affectionately, then began smothering him with kisses.

"Momma's so proud of you, baby!" she said, rocking him in her arms.

"Stop, Ma!" Goldie giggled as he squirmed.

"Oh, so you don't want your momma kissing on you? I bet if I was one of them lil' girls you wouldn't be acting like that!"

Goldie blushed. His mother always knew what to say to smooth things out. That's why he loved her so much. It felt good being praised from a loved one for his hard work, and as long as his mother continued to praise him and acknowledge his hard work, what his father thought did not matter.

"Baby, I'm real proud of you. Go in the kitchen, grab one of them coupons from Little Caesar's off the counter, and order you a pizza with whatever you want on it! When you're finished ordering yours, hand me the phone so I can order something for your brother and 'em," his mother said.

Goldie's face lit up. "I love you, Ma!" he said, then stormed into the house.

"Goldie!" his mother yelled.

"Yes!" Goldie said, turning back around to see what she wanted.

"I think you dropped something," his mother said.

Goldie checked his pockets. He could not figure out what he had dropped. He looked up at his mom.

"What I drop?" he asked, puzzled.

"This!" his mother said, handing him two twenty-dollar bills with a smile on her face.

Goldie took the money and hugged his mom. "I love you, Ma!"

"I gotta make sure I go buy a frame tomorrow so I can hang my baby's certificate up in the living room," Loretta said.

"Then you better buy two, 'cause I'ma do it again," Goldie boasted, sticking out his chest.

His mother smiled and rubbed him on his head. "That's my baby!"

Goldie then disappeared into the living room.

When Loretta walked inside of the bedroom, she could still smell Albert's Grey Flannel cologne lingering in the air. The first thing she did was search for the bill money, which was sitting on the bedroom dresser. She counted the money. The total was right.

"His ass thinks he slick. Tryna rush up out of here before I made it home," she said, taking off her shirt. She sat on the edge of the bed and removed her shoes. "I'm not gonna even sit here and worry myself about where he's at or what he's doin'," she said, while stripping out of the rest of her clothes, throwing on her shower cap and jumping into the shower.

* * * * *

"Come on, Big Ben!" Albert yelled, shaking the dice and then rolling. "Ten motherfuckers!" Albert shouted, picking up all of the bets from around him.

Albert checked his watch. It was ten o'clock. There were still a nice amount of gamblers in the room, and his plans were to break the whole house. After missing his next point, he stood up off his knee.

"I gotta piss ya'll. I'll be right back!" he told the crowd.

"Aw, nigga, I know you ain't running?" one of the gamblers yelled.

"Nigga, I told you I had to piss! What you wanna do, come watch, motherfucker?" Albert joked.

There was uproar of laughter from the crowd, and Albert smirked. "I told you I'll be back!" Then he disappeared to the bathroom.

While pissing, he gathered his thoughts. After draining his member, he flushed the toilet, washed his hands, and then counted his earnings. The total was shocking.

"Fifty-five hundred!" Albert said, smiling as he tucked two grand into his right sock.

Today had to be Albert's lucky day! He looked in the bathroom mirror, rubbed on his face, and smiled. His mind told him to walk away with the fifty-five hundred, but greed convinced him to stay. Besides, he was hot!

When Albert opened the bathroom door, to his surprise, a woman wearing a "move something" dress was standing outside of the door waiting on him.

"Hey, cutie!" the beautiful woman said, close enough to smell Albert's breath.

"How you doin'?" Albert nervously answered.

The woman standing in front of him was beautiful. She had beautiful long hair, a light-skinned complexion, and a smile that could have been on a Colgate commercial. Her body was banging. She had thick hips, a fat ass, and a waist that looked like you could wrap both hands around it.

The woman licked her luscious ups and ran her finger down the center of Albert's chest, all the way down to his navel. She moved in closer, brushing her body up against Albert's.

Then she grabbed his manhood and whispered softly into his ear, "I want you."

Albert nervously pulled away, studying the flirtatious woman.

The woman smiled. "You scared of me?" she taunted.

"I gotta go!" Albert said, brushing his back up against the wall as he passed by the woman.

* * * * *

After all the kids were fast asleep, Loretta headed downstairs and started on her household chores. She turned on the stereo and danced around the house to Frankie Beverley and Maze as she cleaned. Basically, she was trying to keep herself busy and stay awake until Albert came home. They desperately needed to talk. To her, it seemed like Albert was right back to doing what she had kicked him out over.

By midnight, Loretta had the entire apartment spotless. All of the laundry was separated and sitting in the hallway in laundry baskets so she could be one of the first ones to arrive at the laundromat in the morning.

"I'll just take a little nap," she said, plopping down and stretching out on the sofa. "I'll hear Albert's keys when he's coming in the door," she said, getting comfortable. Before she knew it, she had dosed off.

* * * * *

"Come on, Nina Ross!" Albert yelled, while shaking and rolling the dice. "Nine motherfuckers!" Albert shouted, while picking up the enormous pile of money off the floor that resembled a pile of leaves that had fallen off a tree in fall.

"Fuck!" Dollar yelled. "I'm through!" he said, standing up from off of his knee, as both his women came over and helped him throw on his mink. "I'll catch you cats later!" At that, he disappeared out the door with his hands wrapped around both women.

At the time, Albert was busy counting his winnings. In his mind, he knew he had hit for ten grand at least. He had broken the whole house.

Rufus, a petty hustler and heroin addict, had left the gambling house a lil' over thirty minutes ago to grab some more money. Seventy percent of the jackpot Albert had won had come from Rufus.

"What? You niggas ain't got no more money?" Albert asked arrogantly, turning all of the bills the same way and then checking his watch. "Damn, it's three o'clock in the damn morning! I know

Loretta's probably mad as hell right now, thinking that I'm out here cheating!"

Albert smiled while he continued counting his money. "I wanna see the look on her face when she sees all of this damn money!"

* * * * *

Meanwhile, Loretta's body was stretched across the sofa, knocked out. She had dosed off a couple of hours ago, awaiting Albert's arrival. When she woke up, she sat up, stretched her arms, and let off a light yawn. Once she regained her vision, she looked over at the clock and noticed it was three o'clock in the morning. Furious, she jumped up off the sofa and stormed into the bedroom.

"I'm sick of this shit! Right when I thought he was tryna do right, he pulls this shit! This is it! This is the last damn straw!"

She plopped down on the edge of the bed, then buried her head in her hands and started crying. "I can't take this anymore! I can't believe the nerve of this man, acting like me and my babies don't even exist! If that skinny bitch is who he wanna be with, then that's where he need to pack his shit and go!"

Loretta wiped away her tears. Devastated, she jumped up off the bed and started packing all of Albert's belongings.

"Matter of fact, I'ma pack his shit for him!"

* * * * *

When Rufus arrived back at the gambling house, he parked two houses down, got out of the car, and left the engine running. The crowd had thinned out. It was true he had made a trip home, but not to grab more money.

Realistically, out of the seven thousand that Rufus had lost in the dice game, only five hundred was really his. He had just finished the last of a package Snake had fronted him to get on. Scheming, he thought he could use Snake's money to make a quick flip in the dice game. That didn't work. Albert was hot! Their five-dollar bets turned into ten; ten-dollar bets turned into twenty, and before Rufus knew it, he was dead broke. Greed always seemed to have its way with Rufus. He was always trying to find some kind of way to get over.

Fresh out of jail, Snake figured he could use Rufus's manpower. Rufus had an impressive "street rep". He knew how to utilize his 6'7", 280-pound masculine frame to muscle whatever it was that he wanted.

When Rufus arrived on the side of the house, he cautiously peeped inside of the living room window. There were only five men inside: three of his men, Albert, and the houseman. Rufus made eye contact with Richie, one of his men, who gave him the nod. Then Rufus pulled out his gun and patiently waited on the side of the house for Albert to come out.

Five minutes later, Albert appeared on the front porch. He placed his hat on top of his head and took in the mornings' air, as he surveyed the street. He was loaded. Foolishly, not only had he left his pistol in the car, he had also parked up the street.

"Yeah, you were the man tonight, Albert!" Richie said, as Rufus's cue.

Rufus appeared from around the corner, with no mask and his gun pointed straight at Albert's dome.

Albert stood frozen and let off an evil grin.

"I know you didn't think you was finna' leave with all of that loot, did you?" Rufus asked. "Check that nigga! His socks, too!" Rufus instructed his men.

"Hey, Rufus, what's going--?"

Before the houseman could finish his sentence, two of Rufus's men abruptly grabbed him and commenced to beating the shit out of him.

Rufus smiled as he watched. He loved that shit!

"Nigga! You think you just gonna rob me with no mask and I don't do nothing?" Albert asked.

Albert's body felt five pounds lighter once Rufus's men had stripped him of all his money. He felt like a general who had been demoted to a private.

Observing Albert's anger, Rufus walked closer and smiled. "You ain't mad is ya?" he taunted.

Albert gritted his teeth.

"Nigga! You ain't no street nigga! You ain't made for these streets! You ain't no grimey nigga! See, you ain't on point about a lot of shit! The female that was waiting on you when you came out of the bathroom, nigga, I sent her! Remember when she was all rubbing on you and shit? Nigga, I had her seeing if you had a piece!" Rufus said.

Richie saw a car coming down the street. "Rufus, there go a car!"

The split second when Rufus turned his head, Albert violently head butted him.

"Ahhh shit!" Rufus yelled, as he tumbled down the stairs, landing flat on his back.

Albert jumped on top of him and brutally went to beating the shit out of him. In between blows, Albert and Rufus struggled for possession of the gun. Richie and Rufus's two other men managed to pull Albert off Rufus.

Rufus swiftly hopped up with blood dripping from everywhere. He smiled at Albert, and then spit out a mouth full of blood.

"You got more heart than I thought you had! And here I was thinking that all red niggas was soft!" Rufus joked.

Albert tried to furiously charge towards Rufus, but six hands held him back. Albert was breathing heavily and snorting like a bull.

Rufus pointed his .38 special at Albert. With vengeance, Albert looked Rufus straight in the eyes. Rufus grinned before firing three shots, which hit Albert in his upper torso.

Rufus's men nervously dropped Albert's body, and in shock, then stared at Rufus in disbelief.

"Let's get out of here!" Rufus ordered, as him and his men quickly took off.

While resting on the sidewalk on his back, Albert stared up at the sky. He tried to move, but he couldn't.

"Gotta…get …up," he told himself.

Him and Loretta's wedding flashed in front of him, then their honeymoon, and then the day Melissa was born. As the approaching sirens echoed in his ears, he became drowsy and struggled to keep his eyes open.

"Gotta…try…and…move!" he told himself.

Earlier that day flashed in front of him. Goldie was cheerfully meeting him at the front door with his report card behind his back. What did his son make?

"Gotta…make…it…home!" he encouraged himself.

Albert felt an excruciating pain in his chest. His vision became blurry. He had to fight; he had things he needed to take care of, things he needed to make right. He couldn't afford to leave Loretta and the kids behind, not like this. He couldn't let them down; he was their provider.

"Albert...we're ready!" Albert heard a spooky voice say.

"No, no, no!" Albert screamed, but his lips did not move.

"Don't try and fight it, Albert. Just relax and let go!" the voice said.

Albert's entire life flashed in front of him in thirty seconds. He tried, but he could not fight anymore. Tears rolled down his eyes, and then he closed them.

"Now, that wasn't so hard now, Albert, was it?" the voice said.

CHAPTER SEVEN

For some strange reason, it seemed as if it always rained on Saturday funerals towards the end of the year. Everyone in attendance stood quiet, taking in every word during the reading of the eulogy. Loretta was trying hard to conceal her tears by hiding her face under her veil, with an oversized hat. The rain made it challenging to distinguish whether it was droplets of rain or tears running down everyone's faces.

Goldie maintained his composure. He could not find it in him to cry. Did he hate his father that much, or had all the pain he endured over the years caused him to become numb?

Loretta reached over and compassionately rubbed Goldie's back. She noticed that out of all of her children, he was the only one who wasn't weeping.

After the preacher finished with his sermon, everyone came over, one by one, and gave Loretta and the kids grieving hugs. Loretta graciously thanked everybody for their support.

Once the crowd started thinning out, the funeral home director assisted Adriana and the baby with an umbrella back to the limo to give Loretta and the kids a few minutes alone.

Loretta opened up her arms. "Come here, ya'll," she told her children. Everyone gathered and shared in a group hug. "Don't worry, we got each other!" Loretta said, encouragingly.

Goldie observed the pain and frustration in his mother's eyes. His blood started boiling, and he gritted his teeth. Now, he hated his father even more for leaving his mother all alone. If they were barely making it when his father was alive, he could only imagine what things were going to be like without him.

After everyone had taken turns saying their last goodbyes, Goldie was the last one up.

"Take your time, baby. Get it all out of your system," his mother said, rubbing him on the back.

Loretta gave the funeral director a nod, indicating she was ready for him to escort her and the kids back to the limo, where Albert's parents, Adriana, and the baby were waiting. Once Loretta reached the limo, she glanced back to check on Goldie, who was standing erect, overlooking his father's casket.

Goldie stared up at the dark, gloomy sky, as the rain trickled down on his face. It was then when reality hit him. He realized his father was gone off the face of the earth, and was never coming back. That meant they would never spend a Father's Day together, he would not be present in the stands at his graduation, and most of all, he would not be present to see the woman he chose as his wife.

Goldie took a deep breath and then directed his attention to where his father's casket was resting. Thanks to Dollar and a couple of his father's friends, Albert had gone out in style. He was peacefully resting in an almond casket with gold trimming. Dollar had even buried him in an expensive white Italian suit.

Goldie took another deep breath, then kneeled down and let it all out. "You know…when I was little, I use to wanna be just like you! Then you changed! That lady…whatever her name is…ever since you started messing with her, you just started neglecting us! You were always too damn busy! Not once…not one time did you ever tell me you loved me or 'Son, I'm proud of you and your grades'! You ain't even notice when I started acting up in school to try and get your attention!"

Tears began rapidly pouring out of Goldie's eyes, and he felt a sharp pain in his chest, as if he had heartburn.

"We never did shit together!" Goldie lashed out. "It was always about you, and everybody else was last! Momma should have been done left your ass!" he said, wiping his nose and sniffling.

The clouds began to darken and the rain started pouring even harder. The wind whistled, but Goldie was numb and could not feel a single drop of rain. He reached into his suit pocket, pulled out his report card, and belligerently tossed it on top of his father's casket.

"Just in case you wanted to know, I made the Dean's list. That's all A's in case you don't know! If you weren't in so much of a hurry Friday, it would have only taken you two minutes of your precious time to see it for yourself!" Goldie felt relieved getting that off his chest.

Lightning illuminated the sky. The funeral director honked his horn. Goldie turned around and made a gesture to give him a minute.

"You don't have to worry about Momma. I'll make sure that she be alright! I'm the man of the house now, and it's my will to do a better job than you did! I'ma find a way to move Momma outta the projects and make sure that Jeff go to college, even if it kills me!" Goldie said, hitting on his chest.

His tears began to compete with the rain. "If I ever have kids...I'ma make sure they never go through what you put me through!"

He paused for a minute. "I'm picking up where you left off, and I'm gonna straighten everything out!" Goldie said as he confidently stood up and adjusted his jacket. "Take care, Albert...because deep down inside, you don't deserve to be called father!"

Goldie wiped away all of his childish tears, then walked away a man.

CHAPTER EIGHT

For hours, Goldie had been sprinting up and down the basketball court, trying to clear his mind. Now, his entire body dripped sweat.

"Five…four…three…two…one!" Goldie said, before releasing a shot from the three-pointer line, hitting all net.

Snake clapped as he walked onto the basketball court. "Nice shot, lil' man!"

Goldie turned around, surprised to hear his voice. "How long have you been standing there?" he asked.

"A few minutes," Snake said.

Goldie shot a lay-up. Ever since six o'clock that morning, he had been energetically running up and down the court, shooting shot after shot and trying to escape from the reality that his father was gone. It was nine o'clock.

"Listen, Goldie! I know this is hard for you," Snake said, walking over to him.

Goldie continued shooting. Ever since the funeral yesterday, he had not been able to sleep. Last night, he stayed up all night, comforting his mom. Although she had managed to keep her composure during the funeral, it was not until later on that night when reality hit her and she realized Albert was gone.

Before Goldie could shoot another shot, Snake grabbed the basketball from out of his hands. "Listen, Goldie! Nigga...you like the lil' brother I never had! Your beef is my beef!" Snake declared, hitting his right closed fist aggressively against his chest.

"Whoever this motherfucker is that killed your father, I'll find him!" Snake assured. "My people got their ears to the streets. So believe me, I'll find this motherfucker and take care of that for you!"

Goldie boldly stepped in front of Snake's face, looked him in the eyes, and said, "Then you better find him before me!"

Snake was tickled. "Chill out, lil' man! Everybody ain't no killer. It takes a coldhearted motherfucker, or somebody who has been pushed way over the edge!"

Goldie snatched his basketball back out of Snake's hand. "Like I told you, you better find him before me!" he retorted.

Snake smiled. *Shorty's just talking. I have to admit though...the lil' nigga got a lot of heart,* he said to himself. "Listen, Shorty...like I said...I'ma find this motherfucker, and put his ass to rest. That's on my word!"

Goldie walked back in front of Snake, like he was seven feet tall. "If you really wanna do something for me, you'll let me handle it myself when you find him!"

Snake started laughing, and then rubbed him on the head. Goldie just stared at him, not cracking a smile.

Snake observed how serious he seemed to be, and it puzzled him. He threw his hand on Goldie's shoulder. "Look here, Shorty, I got a couple of moves that I need to make. If I hear something, I'll get at you!" Snake said, while reaching out his closed fist and giving him dap before departing.

* * * * *

"Damn! Pass the stem, Rufus!" Gina yelled, agitated.

"That's all you wanna do all day...smoke...smoke... smoke!" Rufus yelled, as he handed Gina the stem.

"Hand me the pusher!" Gina impatiently said.

Rufus just shook his head, then handed her the pusher.

He had been hiding out for a little over a week now. Turns out, not only had Albert died that night, the houseman Sonny had also died three days later from brain damage.

While creeping in and out of the hood, Rufus had bumped into Gina a couple of days ago while he was copping a bundle of heroin. After the heroin ran out, Gina had cunningly convinced him to try crack. Her plan worked perfectly, and Rufus immediately became hooked. Gina had blown his mind. Once she loaded up the stem for him, then sucked his dick while he took his first hit, he was never the same.

"Baby, we're all out of dope!" Gina cried.

Rufus was in a daze. The crack gave him a different high.

"Rufus, do you hear me?" Gina pouted.

Balled up in a corner, nervously rocking back and forth like a little kid, his eyes were glossy. Images of Albert flashed in front of his face, causing him to jump up in fear.

"No...no...no...get away from me!" he frantically yelled, swinging at the air.

"What the hell is wrong with you, Rufus?" Gina nervously yelled.

Rufus deliriously shook his head, while covering his ears and trying to tune out the annoying voices.

"You think you gonna get away with this?" Rufus kept hearing Albert's voice echo in his ear.

"Leave me alone!" Rufus yelled, as he continued to swing at the air.

Gina cautiously stepped back. *This motherfucker is crazy,* she said to herself.

Rufus powerlessly dropped to his knees in front of Gina, then cried, "No...no...make them noises go away. I swear...I swear, Gina...I didn't mean to kill him...I swear I didn't!"

Gina was puzzled. "Kill who?"

"I swear...oh God...I swear, Gina!" Rufus continued to weep.

Gina was curious about who Rufus was talking about. She didn't know if it was the crack or the smoking head she had given him earlier that had him confessing. Rufus was a big man, so Gina kneeled down to him and proceeded with caution. "Tell me what's the matter, Daddy?" Gina asked, while massaging Rufus's back.

Rufus buried his head in her 36 double D's. "I didn't wanna kill him, Gina...I swear!"

"Who the fuck is he talking about?" Gina mumbled to herself, rubbing his head.

Rufus wiped his nose. "Albert, Gina...I didn't mean to kill him!" Rufus confessed.

Gina's eyes lit up with dollar signs in them. She smiled while comforting Rufus, already spending the reward money in her head. Word on the street was that Snake had out a $5,000 reward for

Albert's killer. Somehow, Gina mysteriously always happened to be at the right place at the right time.

"It's gonna be alright, baby!" Gina said, rocking him back and forth.

Rufus had no idea he had just confessed to the wrong bitch. The crack had him so much out of his character, the treacherous gangster in him had been converted into a big ole' teddy bear.

"Momma's gonna go and get you just what you need to ease your pain. I need a hundred dollars, though," Gina said, holding out her hand.

Rufus willfully reached into his pockets and handed Gina five twenty-dollar bills. He noticed his wad was getting low. He had blown sixty-five hundred of the seven grand he owed Snake.

"I need the keys," Gina added.

"Hurry back!" Rufus said, willingly handing over the keys.

Gina kissed him on the forehead. "I promise you...after tonight, you'll finally be able to get you some real rest. When you wake up...I promise you, you'll be right where you suppose to be," Gina said sarcastically, and then disappeared out of the door.

Gina arrived at the projects in record time. After recklessly parking with one wheel up on the curb, she jumped out of the car and rushed over to Snake's crew. His crew put away their guns when they noticed the reckless driver was Gina.

"Man, what the fuck is wrong with you, rolling up here like that?" Mookie asked, agitated.

"I know who killed Albert...I know who killed Albert!" she screamed, leaning forward with her hands on her knees, and out of breath.

"What you talking about, Gina?" Black Jesus asked with an inquisitive look.

Gina took a deep breath. "I've been at the hotel for two days with Rufus."

"Where the fuck is that motherfucker at?" Mookie asked, ready to put a cap in his ass about Snake's money. "That motherfucker owes Snake seven grand!" he let slip out.

Gina's eyes lit up; maybe that meant more money. She placed her hand on her hips. "Let me finish! Two days ago, Rufus made me get a room for him in my name. We've been there for two days straight now. I even got him smoking!" Gina boasted.

Snake's crew looked at her shocked.

"Today, all of a sudden, this motherfucker takes a hit and starts acting all crazy! He starts crying like a lil' bitch and shit, talking about he ain't mean to kill Albert!" Gina finished.

"What hotel that motherfucker at?" Black Jesus asked.

"Unhhh, unhhh…ya'll gotta break me off first!" Gina stubbornly insisted, crossing her arms. "Call Snake! He the only one I'm telling so I make sure I get my five grand!"

"Wait right here!" Black Jesus said, as he walked over to the payphone to make the call.

Snake was cruising the city when his phone rang. He noticed the number was from the payphone at the corner store. "Hello?" he answered.

"Yo, I got somebody over here that say they know where them people at!"

"Who?" Snake asked.

"Gina," Black Jesus said.

Snake laughed. Gina always was at the right place at the right time when it came to anything concerning money. "Did you check it out?" Snake asked.

"The bitch won't budge! She tripping, talking 'bout she ain't telling nobody but you where he at 'cause she want her $5,000!"

Snake laughed again. Gina was a crackhead, but she wasn't no dummy. "Go ahead and break her off a lil' bit of that, and if shit check out, fuck the money, pay her!" Snake said.

"Alright!" Black Jesus said.

"If shit do check out, grab that nigga and call me as soon as ya'll got him! Snake said.

"Peace," Black Jesus said, hanging up the payphone.

Meanwhile, Rufus was impatiently pacing his hotel room. He checked his watch. It was 5:30 P.M. "Where the hell this bitch at?"

Gina had been gone ever since noon. Rufus was debating on whether he should catch a cab into the hood and go search for her and his car, but where would he start? Knowing Gina, she could be anywhere.

As Rufus paced the room, his high began to wear off, allowing him to think more clearly. Then it dawned on him. He had just confessed about a damn murder to a crackhead. Frustrated, he plopped down on the edge of the bed and buried his head into his hands. "Damn!" Rufus screamed.

Knowing Snake, he was sure there was some kind of reward out on the street for any information on his whereabouts. Rufus knew he had to get rid of Gina. Now, she was the only witness. After the robbery, he had killed all three of his men as a precaution.

Rufus peeped out of the curtains when he heard a car pull in front of the hotel's window. It was Gina.

"This bitch better have a damn good excuse!" Rufus said, as he continued to peep out of the curtains. "It don't even matter. I'ma kill this bitch anyway," he arrogantly said to himself. "Maybe I'll just kill her with my bare hands so I can watch those pretty eyes pop out of her head," he said, jokingly making a choking gesture with his hands.

Rufus walked over, sat on the edge of the bed, and waited on Gina. Two minutes passed. Rufus irritably hopped up off the bed and peeped back through the curtains. Gina was still sitting in the car, looking in the rearview mirror and putting on lipstick. She had changed clothes and was now sporting a fresh hairdo.

When Gina observed Rufus peeping through the curtains, she smiled, fluttered her eyelashes, and waved.

Rufus smirked.

Gina blew him a kiss. "That's the kiss of death, motherfucker," she mumbled.

Gina reached into her purse and conservatively sprayed a couple of squirts of Poison perfume. She then reached over into the passenger seat, grabbing the liter of Seagram's Gin and her purse, and hopped out the car.

When Gina arrived at the door, she knocked. Rufus opened the door, astonished at what he saw. Gina looked like a new person. Her luscious red lipstick enhanced her perfectly round lips. Her high yellow complexioned skin was lotioned. Her hair was styled in an updated hairdo, and she was wearing a pair of shorts so skimpy that you could see where her pubic hairs were growing back. Gina looked like a black "Daisy Duke." She had her top tied in a knot, displaying her flat stomach. She was now standing six-feet tall thanks to the six-inch stilettos she was rocking.

"You like, Daddy?" Gina asked, spinning around.

"Yeah!" Rufus said, shaking his head, while drooling.

"Here, hold my purse and this bottle for me while I go and get your present from out of the trunk," Gina said.

Rufus obliged. With both of his hands occupied, and his attention on Gina's ass cheeks hanging out of her shorts, he never noticed Snake's crew creeping along the side of the hotel's wall. When he read Gina's eyes, he tried to figure out with whom she was making eye contact.

"Oh shit!" Rufus shouted.

By the time he realized what was going on, he dropped the bottle and Gina's purse, and tried swiftly to reach for his gun, but it was already too late. Snake's crew kicked in the door. Rufus fell to the ground and simultaneously heard three guns cock.

"Motherfucker, you thought you could hide? Don't you know we got eyes everywhere? Tie this motherfucker up!" Black Jesus instructed Peanut and Mookie.

While they were securing Rufus's hands and ankles with duct tape, Black Jesus walked over and picked up the .38 from off of the coffee table. The .38 snub nose confirmed Gina's story was true.

"You stupid motherfucker! You still around here with the damn murder weapon?" Black Jesus asked, shocked.

Just then, an all-black van with limo tint pulled in front of the room and the side door slid open. Black Jesus surveyed the area before motioning for Peanut and Mookie to bring out Rufus's body. Two of Snake's men greeted Peanut and Mookie at the van's door, and Rufus's body was quickly placed inside of the van. At 6'7" and 280 pounds, it wasn't an easy task. Once securing Rufus inside, Black Jesus motioned with his hand and the van pulled off. He walked over to Gina and handed her the rest of the agreed upon amount.

"Thank you!" she said, smiling. "Do I get to keep the clothes?"

"Yeah," Black Jesus said. He pointed his finger at Gina. "If I so much as hear a peep about what just happened, they'll find dinosaur bones before they find your ass!"

Gina swallowed. She knew she would be signing her own death certificate if she talked.

Black Jesus handed her another two hundred dollars. "Tell the front office that you and your boyfriend had a little argument and he pushed you into the door."

A black IROC with dark tinted windows pulled up, and Mookie got out of the car and hopped into the backseat. Black Jesus walked over to the passenger side of the car, then paused and looked back at Gina.

"I'm serious about what I said, Gina! I'd hate for Mrs. Bernadine to have to go before her time!" he threatened.

Gina nodded her head that she understood.

Black Jesus hopped inside of the IROC, and Peanut sped off.

* * * * *

"What's up, Snake?" Goldie asked, observing something poking out of the front of Snake's shirt and the vengeance in his eyes.

"We found that motherfucker that killed your daddy!" Snake said.

Goldie gritted his teeth and his eyes got bloodshot red.

Snake read his face. "Don't worry, lil' man, I'm finna handle that shit for you."

Goldie swiftly rushed up and got in Snake's face. "I told you, I wanna kill that motherfucker myself!"

Snake eased Goldie back with his hand for breathing room. "Hold on, lil' man, me and you are on the same team! Right now, you just talking out of emotions, and you really don't mean what you saying. Everybody ain't no killer, Shorty!"

"I can't speak for everybody; all I can do is speak for Goldie!"

Snake studied him. He was dead serious. "Look here, lil' man, I feel your pain, but I can't let you get caught up in this kind of shit! You ain't ready for this type of shit!"

"He fucked up my family!" Goldie screamed. "It's because of him that my momma can't sleep at night! She stuck in debt, wondering how she gonna provide for us. Me, my sisters, and lil brother gotta spend the rest of our life without a father!"

Snake observed the tears pouring out of his eyes. He was empathetic. He felt his pain. He knew how he felt when his mother died. Snake took a deep breath, then stared up at the sky. He shook his head and mumbled to himself, "I don't even know why I'm doing this." Snake bit his bottom lip, unlocked the passenger door, and said, "Get in, Shorty."

* * * * *

The spot was an old abandoned warehouse on the outskirts of town, located in the industrial area. The spot, which was so far out you could fire gunshots and not be heard for a five-mile radius, was perfect for the occasion.

When the car parked, Black Jesus could not believe his eyes when he saw an image resembling a kid sitting in the front seat. "This nigga done lost his damn mind!" he said.

Mookie and Peanut were also puzzled. They looked at each other, then at Black Jesus. Snake got out of the car. He immediately read everyone's curious faces, and knew that he had some explaining to do.

"Yo, Snake, what's wrong with you bringing shorty with you?" Black Jesus asked.

"Chill out, and let me explain."

As Goldie waited patiently in the car, he could tell by reading everyone's facial expressions that he was the topic of discussion. It was obvious; especially the way Snake's whole crew kept periodically glancing over at the car and shaking their heads.

"Listen, man, shorty's real! Rufus killed his daddy! Remember now, this is the same shorty that saw me kill that crackhead motherfucker, and he ain't blow the whistle! Now, I don't know if he's ready for this type of shit, but I at least gotta present him with this opportunity! I owe him one. Besides, this is closure. Shit...I killed two motherfuckers when I was ten, so it's possible," Snake said, shrugging his shoulders and laughing.

"Alright, you're the boss!" Black Jesus said.

"Listen. If shorty can't pull the trigger, I'll let Peanut and Mookie drop him off at the projects. Then me and you will handle this," Snake told Black Jesus.

Black Jesus nodded his head in approval. "Bring that motherfucker out of the van!" Black Jesus ordered Mookie and Peanut.

Rufus was blindfolded, with his hands positioned behind his back and duct tape wrapped around his wrists and ankles.

When Black Jesus snatched the blindfold off Rufus's eyes and he looked around at his environment, he knew it was checkout time. Besides, neither Snake nor none of his men was wearing masks.

Snake motioned for Goldie to get out of the car. Black Jesus just shook his head, really disagreeing with the call, but played his role. Goldie walked over to where Snake was standing and stood next to him.

Snake pointed at Rufus. "Lil' man, that's the motherfucker that killed your daddy," he said.

Black Jesus walked over and handed Snake Rufus's gun. He shrugged his shoulders. "Might as well kill him with the gun he killed his daddy with!" he joked.

Snake shook his head and laughed. "You know...that's real creative. I like that!" Snake checked the gun to see if it was already loaded, which it was. "Lil' man, you ever shot a gun before?"

Goldie shook his head.

Snake kneeled down. "Lil' man, are you sure that you wanna do this? Once you cross this line, you a killer."

Goldie stared into Rufus's eyes with a dreadful look on his face. "Yeah, this is what I wanna do!" he said confidently.

Snake patted him on the back. "Good!" He then walked over to Rufus. "Motherfucker, do you got any last words?"

"Listen, man, I ain't mean to kill him," Rufus pleaded. "It just happened so quick!"

"Ummmm hmmm," Snake said jokingly. "Well, this shit gonna go the same way," he replied sarcastically. He then unfastened his pants and started pissing all over Rufus, drenching his entire body.

Everybody except Goldie started laughing.

"Come here, lil' man," Snake said, motioning for Goldie, who walked over to join him. "You see how I'm holding this here?" Snake asked, pointing his gun at Rufus's dome.

"Yeah, I see!" Goldie said attentively.

"All you gotta do is hold it just like this, then squeeze the trigger whenever you're ready. Now, if you scared, you can just close your eyes when you pull the trigger," Snake said, handing Goldie the gun.

Goldie lifted the gun and pointed it straight at Rufus's head. He belligerently stared Rufus directly in the eyes.

Rufus smirked at him. He didn't think he had the balls to pull the trigger. Rufus studied shorty carefully, and truthfully, the more he stared into Goldie's eyes, the more skeptical he became. Shorty had that same look in his eyes that Albert had before he killed him. The only difference was that shorty's look was more vicious, and he had a gun.

Tears began to pour out of Goldie's eyes like a waterfall. As he stared into Rufus's pupils, all the times him and his father shared played like a movie, the good ones and the bad ones. Then his father's funeral played. He saw the pain on his mother's face as they stood over his father's casket. Goldie bit his bottom lip.

Snake walked over, kneeled down to Goldie's ear, then said, "It's because of this motherfucker your lil' brother and sisters gotta live the rest of their lives without a father. 'Cause of this motherfucker, your momma don't have a husband."

Goldie's hand started trembling and Rufus's eyes got larger than quarters.

"Shoot this motherfucker!" Snake yelled into Goldie's ear.

"I can't!" Goldie said, dropping the gun.

Black Jesus, Mookie, and Peanut all looked over at Snake and just shook their heads.

"It's alright, lil' man," Snake said, looking over at his crew and feeling embarrassed.

As he took the gun out of Goldie's hand, Rufus dropped his head and let out a sigh of relief. He knew he was going to die, but at least now, he had a couple more minutes to spare to get right with God.

Shrugging his shoulders, Snake looked over at Black Jesus, who gave him one of those "I told you so" looks.

All of a sudden, Rufus let out a loud scream. "Ahhhhh!"

Goldie had pulled out his butterfly knife and brutally stabbed Rufus directly in the heart. Goldie looked him directly in the eyes, horrendously turning his knife, while Rufus coughed up blood. Goldie felt empowered as he watched life slowly escape out of Rufus's body.

Everybody stood frozen, completely in shock. They could not believe this action from a fucking ten-year-old. Anybody could pull a trigger, but to stab a motherfucker while looking them directly in the eyes and watching took heart.

Goldie savagely jerked his knife from out of Rufus's lifeless body. Breathing heavily and covered in blood, Goldie stepped back like a gladiator.

"Get that motherfucker up out of here!" Snake ordered Peanut and Mookie with a grin on his face, and then walked over to Goldie with a rag in his hand. "Gimme the knife, Shorty!"

"Naw, I'm keeping it! This here got sentimental value, and I'ma make this a souvenir," Goldie said boldly, then brushed past Snake, walked over to the passenger side of the Nova, and jumped in.

Snake and Black Jesus stared at each other in disbelief, then shook their heads and started laughing.

* * * * *

There was total silence in the car during the entire ride back into town. Goldie was still holding the knife in his right hand with a vice grip.

Snake decided to break the silence. "Yo, Shorty, you alright?"

"I did what I had to do," Goldie said, as he continued to stare out of the window.

"You know that what just happened tonight has to stay between us, right? I mean…you can't even tell your momma," Snake said.

"I don't know what you talking about. I been at the park all night playing basketball," Goldie said like a natural.

Snake looked over at him, smiled, and rubbed him on the top of the head. "It's official now, nigga. You 100% gangster!"

* * * * *

When Goldie entered his apartment, his mother and brother were both stretched out across the living room sofa, knocked out. He tiptoed into the kitchen and grabbed a trash bag from out of the cabinet. After peeping outside of the kitchen to confirm that his mother and his brother were still asleep, he snuck upstairs to his bedroom.

The moment he stepped inside, he began stripping out of his clothes and stuffing them into the trash bag, so he could give them to Snake the next morning when he met him at the bus stop to take him to school. When he heard the front door downstairs open, he quickly stashed the trash bag under his mattress and plopped down on his bed. He heard footsteps coming up the stairs.

Melissa swung his room door open. "Boy, where your lil' butt been at?"

"Close my door, girl! Don't you see I'm in my boxers?" Goldie yelled.

"I'ma tell Momma! Your lil' butt thinks you're grown!" Melissa spat.

"Gurl, I was at the park!"

"I done been to that park two times, and I ain't seen you none time!" Melissa said.

"Whatever!" Goldie said, waving her off.

Melissa rolled her eyes before storming out of the bedroom.

"Stupid girl! Think just because she grown that she run somebody," he mumbled to himself, while on his way to the bathroom.

Before hopping in the shower, he examined himself in the mirror until the water got hot, and then he jumped in.

While the hot water trickled down his neck, relaxing his entire body, the scenes from the night kept replaying inside his head. All that kept flashing before his eyes was the look that Rufus displayed on his face before he died. Tonight, he felt something. Tonight, he felt empowered. Although he had tortured numerous animals, on several occasions, amazed at watching them die a slow death, a human was different. This was his first human.

Feeling rejuvenated and cleansed of Rufus's blood, he eased out of the shower and paused at the mirror, studying himself once again.

"Yeah, now these motherfuckers know that if they ever fuck with me, or anybody in my family, they better come motherfucking correct!" he said, hitting his fist into his hand and nodding his head, while grinning his teeth to the image in the mirror.

CHAPTER NINE

Whoever said when it rains it pours was absolutely right. Loretta didn't know what she was going to do. She was sitting at the dining room table, frustrated, thumbing through a large stack of bills. All of a sudden, she went neurotic and frantically knocked all of the bills off the table. She started crying, the tears pouring like a rainstorm.

She stared up at the ceiling. "Why, Albert...why did you leave me all alone like this?" she sobbed, pounding her fist on the dining room table. "Oh God, what am I gonna do?"

It had been a little over six months since Albert's death, and in that short period, her whole world had managed to make a change for the worst. She had sunken so far in debt that she felt trapped in quicksand. With the debt she was in, she knew it would take a miracle to bail her out.

With both Melissa and Ciera pregnant, the little bit of help she had been getting from them had to now go towards preparing for their future babies. For the past couple of months, Loretta's blood pressure had been sky-high. She was suffering from a deadly combination of stress and depression. Her supervisor tried to support her by charitably giving her every little bit of overtime available. Lately, she had been working so much around the clock that she had barely been around to spend time with the kids. She faulted herself for both Melissa and Ciera's pregnancies.

Loretta took a Newport out of the pack that she secretly kept hid in her bra and lit it. To ease her nerves, smoking was a habit she had picked up from a co-worker a little over two months ago. The tears continued to fall, as she took drag after drag, all the way down to the filter. When she finished, she placed the cigarette butt inside of the ashtray. It wasn't until she put the cigarette out and looked up that she noticed Goldie standing in front of her.

"How long you been standing there?" Loretta asked, feeling embarrassed, as she fixed herself up and wiped away her tears.

Goldie empathetically walked over to his mother with a grimace on his face. She looked like a nervous wreck. Not only had bags settled under her eyes, she looked like somebody had pushed the fast forward button on her life. In only a couple of months, she looked like she had aged a couple of years. Goldie stuck his bottom lip out, while breathing heavily, as his blood suddenly started to boil.

"When you start smoking cigarettes?" he lashed out.

"Wait a minute now! If I'm not mistaken, I'm grown!" his mother reminded him.

"Then why you sitting up there crying?" Goldie asked concerned.

A few tears fell as Loretta stared up at the ceiling. She sighed. "Momma's just having a really tough time and struggling right now, that's all. Come here, baby!" she said, opening her arms in desperate need of a hug.

When Goldie reached her, she took him into her arms and lovingly squeezed him. "Mmmm, Momma needed that!" she said, releasing him two minutes later.

Goldie stepped back and studied his mom. She was deteriorating day by day. He understood the physical and emotional stress she was going through. He knew deep down inside she wanted to be able to spend more time around the house with them, but if she worked less hours, then the bills would only continue to pile up. It was killing Goldie to sit back and watch the woman that had brought him into this world struggling like this.

"Ma, how much do you think it's gonna take to get you all the way caught up with the bills?" Goldie asked.

"Humph! Lord...It's gonna take a couple of thousand at least!" his mother said.

Goldie kissed his mother on the forehead, placed his hands on her shoulders, and stared into her eyes. "Listen, Momma...I promise you I'm gonna take care of this! Okay?"

Loretta stared into her son's hazel eyes. She saw fire, ambition, and determination.

"Listen, Momma, I'm finna go outside," Goldie said, and then militantly headed out of the door.

* * * * *

When Goldie arrived at the park, he quickly pinpointed Snake, who was casually lounging up against his Caddy, macking to some big-booty red-bone, as usual.

Goldie walked over to him. "Yo, Snake! I need to holla at you!"

"Give me a minute, Shorty," Snake said nonchalantly, returning his attention back to the red-bone and continuing his conversation.

Goldie impatiently stepped off to the side and waited on the sidewalk. To remain calm, he walked around in small circles with his hands behind his back. Five minutes passed. Agitated, he walked back over and interrupted Snake.

"Yo, Snake, this is real important," he said in a tone that Snake had never heard him use.

The red-bone tooted up her nose, shot Goldie a "no he didn't" look, rolled her eyes, and then directed her attention back to Snake. Snake studied Goldie's face, then whispered something into the red-bone's ear and patted her on the ass. The red-bone shot Goldie another look that was equivalent to three quick right jabs and a left upper cut, then walked off with an attitude.

"Ummmm...ummmm," Snake said, biting his right fist at the sight of all the ass the red-bone had. "I'ma call you tonight!" he yelled, as he admired her ass.

Snake returned his attention back to Goldie, who for some strange reason seemed very agitated. "Lil' man, what's wrong with you?" Snake asked, with a puzzled look on his face.

"I need to make some money!" Goldie said with authority, and hitting his fist in his hand.

Snake studied him. He had hunger in his eyes. Snake pulled out a wad of money and quickly peeled off a couple of twenties.

"How much you need, lil' man?" he asked, pausing after he had flipped through five twenties.

"Naw, man," Goldie said, waving off Snake's money and feeling insulted. "I'm tired of taking money from you! I ain't no damn charity case! If you feeling like you owe me just because I didn't tell on you, you wrong! I did that shit because I'm real, and I ain't no snitch!" Goldie said, beating on his chest. "I ain't like these other eleven year olds out here!"

Snake attentively listened, taking in every word, while studying Goldie's facial expression and hand gestures. He seemed sincere.

"I need to make money, man, and I need to make it right now! My family's struggling, and they need me! How am I supposed to call myself the man of the house if I can't provide for them? Come on, man. All they can do to me, if something happens, is take me to J.D.C.!" Goldie pleaded, as he walked up to Snake and begged for his assistance.

Snake was all ears. Goldie had put on a star-stunning performance.

"You sure you ready for this?" Snake asked for confirmation, as he crossed his arms and rubbed his chin.

"I gotta be!" Goldie said with conviction.

Snake silently walked over to his car and unlocked the doors. "Get in, Shorty!" he told Goldie, while he eased himself inside. Snake cranked up his car, then broke the silence. "Rule number one, you always listen to me! Rule number two…"

* * * * *

After switching cars, Snake toured the entire city, showing Goldie the ropes to the game. He introduced him to a couple of cats he sold packs to, letting them know that from time to time Goldie might make some of the drop offs. He also rode him around to a couple of his traps to show him the running of a trap.

When they arrived back at the projects, Snake showed him all of the good hiding spots around the park where he could easily access his rocks. Snake gave him ten rocks, and then sat back and let him get his feet wet by handling a couple of transactions.

Thirty minutes later, all ten rocks were gone. Goldie walked over and handed Snake the two hundred dollars.

"Here you go," he said, green to the game.

Snake smiled and pushed the money away. "You just made that, lil' man, not me."

Goldie's face lit up like a 300-watt light bulb.

Snake winked at him, as he stood with his arms folded. "See how easy that was?"

"Yeah!" Goldie said, excited.

"Now that was the easy part. The hard part is not letting the police run up on you and catch you dirty. Understand?" Snake asked.

Goldie nodded his head.

"Can you run, lil' man?" Snake asked.

"Hell yeah!" Goldie said, striking the Heisman pose.

Snake laughed. "Okay, you gonna need them wheels if the 'green team' ever rush up on the block," he said, patting Goldie on the back.

"Don't worry. I'll be ready for them!" Goldie shouted.

"Listen! If they ever do happen to rush up on you, just run over through James Park. We got people that stay in apartments G-8, F-5, and C-1, who will open their back doors for us to run in," Snake instructed.

"Then make sure you let them know who I am! I don't wanna be getting chased, and then run to their back door and they don't open it because they don't know who I am," Goldie said.

Snake smiled. He liked the way Goldie was already thinking ahead. "Alright, Shorty, I'll swing by their apartment and take care of that before I go home."

"Appreciate it!" Goldie said.

"Now that you got that lil' two hundred dollars, the real question is what are you gonna do with it?"

"I don't know. I'm probably gonna give my momma most of it for the bills," he said.

Snake shook his head, moving his index finger back and forth. "That's the wrong answer."

Goldie gave him a puzzled look. "What you mean?"

Snake looked at his watch. "The day's still young. I'm talking about flipping that shit, Shorty!"

"Flipping it?" Goldie asked, as if Snake had just spoken in another language.

"Yeah, you know...turning two hundred into four, four into eight. You pretty good with math, so you know what I'm talking about," Snake said.

Goldie was not exactly sure what Snake was talking about, but he liked the way those numbers sounded. "How I do that?" he asked.

"I thought you'd never ask. Gimme the two hundred," Snake said.

At first, Goldie was a little hesitant, but then he willingly handed Snake the money.

"Easy up, Shorty!" Snake said, seeing how hesitant Goldie was to hand over his earnings. Snake then reached into a sandwich bag and pulled out twenty enormous pieces of crack. He walked over to his car, went into the glove compartment, and came back with an empty pill bottle in his hand. He placed the twenty rocks inside of the pill bottle, which he handed to Goldie.

"When you finish with them, you should be done made you four hundred dollars easy," Snake said.

Goldie studied the pill bottle, liking the way four hundred sounded.

"Hey Mookie...Peanut...ya'll come over here for a minute!" Snake yelled.

Mookie and Peanut came over. "What's up, Snake?" the two asked.

Snake rubbed Goldie on the head. "This here is the newest member on the team. He gonna post up with ya'll from time to time so he can make a couple of dollars to help his family out. Right now, his family's hurting, so he's doing the manly thing and stepping up to the plate."

Mookie and Peanut nodded in admiration and welcomed him with opened arms. Goldie was treacherous. He had earned their respect the night he horrendously killed Rufus.

"Ya'll take him under ya'll wings, and throw him into rotation with the sales," Snake ordered.

"Alright," the two said.

"I got a couple of things I gotta go take care of, lil man. GET THAT MONEY!" Snake stressed to Goldie, then hopped into his car and drove off.

When Snake left, Goldie stayed posted up on the block until nine o'clock that night. By nightfall, he had two-hundred dollars in his pockets and ten rocks left in his pill bottle. Peanut and Mookie had schooled him on how to sell his rocks, and showed him a couple tricks of the trade, like how to break a twenty into a dime using his fingernails. For the most part, the two of them had been letting him take turns with them on the sales. Then greed kicked in, and they started skipping him. Before he even knew what was going on, they would competitively dash off to a car with their product in their hands.

Instead of dashing out to customers' cars like Peanut and Mookie, Goldie just sat on the sideline like a rookie and watched everything, becoming familiar with every car that came through. By the end of the night, he knew how the crackhead Bob's car sounded by the knocking engine noise. He knew that white girl Cindy, in the blue Trans Am, always spent a hundred. He could distinguish Ray's car coming down the street, whenever he heard the sound of a dragging muffler.

That night, Goldie just soaked up all of the game. Presently, he was a student, but he knew once he became familiar with the entire operation, he would be on his way to becoming a certified hustler.

CHAPTER TEN

For the past couple of months, Loretta had become curious of where Goldie was getting the large sums of money he kept systematically leaving on her bedroom dresser to pay the bills. Although the extra money was helping her get out of debt, she suspiciously began to wonder if her son was out there doing anything illegal.

Today was Loretta's first day off in five weeks. Therefore, she spent the bulk of her day grocery shopping, cleaning up, and finishing the laundry. Dinner, which was cooking in the crock-pot, was almost ready. She peacefully had the house all to herself for the moment. Jeff had spent the night over at a friend's house; Melissa and Ciera were both at work; and Goldie was at the mall.

Loretta plopped down on the sofa and casually took a sip from her peach Bartles & Jaymes wine cooler. Her body was desperately in need of this day of relaxation. As the day was flowing so smoothly, she could not believe her misfortune. Right slap in the middle of a comical episode of *The Jefferson's*, the TV went into a frenzy, displaying nothing but horizontal lines across the screen. She fumingly walked over and hit it a couple of times. Unsuccessful, she fretfully tried playing with the clothes hanger that served as the ghetto antennae. When that didn't work, she gripped the pliers and turned the knob until she successfully found another station. When she found one, she watched TV for a couple of minutes before dosing off.

* * * * *

After spending several hours and three grand at the mall, Snake and Goldie arrived back at the projects. Snake pulled over to the side of the curb by Goldie's apartment and let him out. Goldie grabbed his bags from out of the back seat.

"Appreciate it Snake! Good looking out!" Goldie said, while reaching inside of the car and giving Snake dap.

"You family, lil man. That's what family do. You still been taking care of them bills for your momma, right?" Snake inquisitively asked.

"Yeah, I've been taking care of the house," Goldie triumphantly declared, with his chest poked out.

Snake got a little sentimental for a moment, pondering on the thought that his mother was gone. He wished his mother were still alive so he could nourish her with expensive gifts or anything her heart desired. Deep down inside, he knew his mother was looking over him.

"Always make sure your momma's straight!" Snake emphasized. 'Cause when she gone, she's gone!" A little choked up, Snake wiped a tear before it fell. "So you got everything almost caught up?" he asked.

"I think so!" Goldie said unsure.

"Peep this! I'm opening up a lil' carwash on 18th Avenue in a couple of weeks. I'ma have you working up there with me, but we still gonna be doin' our thing in the streets. I know it's only a matter of time before your momma starts questioning where you getting all of this money from. I know you starting to run out of lies!" Snake joked.

Goldie laughed. "She has been asking questions."

"With the carwash, I'ma be able to tell her that I'm paying you two hundred dollars a week, or something like that, to ease her mind," Snake said.

"You the boss!" Goldie said sarcastically, then smiled.

"Remember that!" Snake said, smiling and pointing his finger at him. "Alright, lil man, I'ma holla in the morning."

* * * * *

The sound of the front door opening alarmed Loretta. She frantically jumped up off the sofa, simultaneously wiping the slobber she had accumulated during her catnap from off the side of her mouth. When she regained her vision, she realized the unexpected visitor was Goldie.

"Hey, Ma!" Goldie said, walking into the living room.

"Boy, you scared me half to death!" his mother said, placing her hand on her chest.

"I'm sorry," Goldie said, then walked over and kissed her on the forehead. "Here, this is for you."

Loretta looked inside of the bag he handed her and took out the dress. Lifting it up, she stared in awe. "This is beautiful!" she said.

Goldie smiled. This was the way he liked to see her, happy. Her face had its glow back, the bags had disappeared from under her eyes, and she was back to her regular schedule, which allowed her to spend more quality time at home with them.

"So you like it?"

"I love it! How did you know my size?" his mother asked.

Goldie laughed. "I snuck into your closet and peeped at the tag inside one of your dresses."

"This is beautiful," Loretta said, strikingly holding the dress up in front of her body.

"I got it from Mass Brothers!" Goldie boasted.

That alarmed Loretta. Mass Brothers was an expensive store. She eyed Goldie and then patted the sofa. "You need to come and sit down over here."

Goldie dragged his body over to the sofa, sat his bags down, and plopped down next to her.

Loretta earnestly looked him directly in the eyes. "Son, are you out there selling drugs?"

Goldie dropped his head. "I'm only a lookout," he mumbled.

His mother lifted up his chin. "Whatta you mean a lookout?" she asked.

"I just watch for the police. I get paid fifty dollars a day to just stand at the front entrance and watch for the police. If the police come, all I gotta do is let them know through the walkie talkie, then drop it and run," Goldie lied.

"Well, I want you to stop!" his mother commanded.

"I ain't breaking no rules, so I can't go to jail!" Goldie rationalized.

"Well, I still want you to stop!" his mother retorted.

"Why? So you can have a heart attack around here from working so hard!" Goldie said in an outburst.

Loretta was astounded. Goldie had never raised his voice at her.

"Listen, Momma, I'm sorry," Goldie woefully apologized, while empathetically grabbing his mother by the hands. "Daddy's gone now Momma...so I'm the man of the house. It's my obligation to make sure everything is alright. I may be eleven, but I'm smarter than a lot of these grown men out here," Goldie boasted.

Goldie gently rubbed his mother's hands. "I love you, Momma, and it's killing me seeing you stressed out, losing weight, crying all the time, and smoking them cancer sticks. I'm still making the honor roll, so you know what I'm doing ain't affecting my grades. All I'm asking Momma is that you let me be a boy in the day...and a man at night," Goldie begged.

Loretta stared into her son's eyes. He was a spitting image of Albert sitting in front of her. Dire situations had forced her son to become a man before he ever was allowed the chance to become a boy. She no longer saw a little boy sitting in front of her; she now saw a man.

"Momma, I promise you that I'll never go to jail. If anything like that ever happens, I'll stop everything at the drop of a dime," Goldie promised.

Loretta deliberated for a minute, while staring into her son's eyes.

"And you say that you're not selling drugs?" she asked, trying to reason with the situation. Besides, the extra money Goldie had been giving her was helping.

"Nope!" Goldie lied.

Loretta rubbed on her forehead.

"Besides, it's only for a couple more weeks, until I start my job working for Snake up at the carwash," Goldie said.

"Who is this Snake?"

"He's like a big brother to me. He's been looking out for me!" Goldie boasted.

"Well, you tell this Snake, or whatever his name is, that I wanna meet him!"

"Alright," Goldie said.

"In the meantime, go upstairs and get washed up for dinner."

"Okay," Goldie said, then grabbed his bags.

Loretta watched him as he stormed up the stairs. "I don't know what I'm gonna do with that boy," she said, shaking her head and then disappearing into the kitchen.

CHAPTER ELEVEN

On Sunday afternoon at three o'clock, Snake promptly arrived at Goldie's apartment. At 6'4, Snake was built like a basketball player. He carried around an athletic shape of 210 pounds, with washboard abs. Some say if he would have never dropped out of high school, he could have had a promising career as a NBA player. Snake had played hoops with the best of them, and always walked away victorious.

As he stood on the porch, he checked his MCM outfit and then rang the doorbell.

Goldie's mom answered. "Hi! You must be Snake?" she politely asked.

"Yes, ma'am," Snake said, displaying a Colgate smile.

"Come on in," Loretta said.

When Snake stepped inside of the apartment, Goldie ambushed him when he turned down the hallway.

"What's up, Snake?" Goldie greeted in a cheerful mood.

"What's up, lil man?"

Loretta was shocked by the effect Snake had on Goldie. For the first time since his father's death, this was the happiest Loretta had ever seen him. She smiled.

"Have a seat, Snake," she said, motioning for Snake to sit at the dining room table.

When he sat down, Snake felt two pairs of eyes hawking him. Melissa and Ciera were sitting on the living room sofa, looking over at Snake and letting off schoolgirl giggles. Snake just modestly smiled at them and waved. Melissa and Ciera were both cute, but there was no way Snake would ever cross the line. They were like family to him.

Goldie's little brother Jeff stared over at Snake, as he pulled his chair up to the table.

"What's up, lil man? You must be Jeff?" Snake asked.

Jeff smiled. "Yep!"

As Snake surveyed the table, he was impressed with the abundant smorgasbord in front of him. The table was set with your typical African American Sunday dinner: cornbread, collard greens, chitterlings and rice, macaroni and cheese, and peach cobbler for dessert.

Once everyone was seated at the table, everyone held hands, while Loretta led in grace. Melissa and Ciera were in heaven, blessed with the opportunity to be able to hold Snake's soft hands during grace. When grace was finished, everyone dug in. Halfway through the meal, Loretta addressed the issue she had originally invited Snake over to dinner for.

"So Snake!"

"Ummm hmmm," Snake said, with a mouth full of collard greens.

"I'm concerned about where Goldie has been getting these large sums of money from."

Goldie almost choked on his food. He eyed Snake, waiting on his response.

"Well, ma'am, I'm responsible. Goldie's like a little brother to me, so I spoil him like one. Both of my parents are deceased, and they left me with a nice piece of change. So, as long as I have, Goldie has," Snake replied.

"Then what is this he's telling me about him being some lookout or something?" Loretta asked.

"I have no knowledge about that one, ma'am," Snake fabricated.

Loretta eyed Goldie. "Boy, who are these people who you suppose to be looking out for?" she asked in an aggravated tone.

When Goldie did not answer, Snake intervened. "Ma'am, I'll check that out personally, myself! With the new carwash I'm setting up, Goldie will be around me 24/7, and I'll be responsible for him. I assure you...he'll be in good hands."

Melissa and Ciera just sat and shook their heads. They could not believe the crock of shit Snake was feeding their mother. Snake was one of the most treacherous drug dealers ever to come out of the south side of St. Pete, but what boggled the two was why he was so head over heels with Goldie. Something was definitely fishy.

"Listen, ma'am, Goldie's a smart young man. I want to teach him how to successfully run a business, while at the same time allow him the chance to make a couple of dollars to help you out around the house," Snake said.

Loretta studied Snake. He seemed sincere, but still, her mother's intuition felt a little uneasy.

"Listen, Snake, if anything happens to my baby, you have me to answer to!" Loretta made clear. "The only reason why I'm doing this is because I've never seen Goldie look up to anybody like he does with you."

Goldie looked over at Snake and smiled. Snake winked at him.

"But I'm telling you this...the minute his grades drop I'm pulling the plug! Now on the business side," Loretta said smiling, then entwined her hands together and sat them on the table, "how much are you gonna be paying my baby a week?"

"Well, it really depends on how lucrative business is," Snake replied, using a word he had just heard on TV. "For the most part, he'll get five dollars for every car he washes."

"Alright now! Don't be trying to beat my baby out of his money!" she joked.

"Never that! That's the last thing you gotta worry about. Playing fair is the only way I know how to play," Snake swore.

"Alright then," Loretta said, extending her hand.

Snake stood up and shook her hand. "Dinner was great, ma'am. I assure you on my life, your son is in good hands with me."

"He better be!" Loretta joked. "Goldie, get up and walk your company to the door," his mother said, motioning for him to get up.

Goldie got up and escorted Snake to the front door. Melissa and Ciera both giggled, admiring Snake's backside as he walked off.

Loretta popped Ciera on the shoulder. "That's why ya'll hot butts pregnant now!"

"He fine though, Momma!" Melissa said.

When Goldie turned the hallway, he peeped back around the corner to make sure everybody was still at the dinner table.

"Here!" he said, boastfully handing Snake a wad of money.

"What's this?" Snake whispered, smiling.

"Eight hundred," Goldie whispered back. "I kept two-fifty for pocket change."

"You ain't bullshitting, is you, Shorty?" Snake asked, studying the wad of money.

"I told you I was serious," Goldie said in a confident tone, with a look on his face that told Snake he had a promising future.

Snake gave Goldie dap. "Alright, I'll catch up with you tomorrow."

Goldie cheerfully walked back into the dining room after Snake exited.

CHAPTER TWELVE

The next afternoon, Snake was parked at Goldie's bus stop, awaiting his arrival. As he waited, he thought about how jealous his crew had been acting lately. Truthfully, he and Goldie had been spending a lot of time together lately. Snake had taken Goldie under his wing and taught him the ins and outs of the game, including how to cook the product up. For his age, Goldie was far ahead of his time.

Fuck 'em! They need me more than I need them, he told himself. To Snake, Goldie had saved his life in a sense. Besides, he was the future.

When Goldie's bus pulled up, it tickled Snake's fancy to see all of the kids' heads sticking out of the window, sweating his car.

"Owwee dang!" was what all of the kids were screaming.

Snake eased out of the car, then walked to the front and leaned against the hood with his arms folded. The school bus came to a halt, and when the doors opened, all of the kids energetically unloaded off the bus. Each kid glanced over at Snake's car while exiting.

Goldie was the last one to exit. He overbearingly eased down the stairs, walking slowly, like there was a red carpet rolled out for him. Tina was waiting on him when he stepped off the bus, but Goldie brushed right by her and walked over to Snake.

I know he just didn't, Tina said to herself, shifting her weight and throwing her hands on her hips.

"What's up, nigga?" Goldie asked Snake.

"What's popping, lil' man?" Snake replied, as the two shared in their signature hug.

As Goldie strolled over to the passenger side of the car, Tina was standing with her arms folded, mouth poked out, and impatiently waiting for Goldie to say something to her.

"So you ain't walking me home?" Tina asked with an attitude.

"Naw!" Goldie said, getting inside of Snake's car.

Snake looked back and forth at the two, then laughed.

"I'ma call you later on!" Goldie stuck his head out of the window and yelled.

Tina jerked her body, and then stormed down the sidewalk with an attitude.

"Damn, lil' man, you tough on the females, ain't you?" Snake asked, easing inside the car.

"She can't make me no money!" Goldie said like a pimp.

Snake laughed, while rubbing him on top of the head. Suddenly, an idea came to mind. Snake looked over at him.

"You wanna drive?" he asked.

Goldie's face lit up. He looked around at the nice size crowd that was still hanging around.

"Hell yeah!" he yelled.

"Switch with me," Snake said, hopping out of the car.

Goldie was grinning from ear to ear, as he adjusted the seat.

"Alright now, just crank up the car, throw it in drive, then drive off real slow like I showed you," Snake instructed.

"Owwee, look ya'll...Goldie driving!" one of the kids shouted.

"Owwee!" everybody said.

Goldie turned up the volume on the Alpine system, then leaned forward with both hands on the steering wheel and slowly cruised at a turtle's pace, riding through the projects like he was in a parade, bumping the Gucci Crew.

* * * * *

After switching cars at his auntie's house, Snake hopped off the interstate. After driving a couple of blocks, Snake turned down a well-paved alley that led to the back of a restaurant. He reached into the backseat and grabbed two bookbags.

"I'll be right back, lil' man," Snake said, hopping out of the car.

Snake threw one of the bags over his shoulder, while holding the other one in his hand. He surveyed the alley before sliding into the backdoor of the restaurant.

As Goldie sat tight, he didn't have a clue what was going on. After five minutes had passed, a slightly bald, chubby man appeared, wearing one of those overpriced Miami Vice style suits. His top three buttons were unbuttoned, exposing several gold chains that rested on top of his furry chest. He took his toothpick out of his mouth, then thoroughly surveyed the area. He acknowledged Goldie with a nod, and grinned when Goldie did not respond.

Goldie laughed. "Who the hell he think he scaring?" he said to himself.

The man adjusted his pants, as far as his pudgy stomach would allow him, and then disappeared back inside of the restaurant.

Goldie sat patiently for another ten minutes, when all of a sudden, he heard arguing coming from inside of the restaurant. It sounded like somebody was ticked-off with Snake. Instinctively, he reached up under the driver's seat, and eased Snake's .38 snub nose up under his shirt and on his lap. He was puzzled; he didn't know if Snake was in danger or what.

Suddenly, Snake and three other men appeared out of the restaurant's back door. Goldie made eye contact with Snake, while clinching onto the gun. Snake gave him the nod that he was all right. Goldie just gritted his teeth, as he watched a short, fat, bald man continue to scold Snake. Judging by his appearance and his accent, the man looked like he was Cuban or something. He, too, was wearing one of those overpriced Miami Vice style suits. Goldie locked his eyes in on him. He was wearing a phenomenal pinky ring that let off an extravagant glare whenever he moved his hand. His necklaces were excessive. Only one word Goldie knew to describe this man...POWER.

Regardless of the fact, Goldie could not believe Snake was actually just standing there and letting this short-ass man point his finger in his face and yell at him. Goldie was furious; he had never seen Snake taking shit from anyone. At this particular time, he was still young and naive to what all of the rules of the game were.

When the short man's voice went hoarse, he excused Snake, and Snake hopped inside of the car agitated. Once inside, he threw the duffle bag in the backseat. While Snake backed up, Goldie stole one last look at the only man he had ever seen disrespect Snake.

Once Snake pulled out of the alley, Goldie eased the gun from under his shirt and handed it to him.

"Here," Goldie said with an attitude.

Snake was blown away. He looked at Goldie, then at the gun, and back at Goldie.

"What you doing with my gun?" he asked stunned.

"I heard ya'll in their arguing, so I grabbed it so I can have your back," Goldie said.

For a moment, Snake envied Goldie. He was a natural, and undoubtedly had the heart of a lion. For a couple of minutes, they just rode in total silence. During those couple of minutes, Snake periodically glanced over at Goldie, analyzing him. He looked like he was very agitated. Snake knew what it was. Goldie had never witnessed him take shit from anyone, until today. He knew Goldie idolized him. Likewise, little did Goldie know, Snake also idolized him. Snake idolized the fact that deep down inside his heart, he knew Goldie would grow up to be a more advantageous hustler. Goldie was supernatural, and was way, way, way ahead of the game.

Snake looked over at him. "Yo, Goldie!"

"What's up?" Goldie said, slowly turning his head around, as if he did not want to hear what he had to say.

"I know what you're thinking, lil' man! Just always remember...in this game...if you ever wanna go anywhere... everybody gotta play their role!"

CHAPTER THIRTEEN

The temperature outside was a scorching 97 degrees. Summer was officially here. Today was the big day, the grand opening of S & G Carwash. Business was off the chain. Snake had gone all out. Not only were there decorative balloons hanging everywhere, there were clowns for the kids, as well as hot dogs and refreshments for everyone. Even the local radio station, WRXB, attended, broadcasting live. The carwash looked like one great big car show. All of the dope boys had come out to show Snake their support.

"Look at him, Mitch. He thinks he's a fucking God or something," Detective Ross said, posted up across the street.

He and Mitch had been parked across the street for a little over an hour. Even though today was Detective Ross's day off, he would not dare miss the grand opening of S & G Carwash. Today, he was hoping to stumble upon a clue to something. Maybe he would get lucky today, and Snake's supplier would drop by to get his car washed. Detective Ross wanted Snake bad.

"Hey, Ross, isn't that the kid who we brought down to the station to look at those mug shots and try and identify the shooter in that homicide in the projects?" Mitch asked.

Detective Ross looked through his binoculars, zooming in on the kid. "You know what, Mitch...you're absolutely right!"

"I thought so," Mitch said, rubbing his goatee.

"Wait a minute!" Detective Ross snapped, rubbing on his chin.

Mitch turned around and faced him. "Are you thinking what I'm thinking?"

"Yeah...son-of-a-bitch! That fucking kid hustled the shit out of us! That lil' fucker never had any intentions on telling us who the shooter was from the start!" Ross yelled, agitated.

"Can't we bring him back in for questioning?" Mitch asked.

Detective Ross sighed, blowing the hair that hung over his forehead. "We had our shot, Mitch! By now, Snake probably has him so far gone that we don't stand a chance. The kid probably looks up to Snake; he'll never rat him out. These kids in the ghetto...they're being taught to hate us. These kids nowadays are growing up fast," Ross lectured.

"What about your C.I.?" Mitch asked.

"Who, Butter?" Ross said, not too enthused.

"Yeah, him," Mitch said, nodding his head.

Ross lit a Marlboro, took a couple of puffs, then exhaled. "I think the son-of-a-bitch is straddling the fence on me. He keeps feeding this bullshit...about Snake not allowing anyone to get close to him, except his childhood friends. He says his peoples would rather die than rat him out."

"So you're sold that Snake was the shooter?" Mitch probed.

"I'd be willing to bet my pension on it!" Ross said with confidence.

"You have to admit...this guy is good. He covers all his tracks!"

Ross stared at Mitch with a disgusted look. "What are you...one of his lil fans or something, Mitch?" Ross asked, pissed.

"Geeezzzz, I'm sorry. I didn't know this was personal with you!" Mitch said defensively.

"I take my job very serious. So, it's personal with every drug dealer on the street!" Ross declared.

The two sat in total silence. Mitch cracked his window for some fresh air, while Ross continued to puff on his cancer stick and hawk the carwash.

"I'm watching you, Snake! You'll make a mistake. I know you will," Ross said, while smiling and exposing his cigarette-stained teeth. "And when you do, my friend...I'll be right there all over your fuckin' ass!"

For the entire day, cars were pulling in dirty and leaving out sparkling clean. Snake had handpicked all of his employees, all of which were hard workers, because customer service was his number one priority. His mission statement was to make sure that every customer left with a clean car, a smile on their face, and were willing to return.

Loretta had even popped up to show her support. After running all of her errands, she stopped by to treat the family's car to the five-dollar special. Even though the car really did not need to be washed, checking up on Goldie was her real reason for stopping by.

When Loretta pulled up to the carwash, Goldie was actively washing a car. Seeing her baby working hard created a smile upon her face. Goldie looked like a grown man, with his squirt bottle attached to his pants and his rags in his back pockets.

When Loretta honked her horn, Goldie looked up and acknowledged his mom. "Yo, Rudy! Finish up on this car here. I'm finna go over and knock my momma's car out the way!" Goldie said, walking over to their car.

"Look at my baby!" Loretta said, admiring her son as he vacuumed out the car.

Goldie smiled, then poked out his chest and pointed at the title on his shirt.

Loretta could not believe what the shirt said. She crossed her arms, and then moved her mouth to the side. "Assistant manager?" she asked, humored.

"Yep!" Goldie boasted.

"Boy, you too much!" Loretta said, laughing as she shook her head.

Fifteen minutes and three hot dogs later, Loretta came out of the waiting area to a sparkling car. The car was spotless, and the windows were so clean that they looked like they were down. Loretta nodded her head in approval. When she walked over to the car, Goldie was standing beside it as if he was a limousine driver. He was standing with his rag over his shoulder, a smile on his face, and the car keys in the air. Loretta walked around the car and inspected it.

"So, you like my work, huh?" Goldie bragged.

Truthfully, Loretta was impressed. She reached into her wallet, pulled out a five-dollar bill, and handed it to Goldie.

Goldie felt offended and pushed the money away. "I can't charge you! This is on the house!"

"Boy! Take this money!" his mother ordered.

Against his will, Goldie took the money and tucked it in his pocket.

His mother stood by the door, tapping her feet, with her hands on her hips. "I'm waiting," she said.

Goldie was baffled. "What?"

"Not only because I'm your mother, but also because I'm a lady...don't you know that a gentleman always opens the door for a woman?"

"Sorry!" Goldie said, jotting that down in his memory, then rushing and opening the door for his mother like a perfect gentleman.

His mother kissed him on the cheek. "That's my baby! I'll see you when you get home tonight! I'm proud of you, baby!" she yelled out of the window, then waved goodbye and blended into traffic.

Goldie watched as the family's car disappeared down the road. "I gotta remind myself next week to throw on a coat of wax," he said, then went back to work.

By seven o'clock that evening, everyone except Snake and Goldie had cleaned up their stations and called it a night. Snake was in his office behind his desk, engaged in punching numbers into the calculator. Goldie was assisting him with totaling the day's earnings by helpfully separating all of the bills and stacking them in separate stacks. Business had turned out surprisingly better than Snake had anticipated for the first day. Two grand was not bad for a day's work, especially since carwashes were 60% cheaper that day.

Snake's decision to hold off until the second week of June for the grand opening was a smart decision. Goldie's full-time help was definitely a plus.

"Here you go, lil 'man," Snake said, handing Goldie two hundred dollars.

"Thank you, Snake!"

Snake stood up from behind his desk, grabbed the bank bag, then walked over and flicked off the office lights. "Let's go home, Shorty!"

Goldie walked to the door, then Snake threw his hand around him and the two left.

Detective Ross watched as they walked out of the carwash. "I knew it...I knew it...I knew there was some kind of connection between the two," Ross said to himself.

Ross had devoted his entire day to staking-out Snake. After getting aggravated with Mitch's bickering, Ross dropped him off at the precinct and returned to stake Snake out himself.

"I got my eye on you, Snake," Ross said, as he watched Snake and Goldie playfully play with each other before hopping into the car.

"You can smile now, Snake, but you won't be so happy when I get you behind bars. Just wait. I'm gonna nail you, Snake...if it's the last thing I do!"

Ross watched Snake's car disappear down the street. He contemplated on following him, but he was too tired and decided to call it a day.

* * * * *

By mid-August, S & G Carwash was the most talked about carwash on the south side of St. Pete. People of all races and ages became faithful, weekly customers. Business had been so lucrative, Snake knocked down one of the waiting room walls and expanded it an additional ten feet in length.

On a regular day, business would gross anywhere from $700 to $1000. Fridays and weekends were when all of the real money poured in, bringing in anywhere from $1500 to $2000. Snake even extended his services, offering buffing, waxing, carpet shampooing, and headliner installation.

By January, Snake had purchased the adjacent building and opened up a mechanic shop. The shop performed minor mechanic work like: oil changes, tune-ups, brakes, and minor radiator work. He created a one-stop spot and was able to beat other competitors' prices, which made everyone in the community on a budget happy.

Snake could not take credit for the mechanic shop; it was Goldie's idea. Goldie had made a difference in Snake's life and in his pockets, both in his legal businesses and his illegal street affairs.

CHAPTER FOURTEEN

Goldie could not pinpoint exactly when it started to happen, but somewhere during the summer of '88, his body started undergoing changes. Although mentally he was already a man, puberty had finally allowed his body to catch up with his mind.

As he observantly stood naked in front of the bathroom mirror, he examined his new body. In the past couple of months, not only had his voice become deeper, he had also grown a mustache and accumulated a couple strands of hair on his chin.

Goldie lifted up his arms and examined his armpits. Hair was growing at a rapid pace. He worked his way down south, staring at his pubic area, which was full of hair. Not only that but a trail of hair led from his navel all the way down to his pubic area. However, what really amazed him was how much bigger his penis had grown. It seemed like one morning he just woke up and BAM! It had grown twice as big.

He slid on a pair of silk boxers to conceal the dangerous weapon, then headed to his bedroom and got dressed. He was exhausted and really didn't feel like going to school today. It wasn't until three o'clock in the morning when he finally managed to get a couple of hours of shut-eye, and here it was seven o'clock.

"Goldie!" his mother yelled from downstairs.

"I'm coming!" he yelled back, lacing up his Colorado boots.

Melissa appeared at Goldie's doorway. "Umm hmm...tired, ain't you?" She poked at him.

Goldie stood up, threw his bookbag over his shoulder, and then looked Melissa in the eyes. "Listen here…as long as I'm making money, I ain't never tired. Remember that," he said, brushing pass Melissa and leaving her standing by herself.

Since it was the beginning of December and a little chilly outside, Goldie was rocking a Louis Vuitton sweat suit he had picked up from Maximo Mall.

When Goldie reached the bottom of the stairs, his mother was awaiting him in the kitchen, with a sausage, egg, and cheese sandwich wrapped in a paper napkin.

Loretta was baffled when she noticed something unusual about her son. *What's wrong with this boy?*

"Thank you, Ma!" Goldie said, grabbing his sandwich.

Loretta looked down at Goldie's pants and then up at him. "Boy what's wrong with you?"

"What?" Goldie asked, clueless.

"Boy, you need to check yourself before you come down them stairs."

"What you talking about?" Goldie asked, lost.

"I'm talking about your pants," Loretta said, pointing at his sweatpants.

Goldie looked down at his sweatpants. "What's wrong with my pants?"

"Why they poking out like that?" she asked.

Goldie tugged on his pants. "This the way these pants made!"

His mother waved him off. "Boy, just go on to school," she said, placing her hand on her forehead.

Goldie threw his bookbag over his shoulder, then glanced at his mother like she was tripping. He shook his head at her before disappearing out the front door.

Loretta stood in total shock. She had noticed the bulge in the front of Goldie's pants when he was walking down the stairs, and thought he had an erection. Surprisingly, she came to realize it was all naturally him. Just as she had expected, a couple of weeks ago, her son had experienced puberty and was now a man. When she noticed the change in his voice, she figured he was hitting puberty, and after what she just saw, that confirmed everything.

"Poor lil' girls! He gonna hurt somebody with that damn thang!" she said to herself, as she shook her head and started on the dishes.

* * * * *

Mrs. Bowers was standing at the chalkboard, writing down the day's lesson. All of the kids, except Goldie, had their writing utensils in their hand and a sheet of paper in front of them. When Mrs. Bowers finished writing and turned around, she noticed everyone, except Goldie, diligently working. She sat down to her desk, and then stared over her Coca Cola bottle bifocals.

Goldie's body was beat, which is why he was resting his head on his desk, trying to slide in a quick catnap. For a Thursday night, last night's cash flow created the illusion that it was a Friday. Goldie had stepped his game up a notch. Now, whenever he wasn't helping Snake out at the carwash, he posted up on the block, hustling until midnight with all of the older cats. Since he ran faster than the older hustlers did, he used it to his advantage, sprinting to cars with his product already in his hands.

Goldie had his sisters on his payroll, and paid them ten dollars a night to let him stay out to right before his mother came home. Making four hundred a night easily, he had become the breadwinner of his family. Not only had he completely pulled his mother out of debt, he had furnished the living room with a 27-inch television, a VCR, and a new stereo. Now when they opened the refrigerator, food was bound to fall out. Thanks to all of the crackheads' food stamps, he finally actually got a chance to eat the food he seen on the commercials.

"Walker!" Mrs. Bowers yelled, interrupting Goldie's sleep.

"Yeah!" Goldie said, sluggishly lifting up his head, while rubbing his face.

"If you'll join us, we're going over the questions on the board. Question number three, three-hundred and twelve times two-hundred?" Mrs. Bowers asked, trying to humiliate him.

"Sixty-two thousand four hundred," Goldie said in a groggy voice, while stretching out his arms and wondering how long he had been asleep.

Mrs. Bowers looked on her answer sheet and was appalled when she saw the answer to the question was exactly what Goldie had said it was. She looked on Goldie's desk. It was empty.

That's impossible. How could he have answered something that complex so swiftly, she asked herself.

"Question number seven, eight-hundred and forty times six-hundred?"

"Five-hundred and four thousand," Goldie said, wiping the slob from off the side of his mouth before anyone could see it.

Goldie was right again. Mrs. Bowers grew agitated. She was trying to humiliate Goldie, but he was humiliating her. The classroom was quiet. The whole class was baffled. Goldie was spooky. Everyone was trying to figure out how Goldie just woke up out of his sleep and answered those complicated problems off the top of his head so quickly. Those kinds of questions usually took the average eighth grader thirty seconds to figure out.

"A thousand times two-thousand!" Mrs. Bowers challenged, as she walked towards Goldie's desk, refusing to lose.

Goldie smiled. "Would two-million be the answer?" he said arrogantly.

Mrs. Bowers had steam coming off the top of her head, as she stood frozen with her mouth wide-opened. With the uproar of laughter from the students, Mrs. Bowers turned red. Antagonizing, Goldie smiled at her. The school bell rang, interrupting the duel, and all of the students exited the classroom, laughing.

Goldie was the last one to leave. When he stood, Mrs. Bowers was still standing in front of his desk, blocking the aisle.

"You know, if you applied yourself to your studies, you could go far," she poked.

Goldie smirked and squeezed by Mrs. Bowers with a cool, confident stride.

"You're letting your talents go to waste!" she yelled.

Goldie paused at the door, holding a wad of money in the air. "You can have all of the brains you want in the world, but this is what makes the world go round'!" he said, then stuffed his money back in his pocket, threw up a peace sign, and strutted out of the classroom.

When Goldie arrived in the cafeteria, he scanned the area, searching for Tina.

"Hey, Goldie!" Nikki said.

"What's up, Nikki?" Goldie said, grabbing his tray.

"You," Nikki said, courageously moving in closer and fondling with his shirt.

Alarmed with Nikki's courageous move, he smiled. "What you doin' in line?" Goldie asked, when he noticed she did not have a tray.

"I just came to speak," Nikki said.

"What's up?" Goldie replied, reaching into his pocket and paying the cashier.

Goldie scanned the lunchroom, searching for a table and looking for Tina.

"You know, I was just thinking. Since my momma doesn't get off until twelve o'clock tonight, I was wondering if you wanted to come over tonight," Nikki asked, flirtatiously running her finger down Goldie's chest.

"Oh yeah! For what, though?" Goldie asked with a devilish grin.

"Whatever you want," Nikki said in a seductive voice that made her lips seem like they were moving in slow motion. "Here's my number. Call me when you're on the way."

"Alright," Goldie said, grinning.

Nikki looked over to where her girls were sitting and winked at them. "I'll see you later on then. Bye!" she said, then cheerfully walked over to a table full of giggling girls.

Goldie stuffed Nikki's number into his pocket, then surveyed the cafeteria again searching for Tina. He located her.

Tina was sitting at a table all by herself, and had witnessed the little soap opera between Nikki and Goldie. Tina saw Goldie heading her way. Furious, she jumped up and headed to dump her tray.

"Tina!" she heard Goldie yelling. She just rolled her eyes at him and kept on walking. He sat his tray down on the table and then took off after her, not knowing what was wrong.

Nikki watched Goldie chasing after Tina and smiled. *Little miss prissy, think that she all better than everybody else. I'll see how she acts when I take her man,* she said to herself. Nikki smirked, and then went back to her conversation with her girls.

Goldie finally caught up with Tina and grabbed her arm, spinning her around. "Man, what's wrong with you?"

"Don't act stupid! You know why I'm mad!" she said, folding her arms.

"What?" Goldie asked for clarification.

Tina pointed her finger at Goldie. "Ever since you been making your lil' money and wearing all of your fancy lil' clothes, you done changed!" she said, hitting him with a thousand milligrams of reality.

Goldie was shocked at Tina's allegations. He was speechless. *Have I changed,* he wondered.

"You don't even see it, do you?" Tina asked, while twisting her lips and shaking her head.

Goldie didn't answer.

"Then every time I turn around, there's always some different girl all up in your face!" Tina yelled.

"Listen, you know you my girl," Goldie said, taking Tina into his arms and planting a soft, intimate kiss on her lips.

The kiss lasted for every bit of two minutes. When Tina opened her eyes, Goldie went Hollywood. He knew he needed a star-studded performance to preserve his relationship.

Goldie lifted up Tina's left hand, displaying three gold rings he had given her, which he purchased from a rich crackhead, cleaned up, and threw in a Zales box.

"None of these girls compare to you! Who wearing rings on they fingers, huh?" Goldie asked, lifting up Tina's chin. Goldie lifted up the two gold necklaces he had also given her. "You even got necklaces! What they got, huh? Nothing!" Goldie preached.

He planted another kiss on her lips, then stared into her eyes. "You're my girl...not none of these other girls...and remember that!" Goldie declared.

With his words, Tina felt as light as a feather.

Goldie knew he had her, so he started playfully planting kisses all over her face until she started laughing.

"Boy, stop! Stop, Goldie!" Tina said, squirming and giggling.

Goldie threw his arm around Tina. "Now come on. Let me walk you to your class so these females know who my lady is," he said, as the two of them walked down the hallway.

* * * * *

During the bus ride home, Goldie and Tina talked like two lovebirds. Things were going smoothly, until Goldie popped the question.

"So, Tina...when we gonna do it?" he asked, turning around and facing her.

"I told you, Goldie...I'm not ready yet," Tina said defensively.

"Why not? Everyone else that go together doin' it!" Goldie spat.

"'Cause I'm not everybody else!" Tina shouted, beginning to feel uncomfortable.

Goldie bit his tongue and just stared out the window. He really had feelings for Tina. The two of them had been courting for a little over two years, and Goldie was growing tired of all the kissing and grinding. Although he was a virgin himself, his hormones were raging, and he was eager to experience what sex felt like. He had already made up his mind what he was going to do. He was going to ask Tina one more time, and if she was not willing to do it, then he was going to find somebody who was, and he knew just who that somebody was going to be.

Tina and Goldie got in an argument, as he walked her home.

"Listen, Goldie, I told you I'm just not ready!" Tina said, slamming her door and leaving Goldie standing on the porch alone.

Goldie threw his bookbag over his shoulder and walked off. "Okay, if that's how she wanna act, fuck this shit!" Goldie said, storming down the sidewalk.

When he arrived home, he threw his bookbag on the sofa and took out Nikki's number. He nodded his head, as he stared at the number, then picked up the phone and dialed.

Nikki answered on the third ring. "Hello?" she answered, sounding excited.

"What's up?"

"Nothing...what's up with you?" she asked, smiling on the other end of the phone.

"We still on for tonight, right?" Goldie asked for confirmation.

"Yeah!" Nikki said, giggling.

"Alright...don't be faking now," Goldie joked.

"Whatta you mean?" Nikki asked.

"You know what I mean. We still gonna do it, right?"

"Yeah, if that's what you wanna do," Nikki said.

"Alright now...don't be having me come over there for nothing," Goldie said, smiling.

"I ain't! But what about Tina?" Nikki just had to ask.

"What, you gonna tell her or something?"

"I mean...after we do it...are you gonna quit her and go with me?" Nikki asked.

Goldie held the phone away from his ear. Tina was his girl. Even though the two of them had not done it yet, he still had feelings for her, and did not have any intentions on leaving her no time soon. On the other hand, he knew he had to tell Nikki what she wanted to hear.

"Goldie...Goldie...Goldie!" Nikki kept repeating on the other end of the phone.

Goldie put the receiver back to his ear. "My bad, Nikki, I put the phone down to change the channel on the TV. Now what was you saying?"

"I said, after we do it, we gonna be together, right?"

"Fo' sho'!" Goldie said, lying through his teeth.

Nikki's face lit up like a 300-watt light bulb. "So what time are you coming over?"

"It's on you!" Goldie threw at her.

"Alright then, come over around eight o'clock."

"Alright, I'll be 'round there at eight," Goldie said, then hung up the phone and slipped into his hustling attire.

* * * * *

By nightfall, Goldie's pockets were bulging, with only ten rocks left. He was feeling good. He had eight hundred dollars in his pocket, a slight buzz, and in a few minutes, he wouldn't be a virgin anymore. Life was good. Goldie felt grown. He had convinced Snake to let him take a couple of swigs out of his cup, and taken a couple puffs from the joint Peanut and Mookie were passing around.

"What time is it?" Goldie asked Peanut.

"Damn, lil' nigga! All this damn money you making and you ain't got no watch?" Peanut asked, as he puffed on the joint.

Goldie made a mental note to pick up a watch from the mall that weekend.

"It's 8:15," Mookie said.

"Oh shit! I gotta dip!" Goldie said, while walking over to the bushes and grabbing his rocks out of a potato chip bag. "I'ma holla!" he said, taking off down the sidewalk.

"Where your lil' ass going?" Peanut yelled.

"Nigga, mind your business!" Goldie yelled back.

Goldie rushed up the walkway that led to Nikki's front door and rang the doorbell. The porch light came on, then Nikki opened the door.

"You late!" Nikki said, with a slight attitude, standing with her hands on her hips.

Goldie observantly examined her from the toes up. Nikki had gone all out. Her toes were a freshly painted red, complementing her matching lace bra and panty set. Goldie smiled when he arrived at her breasts. Her breasts looked perkier in this particular bra. For fourteen years old, Nikki was well developed.

"Come in," Nikki said, stepping to the side.

Goldie entered the apartment, waiting in the hallway for Nikki to close the door. Goldie nodded his head in approval, as he heard the tunes of Freddy Jackson coming from the living room.

"Follow me," Nikki said, motioning with her finger with a seductive look on her face.

Goldie followed her into the living room, plopped down on the sofa, and observed his surroundings. Nikki's mom had really hooked their place up. A wicker set sat off to the side of the sofa, while two oversized matching fans hung overhead. Their sofa was an updated floral print that matched perfectly with the gigantic picture of a harvest, trimmed in a gold frame. Pictures of Nikki and her mother were everywhere, but not a single picture of Nikki's father was nowhere in sight. Since Nikki was an only child, judging by the pictures, Goldie assumed her and her mother were close.

Nikki walked over to the stereo, kneeled down, took out her Keith Sweat album, and placed the needle on the record. Before she made it back to the sofa, the sounds of "Make It Last Forever" came blasting through the speakers. Nikki plopped down on the sofa next to Goldie, dangling her one leg, while cocking the other one up on the sofa. Nikki was exposing all of the goods. Goldie looked over at Nikki, and then nervously took a deep swallow. It was not until he looked in between her legs when he noticed how hairy she was. His palms started to sweat.

Nikki had spent several nerve-wrecking hours preparing. She spent thirty minutes alone curling her hair with the curling iron. She spent another ten finding the right shade of red lipstick to complement her high-yellow complexion, and match her bra and panty set. Since people always told her she looked like Salt from the group Salt & Pepa, she often imitated her, dressing like her and wearing her hair the same way.

"So how do I look?" Nikki asked, self-confident.

"Good!" Goldie replied, as his erection whispered, "Let's get down to business" in his ear.

"So...you ain't gonna come over and kiss me or nothing?" Nikki said like a vet.

"Ohhh...you wanna do it right here?" Goldie asked, raising his eyebrows.

"It's up to you. I can just lay a towel up under me."

"What about your room?" Goldie suggested.

"We can go up there. I don't care," Nikki said, shrugging her shoulders.

Nikki stood and reached out her hand to lead him upstairs.

When the two arrived in Nikki's room, she immediately began removing all of her teddy bears from off her bed, sitting them on the floor. As he scanned the room, Goldie plopped down on the edge of the bed and eased out of his shoes. Nikki had posters of all of her favorite rappers and celebrities hanging on her wall.

While Goldie continued to undress, Nikki shuffled through her tape collection. She found the one she was looking for. She slid the tape marked "slow jams" into her radio, pressed play, turned up the volume, then eased into the bed, slipping up under the covers.

Goldie was standing in his boxers, overlooking her, when "Let Me Love You Down" by Ready For The World came on.

Nikki giggled. "You must ain't never do this before?" she asked, with a smirk on her face. Nikki covered her mouth, then pointed at him. "Owweee...you still a virgin, ain't you?" she asked.

"Girl, you tripping!" Goldie said defensively.

Nikki sat up in the bed and folded her arms. "Then why you still dressed then?"

Before she could utter another word, Goldie simultaneously stripped out of his boxers and jumped up under the covers with her. For a moment, the two just stared into each other's eyes. Nikki initiated the kiss. After two minutes of tongue wrestling, Goldie's manhood was harder than Chinese arithmetic. Inexperienced, he began rubbing his manhood in between her legs, searching for the hole. Little did he know, Nikki still had her legs partially closed. Goldie continued grinding. He didn't know what he was rubbing up against, but whatever it was, it felt good. Nikki playfully trapped his penis between her legs.

"What you doing?" Goldie asked, agitated.

"Boy, you humping my leg!" Nikki said, rolling her eyes and shaking her head. "Here...let me put it in," she said, grabbing Goldie's manhood.

Oh shit, Nikki said to herself, as she felt along Goldie's member.

Nikki's eyes almost popped out of her head. Not only was Goldie's thang long, it was extremely fat. She wondered if he had elephant in his blood. She looked up at him with a petrified look on her face.

"Damn, what's wrong with you? Why you looking like you done seen a ghost or something?" he arrogantly asked, with a smirk on his face.

Nikki wanted to say, "Fuck this shit!" There was no way she could fit all of that inside of her without doing any damage.

"Put it in," Goldie whispered.

"But it's gonna hurt," Nikki pouted.

"I thought you said you wanted to go with me," Goldie said, using reverse psychology.

Peer pressure got the best of Nikki. "Alright," she said, closing her eyes, then slowly easing Goldie's manhood inside of her. "Unnhhhh!" she cried, with only the tip of the head inside of her.

Once the tip of Goldie's manhood entered inside of Nikki, he was in heaven. His eyes rolled in the back of his head, like a heroin addict with a fix running through his veins. While stroking Nikki, Goldie still could not believe he was actually doing it. Little by little, more and more of Goldie's manhood worked its way inside of Nikki.

"Unnnhh! Go slow; it hurts!" Nikki cried, placing her hand on Goldie's chest, trying to control his depth.

Goldie began rotating his hips in a circular motion, just as he had seen the porn stars on the porno tapes do. Nikki courageously joined him, biting her bottom lip, while seductively staring into his eyes. The two moved in a rhythm. The more the two moved, the more Goldie eased inside of Nikki. He became eager. He grabbed Nikki's legs, positioned them in the air, then smoothly glided in and out of her.

With each brutal thrust, Nikki scooted back further and further, until finally, Goldie had her defensively pinned up against the headboard. The more Goldie thrust, the more Nikki agonizingly screamed. Goldie felt like Nikki's insides had tentacles the way it squeezed his manhood. He grew frustrated when his manhood kept bending and wouldn't go any further inside of Nikki.

Suddenly, he felt an unfamiliar tingle in his manhood. He was not sure if he should keep stroking or pull out. Before he knew it, he felt a sensation that felt like he was peeing inside of Nikki. Paranoid, he pulled out and erupted like a volcano.

"Goldie, no! Not all over my sheets!" Nikki yelled.

Nikki was too late; Goldie had already unloaded all over her leg and sheets.

"Dang!" Nikki said, looking down at her leg and then jumping out of the bed.

It wasn't until she stood up that she realized there was blood all over her sheets. She slipped on her panties and embarrassingly rushed into the bathroom, holding herself. Sex with Goldie had been better than she had expected. Her only gripe was that her period was not due for another two days, and Goldie had managed to mash the fast forward button.

Goldie stripped Nikki's sheets off her bed and threw them on the floor. Then, he lay down on the bare mattress and stared up at the ceiling. If he were a smoker, it would have been the ideal time to smoke a cigarette. "Damn that shit felt good!" he said, rubbing on his stomach.

From that day on, Goldie became a sex addict.

CHAPTER FIFTEEN

When Monday came around, Nikki could not wait to see the look on Tina's face when she found out Goldie had quit her for Nikki. She had held up to her end of the bargain, and now it was time for Goldie to hold up to his.

"He better, after all of that damn pain he put me through," Nikki mumbled to herself, still experiencing a little soreness in her vagina.

When third period came around, Nikki was standing in the hallway searching for Goldie. She could not believe what her eyes saw. Goldie was cheerfully strolling down the hallway, laughing and giggling with his arm wrapped around Tina.

Goldie looked up at Nikki, who was fuming. She crossed her arms and shifted her weight. Puzzled, Tina just stared at the two.

"What you doing with my man?" Nikki lashed out.

Tina gave Nikki a disgusted look. "Excuse me? Whatta you mean your man?" she asked, throwing her hands on her hips.

"You heard me. Tell her, Goldie!" Nikki spat, walking over and standing in front of the two.

Tina looked over at Goldie, waiting for an explanation.

"What? I don't know what she's talking about!" Goldie lied, giving Tina the puppy eyes.

"So you don't know what I'm talking about? Let me refresh your memory for you, Goldie. Remember Friday night?"

Goldie gave Nikki the look of death.

Tina turned Goldie's head around. "What's suppose to have happened Friday night, Goldie?" she asked in an irritated voice.

"He was all up in me. That's what happened!" Nikki blurted.

"Owwweeee!" a couple of girls in the crowd of onlookers screamed, throwing their hands up to their mouths.

Goldie turned around to Tina. "Look, I was on the block Friday night. I don't know what this crazy girl talking about," he said, pointing his thumb at Nikki.

Nikki could not believe Goldie was trying to play her. Today was the day he was supposed to have been on her arm, while she strolled past Tina laughing in her face. Instead, the tables were turned and the joke was on her.

"Come on, Tina, let me finish walking you to your class," Goldie said, throwing his arm around her, then eyeing Nikki as he walked off.

"Bye, Nikki," Tina said sarcastically, as she smirked and walked off.

Nikki stood crushed. Goldie had used her. She felt dirty. Distraught, she ran into the girls' bathroom. The minute she locked the stall's door, tears began to pour like a thunderstorm.

"I hate boys!" she yelled.

Nikki's best friends, Charita and Kim, were standing in the hallway and had seen everything.

"Let's go check on her," Kim suggested.

"Yeah, we better," Charita said, as the two of them headed towards the bathroom.

Once inside, they just followed the sounds of sniffling and crying.

Charita knocked on the stall. "Nikki, are you alright, gurl?"

"I hate boys!" Nikki sniffled.

The school bell rang. Charita and Kim looked at each other. Kim shrugged her shoulders.

"Ya'll gonna be tardy!" Nikki said in a pitiful voice.

"Bump class! You're our homegirl, and we ain't leaving unless all three of us leave together!" Kim stated.

There was silence for a minute. Kim and Charita whispered to each other. Charita waved Kim on. Kim looked at Charita, rolled her eyes, then walked up and leaned her head on the door.

"Nikki...come on out here and talk to us, gurl!" Kim pleaded.

There was silence for a couple of seconds, then the stall door opened. When Nikki came out, her eyes were bloodshot red, and her nose was redder than Rudolph's.

"Come here!" Charita said, opening up her arms for Nikki.

Nikki walked over and gave Charita a hug, then turned around and gave Kim one, also.

"Thank you, ya'll!" Nikki said, wiping her red nose.

"That's what homegirls are for!" Kim said.

"That's right!" Charita said.

The three shared in a group hug.

"I love ya'll!" Nikki said.

Since the three were already ten minutes late, they all decided to skip class in the bathroom and share the latest gossip with each other.

* * * * *

That afternoon, Nikki could not wait to get home from school to curse Goldie out. Even though her girls helped her feel a little better, her mind was not at ease. He owed her an explanation.

Goldie was changing out of his school clothes, when he heard the phone ring. Just by the way the phone was distinctively ringing, he knew it was Nikki. For some strange reason, it seemed like someone had turned up the volume on the ringer. Goldie took a deep breath, and then walked over to answer the phone.

"He gotta tell me something," Nikki said, hyping herself up as she paced the living room, waiting on Goldie to pick up.

"Hello," Goldie answered.

"Why you lie?" the caller screamed through the phone.

Goldie moved the phone away from his ear. "Got damn!" he cursed.

Nikki was on the other end babbling a hundred miles an hour.

"All I wanna know is why you lied?" was all he caught when he put the phone back to his ear.

"Listen, you tripping!" Goldie told Nikki.

"How am I tripping?" Nikki asked defensively.

Goldie lay back on the bed and stared up at the ceiling, while rubbing on his chin. He needed to come up with a good lie, and he needed to do it quick. An idea hit him. He smiled, and then went into action.

"See, you don't even know everything! I told you that we gonna be together! I just need a couple weeks," he said.

"A couple of weeks?" Nikki shouted.

Goldie was silent.

"Goldie...Goldie...you still on the phone?"

"Yeah...I'm still here," Goldie said in a melodramatic voice.

"Goldie, what's wrong?" Nikki asked sympathetically.

Goldie sighed, and then turned into Denzel. "I'm not even supposed to be telling you this, but I want you to understand why I did what I did."

"What?" Nikki asked.

"I'm serious now, Nikki. What I'm about to tell you, you gotta promise you won't tell nobody, not even Charita and 'em!"

"I promise. What is it?" Nikki asked impatiently.

"Tina got a brain tumor," Goldie lied.

"Fo' real?" Nikki said, throwing her hand up to her mouth.

"Yeah, they suppose to perform an operation on her in a couple of weeks. Her momma made me promise I wouldn't upset her, and that I'd keep her happy until the operation. That's the only reason why I told you a couple of weeks," Goldie said.

"Dang...I didn't even know. Can she die?" Nikki asked, sounding a little choked up.

Goldie sighed. "They said it's a 50/50 chance," he lied.

"Dang...I feel so bad because I'm always jugging at her."

"Yeah, that's the only reason why I did what I did today. I just hope you can find it in your heart to forgive me," Goldie said, trying his luck.

"I understand...and I forgive you, Goldie," Nikki said, taking the bait.

Goldie turned it up a little. "It's just so hard, Nikki, especially when I really wanna be with you," he said, going Hollywood on her.

Nikki felt sorry for Tina. Even though she hated her guts, she still was a compassionate person. She did not hate Tina to the point where she wanted to see her dead.

"This is all too much for me," Goldie said, faking as if he was sobbing and blowing his nose.

"Don't cry, Goldie. It's gonna be alright," Nikki replied in a compassionate voice, trying to comfort him.

"But I really wanna be with you!" Goldie said, pouring it on.

"Don't worry. You said it's only for a couple of weeks. It's not that bad. A couple of weeks won't hurt either of us," Nikki reasoned.

"I mean...if you see us together, you ain't gonna get mad like you did today, is you?"

"No, because now I understand," Nikki declared.

"You promise you gonna wait on me?"

"I promise," Nikki said, touched that Goldie had asked her to wait on him.

Goldie stretched his body out across the bed and smiled. He felt he deserved a standing ovation and an Oscar for his performance. Since things were going so smooth, he decided to test his luck.

"Well, I guess that means we won't be doing it no more."

"Don't ya'll do it?" Nikki asked, being nosey.

"We use to do it, but not since she been diagnosed. Her stuff ain't like yours, though! Damn, a nigga's getting a hard-on just thinking about your stuff!" Goldie said, blowing up her head.

"Fo' real?" Nikki asked, smiling.

Goldie tugged on his manhood. "Ever since Friday I can't stop thinking about you. So, when you gonna let me come over again?"

"How about Friday?" Nikki asked.

Goldie's face lit up. He wanted to jump in the air like one of those people on the Toyota commercials. "Same time?" Goldie asked.

"Yeah!" Nikki giggled.

"Listen, just remember, only a couple of weeks. Just know that every time you see us together, in my heart, I really wanna be with you. So, if I pass by you and don't speak, just keep telling yourself a few more weeks and you'll be on my arm."

"Alright!" Nikki said, totally brainwashed.

"Bye, future girlfriend!" Goldie said sarcastically.

"Bye," Nikki said, with a schoolgirl giggle, then hung up the phone.

Goldie sat the cordless phone back on the base, then smiled. He felt like he had handled the situation like a champ. Not only had he bought himself more time with Nikki, but also he still was going to be able to hit it. Goldie stood up, stuffed a couple of dollars in his pocket, then grabbed his sack and hit the block.

CHAPTER SIXTEEN

Business on the streets was slow for a Monday, so after checking a couple of his traps, Snake swung by the carwash to look over the books. He didn't want the carwash to seem like it was just a front, so whenever he had spare time, he always showed his face and mingled with customers.

As Snake pulled in front of the carwash, business looked like it was doing all right for a Monday. Two of his employees were standing around joking, but quickly grabbed a broom when they saw Snake exiting the car.

"How you doin', boss?" the two employees said.

"Ya'll got one mo' time for me to catch ya'll fucking around!" Snake warned the two, as he walked inside of the lobby. "How you doin', how you doin'?" he then said, greeting two customers as he headed towards his office.

Detective Ross and Mitch had just pulled into the alley across the street from the carwash.

Snake was just stepping back outside to get some fresh air, when he glanced across the street and saw Ross parked on the side of the abandoned restaurant. At their last meeting, Butter had tipped Snake off, and told him that Ross was watching his carwash.

Snake took his toothpick out of his mouth and shook his head. *That damn Ross just doesn't give up, do he?*

Snake walked around to the different stations with a clipboard in his hand, checking up on all of the equipment and doing inventory, like a real businessman.

"Get away from me begging!" Snake heard a lady customer shout.

Snake walked to the front of the carwash to see what all of the commotion was about.

"What's the problem, ma'am?" Snake asked the customer.

"Him!" the lady replied, pointing at Fingers.

When Fingers heard the sound of Snake's voice from behind him, he wanted to take off running.

"Ah, yo!" Snake said, spinning Fingers around.

Fingers let off a petrified, snaggle-toothed smile and waved a terrified wave. "Hi, Snake," he said.

"What you doin' up here messing with my customers?" Snake yelled.

Fingers started explaining. "My bad, Snake! I didn't know you were in," he said, wishing he could take his statement back.

"So you telling me you do this shit when I ain't here?"

"No...no...no...no," Fingers said, waving his hand.

Snake thought about kicking Fingers in the ass, but an idea came to mind. "Come here," he said, grabbing Fingers by the neck and walking him around the building.

When the two arrived around the building, Snake released Finger's neck. Fingers rubbed his neck. Snake had to have had a vice grip on him, because even though Fingers was blacker than Wesley Snipes, you could still see the impression from Snake's fingers on his neck. Fingers balled up and prepared for a blow.

"Nigga, ain't nobody finna hit yo' ass!" Snake shouted.

Puzzled, Fingers stood up.

Snake smiled. "I got a job for you, and this is what I want you to do..."

* * * * *

Ross lit a Marlboro.

"Jesus! Do you mind?" Mitch asked, fanning the smoke from in front of him.

"Let your window down!" Ross said arrogantly.

"Son-of-a-bitch," Mitch mumbled under his breath, while letting down his window.

Fingers stood behind the abandoned restaurant, with his back up against the wall. He peeped around the corner, and saw two heads inside of the unmarked car. Planning his attack, he noticed only one window on the car was down, so of course, that had to be the side he had to sneak up on. Cautiously, he crept along the side of the wall, and then eased behind the trunk of the car. He grabbed a piece of newspaper out of all of the clutter on the ground. He peeped around the trunk of the car. The passenger's window was still down. Fingers mischievously smiled, then rolled up the newspaper and lit it. With the lit newspaper, he lit each of the fuses on the firecrackers, then eased along the side of the car to the passenger's window and threw the firecrackers inside of the car.

Ross and Mitch were so busy hawking Snake that they never saw the firecrackers come inside of the car. Instinctively, both detectives frighteningly scooted down in their seats and frantically reached for their revolvers when the firecrackers sounded off.

"Son-of-a-bitches!" Ross cursed. "Somebody's shooting at us, Mitch!"

Fingers heard the firecrackers sounding off. When he made it back around the building, he stole one last look at the unmarked car. "Easiest fifty bucks I ever made!" Fingers boasted, then took off running down the alley, laughing.

Detective Ross and Mitch were still scooted down in their seats, with their guns protectively positioned on their chests. The shooting stopped.

"I think they're gone!" Mitch looked over and whispered to Ross.

Detective Ross sniffed the air. He smelt smoke. It was not until he looked down that he realized his cigarette was burning a hole in his favorite shirt. Ross quickly grabbed the lit cigarette from off of his stomach, but it was already too late. His favorite shirt was ruined.

When Mitch glanced down on the floor, he embarrassingly sat up in his seat and felt like a jerk.

"What are you doing? How do you know they are gone?" Ross asked with concern, while still lying on his back with his gun glued to his chest.

"It was a prank, Ross!" Mitch said, picking up the firecrackers and showing them to Ross.

Ross was furious. He sat up in his seat. He examined his favorite shirt one last time, gritted his teeth, and then savagely stared back across the street at Snake. What he saw when he did made matters even worst. Snake was standing across the street with a pair of high-powered binoculars glued to his eyes, staring directly at him.

"Yeah, motherfuckers...while you watching me, I'm motherfuckin' watching you," Snake mumbled to himself.

Snake smiled. As he stared through the binoculars, he read Ross's facial expression and knew exactly what he was thinking.

Ross's pale face instantly turned fire engine red. Snake decided to add lighter fluid to the fire, so he arrogantly waved at him.

"Son-of-a-bitch! Our cover's blown! Let's get out of here!" Ross said, immediately cranking up the car.

Snake watched as Ross's unmarked car disappeared down the street. "Yeah, that outta teach your bitch ass!" he said, then headed back inside of the carwash.

CHAPTER SEVENTEEN

The year was winding down, and Christmas was only a couple of weeks away. A little over four weeks had passed since Goldie's award-winning conversation with Nikki on the phone. Since then, he repeatedly performed his same routine: chilling with Tina at school in the daytime, hustling at night, and knocking Nikki off every Friday night. Truthfully, he was surprised at how well Nikki was taking everything. Now, whenever she saw them strolling down the hallway, she would always speak.

"Hey, Tina...hey, Goldie," Nikki said cheerfully.

Tina gave Nikki a phony wave, as her and Goldie walked pass Nikki. When Tina was not paying attention, Goldie looked back, and then he and Nikki made eye contact. Nikki winked at him and threw up her thumb. Goldie smiled and winked back. Nikki blew him a kiss, then threw an imaginary phone up to her ear and cheerfully walked off.

As Goldie joyfully walked Tina down the hallway, he felt like he was sitting on top of the world. Girls were easy to manipulate. Now, he saw why Snake kept a couple of females who all knew about each other in his stable.

When gym class rolled around, Nikki didn't know why her eyes kept making their way over to Tina. *She doesn't look sick,* she thought to herself.

Actually, Tina was starting to fill out. Her breasts were getting bigger, her hips were more curvaceous, and her butt was starting to poke out a little more.

When it was Tina's turn to serve the volleyball, she couldn't figure out why Nikki kept staring at her. She made a mental note to make sure to address her as soon as they got back in the locker room. Tina held the ball in the air, and then served a powerful serve with heat.

"Unhhh!" one of the defenders cried, as the ball bounced right off the palm of her hands and went out of bounds.

Tina's team jumped up and down. She had scored the winning point.

The coach blew the whistle. "Shower time!" Mrs. Wiggins yelled.

Tina walked inside of the locker room, opened her locker, then grabbed her clothes and headed to the showers to freshen up. Seven minutes later, she was sitting on the bench and sliding into her pants. When she stood to button up her pants, she felt a pair of eyes from across the room hawking her. That pair of eyes belonged to Nikki.

When Tina caught her staring, Nikki tried to play it off by looking the other way. It was too late, though; she was busted. Tina quickly slid her shirt over her head, and then furiously stormed over to Nikki's locker.

Nikki was bent down tying her shoes, and was surprised when she looked up and saw Tina standing in front of her with her hands on her hips.

"Why you keep staring at me?" Tina asked with an attitude.

"Gurl, you trippin'! Ain't nobody staring at you!" Nikki said nonchalantly, while grabbing her belongings from out of her locker.

Tina slammed Nikki's locker shut. Nikki challengingly opened her locker back up, trying to ignore Tina. Tina wanted a piece of Nikki, so she spun Nikki's shoulders around. Nikki defensively jumped up, and the two stood in front of each other's faces, close enough to smell each other's breath. The locker room was quieter than a library.

"Hey, what's going on over here?" Mrs. Wiggins asked, making her way through the crowd.

Neither girl spoke a word. They both stood frozen, breathing heavily, and prepared to tear each other apart. Both girls had impressive fight records, and really respected each other's fighting skills. The only advantage Nikki had was Tina had long hair.

Mrs. Wiggins blew her whistle, and then separated the two. "Do we have a problem here?" she asked.

"She started it!" Nikki blurted.

Tina got back in Nikki's face. "That's only because you won't stop staring at me!" she spat. "Get over it; Goldie's my man!" she said, waving off Nikki.

"That's only because you sick!" Nikki let slip, before covering her mouth.

"What did you just say?" Tina asked with a grimace on her face. "Sick? I'm healthier than you!" Tina added, rolling her eyes at Nikki. "And besides, I just took my cheerleading physical, and ain't nothing wrong with me, baby!" Tina shifted her weight and snapped her fingers in front of Nikki's face.

Nikki felt like shit. Not once, but this now made twice that Goldie had played her. She was heated. He never had any intentions on being with her. She was just a little sex toy to him. Nikki felt used, like a whore. She desperately wanted revenge, and she knew just how to get it. To be victorious, she knew she had to put her pride to the side and take sides with the enemy.

"Listen, Tina, I don't hate you!" Nikki said, neutrally walking over to Tina with her arms folded. "Gurl, Goldie is playing both of us!" she said, trying to convince Tina.

Tina twisted her mouth. "How do you figure that?" she asked, also folding her arms.

"I admit...we have our differences, but I swear, me and Goldie have been doin' it!" Nikki said, spilling her guts.

Tina sucked her teeth, and then started patting her left foot on the ground, while staring up at the ceiling. "Prove it then!" she challenged Nikki.

"I'll get him to admit it himself!" Nikki swore.

The school bell rung.

"And how are you gonna do that?" Tina asked, walking over to grab her belongings.

Nikki smiled, and followed behind her. "All we gotta do is this..."

* * * * *

During the entire bus ride home, Goldie was wondering why Tina had not spoken a word to him. He looked over at her. She was staring out of the window. Something was on her mind; she seemed so distant. A couple of minutes later, the bus pulled in front of the bus stop. All of the kids grabbed their belongings and started exiting the bus. Tina, who was in her own little world, was the last one to get off the bus. Goldie stood on the curb, waiting for her.

Goldie studied her body language as she stepped off the bus. She looked like somebody close to her had died.

"I wonder what the hell is wrong with her," Goldie mumbled.

Tina stepped off the bus, then rambunctiously walked right pass Goldie.

"What the---?" Goldie said, standing puzzled, with a confused look on his face. He ran and caught up with Tina, then spun her around. "Dang, what's up with you?"

Tina pulled away, walking pass Goldie again. "I got something I gotta do!" was all she said, as she stormed up the sidewalk with an attitude.

Goldie rubbed his head. He was confused. He watched Tina's head get smaller and smaller. "Boy, I tell ya'...girls and they damn periods!" he said, shaking his head, then headed towards his apartment.

When Goldie arrived on his front porch, he stared at the parking lot, and could not figure out why their car was not parked out front. Today was his mother's day off. He grabbed his key from out of his pocket, opened the door, and shot straight upstairs. As he traveled up the stairs, he was surprised not to be greeted by the cries of his little nephew, Deontae. This was usually around the time he performed his daily tonsils exercise.

Curiosity made Goldie peep inside his sister's room. She wasn't there. She and Deontae were gone. Then it dawned on him. He remembered his mother and sister's conversation last week about Deontae's three o'clock appointment today. After having little Deon, Melissa had moved in with her boyfriend, leaving Ciera and Deontae the room all to themselves.

Goldie walked into his room and sat down on the bed. He threw his bookbag at the foot of the bed, and then fell back. He could not figure out what had gotten into Tina today. The minute he bent down to un-lace his shoelaces, the phone rang.

Goldie reached over and grabbed the cordless. "Hello?"

"What's up with ya'?" Nikki asked in an energetic voice.

"Who dis?" Goldie asked, with a crazy look on his face, taking the phone away from his ear and looking at it.

"Boy, you trippin'! This Nikki!"

"Nikki? What's up?" Goldie asked.

"I'm just calling to see when we gonna do it again!" Nikki said, over-aggressively.

"Do what?" Goldie retorted.

"Boy, stop acting crazy. Have sex, that's what!" Nikki said, waiting on him to take the bait.

Goldie's intuition told him something was not right. Nikki did not sound like herself; she sounded too persistent. Besides, all of their conversations always started with them talking about what happened at school. Goldie listened to the background closely. He attentively could hear two different television shows playing in the background. He had a hunch Nikki was up to no good.

"Goldie, are you still there?" Nikki asked.

"Hold up for a minute. My momma calling me to do something," Goldie lied, then placed the phone down on the bed.

He stood up and rubbed on his chin. *Nikki is on the three-way with somebody, but with who? Aw, damn!* Goldie hit himself on the forehead. *All of the signs are right in front of me...Tina!*

Goldie dashed into Ciera's room and picked up the phone. Since his sister had her own line, he investigatory dialed Nikki's number. He got a busy signal. He smiled, hung up the phone, and returned to his room.

He picked the phone up off the bed. "Now who you said dis' is?" Goldie asked.

"Nikki, boy! Now answer my question. When we gonna do it again?" Nikki said, overdoing it a little.

Goldie switched into Denzel mode. "Do what again? What you talking about? And how did you get my number?" Goldie asked.

"You gave me your number!" Nikki shouted.

"I ain't give you shit!" Goldie said convincingly.

"So you sayin' you ain't give me your number?"

"Hell naw! Listen, it's only one girl I love, and that's Tina!" Goldie boasted.

Tina's face lit up on the other end of the phone.

"Listen, man...I don't know how you got my number, but you need to lose it!" Goldie said.

Nikki's blood was boiling on the other end. This was her third strike with Goldie. She dropped her bat, and the umpire called her out.

"Now, if you'll excuse me, I got shit to do!" Goldie said, and then hung up.

Nikki was speechless. Tina was still on the line, waiting on her to say something.

"Hello! Nikki, you still there?" Tina asked.

"I'm here," Nikki replied in a pitiful voice.

"If you don't mind, I hope you'll leave me and Goldie alone now. I love him, and you just heard it yourself, he loves me! Find yourself your own man!" Tina said, and then slammed the phone in Nikki's ear.

Tina felt bad when she hung up. She had misjudged Goldie. She cheerfully plopped down on her bed, smiling as she hugged her pillow, imagining that it was Goldie. She was in love. She picked up the phone and dialed Goldie's number.

Goldie pulled his Polo hoodie over his head, then grabbed a couple of rocks out of his mattress, which was also loaded with money. He was sitting on a little over eleven grand. Christmas was around the corner, and he had big things on his agenda for his family and Tina. After grabbing his sack, the phone rang.

He reached over and answered it. "Hello."

"What you doing?" Tina asked in a cheerful mood.

Goldie smiled, then sat down on the edge of the bed. "What's up, Tina?"

"I just called to apologize for how I was acting today."

"Yeah, you was trippin'!" Goldie told her.

"I wanna make it up to you!" Tina said.

"Oh yeah?" Goldie replied, wondering where she was going.

"Yeah!"

"How?" Goldie asked.

"I'm ready to do it!" Tina said, while smiling and twirling the phone cord.

Goldie jumped up. "You ready to do what?" he said, not believing he heard what he just heard.

"You heard me, silly...I'm ready to do *it*!" Tina said, in a voice that sounded like she had her thumb in her mouth.

Yes! Goldie said to himself. He couldn't believe his luck. Things had actually turned out better than he expected.

"So when you talking about doing it?" Goldie asked.

"I thought about during our Christmas break. I want it to be my Christmas present to you," Tina said.

"Yeah, that'll be straight!" Goldie replied.

"I just want you to know that I love you, and I feel like you love me, too."

"You know I love you," Goldie said, pacing the room, and still in shock.

"I know. That's why I want you to be my first," Tina expressed.

Goldie looked up toward the ceiling and wanted to shake God's hand personally.

"Check this out, Tina. Right now, I'm finna hit the block and get this money. I'll call you from the payphone."

"Alright. Bye, Goldie," Tina said.

"Bye," he said, then hung up. He rubbed his hands together, then exuberantly marched down the stairs and hit the block.

As Goldie cheerfully strolled down the sidewalk, while thinking about his future with Tina, he was in such a good mood that he snapped his fingers as he sung one of Freddie Jackson's songs.

"You are my lady..."

CHAPTER EIGHTEEN

The next morning, Goldie was awakened by the smell of homemade biscuits, smoked bacon, eggs, and cheese grits. Today was Christmas Eve. He sat up in his bed, stretched his arms in the air, and slipped into his bedroom slippers. He stood up, tugged on his early morning erection, and then headed to the bathroom to freshen up.

Once inside, he flicked on the light, walked over to the sink, and turned the hot water on. He let the water run for a minute to warm up. While the water was warming up, he walked over to the toilet, lifted up the seat, and then drained his member. Thirty seconds later, he walked back over to the sink to wash his hands.

"Ahhh shit!" he yelled, quickly pulling back his hands.

Just that fast, he had forgotten all about leaving the hot water on. He adjusted the temperature on the water, then finished washing his hands. He grabbed his washcloth from off of the towel rack, ran it up under the water, and proceeded to wash his face. The feeling of the hot rag up against his face rejuvenated his body. Now feeling awake, he grabbed his toothbrush and brushed his teeth. After tightening up his hygiene, he headed back into his room and started getting dressed.

"Goldie, breakfast is ready!" Loretta screamed from downstairs.

"I'm coming!" he yelled back, while studying himself in the full-length mirror on his door.

He snatched off his do-rag, then vainly stroked his waves a couple of times with his brush. He squirted on two conservative squirts of Obsession by Calvin Klein, then grabbed the bag with Tina's gifts in it and headed downstairs.

Loretta was just setting the table, when he came galloping down the stairs in a cheerful mood.

"Good morning, Ma," Goldie said, walking over and kissing her on the cheek.

Loretta gave him an inquisitive look. "What are you so happy about this morning?"

Goldie smiled, then held out his hands and shrugged his shoulders. "Can't I just be happy?"

"Ummmhmmm! Who are those presents in that bag for?" his mother asked, raising an eyebrow. "Is something in there for me?"

Goldie laughed. "I told you we exchanging gifts tomorrow! These are Tina's gifts. We're exchanging gifts today, because her and her mother is doing something special together tomorrow."

"Did her mother have to work today?" Loretta asked from the kitchen.

"Yeah, that's the only way she could get tomorrow off," he replied.

"Well, that's good. At least they'll be able to spend Christmas together."

"I'm just glad that you off tomorrow," Goldie said.

"Believe me, it wasn't easy," his mother said, sitting the plates on the table.

Goldie dug into his plate. "I wanna see the look on your face tomorrow when you open up your gifts," he said.

His mother grew agitated when she saw Jeff sitting on his bicycle that Goldie had purchased for him after being told to stay off it on numerous occasions.

"Jeff, boy, get off of that bicycle and come to this table and eat this food!" Loretta scolded.

"Chill out, Ma. He just anxious, that's all," Goldie said, laughing.

Jeff joined the two at the table with an attitude.

"You better straighten up!" their mother warned Jeff, then turned and faced Goldie. "Getting back to you, mister! You said gifts, so that means there's more than one?" she probed.

Goldie just smiled, then stood up and walked into the kitchen. After scrapping his plate, he placed it in the sink. His mother startled him when he turned around.

"Just give me a hint!" she pleaded.

"Dang, Ma, you only got one more day to wait," Goldie said.

Loretta started playfully tickling him. "So you don't wanna tell me, huh?"

"Stop, Ma!" Goldie giggled.

"Nope... not until you tell me what one of my gifts is!" she said, continuing her assault.

Somehow, Goldie successfully managed to squirm his way out of his mother tickling.

"Dang, Ma, won't you just wait until tomorrow then," he reasoned. Goldie adjusted his Nike sweat suit. "See, you got me all wrinkled now!"

"Boy! Ain't nothing wrong with them clothes!" Loretta spat.

Before leaving, he paused in the living room and glanced over at the nine-foot Christmas tree he had purchased for his family. He got a little emotional and smiled, then nodded in admiration. Numerous gifts were up under the tree, varying in both size and shape. Jeff's Huffy dirt bike sat off to the side. Goldie felt proud. He had stepped up to the plate for his family.

After admiring the living room, he grabbed his bomber jacket off the coat rack, thoroughly checked himself one last time in the hallway mirror, and then he and Tina's gift disappeared out of the front door.

* * * * *

Tina had just finished wrapping the cord around the vacuum, when she heard the doorbell ring.

"I'm coming!" she yelled.

She quickly scanned the living room. It was presentable. She rolled the vacuum into the utility closet. The doorbell rang again.

"I'm coming!" Tina yelled, heading to the front door.

Out of habit, she looked through the peephole. Goldie was standing on the front porch, looking fine as ever. She smiled, took a deep breath, and opened the door.

"Is Tina home?" Goldie jokingly asked with a smile.

"Boy...come on in!" Tina said.

Goldie handed her the bag with her gifts. "I believe these belong to you."

Tina's face lit up like a 300-watt light bulb. Goldie brushed by her and waited in the hallway. Tina locked both locks, and then escorted him into the living room. Goldie made himself comfortable on the inviting sofa.

"This a nice place ya'll got here!" he said, admiring Tina's crib.

"It's alright," Tina replied nonchalantly, while plopping down on the sofa. "If you think this is something, you should've seen the house we use to live in," she boasted.

"Word?" Goldie said.

"I got some pictures. I'll show you," she said, then went to retrieve her photo album. Tina returned to the sofa with her photo album, and then flipped through the pages until she came to pictures of their old house.

"Damn!" Goldie said in amazement. He looked up at Tina. "Ya'll left there for this shit?" he asked in disbelief.

Tina just shook her head and then sat in a daze for a couple of seconds, reminiscing on the good ole' days.

"Tina!" Goldie yelled, snapping her back to the present.

"I'm sorry," Tina apologized, then closed the photo album and went to put it away.

Goldie scanned the living room. "So where you hiding my gift at?" he asked when Tina returned.

"Which one?" Tina asked, while flirtatiously opening up her satin robe to expose her matching bra and panty set.

Goldie felt his palms begin to sweat. There was a lump in his throat. Tina let her breasts lead the way, as she approached him.

"You aren't scared of me, are you?" Tina whispered into his ear.

"Piissss! Girl, you trippin'!" Goldie said, nervous as hell.

Tina let off a devilish grin and licked on her bottom lip. "Okay, I was just making sure," she said, sensually running her finger down his shirt. "So...can I open my gifts now?" she asked.

"Yeah, go ahead," he said.

Tina didn't need to be told twice. The wrapping on the bigger of the gifts was already halfway off. Tina grew even more excited at the sight of the large-sized jewelry box. She looked over at

Goldie and smiled. Goldie nodded his head, and then she opened up the box. When she saw what was inside, she emotionally threw her hands up to her mouth.

"Oh my God! These are beautiful!" Tina said, taking a pair of diamond earrings from out of the box, then rushing to the downstairs bathroom to try them on.

Goldie followed behind her. When he arrived at the bathroom, Tina was turning her head from side to side, admiring the earrings.

"How do they look?" she asked, looking back at him for his opinion.

"Them you!" Goldie said, nodding his head in approval.

Tina turned around and wrapped her arms around his neck. "Owee, thank you, Goldie!" she said, and then kissed him.

"Wait a minute. You ain't seen nothing yet. Open up your other gifts."

"Oops, I almost forgot," Tina replied with a goofy giggle.

Goldie followed her back into the living room and sat on the armrest of the sofa, while Tina unwrapped her other gift. When Tina opened the box inside, her pupils got as big as quarters. She tried to speak, but she was so overwhelmed that the words could not come out. She fanned herself, then reached inside of the box and pulled out the ankle bracelet, and the matching herringbone chain and nameplate. She jumped up and down like she had just won the showcase on *The Price is Right*.

"So you like it?" Goldie asked.

"Like it? I love it! I gotta go see how everything looks together!" she said, rushing back into the bathroom mirror.

Tina shot out of the living room like a bat out of hell. Goldie just shook his head, then followed behind her. Once again, Tina was in the bathroom mirror, grinning from ear to ear, while holding her nameplate up against her shirt. Goldie stood in the doorway and smiled in admiration.

"Here, let me help you put it on," Goldie said, while easing behind her and putting on the chain for her. "There you go." He took a step back and let her admire herself in the mirror.

Tina rubbed on her nameplate, as she stared into the mirror and let off a schoolgirl chuckle. She turned around and stared into Goldie's eyes. The two stood frozen; neither spoke a word. Tina stepped forward, and then initiated what evolved into a tongue-wrestling contest. Three minutes later, Tina pulled away. She stared into Goldie's eyes, then nodded her head and passionately grabbed his hand.

"Now, it's time for your gifts," she said, and then led him up the stairs to her bedroom.

CHAPTER NINETEEN

Jackie was just finishing her rounds, and heading to the breakroom for her fifteen-minute break. Her feet were killing her. For the past couple of months, she had been busting her butt, working overtime, trying her best to accommodate Tina with the type of lifestyle she was accustomed to living. She refused any help from Tina's father. Although he was wealthy, Jackie was independent and preferred providing for Tina on her own. Besides, he was the reason their family had parted anyways. For years, Jackie had tolerated the physical and emotional abuse, until she got fed up. At first, she use to believe she couldn't make it without Stephen, until one day she flicked on the TV and watched an episode on Oprah, where a woman in her identical situation had built up the strength to walk away. That episode motivated her, and she began planning her escape.

For the next couple of months, she placed herself on a strict budget, saving every single penny Stephen gave her. She stuck things out, routinely having Stephen's dinner ready by six and bathwater ready by seven. So many nights, she stared off into space, while giving him meaningless sex, telling herself that one day it would all be over. Then that day came.

After six months of planning, it was time. Over those six months, Jackie had managed to save up a little over fifteen thousand dollars to cover all of their relocation expenses. One of her college friends, Audrey, convinced her to move down to St. Petersburg, Florida, and Jackie's transition worked out perfectly.

Since Audrey was the leasing officer for Jamestown Apartments, she secured Jackie an apartment. Finding a job came easy for Jackie. Since she was in the medical field, it did not take long for her to secure a job at Bayfront Medical Center.

As Jackie sat in the breakroom all by herself, she remembered that sentimental Monday as if it was yesterday...

That Monday, Jackie patiently waited on Stephen to finish his breakfast and leave for work. The minute Stephen's BMW pulled out of the driveway, she stormed upstairs and started packing her and Tina's clothes. She had prepared herself by washing all of the laundry that Sunday. She left a lot of things behind, only taking things of importance. By 9:00 a.m., the moving company had arrived, and were actively breaking down Tina's bed and transferring all of her belongings to their truck.

After packing everything, Jackie remembered how emotional she got when she took one last look at the living room of the beautiful 4,000 square foot mini-mansion she would no longer call home. She got a little teary-eyed, then took off her two-karat wedding ring, sat it on the coffee table, and left a Dear John letter. Next, she called Tina's private school to inform them she was on the way to pick her up, and gathered the last of her personal belongings. She paused at the front door, sighed, and then disappeared out of the front door, never looking back.

That afternoon when Stephen arrived home and noticed that Jackie's Jaguar wasn't parked out front, he knew something was wrong. He recklessly parked in the driveway and rushed inside of the house.

"Tina...Tina!" he frantically yelled all throughout the house.

He sprinted up the stairs. His legs buckled when he opened Tina's bedroom door. Stephen got lightheaded when he noticed all of Tina's furniture and clothes were gone. Delirious, he rushed into their bedroom. Same thing. All of Jackie's clothes were missing, but all of their bedroom furniture was intact.

Stephen grabbed the cordless phone, then charged down the stairs. He immediately dialed Jackie's pager number, while pacing in the living room. He got the shock of his life; her pager number was disconnected, Stephen felt the living room spinning. He grabbed his head and rubbed his temples. He plopped down on the sofa, crushed. That's when he noticed Jackie's wedding ring and a note sitting on the coffee table. He picked the note up. The note was brief. It only had three words: "ENOUGH IS ENOUGH."

"Jackie!" her boss, Patty, yelled.

"Sorry!" Jackie said, snapping out of her daze. "Is break over?"

"Never mind break. You can go ahead and knock-off early," Patty said.

Jackie's face lit up. "Thanks, Patty!" she said in a cheerful mood.

"Have a Merry Christmas!" Patty said, before disappearing through the breakroom's doors.

Jackie checked her watch. It was only 12:30. She thought about calling Tina and letting her know that she was on her way home, but decided to surprise her.

She walked over to the time clock, punched out, and then headed home.

* * * * *

Meanwhile, Tina and Goldie were upstairs in her bedroom. Goldie was sitting on the edge of Tina's bed, observantly scanning her room. Her room was fit for a princess. Goldie was blown away. Surprisingly, Tina's bed happened to be the same size as his mom's bed. Tina had it going on. Her bed was a queen-sized canopy bed, with a floral bed set and matching wallpaper that accented the entire room.

"Your room tight!" Goldie told her.

"Thank you," Tina said, while sitting next to him and handing him a gift. "Here, open it up!"

Goldie looked over at her and smiled. While he opened the gift, Tina tried to read his face, waiting on his reaction. Goldie was a little choked up. On the week his father passed away, his family was scheduled to take family pictures at Olan Mills. Unfortunately, they never got the chance. Goldie didn't know how Tina had did it, but somehow, she managed to find an artist to airbrush his entire family's faces on a pair of stonewashed overalls.

"So, do you like it?" Tina asked.

Goldie reached over and hugged her, then kissed her on the forehead. "I love it!"

After hugging for a couple of seconds, the two released each other. Tina grabbed the pair of overalls out of Goldie's hand and threw them on the chair. Then she sensually stood up in front of him and seductively eased out of her robe.

"Now it's time for your other present," Tina said, with a mischievous smile.

She pranced over to her radio and slid in one of her slow tapes. Goldie was speechless. Little, shy Tina had made a three-sixty. She stood in front of him and seductively slipped off her bra. She strip teased him a little, dancing her way out of her panties. Goldie massaged his manhood, as he thoroughly examined her naked body from head to toe. She was flawless.

"Finished?" Tina asked, giggling as she eased up under the covers. She impatiently looked at Goldie. "Well, aren't you gonna take off your clothes?"

Goldie was still in disbelief that all of this was happening. Tina was ready. God had finally granted him his wish. He walked over to the foot of the bed, and without hesitation, stripped out of all his clothes.

The bare sight of Goldie's naked body made Tina's eyes almost pop out of her head. She instantly caught butterflies. There was no way the laws of physics could allow something that big to fit inside of her. If just sticking in a Tampon hurt, she could only imagine what damage Goldie's monster would do to her insides.

Goldie eased into the bed. He could tell by the look on Tina's face that something had her uneasy.

"What's the matter with you?"

"No, what's the matter with you?" Tina asked, raising her eyebrows.

"Whatta you mean?" Goldie asked with a smirk, playing dumb.

"Your thang...why is it so big?"

Goldie arrogantly laughed. "God just blessed me, that's all!" he boasted.

"Yeah, but how is all of that suppose to fit in me?" Tina needed to know.

"Listen, I'm not gonna try and hurt you!" Goldie stressed. "I'm just gonna ease a little bit in at a time. I'ma hold your hands, so if it starts hurting, you can just squeeze my hands. Okay?" Goldie leaned forward and kissed her on the lips.

"Okay," Tina said, feeling a little more relaxed.

Goldie cunningly eased his way on top of her. He warmly planted another passionate kiss on her lips, then reached down and grabbed his manhood.

Before he could insert it, Tina sat up. "Goldie, make sure that you be gentle."

"I promise," he said with a warm smile, ready to get down to business.

"What about a rubber?" Tina asked.

"Listen, I'ma pull out when I nut. Believe me...I don't want no baby either!"

"You better pull out, too!" Tina said, then laid back and closed her eyes.

Goldie slowly inserted the tip inside of her.

"Unhhh!" Tina moaned, clawing his back.

"Don't worry, boo. That's just how it feels at first," he softly whispered into her ear. "I promise I'm not gonna hurt you," he added, staring into her eyes.

Goldie planted another intimate kiss on her lips. She was mesmerized.

"Just be gentle, Goldie," she reasoned.

"Okay." Goldie slowly eased another inch inside of her.

"Unhhh! It hurts, Goldie!" Tina cried in pain. "I thought you said you was gonna let me hold your hands?"

"Listen, Tina, I gotta get it in first," he replied in frustration.

"But it's in!" Tina cried.

Goldie took a deep breath. He didn't want to say the wrong thing and miss out. "Listen, just let me get a little bit more in, then I'll hold your hands. Okay, baby?"

"But it hurts!" Tina complained.

"Trust me, baby...in a few minutes the pleasure gonna override the pain." During his little pep talk, Goldie cunningly managed to slide another inch inside of Tina.

He was growing frustrated. Things were not going as smooth as he expected. "Listen, Tina, you gonna have to help me out here!"

"How?" she asked.

"I need you to just feel the music...and move your hips around a little bit...like you hula-hooping," Goldie coached.

"Like this?" Tina asked, sensually rotating her hips.

Goldie felt another inch ease inside of her. "Yeah, just like that," he said, cheering her on and matching her rhythm. "Give me your hands," he instructed.

Tina did as told. Once Goldie had her fingers entwined with his, he slowly began to ease more and more of him inside of her. Tina's body squirmed and scooted, until finally she ran out of space and found herself defensive, pinned up against the headboard. Tina's unpleasant facial expressions made you think she was in a delivery room, delivering a twelve-pound baby. She was undergoing excruciating pain. Her stomach felt bloated, and it felt like Goldie's monster was right below her navel.

Goldie caringly wiped the excessive sweat off her forehead, and then affectionately kissed her on it. In the midst of all the excruciating pain she was experiencing, he amazingly managed to produce a smile on her face. At that moment, he became her knight in shining armor. It touched Tina to know he was sympathetic, and not like all of the other boys in school just trying to get some.

Tina courageously wrapped her arms around Goldie's neck, startling him. She let off a devilish grin, then pulled Goldie's body to hers. "Make love to me," she whispered softly in his ear.

Goldie didn't need a second invitation. He immediately went into action. Tina was a tight fit, but Goldie made things work. The sensational feeling of the warmth inside of her love garden was driving him crazy. Together, their rhythm was flawless. Tina's headboard became an instrument, as it banged up against the wall like a set of drums. The deeper Goldie dug, the more she clawed her nails into his back. Tina was in shear ecstasy, as she violently swung her long, silky hair from side to side. He felt so good inside of her that she courageously wrapped her legs around his lower back. Five minutes later, Tina experienced yet another orgasm. She felt like she was floating on cloud nine. She was in heaven. Tina's moans only aroused Goldie more, and had him on the edge of shooting off. With each stroke, droplets of sweat dripped off his body.

* * * * *

Jackie cheerfully pulled in front of their apartment and parked. She was in such a jolly mood she sang Christmas carols as she reached into the backseat to grab the groceries. Groceries in hand, she used her body to push the door closed, and then headed towards the front door. She sat the groceries on the porch so she could reach into her purse to grab her keys. She paused for a moment, thinking her mind was playing tricks on her. She stepped off the porch and looked up at Tina's bedroom window. Not only was there music blasting from her room, there was a loud thumping sound she kept hearing, like something hitting up against the wall. Furious, she fumbled with her keys, opened the door, and rushed into the kitchen to sit the groceries down. Then she stormed upstairs to Tina's bedroom to see what in the hell was going on.

"Ohhh...Goldie...it feels so good," Tina whispered into his ear, while nibbling on his earlobe and rubbing on his back.

Goldie repositioned himself. He arched his back, while supporting his frame on the palms of his hands, then commenced to pounding Tina's insides to death.

As Jackie walked up the stairs, all kind of thoughts ran through her head. When she heard moans coming from Tina's room, she marched up the stairs two at a time. Once reaching the top, she noticed Tina's bedroom door was cracked. She crept to the door, and when she pushed open the door, her world would never be the same. Jackie's legs buckled. She could not believe her own eyes. The only thing visible was the constant motion of a young boy's ass cheeks, humping up and down on who she assumed had to be her daughter. Goldie and Tina were so caught up that neither noticed Jackie standing in the doorway. Goldie just kept on pumping, and pumping, and pumping. Jackie threw her hand up to her mouth, and then deliriously disappeared out of the doorway.

"Unnhhh!" Goldie moaned, as his eyes rolled in the back of his head.

"Goldie, don't!" Tina screamed, but it was too late. She could feel the warmth of his hot sperm backstroking down her walls.

Goldie's body deflated on top of Tina's, and then he let out a loud, "UGH!"

"Boy!" Tina said, jokingly slapping him on the back.

"Oh, my bad," he replied, with a sarcastic smirk.

All of a sudden, Tina's eyes looked like she had just taken a hit from a crack pipe.

"Oh my God!" she screamed, nervously pushing Goldie off her and dashing for her clothes.

"What the--?" Goldie asked, puzzled.

The minute he turned around, all of his questions were immediately answered. Thank God his reflexes were swift enough to throw up his arm and defensively deflect the pipe-shaped object Tina's mother had just swung at him.

Jackie was furious. She violently charged towards Goldie, swinging another wild swing, but she missed.

Goldie hopped out of the bed. "Wait a minute, ma'am... just let me put on my clothes and I'll go!" Goldie screamed.

Jackie glanced over at Tina, who was standing up against the wall naked, covering her body with her clothes. Jackie gave her a look that said six months punishment and loss of privileges. Just the thought of her knowing that her daughter was no longer a virgin created more tears. All the overtime she had worked, providing her with the finer things in life, the talks about sex...it had all been meaningless.

Jackie fumingly looked over at Goldie. She stood motionless, breathing heavily and snorting like a bull. She inspected Goldie's naked body, and thought her mind was playing tricks on her. She had to do a double take. She covered her mouth, as she said to herself, *This damn boy hung like a damn horse!*

Jackie quickly looked over at her daughter with a sympathetic look on her face. "Did he hurt you?" she asked Tina.

Tina just terrifyingly stood with her back glued to the wall and shook her head.

Jackie scanned the room. It was not until she looked over at the bed when she noticed the enormous red spot. Jackie went delirious. "What did you do to my daughter?" she screamed at the top of her lungs.

"We just had sex!" Goldie tried to explain, knowing that the blood in the bed over-exaggerated what really happened.

"Ahhh!" Jackie screamed, savagely charging towards Goldie, and violently swinging the pipe-shaped object.

Goldie managed to successfully maneuver the object and storm past Jackie. He charged down the steps, struggling to pull up his pants. Jackie was right on his trail in hot pursuit.

"Momma, stop!" Tina yelled, running behind her mother.

When Goldie reached the front door, he quickly swung it open. His adrenaline was pumping. He pulled up his pants and attempted to make a clean getaway. He was unsuccessful. Right when he was almost in the clear, Tina's mother landed a fierce strike on his right shoulder.

"Ahhh shit, lady! I ain't your damn son!" Goldie screamed, as he spun around.

Goldie pulled up his pants, and then stormed out of the front door, barely dodging another one of Jackie's wild swings.

"And don't bring your lil' ruined ass around my baby again!" Jackie yelled at the top of her lungs.

News in the projects traveled fast. Somebody must have heard all of the commotion coming from inside of the apartment and alerted everyone in the projects. When Goldie got a little distance in between him and Tina's mother, he looked up and was shocked to see damn near half of the projects gathered up outside. Everybody had come to be nosey. Goldie was embarrassed. He adjusted his clothes, dropped his head, and eased through the crowd.

"What the fuck are ya'll looking at?" Jackie yelled to all of the onlookers.

"Unnnh unnnh, I know she didn't! Don't get mad at us 'cause your little princess is hotter than a Mexican tamale!" one of the women in the crowd blurted out.

The entire crowd busted out laughing.

"You people are ignorant!" Jackie screamed.

"Welcome to the projects, Mrs. Cedity!" another woman in the crowd yelled.

Jackie's face turned fire engine red. "Fuck ya'll!" she screamed, and then slammed her door.

Little did everyone know that would be the last time any of them would ever see Tina and her mother.

CHAPTER TWENTY

The next morning, Goldie awoke to loud commotion going on downstairs. He glanced at his alarm clock. "Damn, it's 9:30!" he said, placing his feet on the floor and sitting up on the edge of the bed.

He stretched out his arms, and then with his feet, he searched for his Stacy Adams bedroom slippers, which were up under the bed. After locating them, he slid his feet inside and stood up. He stretched one more time, yawned, then tugged on his early morning erection, as he headed towards the bathroom.

Once inside, he grabbed his washcloth from off of the towel rack and washed his face. For some strange reason, today did not seem like Christmas to him.

He was still tired. He had stayed up all last night, worrying about if Tina was all right. He had repeatedly called her house for five hours straight, every fifteen minutes, only to keep getting the recording that said someone had the phone off the hook.

After smothering his face in a hot rag, he stared at himself in the mirror. He could not figure out what was going on with him. The strange feeling that he felt was hard to identify. Was it possible that he had fallen in love at such a young age? Ever since his sexual encounter with Tina, his mind had been playing tricks on him. It just seemed like they had chemistry together. Goldie felt a connection between him and Tina. Sex with Tina had been enchanting, and sex with Nikki had just been sex.

"Goldie...Goldie, look what Momma bought!" Jeff yelled, rushing into the bathroom with his remote control.

Goldie just looked over at him and smiled. He remembered how anxious he used to be on Christmas mornings when he was Jeff's age. Now, Christmas was just another day.

Jeff curiously looked over at Goldie. "What's wrong with you, Goldie?"

"Nothing...I'm just tired," Goldie lied, as he wondered if he was that transparent.

"Momma say we can't open our gifts from you until you come downstairs, and I'm ready to open my gifts now. So you need to hurry up," Jeff said all in one breath.

"Who you think you talking to?"

Jeff studied Goldie's face and saw that he was not in the mood.

"I'll be down when I get dressed!" Goldie said.

"I'ma tell her you said to go ahead and open our gifts," Jeff said, with a missing-tooth smile.

"Do it and see what I do!" Goldie threatened.

"Hurry up then!" Jeff said, as he took off down the stairs.

After brushing his teeth, Goldie washed his face one more time, threw his rag in the hamper, and then headed to his bedroom. Scenes of yesterday played through his head, as he walked down the hallway. He tried to shake the thought of Tina, but he couldn't. As he dressed, he started hallucinating. He had to do a double take. He swore he saw Tina's lips moving on the photo on his dresser.

"I'm tripping," he said, shaking his head.

He looked over at the cordless and thought about dialing Tina's number. "Naw, it's too early," he said to himself.

"Goldie!" Loretta yelled from downstairs.

"Yeah!" he retorted.

"Boy, everybody down here waiting on you! Hurry up down these stairs!" she ordered.

"I'm coming!" Goldie yelled, sitting on the edge of the bed and lacing up his fresh pair of Jordan's. He walked over to the full-length mirror on his bedroom door and checked himself. He looked electrifying in his Nike velour sweat suit. He was sporting his sweat suit with the jacket open, showing off his two-hundred gram Figaro chain with the nugget dollar sign charm he treated himself to for Christmas. He stroked his waves. His haircut was tight, and his waves were thick enough to challenge the best surfers in California. He vainly winked at the image in the mirror, and then galloped down the stairs.

"There he go, Momma! Jeff yelled excitedly, as Goldie appeared.

Goldie observed all of the gift-wrapping everywhere. The party had started without him. Jeff was having the time of his life, carelessly running his remote control car into everyone's ankles and laughing. His nephews were actively lying on their stomachs, playing with plastic toys in their mouth. Jeff mistakenly ran his car into the wrong person's ankle.

"Put that damn car up before I throw that shit away!" his mother yelled.

Jeff protectively picked up his remote control, flipped it over, and cut it off. Then he pouted all the way over to the sofa and plopped down with his car in lap.

Loretta gave Jeff the look. "You better straighten up over there!" she ordered.

"Momma, stop tripping; it's Christmas!" Ciera said.

Loretta looked at her and lifted one of her eyebrows. "Alright now, your ass ain't too grown to get a whooping!"

Ciera laughed. "Please...I'm grown!" she boasted.

"Can we all just get serious for a minute and open our gifts?" Melissa interrupted.

Everybody looked at Melissa and gave her a what's-your-problem look.

"Her period must be on," Ciera whispered into her mother's ear.

"Gurl," Loretta laughed, jokingly slapping her on the back and laughing. "Okay, ya'll, let's open up our gifts from Goldie!" she said, then looked over at Goldie and smiled.

Everybody ambushed the Christmas tree and grabbed their gifts.

"Ahh, ahh, ahhh!" Loretta yelled before everyone tore open their gifts.

Everyone stood frozen; they knew what was coming. Loretta looked over at Goldie, motioning for him. When he walked over to her, she placed both of her hands on his shoulders, bit her bottom lip, then stared up at the ceiling and got a little teary-eyed.

"It's times like these that family needs to stick together," she preached. She massaged Goldie's shoulders. "Having you all here with me today…kids and grandkids…is a gift itself. All of you are what breathes life into me." She sighed. "I just wish Albert was here with us today," she said, staring up at the ceiling.

The living room was quiet. Ever since their father's death, everyone knew their mother always got emotional around holidays.

"It's gonna be alright, Momma!" Goldie said, empathetically patting her on her back.

Loretta looked into Goldie's eyes and saw a reflection of a younger Albert. "You all need to thank your brother," she said, wrapping her arm around Goldie. "Your brother worked some long hours at that carwash to buy ya'll these gifts!"

His sisters looked at each other, as if to say, "Yeah, right, sold a lot of dope."

Loretta patted him on the back and smiled. "Now let's open our gifts!"

Everyone immediately went to work, tearing open their gifts. Goldie's sisters were speechless when they opened their gifts. They just looked at each other, as if to now say, "Dang, lil' brother doing it like this?"

All three of his sisters shouted, "Thank you, Goldie!"

"Aw, baby!" his mother screamed, as she took the tennis bracelet out of the box.

Goldie smiled. "You ain't seen nothing yet!" he boasted. "Wait till you open the other ones!"

Loretta did not waste any time opening the other gifts. She was speechless when she saw a diamond ring glistening. She almost fainted. She quickly took it out of the box, and slid it on her finger. She twirled it in the air, admiring the sparkle.

"Dang, Momma, them real diamonds?" her daughters asked, while coming and looking over her shoulder, admiring the ring.

"Yeah, them real diamonds!" Goldie confirmed.

Loretta was flabbergasted when she opened her other gift. She threw her hands up to her mouth, getting a little choked up. "Come here, baby!" she told Goldie, opening up her arms and crying tears of joy. When Goldie reached her, she smothered him with hugs and kisses. "Thank you, baby!" she said, kissing him on the forehead. "Ciera, come put this necklace on for me!"

After Ciera clamped on her mother's necklace, she looked like a queen. Goldie stood off to the side, feeling proud. All he wanted was for his family to be happy.

"You know what? This is the best Christmas I've ever had!" their mother declared.

Ciera walked over to the stereo, turned on some music, and everybody, except Goldie, started cheerfully dancing. Goldie just sat at the bottom of the stairs, glad to see everybody else happy.

Thirsty, he walked into the kitchen and poured himself a glass of orange juice. When he closed the refrigerator and turned around, his sister, Adriana, startled him.

"Dang, gurl, why you sneaking up on me like that?" Goldie asked, in an agitated voice.

"'Cause...I don't want everybody in my business," Adriana said in a light whisper.

"What business?" Goldie asked, sipping from his cup.

"I need to borrow fifty dollars until next Friday," Adriana begged.

"I'll think about it," Goldie said arrogantly.

Adriana pouted. "Come on now, Goldie. I know you got it!"

Goldie smiled. "Say please," he teased.

Adriana crossed her arms, then stomped her feet. "Come on now, Goldie!" She pouted again.

"Alright!" Goldie reasoned, then reached into his pocket and pulled out a wad of money.

Adriana's face lit up like Christmas lights. "You know...I really needed to borrow a hundred dollars," she said, trying her hand.

Goldie leaned his head back and laughed. "Now all of a sudden when ya see I got a pocket full of money, you need a hundred dollars?"

Adriana saw her game wasn't working.

"Here! You better just take this lil' fifty dollars and run with it!" he said, holding out a fifty-dollar bill.

Adriana reached for the money, but Goldie jokingly snatched it away. "Boy, stop playing!"

"Say 'I'm nothing without you, big brother'," Goldie teased.

"Boy, you crazy. I ain't calling your lil' butt no damn big brother and I'm older than you!" Adriana spat.

Goldie shrugged his shoulders. "Alright then, suit yourself," he said, and then attempted to walk pass her.

Adriana cleverly blocked his path. She fumingly folded her arms, stared up at the ceiling, irritably tapped her foot on the ground, and then mumbled, "I'm nothing without you, big brother," with a grimace on her face.

"Huh?" Goldie asked, coming closer to her and putting his hand up to his ear.

"I said that I'm nothing without you, big brother. Dang, I said it!" She pouted.

Goldie pleasingly smiled, then held out the fifty-dollar bill.

Adriana furiously snatched the money from out of his hand, and then said, "Sissy!" as she stormed out of the kitchen.

"Alright, see if ya butt get anything else from me!" he shouted to the back of her head.

Goldie just stood in the kitchen's entrance, and admired his family having the time of their life in the living room. He took another sip of his orange juice. It really touched him to see his family happy after everything they had been through over the years. He felt pleased to have successfully made everybody's Christmas. However, Tina was the only one who could make his. He stared over at the cordless phone. It was calling him. He contemplated on calling Tina, while he nervously tapped his fingers on the counter. Temptation got the best of him. He snatched the cordless off the base, then immediately dialed Tina's number.

RING...RING...RING.

Tina made an effort to hop off the sofa and answer the phone, until her mother gave her the frightening look of death. She obediently stopped dead in her tracks, and then disturbingly sat back on the sofa. She knew it was Goldie calling.

Her mother calmly got up, curiously walked over to the phone, and picked it up.

"Hello, Tina?" the caller got in before being disconnected.

"Humph," her mother said, as she hung up the phone.

The caller called right back. Tina's mother just eyed her, while the two just sat and listened to the phone ring.

"I hate her ass!" Tina mumbled to herself, as she stared over at her mother.

Last night, the two had packed all of their belongings, and were now waiting on Stephen to arrive this morning to pick them up and take them back home. Tina's mother had broken down last night and called Stephen, telling him everything that had happened. Delirious, Stephen told her he would be on the first flight available to them. Truthfully, it had taken everything in Jackie to make the call. As a mother, she had to make a judgment call, and do what she thought would be in her daughter's best interest. What was she to do? Here she was, busting her butt and working doubles so her daughter could be happy, only to be rewarded by coming home and finding her laying on her back with her legs in a V.

Stephen wanted to make things work, and had agreed to counseling and anything else Jackie saw fit to better their relationship. He just wanted his family back. Together, he knew the three of them could work things out.

Deep down inside, Jackie faulted herself for moving Tina out of an elite neighborhood and into the projects. What did she expect to happen? She should have seen the signs earlier, when Tina's behavior started to change. Tina needed a father in her life, and if Stephen was willing to change, she was willing to give it another try.

* * * * *

After letting the phone ring for what seemed like a hundred times, Goldie sat the cordless back down in its cradle. Just that fast, he had lost his appetite. He felt weak. As he stared up at the ceiling, he got lightheaded and felt like he needed to go lay down. Unstable, he walked over to the bottom of the stairs, then paused and looked over at his family one last time. He smiled. At least they were happy.

In the midst of playing with her grandchildren, Loretta looked up and could tell by the look on Goldie's face that something was wrong.

"Here, get Dontrel," Loretta told Adriana, as she handed Dontrel to her.

Loretta curiously walked over to Goldie and caringly sat next to him on the stairs. "Baby, what's wrong?" she asked, placing her arm around her son.

"Nothing," Goldie replied, lying through his teeth.

His mother sucked her teeth. "Boy, I brought you into this world. Don't you think I know when something is wrong with you?"

Goldie dropped his head and shook it. "It's a long story."

His mother grabbed his hand and patted it. "Okay, Momma's listening."

Goldie began filling his mother in on everything that happened yesterday. He did not hide anything, because the two of them shared that kind of relationship. Goldie noticed how his mother kept shaking her head as he explained. When he finished, his mother just dropped her head and kept on shaking it. There was silence for a minute.

Goldie's mother looked up at him. "You know you was wrong, right?"

"I know...I know," Goldie mumbled.

Loretta stood up, then placed her hands on her hips. "So how long has this been going on? I mean...how long have you been having sex?" his mother asked, with a serious face.

Goldie blushed, and then bashfully dropped his head. "Come on, Ma!" he cried.

His mother earnestly stood with her arms folded. Goldie got the message.

"I only did it a couple of times," he said.

"With how many of them hot little girls?" his mother asked, concerned.

Goldie laughed. "Just two."

"And did you use protection?" she asked.

Ashamed, Goldie dropped his head.

His mother lifted up his chin. "Did you or did you not use protection?"

"I---," Goldie stuttered.

"Boy, I know you not out there having unprotected sex?" his mother asked, agitated.

"I ---," Goldie said, stuttering again.

"Boy, don't lie to me!" his mother shouted.

"I just forgot, that's all," Goldie explained.

"Well, I tell you what! From now on, if your lil' butt think you're grown enough to have sex, you better be grown enough to wear some protection! I don't know who ya'll think gonna be taking care of all these babies! I don't approve of what you're doing, but I do respect your honesty. I don't know what's wrong with you kids these days," his mother lectured, shaking her head.

"Times done changed, Momma!" Goldie said.

"When I was a kid, we were taught to wait until we were married to have sex!"

"How old were you when you first had sex?" Goldie asked.

"Now you're being grown!" his mother said, with a serious face and pointing her finger at him.

"I'm sorry, Momma!" he apologized.

"What you need to do is take your butt over to that girl's house, and apologize to her momma for being over there when you weren't supposed to!"

"I guess you're right," Goldie reasoned.

His mother smiled. "You know that Momma knows best. Now go on!" Loretta said, waving him off.

"Thank you, Ma!" Goldie said, then hugged his mom and disappeared out of the door.

Loretta stood at the front door, shaking her head. She could only imagine what it would be like to come home and catch one of her daughters having sex in her house. She knew if she were Tina's mother, she would either be in jail for child abuse or murder right now. She hoped Tina's mother was sympathetic and accepted Goldie's apology. Her son was in love, and it was written all over his face. Loretta closed the front door.

"That poor lil' girl," she said, shaking her head as she went back to join the rest of the family in the living room.

CHAPTER TWENTY-ONE

Goldie nervously walked up the sidewalk, carefully reciting his apology speech to himself repeatedly. He knew it was going to be a long shot, but he was hoping Tina's mother could find it in her heart to forgive him.

When he reached Tina's front porch, he took a deep breath and rang the doorbell. No one answered. He rang the doorbell a few more times. Still no one answered.

"Damn!" Goldie shouted, stepping off the porch.

He stood clueless on the sidewalk for a couple of seconds, rubbing on his chin.

All of a sudden, an idea came to mind. He searched along the side of the apartment for a rock. Once he found one, he delicately chucked it at Tina's bedroom window. The rock made a light thump.

"Tina!" Goldie shouted.

No one answered. He picked up another rock, this one a little bigger, and chucked it, too. The rock made a loud thump.

"Oops," Goldie said, covering his mouth with his hand and scanning the area.

Mrs. Bernadine, the neighbor, swiftly lifted up her window. "Child, come from that window!" she ordered.

"I'm looking for Tina!" Goldie said, walking towards her window.

"That child's been gone! Her and Jackie left over an hour ago!"

"You don't know when they coming back?" Goldie asked.

"They ain't!" Mrs. Bernadine said.

Goldie knew he did not just hear what he thought he heard. "What?" he shouted.

"That little girl's father flew in this morning, and came and got the both of them!" Mrs. Bernadine gossiped.

Goldie placed his hands on top of his head, and felt like somebody was spinning him around. It seemed like the entire projects were spinning. He was still in disbelief.

"Tina's gone?"

"Ummmmm hmmmm! You can fault yourself!" Mrs. Bernadine spat.

"Huh? Whatta you talking about?" Goldie asked, with a grimace on his face.

"Humph! Child, don't you know that Mrs. Bernadine sees everything. I told Jackie she was asking for trouble when she was working all of them long hours and leaving that poor child home all by herself. I use to see the way the two of you use to carry on over there on that porch after school. I knew that it was only a matter of time! Ummm hmmmmm!"

Goldie painfully stared up at the sky. He still could not believe Tina was gone and was not coming back. He just stood speechless, his mind in another world. He saw Mrs. Bernadine's lips moving, but he had not heard a word after she had told him that Tina was gone. Goldie looked up at the sky and asked God why. How could she just up and leave like that? He was crushed.

"I hope ya'll used protection!" Mrs. Bernadine blurted.

Mrs. Bernadine's words went in one ear and out the other. Goldie felt like someone had taken a dagger and violently stuck it straight through his heart. And on that day, Goldie got his first taste of what love really felt like. He dropped his head, and gathered enough strength for him and his broken heart to walk down the sidewalk.

"You better hope that little girl ain't pregnant!" Mrs. Bernadine shouted out of the window.

Goldie just ignored her, and his head got smaller and smaller.

CHAPTER TWENTY-TWO

It was not until the beginning of February when Goldie fully recovered from his broken heart. Although rumor had it that him and Tina were caught in her apartment having sex, Tina's mom and dad getting back together was the real reason why everyone thought she had moved.

It took a little time and finessing, but after a couple of weeks, Goldie was right back in regular rotation, knocking Nikki off every Friday night. After Tina broke his heart, Goldie vowed never to let another woman get close enough to him to break his heart again. He turned into a straight playboy. Why not? He decided to be like every male figure he knew in the hood, and juggle a couple of women at a time.

"Hell, Snake's got three baby mommas who all know about each other, and they don't trip. So, shit...I should be able to mess with a couple of different females at school and they shouldn't trip," he reasoned with himself.

Therefore, he did just that. Immediately, Goldie began flirting with every fine girl in school who he thought was vulnerable. He used his looks, money, and persuasion to manipulate different girls to get in bed with him. At any given time, you could catch him standing in the ala carte line, generously treating different girls to various items. The girls would always smile and say, "Thank you, Goldie," but little did they know, he was only setting them up.

169

When Valentine's Day rolled around, Goldie went straight Casanova, spending over $300, sending carnations to every girl who was a victim on his list. He just stood in the hallway posted up on his locker, as every girl he had sent flowers to, walked over and affectionately kissed him on the cheek, while handing him their phone numbers. That day, Goldie played Cupid, shooting each girl in the ass with one of his love arrows, as they walked off.

Goldie was surprised with how far throwing around a couple of dollars, spitting a little game, and making a couple of promises got him. Girls were easy to manipulate. Things were going so smoothly for him that he decided to challenge himself and shoot at some of the stuck-up girls to see if his mack game was really on point. They took a little more time, but once he found their weakness, he moved in for the kill. Surprisingly, the stuck-up girls were freakier than the normal ones. As Goldie conquered each girl, he began feeling empowered at the control he had over her. The attention, the sexual episodes, and the thrill of the chase all excited him. One by one, he was knocking down eighth-grade girls like they were a stack of dominoes. Every day after school his private line in his room rung like a receptionist desk. Whenever he was not at home, his mother would grow so agitated, listening to his phone ring, that she would storm up to his room and unplug his phone.

By the end of March, Goldie had become the Panty Bandit. As kinky as it may sound, he had a dresser drawer that stored nothing but his victim's panties. At the present, there were over thirty pairs of panties inside of the drawer.

As the weeks passed, Goldie was becoming more and more popular. He was the man. It did not take long for the girls to start spreading around school how hung Goldie was. Whenever he strolled down the hallway, all eyes were always on him. The girls seemed to stop what they were doing, let off schoolgirl giggles, and then flirtatiously wave. Goldie would always just arrogantly smile, wave back, and confidently continue strutting down the hallway, as if he knew he was the shit.

As the school year winded down, Spring Break was right around the corner. All of the students were anxiously waiting for their week vacation.

Goldie could not wait, either; it meant he would be able to hustle full time. He could use the extra money, because when August came around and he stepped into high school, he wanted to be the flyest thing on the yard.

CHAPTER TWENTY-THREE

The sun's radiant rays beamed down on the projects. Judging by the way all of the teenage girls were parading around in their Daisy Duke's, everyone finally felt relieved to be able to reveal more flesh and showcase everything that had stayed hidden under excessive winter clothes. Spring Break was officially here.

The projects were abundantly full of life. All of the kids were outside, and energetically running around wild all throughout the projects. While some chose to ride their bikes, others roller-skated. The younger girls were actively engaged in practicing cheers, jump roping, or playing hopscotch.

Snake was posted up on the block with the rest of the crew, leaning up against his car and sipping out of a brown paper bag, when Goldie arrived.

"What's up, nigga?" Goldie asked, greeting Snake with his signature handshake.

"What's poppin' with you, Goldie?" Snake asked, as the two embraced.

"Ahhh...ya'll killing me with all of that mushy shit!" Peanut said.

The whole crew started laughing.

"Fuck you, nigga! Goldie's the future!" Snake bragged.

Goldie nodded his head and mean mugged the whole crew. "Yeah, niggas, you heard!" he said, striking a pose and folding his arms.

A potential customer pulled up, and five members of the crew ambushed the car with their project in hand.

Goldie just looked over at Snake and shook his head. "What the money been like?"

Snake checked his watch, then grabbed his crotch and took a swig from his potion. "A lil' paper been coming through, but it's still early. You know it don't pick up until around six."

"Man, I'm hungry!" Goldie complained. "Let's go grab something to eat."

"Your treat?" Snake teased.

"Nigga, you ain't said nothing," Goldie said, reaching into his pocket and pulling out a wad.

"Oh, you stackin' like that now, huh?" Snake joked.

"Fo sho'!" Goldie boasted.

Snake walked over and rubbed him on the top of the head. "Let's go grab something to eat then. Yo, Mookie, ya'll hold shit down 'til we get back!" Snake ordered, while walking over to the driver's side of the car.

"Fo sho'!" Mookie said.

Snake unlocked the doors, and he and Goldie hopped in.

"Hold up! I know you ain't dirty?" Snake asked.

Goldie gave him a crazy look, while Snake gave him a serious look back.

"I'm serious...if you dirty, you better get that shit up off of you!" Snake ordered, as Goldie started easing out of the car. "You know better than that. You know I don't ride dirty in my Caddy!" Snake scolded, as Goldie headed over to stash his rocks.

Goldie ran over by the crew, picked up an empty potato chip bag from off of the ground, and threw his rocks inside. He then ran over and hid the bag inside of the bushes.

"Watch that for me, Mookie!" he yelled out, while heading back to the car. "My bad!" Goldie said, after hopping inside.

"Listen, Goldie, you can't be slipping like that!" he scolded, while pulling off. "When you old enough to drive, and you rolling in something nice, you can't never afford to get caught slipping with nothing on you! You had better believe when them jealous ass police see you driving in something they can't afford, they gonna get in they feelings and pull your ass over. So to save all of the bullshit, always be one step ahead of them muthafuckas and don't be riding dirty," Snake lectured, giving Goldie his lesson for the day.

"I don't understand why you should let them dictate what you do?" Goldie questioned.

"Listen, it ain't about being scared. It's about using your head!" Snake stressed. "Trust me, just listen to me and you gonna go far."

"You mean one day be as rich as you?" Goldie asked, excited.

Snake laughed. "Richer!"

Goldie's face lit up. "Now that's what I'm talking about!"

Snake turned up his music and the two cruised down 16th Street, bopping their heads to the music, heading to Red's Snack Shack.

"Goddamn!" Snake said, instinctively sitting up in his seat.

Snake slowed down at the sight of two big-booty redbones who were invitingly walking up Campbell's Park sidewalk.

"Watch this!" Snake said, tapping Goldie on the chest.

He then slid in Guy's tape, let down all of his windows, and turned up the volume to "Piece of My Love", while creeping down the street.

That got the girls' attention. They turned around, and found themselves instantly blinded by the gold grille on the Cadillac. Both girls then looked at each other.

"Gurl, ain't that Snake?" the one asked the other.

When Snake caught up with them, he pulled over to the curb and threw his car in park. Without a word exchanged, both girls obediently walked towards Snake's car, as if he was their pimp. He was sitting with his seat leaned all the way back, gripping the steering wheel with his right hand, exposing $50,000 in rings.

The bolder of the two kneeled down and flirtatiously stuck her head inside of his window.

"What's up?" Snake arrogantly asked.

"What's up?" the unidentified woman replied.

Snake revealed his eyes from up under his Kangol. "I know you?"

"Naw, but you can get to know me," the girl boldly stated.

"What's ya'll names?" Snake asked.

"Well...I'm Cherry, and that's my homegirl Rhonda," she said, while pointing at Rhonda.

Snake quickly assessed the two. The shyer of the two seemed to be the cutest.

Snake returned his attention back to Cherry. "What's up with your friend, she can't talk?"

"Who Rhonda? She just real quiet, that's all," Cherry said.

Snake looked around Cherry's body and said, "Yo, Rhonda, you scared of real niggas or something?"

"Ain't nobody scared," Rhonda replied.

"I'm saying, though...why you all hanging in the background like you can't talk? A nigga tryna get to know ya'll," Snake said.

Rhonda walked over to the car and kneeled down next to Cherry. "What up?" she asked.

Cherry did not like sharing the spotlight with Rhonda, because she knew Rhonda was prettier than she was. She wanted Rhonda to just sit back and let her do all of the talking.

"So, Snake, what ya'll finna get into," Cherry asked, stealing the spotlight back.

Snake tugged on his manhood. "Shit, me and my lil' nigga was just finna go chill at a room."

Cherry curiously looked over at Goldie with a disturbing look on her face. "How old is he?"

"My lil' nigga's fourteen, but what age gotta do with what we talking about?" Snake asked.

"Unnhh unnhh, you must be talking about another homeboy or something," she replied.

"What the fuck you mean?" Snake shouted defensively.

"Rhonda's eighteen; he too young for her!" Cherry said, automatically claiming Snake for herself.

Snake got agitated. "So what the fuck are you, the spokesman for Rhonda or something? She got a mouth; let her speak her peace. Besides, this shit a package deal. It's either both of us, or ain't shit happening at all," Snake arrogantly stated, cranking up his car and letting them know they had better make a fast decision.

Cherry and Rhonda both exchanged crazy looks. Cherry gave Rhonda the sympathetic, puppy dog eyes, as if pleading with her not to mess it up.

"Hold on one minute, Snake. Let me holla at Rhonda real quick," Cherry told him.

"Handle your business," Snake said, waving her off.

Cherry and Rhonda stepped up on the curb, and then huddled up.

"Cherry, what I'ma do with that lil' ass boy? That boy probably just starting to get hair on his lil' thang," Rhonda joked.

"Listen, Rhonda, this nigga Snake is paid! Don't mess this up girl," Cherry said, giving her a serious look. "Girl this nigga the man; he controls the streets. Shit...for the right price, I'll fuck both of 'em my damn self," Cherry let slip out.

Rhonda just stood with her arms folded, giving Cherry a look like "Do it then!"

Cherry wanted to take her last comment back. She walked over and threw her hands on Rhonda's shoulders. "Listen, girl, just do this for me this one time, please! Shit, ain't you tryna get up some money to go to the concert, too?" she asked.

Rhonda stood speechless for a moment, tapping her foot and debating.

"Damn, what the fuck these bitches doing?" Snake said, looking over at the girls and wondering what was taking so long.

"I don't know," Goldie said.

"Damn, this shit is simple. Either they fucking or they ain't. Shit, we could turn a couple of corners and find some hoes to take to the room," Snake said.

Goldie laughed. "Nigga, you crazy!"

Snake looked over at him and smiled. "Yeah, lil' nigga, I heard you busting up them lil' middle school girls. I'ma see how ya lil' ass handle some grown-woman pussy!"

"Nigga, I can handle mine!" Goldie boasted with a smile.

"We gonna see, nigga...we gonna see," Snake taunted.

The girls walked back over and Cherry kneeled down, sticking her head in the window. "Tell him to get in the backseat," she said, happy she had convinced Rhonda.

Snake looked over at Goldie and smiled. It was on. Goldie smirked, then opened the door and hopped in the backseat. Cherry pranced around the front of the car to hop in the front seat.

"Yeah, a nigga was finna pull off on ya'll ass," Snake joked.

Coincidentally, Goldie and Rhonda happened to hop in the backseat at the same time.

"What up? I'm Goldie," he introduced himself, with a pleasant smile.

"Hey, I'm Rhonda," she said, returning a warm smile.

Snake adjusted his rearview mirror so he could see in the backseat. Goldie gave him a nod that everything was straight. Then Snake threw his Caddy in drive, turned up the music, and pulled off.

During the rest of the ride to the hotel, both couples exchanged small talk. In Snake and Cherry's conversation, she did most of the talking. She talked so much that Snake wanted to put some damn tape on her mouth. He said a couple of words here and there, but mostly just nodded his head.

Cherry was surprised to hear the backseat full with joyous laughter. She curiously turned around in her seat, and was surprised to see a fourteen-year-old holding a conversation with her girl.

After saying a couple of things to make Rhonda laugh, Goldie managed to get her to open up. Judging by the way that she kept bashfully blushing, Goldie took it he was saying all of the right things. Each word that flowed off the tip of his tongue made him more and more confident. At first, he was a little intimidated and not sure if he would be able to entertain an older female. However, once their conversation started flowing, and Goldie managed to produce a smile on her face, it was smooth sailing from there, and Goldie knew he had her.

To Rhonda's surprise, Goldie was extremely mature for his age. His choice of words showed how intelligent he was. Not only that, but she found Goldie's deep, baritone voice extremely sexy. Finally, after blocking out his age, Rhonda found herself physically attracted to Goldie.

Fifteen minutes later, Snake pulled up under the carport of the Downtown Hilton. Cherry was impressed. Not only did Snake have money, he had style and class to go with it. Cherry looked in the backseat at Rhonda, and the two nodded their heads at each other.

The valet approached the passenger side, opened Cherry's door, reached out his hand, and courteously helped her out of the car. Flattered, Cherry exited, fluttering her eyelashes. You could tell she was a Motel 6 girl, and was not use to this kind of treatment.

Before Rhonda ever got a chance to step one foot on the ground, the valet had rushed over and helped her out, as well.

Snake and Goldie helped themselves out, looked at each other, and shook their heads.

The valet walked over to Snake. "Keys, sir, please," he said in a polite voice.

After Snake dropped his keys in the valet's hands, the valet just stood there for a minute, then cleared his throat.

"What, you waiting on a tip or something?" Snake asked agitated. The valet smiled. Snake pulled out a hefty wad, big enough to operate a teller at a bank. Just looking at all that money made the girls drool, and their panties became instantly wet. Money was their aphrodisiac, and both girls had just had a money-gasm.

"Here!" Snake said, handing the valet a twenty-dollar bill.

Cherry's eyes got big. If Snake tipped the valet twenty dollars for just opening their doors, she knew her mind-blowing performance was sure to bring her $200, at least.

"Thank you, sir! Have a nice day!" the valet said, and then rushed off to attend to another car that had pulled up.

As the four strolled inside of the hotel lobby, Cherry wrapped her arm around Snake's waist and asked him, "We getting our own room, ain't we?"

"For what?" Snake blurted, with a look on his face as if Cherry had just asked him to slap his auntie.

Cherry tooted up her nose, pulled away from Snake with an attitude, and went over and sat down in the waiting area.

"Let me see what's wrong with her," Rhonda told Goldie, then walked over and joined Cherry.

Goldie waited in line with Snake. "What's wrong with ya girl?" he asked.

Snake looked over at Cherry. "You know that crazy bitch had the nerve to ask me if we were getting our own room, like she's a nigga's lady or something," Snake said, fuming.

Goldie laughed. "Nigga, you crazy," he said.

* * * * *

Inside of the room was immaculate. There was thick, expensive oriental carpeting that accented the floral designs on the comforters. When you opened the drapes, there was a beautiful, breathtaking view of the pier and downtown St. Petersburg. For a non-smoking room, the room had a surprising fresh smell.

While Goldie and Rhonda were seated on one bed engaged in deep conversation, Snake was over in the other bed, laying on his stomach, and getting a massage from Cherry. Since Cherry was wearing a skirt, he felt the warmth from her love garden, as her goodies rested on his lower back. While enjoying the royal treatment, Snake wondered if Cherry could work her mouth like she worked her hands.

All of a sudden, an idea came to Snake's mind, and he leaned over to whisper something into Cherry's ear. Cherry playfully hit him on the shoulder, then smiled. The two glanced over at Goldie and Rhonda, who were still engaged in deep conversation. Snake grabbed Cherry by the hand, and the two secretly tiptoed towards the bathroom. Before disappearing inside the bathroom, Cherry took one last look back, made eye contact with Rhonda, and winked.

Meanwhile, Goldie and Rhonda had graduated to tasting each other's tongues. Rhonda was amazed at how experienced he was in the kissing department. The way he held her had her breathless. Not only that, but he kissed with such passion. Goldie laid Rhonda down on her back, and then passionately started sucking on her neck.

After coming up for air, he whispered, "You got a man?"

Goldie felt so good on top of Rhonda that she did not want to talk. She just answered him by shaking her head.

Goldie let off a devilish smile. He really did not care if she had a man, but asked out of common courtesy. He went back into action, sensually sucking on her neck. Her moans only heightened Goldie's arousal. Before he knew it, the two found themselves making love with their clothes on. Rhonda wrapped her arms around his neck, while the two gyrated their hips.

When Cherry and Snake returned in the room, they were startled. They stopped dead in their tracks. Snake threw his index finger up to his mouth for Cherry to be quiet, and the two just stood and watched them for a minute.

"Damn, that lil' nigga can work it," Cherry said to herself.

Rhonda looked up and noticed Snake and Cherry watching them.

"Dang, what's going on in here?" Cherry said with a smile on her face.

"Gurl, shut up!" Rhonda said, embarrassingly sitting up and fixing her hair, while blushing.

"You see my lil' homeboy?" Snake said, cheering Goldie on, as he zipped up his pants.

Goldie smiled, then hopped up and headed to the bathroom, concealing his erection.

Cherry rushed over, sat next to Rhonda, and started jokingly picking on her.

"Gurl, let me find out that lil' boy got you wide-open!" Cherry said, slapping her on the leg.

"Gurl, please, I'll drown that lil' boy! He can't do nothing with this!" Rhonda bragged, as she snapped her fingers in front of Cherry's face.

"Alright, now remember what you said," Cherry scolded.

Two drinks and three joints later, everybody had nice buzzes. Snake took that as his cue, so he closed the curtains, turned off the lights, and slid up under the covers with Cherry.

SHOWTIME

Goldie heard giggling coming from the bed that Snake and Cherry shared. When the giggling stopped, those sounds were replaced by slurping sounds. "Ahhh Shiiiit," was all Goldie kept hearing Snake repeating.

Anxious to get busy himself, he whispered in Rhonda's ear, "So what's up?"

"Whatever you want to be up," she whispered seductively, nibbling on his earlobe.

Goldie maneuvered his way on top of Rhonda, and then eased off her shorts. After sliding off her panties, he started sensually planting kisses all over her body, then worked his way up to her lips. Meanwhile, Snake was over in the other bed brutally pounding Cherry.

At first, Rhonda was just in it for the money, but now, she was attracted to Goldie. Right when she began to wonder if Goldie would be able to satisfy her sexually, she got the surprise of her life.

"Unnnnhhhh!" was all she could manage to get out, when Goldie rammed his monstrous rod inside of her.

Rhonda's eyes got as big as an owl's. With each stroke, Goldie traveled deeper and deeper inside of her. Goldie excavated deeper than anyone had ever dug. He felt so good inside of Rhonda that she wrapped her arms around his neck and her feet around his lower back.

Now, the bed they shared became the center of attention. Cherry's moans were drowned out by Rhonda's. Rhonda was in shear ecstasy. She was still is disbelief that a fourteen-year-old was putting it on her like that. Rhonda's moans became so loud that Snake stopped stroking.

"What's the matter with you?" Cherry asked.

"My lil' homey fucking the shit out of ya gurl," Snake boasted.

Deep down inside, Cherry wanted to tell him how much she wished she were in the other bed. Truthfully, Snake was working himself more than he was working her. He had to have money, because he was lacking in the dick department. Cherry wanted to tell him to get up, but she played along, making him feel like he was really doing something.

"Oh shit, GOLDIE!" was all Rhonda kept repeating.

Snake took that as a challenge, and immediately went back to work pounding Cherry's insides.

"Oh shit!" Cherry faked.

Snake thought he was handling his business. Little did he know he wasn't the one responsible for Cherry's moaning. Cherry was getting off on the sounds of Rhonda's moans, and the help of a couple of her fingers massaging her clit.

For twenty straight minutes, Goldie made the headboard sing. Rhonda could not believe what was going on. She had already experienced four orgasms and was currently working on her fifth.

"Oh shit, Goldie! Damn, baby, you feel so good!" Rhonda moaned, as her juices overflowed out of her love garden.

"Damn, ya gurl loud over there!" Snake told Cherry.

"Well, at least somebody's enjoying themself," Cherry mumbled.

Snake stopped stroking. "So what the fuck you tryna say?" he asked with an attitude.

"Are you finished?" Cherry asked, ready to throw on her clothes.

Snake pulled out of Cherry. His ego had been crushed, and sitting and listening to Goldie still going like the Energizer Bunny did not help things either. Curiosity was killing Snake. He threw on his boxers, then walked over to the light switch and flicked on the lights.

The lights coming on did not seem to distract Goldie one bit. Sweat dripped from his masculine body, as he smoothly glided in and out of Rhonda with nice controlled strokes.

"Goddamn!" Goldie moaned with a grimace as he leaned his head back, and then increased his pace.

Rhonda's head was buried in the sheets, as she gripped the comforter, slowly pulling more and more of the bedding off the bed, while Goldie rammed his rod inside of her.

All of a sudden, Goldie leaned forward, and let out a grunt. He quickly pulled out of Rhonda, collapsing on the bed, exhausted.

"Damn, baby!" Rhonda said, massaging her clit as she rolled back and forth on her back.

Goldie victoriously stood up at the foot of the bed, naked, glistening with sweat.

Snake looked at Goldie's naked body and could not believe his eyes. By no means was he gay, but he was speechless.

"Damn, this nigga's daddy must have been a horse!" Snake said, looking at Goldie and shaking his head.

Snake glanced down inside of his boxers and felt like he was the fourteen year old, not Goldie. He looked over at Cherry, who was rubbing on herself and looking over at Goldie like she wanted to tear him apart. Snake got mad.

"I tell you what...since a nigga can't please your muthafuckin' ass, put on your shit so I can take your ass home!" Snake ordered.

Cherry rolled her eyes at him and tooted up her nose. She reached down on the floor, grabbed her panties, and quickly slid them on. She then rose to her feet and started putting on her clothes.

While looking over at Snake, she mumbled, "Lil' dick motherfucker."

After Snake finished dressing, he grabbed his keys and stormed towards the door.

"I'll be out in the car!" he said, before exiting the room.

Rhonda curiously looked over at Cherry. "What seems to be his problem?"

"Child, I ain't stunnin' his lil' dick ass!" Cherry replied.

"Hold up now. I ain't finna sit here and let ya'll talk about my homeboy!" Goldie said, defending Snake.

"Well, all I can say is that I enjoyed myself," Rhonda said sarcastically, then started massaging Goldie's shoulders.

Cherry looked over at her and rolled her eyes. Rhonda stuck her tongue out at her.

Frustrated, Cherry threw her purse over her shoulder and grabbed the rest of her belongings. "I'll be downstairs!" she said, then stormed out of the door.

Rhonda and Goldie just stared at each other, and then busted out laughing. They laughed together for a couple of minutes.

"We better go," Rhonda said, standing up.

Goldie stood up, scanned the room to make sure he wasn't leaving anything behind, and then said, "Let's dip."

* * * * *

"Where am I dropping ya'll off at?" Snake asked Cherry after everyone was in the car.

"Just take me home!" Cherry blurted, waving him off as she stared out of the window.

Rhonda stuck her head in the front seat. "I'm going to your house, Cherry?"

"I don't care, but I got a date at nine," Cherry said, taunting Snake.

Rhonda checked her watch. "It's 7:30 now!"

"Well, you just gonna have to catch a cab from my house," Cherry said.

"Ho, you know a cab gonna cost me at least twenty dollars from your house," Rhonda spat, not believing how inconsiderate Cherry was being.

"That's on you!" Cherry said arrogantly.

Rhonda distressfully sat back in her seat and crossed her arms. "You a selfish motherfucker, Cherry!" she spat.

Not liking what was going down, Goldie caringly grabbed Rhonda's hand and patted it. "Don't worry, boo. I got you!" he said, then reached into his pocket and handed her two twenty-dollar bills.

Rhonda affectionately kissed him on the check. "Thank you, Goldie."

Goldie smiled. "I ain't tripping! That's forty dollars, just in case you want the cab driver to circle the block one time," he joked.

Snake glanced into the backseat through his rearview mirror. When he and Goldie made eye contact, he nodded his head in approval. Goldie had game.

The minute Snake pulled in front of Cherry's house, she hopped out of the car and slammed the door behind her.

Snake jumped out of the car heated. "Alright, bitch, slam my shit like that again!"

"Don't worry. You don't ever have to worry 'bout me riding in the car with your lil' dick ass again. Humph! I should've picked Goldie instead of you!" Cherry said, adding lighter fluid to the fire.

Before Snake got the chance to say a word, Cherry disappeared inside of the house. Embarrassed, Snake looked over at Rhonda and Goldie. The two were leaning up against Snake's car, fighting to hold in their laughs. Snake fumingly gritted his teeth, and then eased back inside of the car.

"Listen, Goldie, I really enjoyed myself tonight," Rhonda said.

"Me, too!" Goldie replied.

"Here's my beeper number and my home phone number. Call me whenever you want," she said.

Goldie looked at the piece of paper and smiled. "Alright, I'ma do that."

Rhonda stepped forward and kissed him on the forehead. "Listen, I gotta go."

Goldie stepped forward and stuck his tongue inside of her mouth. Rhonda's knees got weak. The kiss lasted for a couple of minutes, before Rhonda pulled away. As the two held hands and stared into each other's eyes, Rhonda felt herself falling for Goldie.

"I really gotta go," she said, then waved goodbye and headed towards the house.

Goldie made his way around to the passenger side of the car. Rhonda looked back one last time, blew Goldie a kiss, and then disappeared inside of the house.

Goldie hopped inside of the car with a smile on his face. Snake looked over at him, shook his head, then cranked up the car and drove off.

The two rode in silence for a couple of minutes, before Goldie turned in his seat to face Snake and asked, "So how did I do?"

CHAPTER TWENTY-FOUR

For the next couple of days, Snake spent most of his leisure time preparing for his 24th birthday bash. Not only was he planning to have a huge picnic, he was also planning to have a huge after-party.

Snake had gone through pure hell with the parks department to obtain a permit to hold his birthday bash at Bartlett Park. The city was not too keen of thousands of black folks gathering in one particular area. That meant more security and more work for them.

Tomorrow was the big day, and Snake had his street team paint the city with flyers, posting them at all the key hangout spots and on telephone poles throughout the hood.

As Snake toured the city, he reflected on how far he had came over the years. He had come from nothing, and now, he was sitting on top of the world. He never thought he would make it this far. Based on his lifestyle, he never saw himself living a day past twenty-one.

As Snake traveled down 16th Street, he wondered if he would ever be able to leave the game. He was sitting on a little over $800,000, and both of his businesses were doing exceptionally well and bringing in legitimate money. Combined, both businesses were clearing over $4,000 a week.

And now that he was buying bricks instead of individual quarters, he was killing them in the streets. Cheaper prices allowed him to cut bigger rocks, killing the competition. Snake had niggas from all of the surrounding counties coming to cop work. In the last couple of weeks, clientele had nearly doubled. Everybody on his team was getting major money. Black Jesus had branched off to Jacksonville to do his thing, but stayed loyal and continued coming down every weekend to cop work off Snake, then head back up   I-95.

Since Snake was moving up, he decided to upgrade, and sold his Caddy to Peanut for $15,000. Not wanting to be outdone by Peanut, Mookie copped himself a '73 Chevy convertible and tricked it all the way out. Snake's entire crew was living their dreams. Money was being distributed through the whole crew and everybody was happy.

Even Goldie was getting his fair share of the pie. Although he was not old enough to drive, that did not stop Rhonda from handing over her car keys without any hesitation. Goldie had her wide-open. Whenever Goldie was not hustling, the two of them were always cooped up inside of a hotel having raunchy sex. To keep Rhonda happy, Goldie would throw a few dollars her way. He even paid one of the crackheads in the hood to tint her windows and copped a pair of five-star rims that some niggas in the hood stole off a car in Tampa.

As Snake pulled into the projects, he admired his surroundings. This was home. From the little kids running around bare-footed, to the crackhead trying to sell her food stamps for a hit of crack, this was home.

"What's up, nigga?"Goldie asked, after Snake parked.

Snake smiled. "I see you out here getting this money!"

"You know it!" Goldie boasted.

Goldie and Snake took a seat on one of the park benches and conversed for the next couple of minutes. Goldie excused himself whenever a crackhead came up, and stepped to the side to make the sell. Snake just watched him. He was a natural. He had picked up on the game quicker than anyone he had ever seen.

By the time 9:00 p.m. came around that Friday night, music was blasting, weed was in the air, money was pouring in, and cups filled. Peanut and Mookie had showed up a couple of hours ago and jumped right into the rotation with Goldie. The park looked like one big block party.

While everyone else was enjoying themselves, Snake was busy staring off in a daze. He could not believe he had lived this long. He had beaten the odds. He took another sip of his potent potion. The more he sipped on his drink the more he contemplated on leaving the game. He had every luxury a man could want. He held up his cup and wondered if the alcohol had him feeling soft. Did he still possess the hunger for the game? Had he outgrown the ghetto?

"Yo, Snake! What you buying yourself for your birthday?" Peanut asked.

Snake snapped out of his daze. "Huh?"

"I said...what you buying yourself for your birthday?"

Snake smiled. "Let's just say I'm buying myself a lil' toy that's gonna separate me from everybody else out here that thinks they getting a lil' money," Snake bragged.

Snake could not wait until tomorrow. He wanted to see the look on everybody's face when he showcased his birthday present. Thanks to Sal and his connections down in Miami, Snake's birthday gift was going to be a real head-turner.

"Alright, niggas, I gotta go home and get rested up for tomorrow," Snake said, walking around and giving everyone dap.

"Alright, nigga, we gonna holla at you tomorrow then!" Peanut said.

Snake threw up a peace sign, and then walked over to his car, hopped in, and pulled off.

Peanut waited until Snake disappeared down the road. "Yo, Mookie! Is it me or has Snake been acting kind of funny lately?"

"Whatta you mean acting funny?" Mookie asked.

"I mean...it's like he ain't hungry no more," Peanut replied.

Mookie took a couple of puffs from his joint. "Shit...he rich. He can do what the fuck he wanna do!"

Peanut gave him a disgusted look. "Fuck you, nigga. I should have known not to ask your stupid ass!"

"I'm just telling you like it is! The man paid!" Mookie said.

"Boy, I tell ya...you stay pulling a nigga's dick!" Peanut scolded.

"Nigga, you be acting like you jealous of the man or something!" Mookie spat.

"Nigga, what the fuck I gotta be jealous of him for?" Peanut asked, agitated. "Nigga, I got money!"

"Not like Snake!" Mookie taunted. "You know what? I know what it is. You wanna be like Snake."

"Nigga, I don't wanna be like any muthafuckin' Snake! Nigga, I'm my own man!" Peanut shouted, hitting himself on the chest as if he was King Kong.

"Yeah...well why you keep the Caddy painted the same color Snake had it instead of painting it?" Mookie asked.

Peanut was speechless. He was envious of Snake, but he would never reveal his hand. Snake had it all: money, power, respect, an impressive street rep, and a shit load of fine ass females. People never looked at them for who they were; they just labeled them as Snake's crew. Peanut was growing tired of that shit, and had plans of doing his own thing once he got his money right.

"Look, man, ya'll need to stop all of that damn arguing, and concentrate on getting this damn money out here!" Goldie chanted.

Peanut and Mookie looked at each other, and then started laughing.

"Nigga, shut your lil' ass up, tryna be grown," Peanut said, laughing.

"Yeah, but your sister like it!" Goldie shot back at him.

"Nigga, your lil' ruined ass better not be fucking with my lil' sister!" Peanut said, then started playfully chasing him around the park bench.

* * * * *

"Damn, it's eight o'clock!" Snake said.

Snake's body still felt exhausted. Even though he had turned it in early last night, his body still felt like he had only given it two hours of sleep. He swung his long legs around the bed. A smile appeared on his face when he glanced over at the calendar. After slipping into his slippers, he trotted over to his full-length mirror and stared at the handsome image in the mirror.

"What's happening with ya, birthday boy?" Snake asked, stroking the waves on his perfectly cut, tight fade.

Conceited, he playfully blew a kiss at the image in the mirror, then smiled and headed towards the bathroom. He was in such a jovial mood that he moonwalked all the way down the hallway. When he arrived inside of the bathroom, he prepared the water for his shower, while he brushed his teeth.

After showering and drying off, Snake headed back into his bedroom, threw on a pair of silk boxers, and turned on his stereo to pep things up. He energetically danced around the room, all the way to his walk-in closet. He carefully thumbed through his clothes, searching for the ideal outfit. Once he found it, he laid it across his bed.

In need of some fresh air, he opened the sliding glass door and walked outside onto his balcony. The ocean view was breathtaking. He still was in disbelief that he had come from a snotty-nosed kid, living in the ghetto, to now wearing Gucci loafers and living in a mini-mansion with the Gulf of Mexico in his backyard. It did not come easy, though. Over the years, Snake had put in mad work to be where he was today. He admirably observed his surroundings. All of his neighbors were the cream of the crop. He no longer looked outside of his front door and saw alcoholics, hustlers, prostitutes, and patrol cars. He now saw perfectly manicured lawns, and could peacefully fall asleep listening to the relaxing sounds of the waves hitting up against the seawall.

Snake walked back inside and glanced over at the clock. It was 9:00. He walked over to his bed and started removing the plastic off his cream Italian-made linens, then slid his legs into them. Next, he grabbed his silk Gucci shirt from off the hanger and slid it on. It fit his masculine chest perfectly. He made another trip across the extremely plush, ice-cold carpet, courtesy of the ice cold AC, back into his walk-in closet. He slid into his tan Gucci loafers, then reached up on his shelf and grabbed his matching Gucci belt and matching Gucci fedora. As he walked back into the room, he ran his belt through the loops of his slacks. He arrogantly paused in front of the full-length mirror and struck a pose. He carefully tucked his shirt inside of his slacks and made all the proper adjustments. He smiled, then reached on his dresser and threw on his fedora to tip things off. He tilted it to the side for a little gangsta lean. Now he was ready. He squirted on two squirts of Polo cologne, grabbed his car keys, and headed downstairs.

When he arrived downstairs, he cracked open his safe and grabbed $10,000 worth of hundred dollar bills. He threw on all his jewelry, and then headed towards the garage. Snake could not wait to see the look on everybody's faces when he pulled up to the park this afternoon.

Snake paused at the garage door, took a deep breath, and flicked on the lights. He just stood in admiration, shaking his head. He was the man. Sitting in the middle of his three-car garage, all by itself, was a brand spanking new, acrylic white, 1989 convertible Rolls Royce Corniche, with a tan top and tan hides. Sal had turned him on to one of his friends who worked for a Rolls Royce dealer down in Miami. Sal's friend pulled a couple of strings, and after a quarter-of-a million in cash, Snake drove the beauty right off the lot, with no questions asked. It was official now; Snake was rolling with the big boys.

As Snake walked around his baby, he ran his hands along the body. Every piece of chrome visible was perfectly shined. He was still in disbelief that he was actually the owner. He opened the driver's side door and eased into the leather seat. He never felt anything so comfortable. He felt like he was sitting on top of a thousand pillows. He adjusted his rearview mirror, admired the interior one last time, and nodded in admiration. Next, he grabbed his garage door opener and activated it. He cranked it up and prepared for take-off. The engine purred like a kitten. This upgrade was a thousand steps ahead of his Cadillac.

Delicately, Snake threw his baby in reverse. Once he had completely backed out of the garage, he closed the garage and cautiously backed into the road. Surprisingly, his next-door neighbor Phil was standing out front watering his lawn. Phil's mouth dropped to the ground, as he wet both of his shoes with the water hose, while staring at the newest Rolls Royce Corniche.

"Morning, Phil!" Snake said, waving sarcastically.

Phil nonchalantly waved back.

Snake tilted back his head and laughed. "Damn it feels good to be on top!" he chanted, as he toured down the street, driving slower than a turtle for all his on-lookers.

* * * * *

By noon, Snake was done running all of his errands, and was en route to Bartlett Park. When he arrived at the light on 18th

Avenue and 9th Street, he could tell by the bumper-to-bumper traffic that the park should have a nice size crowd. He felt fortunate that he was not one of those drivers who had to wait in traffic. The security he hired had barricaded off one of the back roads that led to the park exclusively for Snake to make his grand entrance.

Security graciously started removing all of the cones when Snake arrived at the barricade. As he drove through, security nodded their heads in admiration. Snake just smiled and arrogantly nodded his head in response. Approaching the park, he could hear the music blasting from a couple of blocks away. When he arrived at the street that led to the parking lot, the park was more crowded than he had anticipated. There was not a single parking space in the area, except for his designated parking space. He smiled as he saw his designated parking space, which was actually two spaces in length, blocked off with cones and yellow tape.

Security gave Snake the royal treatment, and immediately went into action removing the cones and tape so he could park. At that moment, everybody stopped what they were doing and stared in awe. Snake loved the attention. He felt like he had the entire city in the palm of his hands. Being the show-off that he was, he decided to leave the top down so everyone who passed by could look inside and weep.

"Damn, nigga, you doing it like this!" Mookie asked, throwing his fist up to his mouth as he walked around and inspected Snake's Rolls Royce.

Snake arrogantly smiled as he opened up the door, planted his Gucci loafers on the ground, and eased out of the car, delicately closed the door like it was made of glass.

Peanut was just walking up the sidewalk, when Snake hopped out of the car. Up until Snake's arrival, his Caddy had been the center of attention. All of that changed the minute Snake pulled up. Now, every gold-digging female wearing a skimpy outfit had vanished from around Peanut's Caddy and made their way over to where Snake was parked.

Peanut walked over to Snake and gave him a fake hug.

"What's up, nigga?" he asked, as he embraced Snake. During the hug, Peanut glanced at Snake's neck and noticed he was wearing every piece of jewelry that he owned. *This show-off ass nigga,* he said to himself.

After the two let go of each other Snake rubbed his hands together, while smiling at all of the vulnerable women standing around them, begging to be picked for a one-night stand. All Snake had to do was say the word, and any of them would have thrown their morals out the window for the rest of the day to become his personal sex toy.

The temperature was a nice, sunny, 90 degrees outside on this particular Saturday. Today was perfect for a cookout. Snake had gone all out. Not only had he brought up Jam Pony Express' D.J., there was also enough food and drinks available to feed a nice size portion of the city. Money did not matter to Snake; it was his 24th birthday. Snake had hired two cooks to work the barbecue grills from sun up to sundown. Several of his female friends had also pitched in and prepared several dishes, such as potato salad, macaroni, string beans, and various desserts. Everybody was fixing plates and taking advantage of the free food. Little kids were playfully giggling, while grabbing sodas out of the coolers and taking off running to the playground.

"Hi, birthday boy!" a thick redbone named Sharon said, making her way over to Snake and giving him an affectionate hug.

"Damn!" Snake's entire crew said, grabbing their dicks.

Sharon was wearing a pair of spandex so tight that you could see the outline of her pussy lips. Her well-toned stomach was flatter than a white girl's ass, and her breasts were sitting up extra perky in her matching sports bra. Her gold ankle bracelets were excessive, fashionably resting on her footies, while she sported a pair of the latest Nikes.

Sharon playfully punched Snake in the shoulder. "So why haven't you called me lately?"

Snake bashfully leaned his head to the side and rubbed on his chin. "You know…a nigga just been real busy, that's all."

"Well, if you're not busy tonight, I got a little birthday present for you that's moister than a Duncan Hines cake," Sharon flirted, sensually running her finger down Snake's chest.

"Damn!" Snake's whole crew said, while again grabbing their dicks and wishing they were Snake.

"Oh yeah?" Snake asked, humored.

"Yeah," Sharon replied seductively, as her perfume continued to seduce Snake.

"Alright then...I'ma make sure I hit you later on."

"So you gonna hit me later on? Ohhhh...I like the way that sounds," Sharon said in a light moan, as she placed her Blow Pop in her mouth, made an impression in her jaw for Snake to use his imagination, and then mischievously walked off with a sarcastic smirk on her face.

Snake and his crew watched as she sashayed off, admiring her voluptuous backside.

"That bitch a freak!" Peanut blurted.

"Boy, I tell ya...some niggas got all the luck!" Mookie said, shaking his head at Snake.

Snake rubbed on his chin. "You just gotta be that nigga," he boasted.

"Ah, yo! Ain't that Rhonda's car over there in traffic?" Mookie asked, pointing toward the Toyota Tercel.

"Damn sure is!" Peanut said.

The whole crew threw their hands up in the air once they saw Goldie sitting on the passenger side.

Goldie stuck his head out of the car. "What's up, niggas?" he shouted.

Everybody waved for him to come over.

"I'ma get out right here," Goldie told Rhonda, anxiously hopping out of the car and running around to the driver's side of the car. He kissed Rhonda on the cheek, and then patted the door. "Appreciate it!" he said, then shot across the street.

"I'ma be at the room. Just beep me when you're ready!" Rhonda shouted out the window.

Goldie turned around. "Alright! You know what time it is when I get back to the room!" he joked.

"Bye, boy! You so crazy!" Rhonda said, smiling from ear to ear as she turned off on one of the back roads to avoid the traffic.

"Damn, nigga, you been spending a lot of time with ole' girl lately. I know she ain't got you pussy whipped?" Peanut said as Goldie approached and gave everyone dap.

"Nigga, please! I'm just working her because she got a car. She's my personal chauffer. You niggas need to step ya'll game up and get ya'll one!" Goldie said.

"So you working her, huh?" Peanut asked.

"Fo' sho'!" Goldie boasted. "Plus she got some good ass pussy!" he added.

The whole crew started laughing.

Goldie stared over at Snake, and then opened up his arms. "Happy birthday, nigga!" he said, as he walked over and hugged Snake.

"Ahhh shit! Here them niggas go with that ole' mushy shit!" Peanut joked. Again, the whole crew started laughing, and Goldie and Snake released each other.

"Fuck you, nigga! It's my birthday, and I'll hug if I want to!" Snake said.

For the next couple of minutes, Snake and his crew posted up and hugged all of the flirtatious women that came over and shook hands with them.

"Yo, Snake! What's up?" a local hustler from out of the hood asked Snake, while walking over. "Happy birthday, nigga!" Pete said, giving him a hug.

"What's up with you, Pete?" Snake asked, attentively looking over Pete's shoulder, not familiar with the three cats that Pete had along with him.

Pete noticed the inquisitive look on Snake's face when the two released each other. "Oh, my bad Snake! These are my three cousins, Andre, Robert, and Richie. They down from Alabama for the weekend," Pete explained.

Snake nodded his head, acknowledging Pete's cousins. "What's up?" he said.

Pete's cousins nodded their heads back. "What's up?" they replied.

Peanut and Mookie were standing and exchanging evil grins with Pete's cousins.

Pete nervously scratched the back of his head. For some strange reason, Snake's crew and his cousins were not hitting it off too well. Pete knew how funny Snake acted around new faces, so he pulled Snake to the side. "Yo, Snake, let me holla at you for a minute."

"I'll be right back," Snake told his crew, then walked over to Pete. "What's up?"

"Listen, Snake, my cousin Andre wanna spend a lil' paper with you," Pete said.

"Like what?" Snake asked.

"I think about thirty thousand," Pete said.

Those numbers got Snake's dick hard, but he did not show it. Snake glanced over at the cousins and assessed them, then returned his attention back to Pete. "Where the money at?"

"They got it," Pete replied.

"What they tryna buy?"

"I don't know. All I know is that there isn't any dope down their way. That's why they came down here. I wanted to hook you up with my cousin Andre so ya'll can talk about all of that."

Snake rubbed on his chin. "And you say they got the money with them?" Snake probed.

"Yeah!" Pete boasted. "You see that B.M.W. parked over there with that bowling ball paint on it and that Ferrari kit?" he asked, pointing over at Andre's Beamer.

"Yeah, I see it!" Snake said.

"I'm telling you, Snake, he got money!"

"Well, tell your cousin to come over here and holla at me," Snake told Pete.

Pete smiled. "Andre! Come over here for a minute!"

Andre walked over and joined the two. "What's up, cuz?" he asked.

Pete patted Andre on the back. "Ya'll two holla," Pete said, then excused himself.

"Your cousin say that you tryna holla at me?" Snake asked.

"Yeah, he told me that you were who I should holla at," Andre said.

"Oh yeah?" Snake asked, looking over at Pete, who was smiling.

"So what you letting them ounces go for?" Andre asked.

"Eight-fifty," Snake said firmly.

Andre did a couple of quick calculations in his head, and then nodded his head. "Alright, give me thirty-six of 'em for thirty thousand," he said.

Snake moved his mouth to the side and played hardball for a minute. "You know I'm losing, but I'll do it," Snake said, knowing he was already getting over. "Have Pete to bring you by the carwash at six o'clock. Tell him to use the alley."

The whole alley thing did not settle too well with Andre, but he did not want to show Snake any signs of fear. "Alright then, six o'clock it is!" Andre said, and then the two shook hands.

"Just make sure you bring that paperwork with you," Snake stressed.

"That's cool!"Andre said, defensively throwing up his hands.

The two headed over to where everybody else was standing.

"So everything's straight?" Pete asked, looking at Andre and Snake.

The two nodded their heads.

"Good!" Pete said, anxiously rubbing his hands together as if he had just closed a million-dollar deal. "Ya'll ready?" he asked his cousins.

"Yeah...let's go back over to the Beamer and post up," Andre said.

"Speaking of Beamers, make sure ya'll drive something different when ya'll come and holla at me. That wouldn't be a good look, having a flashy car with an out-of-state tag pulling up to the carwash. You feel me?" Snake asked.

"I feel you. That's cool, though. We'll drive something different," Andre replied.

"Ya'll go ahead and head over to the car. I'll catch up. I'm gonna holla at Snake for a minute," Pete said.

"Alright," Pete's cousins said, and then blended in with the crowd.

When the three disappeared, Pete smiled at Snake and started rubbing his hands together again. "Now I know you gonna look out for me?"

Snake smiled. "If everything go straight, I'ma look out."

Pete's eyes lit up, and he gave Snake dap. "Alright, I'ma see you at six," he said, then patted Snake on the shoulder and caught up with his cousins.

"What them motherfuckers was talking about?" Peanut asked, as they headed to their cars.

"They just tryna cop a little weight," Snake said.

"Damn! Who Rolls Royce that is?" Goldie asked in a euphoric tone.

Snake smiled, then held up his car keys and showed Goldie the Rolls Royce keychain.

"Got damn! When did you cop this?" he asked Snake, as he walked over and admired it.

"It's my birthday present to myself," Snake said.

"Can I sit in it?" Goldie asked.

After Snake gestured for him to go ahead, Goldie swiftly hopped inside and sat behind the steering wheel.

While Goldie was busy admiring Snake's Corniche, Mookie put a bug in Snake's ear. "Yo, Snake! You really plan on serving them country muthafuckas?"

Snake stared off into nowhere. "Yeah...if they money straight, they can get served," he said.

"Shit! We need to touch them country muthafuckas!" Peanut said.

Snake rubbed on his chin. "You know, you might have yourself a point there, Peanut."

Mookie and Peanut were anxiously licking their lips, waiting on Snake to say the word.

"Check this out! I'ma go switch cars and swing by Mesha's house to grab some work. Ya'll meet me at the carwash at about five-thirty. Grab the vest and some of that big shit, just in case," Snake instructed.

Peanut looked at Snake, and then nodded his head. "Let's do this shit!"

After giving everybody some dap, Goldie exited the car to allow Snake to take his place behind the steering wheel.

He then threw his spaceship in drive, and then out of respect, the crowd obediently parted like the Red Sea.

As Snake exited the park, little did he know, not only had he graduated to the big league on the streets, he had also graduated to the big leagues with the FEDS.

From across the street, Agent Bradshaw stared through his high-powered binoculars, watching as Snake disappeared out of the parking lot. He shook his head with a disgusted look on his face, and then sat his binoculars on the dashboard.

"This kid is getting big time!" Agent Roberts said.

Agent Bradshaw sat in silence. He was pissed. Seeing Snake cruising around in a quarter-million-dollar ride without a worry in the world was like a slap in the face to him.

"Roberts, as soon as we get back to headquarters, I want everything that you have on this guy!" Agent Bradshaw fumingly said, as he pulled off.

CHAPTER TWENTY-FIVE

Snake pulled into the alley that led to his carwash and parked. He had already thoroughly performed his usual procedure, circling the block a couple of times and making sure there were not any cops in the area. The coast was clear.

He checked his watch. "It's quarter after five. Them niggas should be here any minute."

Snake hopped out of his Regal, surveying the area, and then entered the building.

"Hi, boss!"

"What's happening? Tell everybody to go ahead and wrap everything up."

"Will do!"

Snake strolled into his office, flicked on the lights, then plopped down in his plush, leather chair behind his desk. He picked up his office phone and dialed Angie's number.

"Hello," Angie answered on the fourth ring.

"You did that?" Snake asked.

"Don't I always do what you tell me to do?" Angie replied.

Snake laughed. "Just make sure you come as soon as I call you," he said, then hung up.

He pulled a joint from out of his desk drawer, lit it, reclined back in his chair, and stared up at the ceiling, while casually blowing out smoke.

"I hope these niggas ain't got no shit with them," he said, pulling his .45 automatic out of his pants and sitting it on top of his desk.

As a precaution, Snake had only brought a sample ounce along to show Pete's cousins the quality. He had Angie on standby to bring the other thirty-five ounces once he made the phone call. He felt leery about this whole deal. It wasn't everyday that some out-of-towners came into town and spent thirty thousand dollars.

Snake heard a knock at the door. "Who dat?"

His office door swung open, and Peanut and Mookie came charging in.

"What's up, nigga? You ready to do this shit?" Peanut asked, as he walked over and gave him a high-five.

Snake laughed. "Just chill, nigga...just chill!"

"Nigga, I know you ain't having no second thoughts about this shit?" Peanut asked.

Snake just smirked as he rubbed on his chin and turned back and forth in his chair. He entwined his fingers. "Naw, I just got a better plan."

* * * * *

On the other side of town, Pete and his cousins were in Pete's room at their grandmother's house getting everything together. The four had thoroughly gone through each individual stack, making sure there was $1,000 in each.

"Pete, you sure this nigga the man?" Andre asked.

"Shit, nigga, you see what kind of car that nigga drive!" Pete said, trying to convince Andre everything was all right.

Andre threw the last couple of stacks in his bookbag. "Alright, let's do this shit!" he said, as he threw the bookbag over his shoulder.

Pete smiled. "I'll drive!"

* * * * *

Pete turned off 18th Avenue, turning down the alley that led to the back of Snake's carwash. His cousins were a little paranoid, observantly surveying the alley. The only reason why Pete was so calm was he was the only one who did not stand to lose anything if the deal went bad. Pete's cousins were all in. Fifteen grand of the thirty grand was Andre's, seventy-five hundred was Richie's, and the other seventy-five hundred was Robert's.

Pete pulled up behind a Regal, parked, and cut off the car. "Ya'll ready?" he asked his cousins.

His cousins all looked at each other like they were having second thoughts.

"I'm telling you, Pete...this shit better go straight!" Andre said with emphasis.

"Nigga, get your scary ass out of the car," Pete joked, while hopping out of the car. His cousins followed.

Snake was patiently sitting behind his desk, attentively watching Pete and his cousins exit the car on his surveillance monitor. Once the four of them exited the car, Snake grabbed his .45 automatic from off his desk, tucked it in his waistband, and headed to the backdoor.

Pete attempted to knock on the backdoor, but before he could knock, Snake opened it.

"What's happening, fellas?" Snake asked.

"What's up, Snake?" Pete replied. Pete's cousins just nodded.

"Follow me," Snake said, leading them down a long hallway that led to his office. When Snake reached his office, he walked inside and took a seat behind his desk. "Sit down, fellas," he said, motioning with his hands.

Everybody except Andre sat down. "I'm straight, I'll stand," Andre said.

Snake smiled at Andre trying to play the tough guy role. "Suit yourself."

"Let's do this!" Andre said, with a firm grip on his backpack.

Snake lit a joint, then took a couple of puffs and exhaled. Just by observantly reading Andre's body language, he could tell he was nervous. Snake decided to mess with him for a minute, so he stalled. After a couple of minutes, Snake reached into his desk and threw the sample ounce on top of his desk.

"This is what they all look like," he said.

Andre picked up the ounce. He nodded his head, immediately impressed that the cookie did not break when Snake tossed it.

Pete and his cousins gathered around Andre to check out the ounce. Andre twirled the sandwich bag, studying the ounce through the bag, admiring the crystals in the cookie.

"That's that glass!" Robert said, looking over Andre's shoulder.

Andre was impressed with the product, and since the bulk of the money was his, he had the final decision.

"Do the rest of them look just like this?" Andre asked, twirling the cookie.

"Yeah," Snake replied.

"Alright, we'll grab 'em," Andre said.

"You brought the money?" Snake asked, raising his eyebrows.

Andre surveyed Robert and Richie's faces. They both nodded.

Snake reached out his hand. "Come on now, playboy!"

Andre hesitatingly handed over the bag. Snake sat the bag in his lap, unzipped it, then pulled out the stacks of money, sitting them on his desk. Snake grabbed one of the stacks and started counting.

"Where's the rest of the dope?" Andre asked.

Snake picked up the phone and dialed Angie's number. When the phone started ringing, he hit speakerphone, and then placed the receiver back on the base. Snake continued counting the money while the phone rang.

"Hello," Angie answered.

"I'm ready. Bring that," Snake said, then terminated the call.

He continued counting the money, placing the stacks he already counted to the right. Pete's cousins just sat and waited patiently.

Snake looked over and noticed they seemed a little uneasy.

"Relax, fellas, she'll be here in a few minutes."

CHAPTER TWENTY-SIX

"Man, this nigga do shit backwards as fuck!" Peanut said, irritably tapping his fingers on the steering wheel.

"I know, right! He should have just let us run up in that motherfucker, skied-up, and lay those muthafuckas down!" Mookie said, passing Peanut the joint.

Peanut tapped Mookie on the shoulder, then pointed. "There go that stuck-up ass bitch Angie right there!"

Angie's Maxima pulled up and parked in front of the carwash. She grabbed her Louis Vuitton purse, hopped out of the car, and strolled inside.

Peanut puffed on the joint as he watched her voluptuous ass cheeks bounce up and down as she walked. He grabbed his dick. "Damn, I bet that bitch got some good-ass pussy!" he said, shaking his head as he passed Mookie the joint.

Mookie took a couple of puffs and laughed. "We know one thing...your broke ass will never know!" Mookie joked.

"Fuck you, nigga!" Peanut said.

* * * * *

Angie didn't bother to knock when she reached Snake's office; she just stormed straight in.

Pete's cousins almost jumped out of their skins, when Angie flung Snake's office door open.

"Oops! My bad!" Angie said, while throwing her hand up to her mouth and walking over to Snake's desk.

"Damn, you ever heard of knocking before you enter?" Snake asked.

"Sorry," Angie said, in a baby's voice. "Here you go, daddy," she said, pulling out a Ziploc bag containing the remainder of the ounces. "Call me," she told Snake, then blew him a kiss and disappeared out the door.

"Here ya'll go," Snake said, holding up the Ziploc bag.

Andre walked over to his desk, and Snake handed him the ounces. Andre walked back over to Robert and Richie, opened up the Ziploc bag, and checked out the product.

"Yo, Pete, pull ya'll car around to the front so one of my boys can tighten it up for ya'll," Snake said.

"That won't be necessary; we straight," Andre replied.

"I insist!" Snake said with authority in his voice.

"Pete, go ahead and pull the car around to the front," Andre instructed.

* * * * *

Pete hopped out of the car, then outstretched the keys to one of Snake's employees who looked like he was just about to clock out.

Rocky gave Pete a crazy look. "We closed, playboy."

"Snake just told me to pull up front," Pete said.

Before Rocky could reply, Snake walked out. Pete handed his keys back to Rocky with a sarcastic smirk.

"Yo, Rocky! These good people right here, I need you to tighten up they car for them. Give 'em the works!" Snake ordered.

"Alright," Rocky said, shooting Pete a unit, as he walked over to the water hose, not too enthused.

Snake threw his arm around Pete and they headed back inside of the carwash.

For the next thirty minutes, the four drank Heinekens and smoked numerous joints. Everybody was joking and giggling. While Pete and his cousins were busy laughing, Snake secretly made eye contact with Rocky through the garage's side door, and gave him the nod. Rocky nodded back, smiled, and went into action.

Thirty minutes later, Rocky walked into the waiting room and held the set of keys in the air. "I'm finished!"

"You pulled it into the garage?" Snake asked.

"Yeah, it's in there," Rocky retorted.

"Ya'll follow me," Snake said, heading towards the garage.

Everybody looked at each other, boggled.

Pete shrugged his shoulders and said, "Let's just see what's up."

Everybody stood and followed behind Snake.

"Yo, Pete, pop the trunk. I wanna show ya'll something," Snake said once everybody was in the garage.

Pete walked around to the trunk of the car and popped it open.

"Hey, Bobby!" Snake yelled.

"What's up, Snake?" Bobby replied.

"Bring that tool around here!"

Pete and his cousins looked at each other puzzled.

Snake looked over at them. "Now usually I don't show people my hiding spots, but ya'll seem like ya'll good people."

"What you want me to do, Snake?" Bobby asked.

"This is the rental ya'll driving back, ain't it?" Snake asked.

Andre hesitated for a minute before replying. "Yeah."

"Chill out, playboy. I'm just tryna make sure ya'll make it back to Alabama straight. I'm tryna turn ya'll on to what I know works," Snake said, patting Andre on the back for him to loosen up.

Andre let off a fake smile.

"Bobby, stash them ounces in the stash spot for them, and show them how to get back into it when they make it home," Snake instructed.

"Alright, boss. It shouldn't take but about fifteen minutes," Bobby said.

"Yo, Bobby, what time you closing up tonight?" Snake asked.

Bobby wiped the sweat off his forehead, then said, "I'm probably gonna be here until late. After I finish here, I gotta finish hooking up the engine on that Chevy over there. It's due for pick-up tomorrow at five."

"Yeah, you need to make sure you finish up," Snake told him. "Alright, I'm taking it in for the night. Ya'll boys be easy," he said, then waved goodbye to everybody and disappeared out the door.

Pete and his cousins just stood and observantly looked over Bobby's shoulder while he did his thing.

"Just give me a couple more minutes and I'll be finished," Bobby said.

* * * * *

"That should just about do it," Bobby said, tightening up the last screw.

"Alright, Bobby, I appreciate everything," Pete said.

After Bobby closed the trunk, everybody hopped in the car. Pete cranked up the car, honked the horn, and then pulled off.

"You'll be back in a few minutes," Bobby mumbled to himself with a smirk on his face.

As Pete traveled down 18th Avenue, he felt relieved that everything had gone as planned. He smiled. He was expecting to get broke off by his cousins and Snake. He looked in his rearview mirror at his cousin's faces and noticed they seemed a little more relaxed.

He looked over at Andre. "I told you Snake was good peoples," he said.

"Yeah, you were right," Andre said with a smile on his face.

Robert started curiously sniffing the air. "Ya'll smell something?" he asked with a funny look on his face.

All of a sudden, Pete noticed smoke coming from up under the hood. "What the...?"

"Pull over in that parking lot," Andre ordered.

Pete pulled over, and everybody hopped out of the car agitated.

"Shit! Pop the hood, Pete," Andre said.

Pete stuck his hand through the window, and then popped the hood.

When Andre lifted up the hood, he immediately started fanning smoke from out of his face.

"Damn, I can't believe this damn shit!" Andre said, shaking his head.

"What's the matter?" Robert asked, walking over and looking over Andre's shoulder.

"Shit look like it's leaking oil!" Andre replied, rubbing his fingers along the car's engine.

"Damn! Let's take this shit back to Snake's shop and see what his mechanic says," Pete suggested.

Everybody hopped back inside of the car, and Pete headed back to Snake's shop.

When Bobby saw a set of highlights through the shop's front window, he knew everything was going just as planned.

A couple of minutes later, there was a knock on the door. Bobby cleverly ran his hand along the greasy Chevy motor until he accumulated a little grease on his hand, then wiped it all over his jumper. He wanted to make it look like he had been working nonstop ever since they left.

When Bobby arrived at the door, he peeped through the blinds at Pete and his cousins. Bobby could hear the car's engine still running. Opening the door, Bobby switched into acting mode.

"Damn…I'm sorry to bother you, man, but our car just started smoking all of a sudden," Andre said.

"What's the matter?" Bobby asked, holding his cigarette on the side of his mouth.

"I don't know. It's leaking oil from somewhere," Andre said. "We wanna know if you can take a look at it."

"I'll have to call Snake and see what he says. I'm supposed to have this Chevy ready for pick-up by tomorrow at five. If not, Snake will be all over my ass!"

"Just call him and tell him this is real important. We trying to hop on the road and leave tonight," Robert said.

Bobby wiped his hands with a rag. "Alright, I'll call him and see what he says."

He walked over, picked up the phone, dialed Snake's beeper, and then looked around to see if anybody was paying attention. They weren't. When the beep sounded to punch in the phone number, Bobby punched in the shop's number followed by 911. When Bobby saw Andre glance over at him, he started faking like he was talking to Snake.

"Okay, so you say you're on your way?" Bobby said, loud enough for everybody to hear.

Bobby hung up the phone. "He's on his way. He was around the corner getting a little birthday present, if you know what I mean," Bobby said with a smile. "Go ahead and pull into the garage."

* * * * *

Andre impatiently looked at his watch, as he paced the garage. They had been waiting for fifteen minutes now.

Bobby was buried under the hood. Actually, he was just trying to look busy until Snake arrived.

The sound of Snake opening the front door startled everybody.

"What seems to be the problem?" Snake asked, walking over to the car.

"I think it's a leak in a hose and a loose clamp," Bobby said, looking up at him and winking.

"Do we have the parts?" Snake asked.

"Yeah, we got it in stock," Bobby replied.

"How long will it take for you to fix it?" Snake asked.

"Ummmm. . . say about twenty minutes."

"We'll pay for whatever!" Andre blurted.

Snake threw up his hand. "Keep your money."

"I'll get started right now," Bobby said, walking over to his toolbox.

"Come on, ya'll, I'll take ya'll to grab some Popeye's. By the time we get back, ya'll car should be ready," Snake said.

"Damn, I am a little hungry," Pete said, while jokingly rubbing on his stomach.

Twenty minutes later, Snake pulled back in front of his shop.

"Bobby should be finished by now," he said, as everybody exited the car with a full stomach.

Snake glanced across the street, and saw that Peanut and Mookie were still in place.

"Look at them country muthafuckas!" Peanut told Mookie.

"Look, Snake...we appreciate everything," Andre said, as he exited the passenger's seat.

Everybody headed inside of the shop.

"How we looking?" Snake asked Bobby.

Bobby wiped his hands with the rag, then reached through the window of the car and cranked up the car.

Andre let out a sigh of relief.

"Listen to her...purring like a kitten," Bobby boasted.

Snake made eye contact with Bobby, who smiled and nodded his head.

"I went ahead and checked the oil, also, for you fellas. You're all set to hit the road," Bobby said.

Andre walked over to Bobby, and gratefully shook his hand. "I appreciate this, man. Here's a lil' tip," Andre said, handing him a fifty-dollar bill. Andre then walked over to Snake. "I appreciate everything," he said, as he reached out his hand.

"Oh no, the pleasure's been all mine," Snake said sarcastically, while shaking Andre's hands.

As Pete and his cousins hopped into the car, Bobby walked over and let up the garage door.

"Thank you again," Andre yelled out of the window, while Bobby guided Pete as he backed out of the garage.

Pete honked the horn two times, and then pulled off down the street.

Bobby and Snake celebrated by giving each other high-five when their victims disappeared out of sight.

"Country ass niggas!" Snake said.

"Look what I got!" Bobby said, tossing him the taped up Ziploc bag that all of the ounces were in.

Snake swiftly pulled out his .45 automatic when he heard a knock at the door. "Who dat?" he asked, attentively standing with his gun on his side, ready for war.

"Nigga, it's us!" Peanut and Mookie said, storming inside the front door.

They almost jumped out of their skin when they noticed Snake's .45 pointed at them.

"Nigga, put that shit up!" Peanut said, protectively blocking his face with his hands.

Snake smiled, while putting his gun back in his waist. "Niggas, don't be running up in here like that."

"Fuck that! What's up?" Peanut asked.

Snake tossed Peanut the Ziploc bag. Peanut caught it, twirled it, and smiled. Both Peanut and Mookie were astonished.

"Ya'll niggas meet me up at the New Deal for the after party. Drinks and pussy are on me tonight!" Snake said, then smiled and disappeared out the door, whistling.

CHAPTER TWENTY-SEVEN

Robert pulled into a Shell gas station in Lake City off I-75 to get some gas. Andre was a couple of minutes behind him. For the most part, Andre had been pretty much staying seven car lengths behind Robert, trying not to create any suspicion.

Robert reached over, tapped Richie on the chest, and woke him up. "I'm finna go pay for the gas. Get out and pump."

Richie stretched, and then wiped the slobber off the side of his mouth. "Where we at?" he asked, surveying the unfamiliar surroundings.

"Lake City, nigga!" Robert said, while hopping out of the car and slamming the door.

Richie hopped out, also, and asked, "How much you putting in?"

"I'ma fill it up," Robert yelled back, while heading into the station. "That should be enough to take us all the way home."

As Richie opened the gas tank and started pumping the gas, Andre pulled up and parked on the other side of the station. Richie just smirked and acknowledged him with a head gesture. Andre made a head gesture toward the highway patrol that Richie had not noticed parked on the side of a tractor-trailer.

Robert came out of the station with two bags of Combos and two cans of Pepsi, and walked right pass Andre like he was a total stranger. Robert hopped in the passenger seat and reclined it back as far as it could go. "There we go," he said, "nice and comfortable."

"What you doin'?" Richie asked, not paying attention and noticing the gas overflowing out of the tank. "Shit!" Richie yelled, swiftly stepping out of the puddle of gas and pulling the nozzle out.

"Nigga, you driving the last leg home!" Robert said, then pulled his cap down over his eyes.

"Nigga, you ain't slick. This shit ain't halfway!" Richie said, walking around to the driver's side of the car, agitated.

Robert just sat with his arms folded and ignored him.

Richie hopped into the car with an attitude. He looked over at Robert and sucked his teeth, then just started nodding his head. "Alright...you got that," Richie said, then cranked up the car.

Andre was parked over at the air pump, faking like he was putting air in his tires and wondering what the fuck Robert and Richie were arguing over. "I gotta start doing business by my damn self," he mumbled to himself, shaking his head.

After five minutes of arguing, Richie finally pulled out of the gas station and hopped back on I-75. Andre hung up the air pump, then hopped into his Beamer and followed behind them. The minute Andre pulled out the lot the highway patrol turned off his interior dome lights and followed behind him. It was not until Andre looked into his rearview mirror that he noticed him behind him.

"Shit!" he cursed.

Richie was seven cars ahead and had no idea Andre was being trailed.

Andre threw his Beamer on cruise control to insure he did not exceed the speed limit. Anticipation was killing him. He wanted to take another glance in his rearview mirror, but he did not want the highway patrol to think he was panicking. He skillfully managed to glance in his rearview mirror without moving his head, and noticed the highway patrol talking into his walkie-talkie.

"Shit, motherfucker running my damn tag! Boy, I tell ya'...a black man can't even ride around in a luxury car without being harassed," Andre said.

Andre saw a sign up ahead, and then he saw Richie switching lanes. He threw on his blinker and switched lanes, too. After a couple of meters, he looked up and read the sign that said I-10 and realized why Richie had switched lanes. Richie turned off on I-10, Andre followed, and by the grace of God, the highway patrol kept going straight.

"Damn!" Andre said, letting off a sigh of relief, and then pulling out a Newport to calm his nerves.

When Richie passed through Live Oaks, he looked over at Robert, who was knocked out. Richie adjusted his rearview mirror. Andre was right where he was supposed to be.

After finishing off his Newport, Andre let down his window and flicked out the butt. He felt a little more relaxed. He took a deep breath, and then said a silent prayer.

"Please let us make it back home safe with this shit!"

* * * * *

Richie's eyes lit up when he saw the Virginia Street exit. He anxiously woke Robert up as he switched lanes. "Nigga, we home!" he shouted.

Robert woke, familiar with his surroundings. He sat up in his seat, wiped the side of his mouth, and smiled. Richie turned off on the Virginia Street exit, and then looked into his rearview mirror to locate Andre, who was now only four cars behind them.

Although they had reached the city limits, Andre did not start celebrating yet. They still had to make it back to Jackson Heights.

As Richie cruised down Airport Boulevard, he was anxious to make it home to sit down to the table and dice up his nine cookies. Being that there wasn't any dope in town, he knew he could cut his rocks a lot smaller to see more of a profit. An idea came to mind when he glanced over to his right and passed by Springdale Mall. *Yeah, maybe Wanda and me will go cop us a couple of outfits,* Richie thought, already spending a couple of hundred in his head.

Robert was staring out of the window also thinking about what he was going to do after he dumped his nine ounces. Robert had a different agenda, though. Spending money was the last thing on his mind. Robert was hungry! He was thinking about selling his nine ounces for a nice profit, then turning right back around and heading back down to St. Pete to cop thirteen to fourteen more. Robert was about money. He was the hustler of the family. Copping a brick was Robert's ultimate goal. He figured after three or four more trips down to St. Pete that he should be right about where he wanted to be.

Andre was also in his Beamer thinking about what he was going to do with his money. Andre was the brains of the family. He was business-minded. Truthfully, he was only in the game to get a little head start on some of his business ventures. Depending on how Andre grinded his eighteen ounces, he knew he stood to make anywhere from $25,000 to $35,000. Andre's plans were to open a hair salon for his baby momma to launch her career, and depending on how things turned out, dropping a nice size down payment on a house for him and his family.

Richie turned off on Azalea Road, and five minutes later, he was pulling into their driveway. After activating the garage door opener, he drove inside and let the door back down.

Andre pulled into the driveway, cut off the car, and smiled. He was home safe, and could now start celebrating. He hopped out of the car, and then headed inside of the house.

Richie cut off the rental, anxiously popped the trunk, and hopped out of the car. He made his way around to the trunk of the car, then started taking out all of their bags and sitting them on the ground.

"Need this!" Andre yelled, walking into the garage with a flat head screwdriver.

Robert nodded his head. "Now that's what I'm talking about, playboy! Let's get this shit up out of here!" he said, taking the screwdriver out of Andre's hand.

Robert hopped into the trunk of the car and went to work unscrewing all of the screws. He took a piece a loose, and then handed it out of the car to Andre. Andre grabbed the piece and sat it on the ground. Robert took another piece a loose, and also handed it to Andre. Robert smiled when he saw the Ziploc bag. He pulled the bag out, and when he did, he almost fainted. He shook his head in disbelief. How could this shit have happened?

"What, nigga?" Andre asked, reading Robert's facial expression.

Looking like he wanted to cry, Robert just dropped his head and handed Andre the bag.

Andre fumingly twirled the bag in his hands, also in disbelief. His eyes turned bloodshot red. Steam evaporated from off of his head.

"Ahhhh!" Andre yelled. He slung the bag up against the wall, then slowly slid down the wall, sat on the ground, and started massaging his temples.

Robert hopped out of the trunk and started rubbing his chin. "Damn...I'm tryna figure out when the hell they could have switched that shit on us."

Richie was lost. He wasn't that bright, and he didn't have a clue what Robert and Andre were talking about. Curious, he walked over to the Ziploc bag and picked it up. He looked at Robert and Andre with his mouth wide open. Robert and Andre just shook their heads.

"Thirty fuckin' thousand dollars!" Andre shouted, while irritably pacing the garage.

Richie reached into the bag, pulled out one of the cookies, and ate it. Andre and Robert looked at him as if he was retarded.

"Nigga, how the fuck can you eat some muthafuckin' cookies at a time like this and we just got our damn head slapped for thirty muthafuckin' thousand dollars?" Robert shouted.

Richie continued munching on the cookies. "Fuck you, nigga. This shit ain't gonna be no muthafuckin' total loss! I don't know about ya'll, but I'ma eat my seventy-five hundred dollars worth of these muthafuckas! Shit, and they Chips Ahoy, too!" he said.

The garage was quiet for a couple of minutes, before Robert broke the silence. "I ain't going out like this! Get Pete's muthafuckin' ass on the phone!" he ordered.

CHAPTER TWENTY-EIGHT

It was a bright and sunny Sunday. Snake woke up with a hangover. He eased to the edge of the bed, slid his feet into his slippers, stood up, and stretched. He yawned, then headed towards the bathroom to freshen up. The taste of Dom P and Hennessy was still in his mouth. Something told him he should have never mixed the two last night.

Snake turned on the hot water on the sink and let it run for a minute. He grabbed his washcloth off the rack, soaked it up under the hot water, wrung it out, then opened the rag and smothered his face with it.

"Damn that feels good!" he said, leaning his head back.

Feeling a little more awake, he grabbed his toothbrush from out of the holder and brushed his teeth.

He then stared at the man in the mirror. "You a bad motherfucker!" he said to the image of himself. Last night, he had pulled off some real Hugh Hefner type shit. First, he sexed Sharon before the after party, and then Stacy, Marlo, and Shawn, some chicks he met at the after party. He felt drained, and he knew it was going to take his nuts a couple of days to produce more sperm as much as he had nutted yesterday.

After freshening up, he headed back to his bedroom, walked over to his dresser, grabbed his bible, and sat on the edge of the bed. Although he did not attend church, every morning he religiously read a couple of scriptures from the bible. On Sundays, he usually read a little more.

While reading his scriptures, he kept hearing an annoying chirping sound. It was not until he looked down on the floor, that he realized it was his pager. It had vibrated so much that it had worked its way off the dresser. He looked at it, and saw it was Goldie paging him from his house with 9-1-1 behind his number. Snake picked up his cordless and called him back.

"Hello," Goldie answered.

"What's poppin' with ya, young nigga?" Snake asked.

"I need to see you!" Goldie said with urgency in his voice.

Snake laughed.

"I'm serious, man. I need to see you!" Goldie repeated. "I'm dead...and shit's jumping!"

"Alright, I'll be through there in a few minutes," Snake said.

"Alright, but hurry up, man!" Goldie said, then hung up.

Snake hung up the phone, then grabbed his car keys off the dresser and disappeared out the front door. After hopping into his Regal, he headed towards the projects. As he traveled through the city, in his mind, he knew it would be only a matter of hours before Pete started blowing up his pager. He really did not give a fuck, though; he was ready for whatever.

"Fuck them country ass niggas," he mumbled to himself, as he pulled into a McDonald's drive-thru and waited to place his order.

* * * * *

Robert was talking a hundred miles per hour on the other end of the phone. His voice was so loud that Pete had to hold the phone away from his ear. Pete could feel Robert's wrath from over the phone.

Pete was still in disbelief. How could all of this have happened? When did it happen? Pete was discombobulated.

"You said that what was in the Ziploc bags?" Pete asked, pacing the living room.

"Nigga, you heard what the fuck I said! Some muthafuckin' Chips Ahoy cookies!" Robert spat.

Pete took a deep breath. He got light-headed. He could not believe all of this was happening. He sat on the edge of the sofa, and then buried his head in his hands.

"Nigga, muthafuckin' say something!" Robert shouted.

"Listen, let me go over there and see if he knows anything about this," Pete suggested.

"This nigga talking about let him go over there and see if Snake know anything about this," Robert told Andre, covering up the phone's receiver.

Andre rushed over and snatched the phone out of Robert's hand. "Nigga, what the fuck you mean go over there and see if Snake know anything about this? Nigga, he's the one that orchestrated all of this shit!" Andre shouted through the phone.

"Listen, let me go over there and see what's up. I'll call ya'll right back," Pete said.

"You better straighten this shit out!" Andre said.

Pete was left listening to a dial tone. He hung up the phone, then leaned back on the sofa and stared up at the ceiling. He knew what the score was; they had been jacked. He knew Snake would deny any involvement. Snake had really thoroughly thought this one out. Pete knew that accusing anybody with a street rep like Snake's of any foul play without any concrete evidence would be straight up disrespect.

"I'll just go and ask him," Pete told himself.

He walked into his bedroom and threw on his shoes. He stared up at the shoebox in his closet that he rarely pulled down.

"Shit, I'ma grab this just in case," he said to himself, while reaching up and grabbing the Nike shoebox.

He sat the shoebox on his bed, opened it up, and pulled out his .38 snub nose, checking to make sure it was still loaded, which it was.

He stuck it in his waistband, looked in the mirror for a minute, took a deep breath, then grabbed his keys and headed out to his car.

* * * * *

When Snake pulled up to the projects, Goldie let off a sigh of relief. Goldie looked over at the park bench, where he had a couple of crackheads waiting on him, and threw up one finger to tell them to give him a minute.

"What's up, lil' nigga?" Snake said, easing his body out of his Regal.

"Damn, nigga, you got a nigga missing money!" Goldie said, anxious to get his grind on.

Snake rubbed him on top of the head. "All money ain't good money."

"Shit...show me some money that ain't good!" Goldie challenged.

Snake reached into his McDonalds bag, then tossed him a bag of rocks.

"I'll be right back!" Goldie said, rushing over to the park bench to serve the crackheads.

Snake just looked at him and shook his head. Goldie had really turned things up a notch. He had more ambition than any member did in his crew.

For a Sunday, the park was packed. The basketball court was crowded. All of the neighborhood's best players were sporting the newest basketball kicks and putting on an exhibition for all of the females watching the games through the fence.

Snake walked over to one of the benches, sat down at the table, and started eating his breakfast. A few minutes later, Goldie was walking towards him, cheerfully counting a wad of money.

"What's up, nigga?" Goldie said, sitting down next to Snake.

Snake looked over at him. "What's up?"

Goldie handed him a wad of money with a rubber band wrapped around it.

"What's this?" Snake asked.

"That's two grand!" Goldie boasted.

Snake flipped through the wad and started nodding his head. He looked over at Goldie and was impressed. "You ain't bullshitting, are ya?"

Goldie hit his fist in his hand. "I'm tryna get money, man!"

Snake laughed, and then rubbed him on his head. "I'm proud of you, lil' nigga! Let me hold something," Snake said, then playfully started reaching into Goldie's pockets.

Goldie kept slapping his hands away. While the two of them wrestled, Mookie and Peanut approached them.

"Awww, now ain't that cute!" Peanut joked, standing and watching with his arms folded.

All of a sudden, everybody's attention was drawn to a Delta '88 that pulled up and parked. Mookie, Peanut, and Goldie all pulled out their rocks, thinking it was a sale.

When Pete eased out of the car, Peanut reached up under his shirt for his .357 Magnum.

Snake grabbed his hand. "Wait. Let's see what he's talking about first."

With his head down, Pete nervously walked over to where everybody was standing. Everybody was trying to read his body language. Peanut and Mookie were attentively standing with their legs spread apart, arms folded, and grins on their faces.

Pete stopped in front of Snake. "Yo, Snake, can I holla at you for a minute?" he asked in a cracking voice.

Snake smirked. "Yeah, what you wanna holla about?" he calmly asked.

Pete stepped off to the side with Snake, and the two of them went into conference.

"Yo, Snake, my cousin just called me, tripping about somebody switched they dope for some chocolate chip cookies."

"Oh yeah!" Snake said, adjusting his toothpick in his mouth.

"How good do you know that mechanic that works at your shop?"

"Who Bobby?" Snake asked.

"Yeah!"

"I've been knowing him all of my life," Snake replied.

"So who do you think at your shop could have switched the dope?"

Snake scanned the park. All of the basketball players had stopped playing basketball. Everyone was curious of what was about to go down.

"Yo, check this out, Pete. I took that! Your country ass cousins should have never brought they country ass down here tryna cop!" Snake boldly stated.

Peanut and Mookie were standing off to the side, smiling. They were itching for some gangsta shit to jump off.

Pete could not believe what his ears had heard. He thought for sure Snake would have denied any involvement, and here it was he had courageously confessed to everything.

"Listen. Don't ever bring your coward ass around here again disrespecting my spot! Now get the fuck from around here!" Snake said, bravely turning his back and walking back over towards the fellas.

Out of nowhere, Pete courageously pulled his .38 from under his shirt. Everybody on the basketball court and standing around started running. It was not until Snake noticed everybody taking off, when he turned around and saw Pete pointing a gun straight at him. Snake stood frozen, with a grimace on his face.

"Just give us back the money!" Pete shouted nervously.

Peanut, Mookie, and Goldie were all standing with their guns pointed at Pete.

Snake threw up his hand. "Hold up, ya'll. Just let me holla at him."

Mookie had a grimace on his face, and he was itching to pull the trigger, but he did as told.

Snake heroically started walking towards Pete. "Look, man, this done got way out of hand."

"Stop right there!" Pete shouted.

"You gonna shoot me, Pete? What do you think my boys gonna do to you when you shoot me?"

"I don't care! I don't care!" Pete cried.

Snake observantly noticed how bad Pete's hand was shaking. The two were only a couple of feet apart.

Frantic, Pete started rubbing his head. "Why, man, why?" he cried.

"Oh shit, ya'll, put them guns up! There go the police!" Snake told his crew.

Peanut looked at Snake and smiled. Then he, Goldie, and Mookie obediently put their guns behind their backs. Nervously, Pete turned his head to locate the police, which turned out to be the worst mistake of his life.

Snake moved so swift that Pete never stood a chance. Snake hit Pete with a right uppercut so vicious that Pete's body went one way and the gun went the other.

"Motherfucker! You wanna pull a muthafuckin' gun on me?" Snake asked, standing over Pete's body as he started stomping the shit out of his face.

The rest of the crew came over and joined in. With each blow, more and more blood flowed out of Pete's body.

After issuing about fifty horrendous blows, Snake stood up breathing heavily. "Let's get out of here!" Snake said.

Everybody took off and headed their separate ways, leaving Pete laying in a puddle of blood that looked like somebody had poured a gallon of red paint on him. Pete was not moving. A group of nosey people ran over to see if he was dead. Pete had taken a brutal beating.

It took about twenty minutes for the paramedics to arrive. Surprisingly, Pete was not dead. He was unconscious, but he was not dead.

When Detective Ross arrived on the scene, the crowd started thinning out. Everybody the detectives tried to talk to refused to comment. Everyone knew how Snake got down, and nobody wanted to be in Pete's shoes.

"So, do you think this was Snake's work?" Mitch asked Detective Ross.

"What kind of question is that, Mitch?' Detective Ross asked, while lighting a Marlboro and taking a couple of drags. "This is his backyard, Mitch. Of course he had something to do with it!"

"This whole thing is getting pretty ugly," Mitch said.

Ross dropped his cigarette butt and put it out with his shoe. "I want to know the victim's name. Page me as soon as he's conscious. If we can get him to testify against Snake, we may have ourselves a case."

"Alright, I'll get right on it, sir," Mitch replied.

"You might have gone too far this time, Snake. You might have gone too far," Detective Ross said to himself, as he hopped in his cruiser and pulled off, heading back towards the precinct.

CHAPTER TWENTY-NINE

Robert was impatiently pacing the living room of their home. "It's been a couple of hours. I wonder what's taking Pete so long to call us back," he said, frustrated.

"Call Grandma's house and see what's up with that nigga," Andre said.

Robert nodded his head in agreement, and then rushed over to the phone.

"Hello," their grandmother answered on the fourth ring.

"Sorry to bother you, Grandma, but is Pete there?" Robert asked.

"That child's in the hospital! I don't know what type of stuff you boys got yourselves into, but whatever it is, you boys need to stop all of that foolishness!" their grandmother spat.

Robert held the phone away from his ear and looked at it, not believing what he had just heard. He massaged his head. "Is he okay?" Robert said into the receiver.

"He's in a coma!" their grandmother shouted.

"A coma?" Robert repeated in disbelief, while plopping down on the sofa in shock. This was getting way out of hand. "Pete's in a coma," he repeated to himself.

Andre and Richie sensed something was wrong.

"What is it?" Andre whispered.

Robert threw up his finger.

"Robert, do you hear me talking to you?" his grandmother shouted.

"Yes, ma'am," Robert replied.

"You boys stay from down here! You hear me? Whatever done happened just let it 'lone."

"Alright, Grandma, I'll call you back to keep checking on Pete," Robert said.

"Alright, child, and remember what I said!" his grandmother stressed.

"Okay, Grandma, bye," Robert said, and then hung up.

"What happened?" Andre asked.

Robert lifted his head, which was buried in his hands, and said, "Man, Pete's in a coma."

"A coma?" Andre hopped up off the sofa and threw his hands on his waist. "I can't believe this shit!" he said, irritably pacing the living room.

"He must have gone around there and tried to holla at that nigga Snake by himself," Robert said.

"We gotta go back down there!" Andre proclaimed.

"We can't just go down there bullshitting! You think what just happened to Pete can't happen to us?" Richie said.

"Damn, this shit done got outta hand!" Robert said, pacing the room with retribution on his mind.

Andre plopped down on the sofa. "We're responsible for this shit!" he said, now feeling guilty for pressuring Pete to do something.

"Nigga, what the fuck you mean we're responsible?" Robert asked.

"We pressured Pete to go back over there," Andre said.

The room went quiet. Everybody was a little choked up, and felt equally responsible for what had happened to Pete.

Andre was in deep thought. Snake needed to be dealt with, but how? Andre stood up and started calmly pacing the room with his hands behind his back. After five minutes, Andre shouted out, "I got an idea!"

"And what's that?" Robert asked.

Andre smirked. "Here's the plan…"

* * * * *

Bright and early the next morning, Detective Ross was in the projects going from door to door, trying to find someone courageous enough to come forward and finger Snake as the one responsible for initiating yesterday's brutal attack on Pete. He was unsuccessful.

The streets loved Snake. Snake was the ghetto's savior. If the streets were ever looked at as a company, Snake would have been appointed the CEO. He was a one-man wrecking crew that assisted the ghetto better than the good ole' government itself. He was the one that kept dope flowing through the junkies' veins, food on the kitchen tables, maintenance up on all the women, and made it possible for every hustler's dreams to turn into reality.

Detective Ross had tried every trick in the book. Even his $2,500 cash reward could not get a single soul to budge, not even a crack head. Ross wanted to nail Snake bad. He even offered to drop all charges of a couple of local hustlers in the hood, who he knew had pending cases, in exchange for a signed affidavit fingering Snake as the one responsible for the brutal attack. Still, no one budged. Everyone knew Snake's wrath.

Snake's tactics had worked. He had done so many positive things in the community that whenever he did wrong, people tended to overlook many of the negative things. Although many of the people did not approve of his profession, he knew how to utilize the power of persuasion to make them look the other way. He cleverly recycled a lot of money he made by dumping it right back into the ghetto.

For the older residents, he donated generously to Meals on Wheels. He renovated the old neighborhood clubhouse for the elderly, installing brand new shuffleboard courts, an inside air-conditioned exercise gym, and horseshoe pits. He even installed a gazebo on the clubhouse's patio, with tables installed for playing dominoes, cards, checkers, and chess. Every month, he donated a thousand dollars to the clubhouse as prize money for the regularly scheduled bingo games held on Wednesdays and Saturdays.

For the kids, whenever report card day rolled around, Snake posted up at their bus stop with a wad of money, waiting on the kids to reward them for all the A's and B's on their report cards, which gave them the incentive to do well in school. He even enforced a strict "Save the Kids" rule upon his crew, stipulating that no sales were ever to be made around any kids. He even threw regular cookouts at the park on the first Saturday of every month, completely shutting down shop for the day and showing everyone in the community that he had a compassionate side.

Although Snake's action weren't justifiable, his conscious felt a little bit better knowing that he had at least tried to make a positive difference in the hood.

As he cruised the city's streets in his newly acquired Honda Accord, he seriously debated on whether it was time to walk away from the game. Why not? He had enough stashed to walk away from the game and never have to look back. He was living every man's dream. He was the owner of two successful, legitimate businesses, and lived in a mini-mansion in Tierra Verde, one of the most prestigious communities in St. Petersburg.

He was just growing tired of looking over his shoulder. He did not possess the hunger for the dope game anymore. He was ready to settle down and be more of a father to his kids. He wanted to see the world.

Therefore, he made a decision. After one more good flip, he concluded he would leave the game.

* * * * *

Halfway to Peanut's house, Snake picked up his cellular and called Peanut. The phone rang a couple of times.

"Hello!" Peanut answered loudly, trying to talk over the loud music playing in the background.

"Nigga, turn that shit down!" Snake yelled through the phone.

The phone went quiet on Peanut's end for a minute, and then Peanut came back to the phone. "What's up, nigga?" he said.

"You ready?" Snake asked.

"Yeah, when you coming through?" Peanut asked.

"I'm outside," Snake said, and then the phone went dead.

Peanut peeped through his curtains, and saw Snake's Honda Accord parked in front of his house. He grabbed the money he owed Snake off the dining room table and bounced out of the house.

When Peanut hopped inside of the car, Snake was in a heated conversation with someone on his cellular. Snake threw up his index finger, indicating for him to give him a minute.

"Listen, Sal, we'll talk about this later," Snake said, and then listened to Sal's last couple of words before hanging up.

"Man, I hope you weren't talking about what I think you were talking about?" Peanut said.

Snake looked him directly in the eyes. "I'm getting out, playboy."

Peanut started shaking his head and rubbing on his temples. "Man...when was you gonna tell us?" Peanut asked, agitated.

"I know, I know, I know. Listen, I ain't gonna leave ya'll hanging. I'ma help ya'll get ya'll money right."

"Why don't you just give us the connect?" Peanut asked, trying his hand.

"It ain't that easy, playboy. I'll holla at my people and see what they say," Snake replied.

"Damn, Snake, I can't believe you just leaving like this," Peanut said, shaking his head and staring out of the window.

"That's the money?" Snake asked, observing the stacks sitting on his lap.

"Yeah...here you go," Peanut said nonchalantly, while handing it over.

Snake sat the money in his lap, removed the rubber bands off each stack, and counted. Meanwhile, Peanut was heated. He just sat in total silence and stared out of the window.

"Everything's here," Snake said, then reached over, opened up the glove compartment, and threw the ten grand in it.

Snake looked over at Peanut, whose eyes were bloodshot red. Snake caringly placed his hand on Peanut's shoulder. "Listen, Peanut, I feel your pain. I just ain't hungry no more."

"Then why won't you just grab all of the work and let me move it?" Peanut asked.

Snake took a deep breath. "I tell you what I'ma do. I'ma cop five bricks from my connect and let ya'll just work 'em and pay me back what I paid for 'em."

Smiling, Peanut turned around in his seat with a newfound attitude. "Alright then, if leaving the game is what you really want, then I support ya," he said, extending his hand for a shake.

"That's good to know, playboy," Snake said, reaching out and shaking his hand. "I gotta go make a run. I'ma holla at ya when I got that for ya'll."

"Alright then," Peanut said, hopping out of the car.

Snake honked the horn two times, and then pulled off.

* * * * *

"And when did you arrive at this decision?" Sal asked, as he leaned back in his favorite booth and exhaled the smoke from his Cuban cigar.

"I just ain't feeling it no more, Sal," Snake said.

Sal distastefully stared at him, and then made a hand gesture. "So this is the fucking thanks I get for rescuing you out of the ghetto? A fucking slap in the face? Do you remember when you had nothing?" Sal reminded him.

Snake dropped his head and started distressfully massaging his temples. "I remember," he mumbled.

"You know how many fucking guys would die to be in your shoes?" Sal asked, leaping up and slamming his heavy, hairy hands on the table.

"I know," Snake said in a pitiful voice.

"Look at me when I'm talking to you!" Sal ordered, irritably slamming his hand on the table.

Two of Sal's men walked over and tapped Snake on the shoulder, then motioned for him to show their boss some respect. Snake lifted up his head, pathetically looking into Sal's eyes. Sal took a couple of drags from his cigar and rudely blew his smoke in Snake's face. The two sat in total silence and let their eyes do all of the talking.

Snake squirmed in his seat. His heart started beating fast. He felt uncomfortable, and did not know what to expect out of Sal.

Sal disgracefully shook his head at Snake. "I remember when you were just a petty street hustler like your crew, running around nickel and diming, until I came along. I misjudged you, Snake. I thought I saw spunk and fire in your eyes. I really thought you were one of the ones that were in it for the haul. I guess I was wrong."

Snake sat in total silence, nervously fiddling with his hands.

Sal continued. "I just don't understand you kids today! Got damnit, I made you Snake!" Sal shouted, once again slamming his hand on the table.

Snake alarmingly jumped, then leaned back in his chair.

Sal looked at the ring he had given Snake and contemplated on taking it back. He lifted up Snake's hand. "You see this ring? This ring represents power! As long as you have this ring, you'll never go broke. What good is it to you if you're walking away?"

Snake rubbed on the ring. "How about I pay you for it?" Snake asked.

"It's priceless!" Sal said.

"Well how about I make a generous forty thousand dollar donation to you," Snake bribed.

Sal rubbed on his chin. "That could be a day at the dog track. When can you come up with the money?" Sal asked.

"Give me a week," Snake replied.

Sal disturbingly snatched his napkin from off of his shirt, and then tossed it on the remains of his meal. "You have my blessings on your retirement, and I'll give you a week to come up with the money."

Snake gave Sal a surprised look. *Is it really gonna be that easy,* he thought.

"Snake, just out of curiosity, were does your money stand?" Sal asked.

"I got a couple hundred thousand saved up," Snake said.

Sal and his crew started laughing. Snake curiously looked around at everybody and tried to figure out what in the hell was so funny.

Sal was leaning on the table, struggling to keep his balance. He was laughing so hard that his face had turned fire engine red. Sal raised his hand, indicating for Snake to give him a moment while he caught his breath.

"You mean to tell me after all these years that we've been doing business you haven't managed to stash away a million dollars in cash yet?" Sal asked.

Snake sunk down in his seat, feeling like a peon.

Sal walked behind Snake and threw his hands on his shoulders. "I'm gonna make you a deal you can't refuse."

"What's that?" Snake asked.

"How much have I've been selling you kilos for?"

"Twenty-two, but you've been letting me get five of them for a hundred thousand," Snake replied.

"How much money can you come up with by tomorrow?" Sal asked, figuring that at least he should make a couple of dollars off Snake before he let him walk away.

"Everything's kind of scattered out right now. Plus, I still got a lot of money on the streets."

Sal patted him on the shoulder. "Just gather up everything you can put together, and come and see me. The more the merrier!" Sal joked.

Snake stood up, and then he and Sal shook hands. "No hard feelings?" Snake asked.

"No hard feelings," Sal replied.

"Alright then, I'll see ya tomorrow," Snake said, then waved goodbye to everybody and disappeared out of the restaurant.

When Snake hopped into his car, he let out a sigh of relief. He was surprised Sal had let him out of the game.

After stopping by his Aunt Maggie's house to pick up $162,000 in cash that he had stashed there, he headed home to get some much-needed rest.

CHAPTER THIRTY

While Snake was fast asleep, little did he know he had unexpected guests.

Andre let off a sigh of relief the minute he reached the St. Petersburg city limits.

He reached over and tapped Robert. "We here, nigga!"

Robert wiped the side of his mouth off, sat up in his seat, and started rubbing his eyes. He stretched, and then tugged on his manhood.

"Damn, I gotta piss!" he cried.

Andre adjusted his rearview mirror. Monica and her home girls were right on his tail.

Andre threw on his right blinker when he approached the 54th Avenue North exit, then merged over into the turning lane. Monica did the same.

"Man, pull over to a gas station or something!" Robert cried, squeezing his manhood.

Andre ignored Robert's statement. As he took the exit, luckily for Robert there was a gas station on the right-hand side of the road. Andre pulled into the gas station and parked next to the gas tanks. Monica pulled in behind him.

Before Andre ever got a chance to throw the car in park, Robert shot out of the car like a bat out of hell, and stormed into the gas station.

Andre just shook his head, as he eased out of the car to pump the gas.

Monica let down her window and asked, "You gonna pump our gas, too?"

Andre looked over at her and smirked. "What's wrong with ya'll hands?"

"Owwwweeeee, you make me sick!" Monica said as she hopped out with a disgusted look on her face, and pouted all the way over to the gas tank, while her friends Pam and Denise watched from inside the car.

"One of ya'll can go inside and pay!" Monica yelled to her girls.

"Ummm, she got an attitude," Pam mumbled to Denise. "I'll go inside. I gotta pee anyway," Pam said, grabbing her purse and hopping out of the car.

As Pam entered the gas station, Robert was exiting.

"Nigga, did you pay for the gas?" Andre asked.

"Yeah, nigga!" Robert shouted, as he hopped inside of the car.

The slamming of Robert's door woke Richie, who had been knocked out in the backseat throughout the entire duration of the trip.

Andre hopped back inside of the car.

"Where we at?" Richie asked, as he stretched in the backseat, unfamiliar with his surroundings.

"We here," Andre told him.

Monica impatiently honked her horn, indicating that she was ready to go. Andre cranked up the car, and then pulled out of the gas station with Monica right on his tail.

Ten minutes later, Andre was pulling up under the carport of the Howard Johnson. He parked, flipped down the sun visor, and grabbed his fake I.D.

"I'm finna go grab the rooms. I'll be right back," Andre yelled to Monica, as he headed towards the front lobby.

A couple of minutes later, he returned to the car with two sets of room keys in his hand. He cranked up the car, and then stuck his hand out of the window for Monica to follow him.

Andre drove to the back of the hotel and parked in front of their room. Monica parked beside him. After Andre popped the trunk, Richie and Robert hopped out and started grabbing their bags. The girls also gathered their belongings.

Andre walked over to Monica and handed her a key. "Here go ya'll room key."

Monica pouted. "I thought we were getting a room together," she said, flirtatiously rubbing up against Andre. She was horny and desperately in need of a fix.

Andre eased her back for a little breathing room. "I told you… this is business!" he reminded her.

"You make me sick!" Monica pouted, as she tooted up her nose and headed towards the room, heated.

CHAPTER THIRTY-ONE

The next morning, the sound of Snake's pager sounding off served as a substitute for his alarm clock. He reached up under the covers and grabbed his pager off his pants, then looked at the number. It took him a couple of seconds to regain his vision. Open-eyed, he abruptly sat up in the bed, realizing it was Sal paging him.

"Oh shit!" he yelled, leaping out of the bed and grabbing the cordless phone all in one motion. He dialed Sal's number, as he headed towards the bathroom.

"Hello," Sal answered calmly on the fifth ring.

"It's me," Snake said into the receiver, while running warm water on his washrag and preparing to wash his face.

"Are you ready to see me yet?" Sal asked.

Snake looked down at the Gucci watch on his wrist. It was eight o'clock in the morning. "Sal, whatta you say we do lunch?" he said in code, acknowledging he would be ready to handle business at noon.

"Very well, I'll see you then," Sal replied, then hung up.

Snake stared at the image in the mirror, vainly rubbing on his goatee. "Yep, a couple more days and you're a free man," he said, then winked.

He walked over to the shower, undressed out of yesterday's clothes, and hopped into the steamy, hot water.

* * * * *

Meanwhile, on the other side of town, Monica, Pam, and Denise were just waking up in their hotel room.

"Shit, I'm hungry, Monica! Girl, call Andre's room and see if they up yet," Pam cried, standing in front of the bathroom mirror in her panties, curling her hair.

Monica looked over at the clock radio. It was 9:00 a.m.

"Yeah, call them, because I'm hungry, too," Denise complained, sitting on the edge of the bed polishing her toes.

"I'm finna call right now," Monica said, picking up the phone and dialing the guys' room number. The phone rang about fifteen times. "I know they ain't still over there sleep. I can't believe this shit. They got us all the way down here, and can't even take us to get no damn breakfast," Monica mumbled to herself.

She hung up the phone after the twentieth ring, then curiously walked over to the window and pulled back the curtains. The rental car was still parked in the same spot. Monica instantly caught an attitude.

"Get dressed, ya'll. We going to get ourselves some breakfast," Monica ordered, feeling liberated.

"Now that's what I'm talking about, girl!" Pam chanted.

Twenty minutes later, the girls were fully dressed and strolling out the door.

"You want me to go knock on their door?" Denise asked, standing in between the two rooms.

"Naw, never mind them, come on, girl," Monica said, unlocking the car.

Once she hopped in, she lowered the top to the Mustang convertible, popped in a 2 Live Crew tape, and turned the volume up as far as it could go. Pam rushed over to the passenger side door, and Denise took her place in the backseat.

"What the fuck!" Andre shouted. The sound of loud music blasting in the parking lot woke him. "I wonder who the fuck out there playing all of that damn loud-ass music at this time of morning," he said, tugging on his early morning erection, as he headed to the window.

He pulled back the curtains just as Monica was pulling out of the parking lot. "Where the fuck these stupid-ass hoes think they going?" he mumbled to himself, rushing to the door.

He furiously flung the door open. "Hey! Where the fuck ya'll think ya'll going?" he yelled, but there was no use. His voice was drowned out by Luke's rap lyrics.

Andre stopped yelling when he realized he was only wasting his breath. He watched the girls disappear down the road, as they danced in the car with their hands up in the air like they were on a roller coaster ride.

*****

By 11:00 a.m., Snake had just about gathered everything he could put his hands on. He was heading into town with $310,000 inside a duffle bag, which was in the trunk of his Honda. Besides fifty to sixty-thousand cash wise, he was all in. After this last flip, the game would be officially over for him.

As he cruised the city, he worked a couple of numbers in his head. If everything went as planned, depending on how many bricks Sal threw him for the $310,000, this last flip would put him well over $600,000 to $700,000 in cash, which was all he needed.

Spending a quarter-of-a-million on his Corniche was the only thing that put a dent in his stash, but Snake still felt like he was on top. Both businesses were still doing exceptionally well. With all of his assets combined, he was still worth over more than a million dollars. His house on Tierra Verde was appraised at over $350,000, his Corniche was still valued at least $200,000, and his financial advisor had over $150,000 in Mesha's name scattered around in different stocks and bonds. Not only that, his jewelry alone was appraised at well over $125,000.

Snake's appetite drove him into the parking lot of Shirley's.

"Mmmm!" Snake said, sniffing the aroma of the soul food as he hopped out to go inside to grab a bite to eat.

*****

Andre angrily paced the hotel room, heated. Two hours had passed since the girls left. "I wonder where the fuck these silly hoes at?" he said.

"It was your silly idea to bring them down here," Robert said, antagonizing him.

Richie looked over at Andre, as if he was waiting on his response.

"You know what? Fuck you, Robert!" Andre spat, boldly walking over and getting in Robert's face.

Robert defensively jumped up off the bed. Richie jumped in between the two and intervened.

"Both of ya'll need to just chill out!" he said, eyeing them.

As the two stubbornly stared into each other's eyes, a car blasting its stereo system pulled in front of the hotel room. Andre raced to the window and pulled back the curtains. He didn't even have to say a word. The way he charged out of the front door, told Robert and Richie who was parked out front.

"What the fuck is wrong with ya'll?" Andre asked, approaching the Mustang with rage in his eyes.

All three girls were at a loss for words. They just looked at Andre like he was deranged.

"What are you talking about, Andre?" Monica asked, puzzled.

Not bothering to say another word, he forcefully opened Monica's door and grabbed her by her braids, then pulled her out of the car.

"Ouch! Let me go!" Monica cried defensively.

"Oh, hell naw! Let her go!" Pam and Denise ordered, protectively charging out of the car and rushing to their girls' defense.

Coincidentally, Robert and Richie were just stepping out of the room, when they saw the girls rushing towards Andre with their shoes in their hands. The two charged the girls and intervened. Robert grabbed Pam, while Richie grabbed Denise.

"Unhh unhh, he better let her go!" the girls ordered, struggling to get loose.

"I brought ya'll down here to handle business, not sightsee!" Andre told Monica.

"Chill out, cuz!" Richie said.

"Nigga, shut the fuck up!" Andre yelled.

After forcefully dragging Monica inside of the room, Andre pushed her down on one of the beds.

"What's wrong with you?" Monica asked with a terrified look on her face, as she pushed her left breast back inside of her bra.

Slightly out of breath, Andre took a moment to compose himself, and then he pointed his finger at Monica. "Where the fuck ya'll been for two whole hours?"

Monica sat up in the bed and straightened herself up. "We went to get something to eat. I called ya'll room and let the phone ring about twenty times, then hung up."

"Dang, why you tripping? We brought ya'll back something to eat," Pam said sarcastically, and then hit Robert in the chest with a McDonald's bag.

Robert looked inside of the bag.

"The orange juice is out in the car," Denise told him, while rolling her eyes. Then she shifted her weight and headed out to the car to retrieve the orange juice.

"I don't care what you say. That shit still didn't take no damn two hours!" Robert spat.

Monica knew she needed to come up with a lie, and she needed to do it quick. She could never tell Andre about the three fine-ass boys they met and ate breakfast with at McDonald's. Florida boys had it going on! They had been so caught up laughing and giggling that they had lost track of time.

Pam rescued Monica. "You need to stop yelling at her! We got lost, dang! We accidentally made a wrong turn and got lost."

"Ya'll got lost, huh?" Andre asked. "Then where ya'll get lost at?" he challenged.

"St. Pete Beach," was the first thing to come out of Pam's mouth.

Andre looked over at Monica, and then back at Pam. Something was fishy.

"I tell you what, from now on...if anybody leaves this hotel, we leaving together!" he said, laying down the law. "Ya'll understand?"

"Dang, we understand," the girls said with attitudes.

"Good! 'Cause I'm paying ya'll to take care of business, not muthafuckin' sightsee! This ain't no damn vacation; this is business!" Andre said.

"You want one of these sandwiches, cuz?" Robert asked, nibbling on his sausage egg Mcmuffin.

"You damn right I do!" Andre shouted with a grimace.

Robert tossed him two sandwiches.

"Go on back to ya'll room. I'll call you when I'm ready to go," Andre told the girls.

"Punk motherfucker," Pam mumbled under her breath as they exited the room.

* * * * *

By noon, Snake was turning down the alley that led to the back of Sal's restaurant. He cautiously scanned the area as he approached the back of the restaurant. Hector, one of Sal's men, was standing out back puffing on a cancer stick. Snake pulled into the back of the restaurant, and then parked. His presence alarmed Hector. Edgy, Hector reached inside of his jacket and pulled out his Colt 45.

Snake shook his head as he stared at him through the windshield. "This crazy muthafucka," he mumbled to himself, shaking his head as he turned off the ignition.

Gun in hand, Hector kneeled down to distinguish who the driver of the Honda was. He slapped himself on the forehead and put his gun away when he realized Snake was the driver.

"Man, what the fuck is wrong with your crazy ass! You must be out here tooting that shit! Here, the money's in the trunk," Snake said, tossing him his car keys.

Hector caught the keys in mid-air. "The boss is expecting you inside," he said, while rubbing his nostrils and then looking at his fingers to see if there was any visible evidence that he had been snorting.

Snake shook his head in disappointment as he brushed passed him and walked inside of the restaurant.

Sal was sharing a corny joke with a couple of his men when he entered the dining area. He patiently waited until Sal got to the punch line. The room instantly went quiet after Sal finished telling his joke. Sal held out his hands. "You get it?" All of Sal's men started laughing.

"You're hysterical, boss!" one of the men shouted.

"Yeah, you should've been in comedy, boss," another man exaggerated.

Snake just stood against the wall and shook his head. Sal had just told the corniest joke he had ever heard. "He gotta be paying those motherfuckers well," Snake mumbled to himself.

Sal noticed him. "Hey…well, whatta you know, if it isn't my ole' friend who's retiring on us!" Sal joked, holding out his hands.

Sal's crew started laughing again.

"Come on over. Have a seat," Sal said, motioning for Snake, while sitting at his favorite booth and puffing on a Cuban cigar.

Snake walked over and joined him.

Hector walked into the room. "Excuse me, boss. Whatta you want me to do with this bag?" he asked, holding up Snake's duffle bag.

Sal leaned over and whispered to Snake, "How much did you bring me?"

"Three-hundred and ten thousand," Snake replied.

Sal leaned back in his seat. "Hmmm, I was expecting a little more, but I guess that'll do."

Sal returned his attention to Hector. "Hector, you and the boys go in the storage room and count the money in the bag."

"Will do, boss," Hector said, then disappeared.

"Rapido!" Sal yelled, snapping his fingers in the air to a couple of his other men who obviously were not moving fast enough for him.

Sal waited until his men disappeared out of the dining area. "Sorry about that. Now where were we?" he asked.

"You were saying something about…"

"Oh yes, now I remember," Sal said, rudely cutting Snake off in mid-sentence. "I'm a man of my word, Snake. I gave you my word yesterday that I was gonna give you a deal that you couldn't refuse, and I plan on doing just that."

Sal lit another Cuban cigar. "Since this is gonna be our last time doing business, I figured I'd throw in a little going-away present for you," Sal said, with a warm smile.

Snake smiled and nodded his head. "That'll be straight!"

Sal took a couple of puffs from his cigar, and then said, "How does twenty kilos for your $310,000 sound?"

Snake's face lit up, as he quickly did the math in his head. "That's about $15,500 a kilo," he mumbled to himself, as he rubbed on his chin.

"How does it sound?" Sal asked.

"Hell yeah!" Snake replied, gratefully reaching out his hand to shake on the deal, with a Kool-Aid smile on his face.

"Good, I'll have the boys grab them for you," Sal said, shaking his hand.

Sal called one of his men over, and then whispered something in his ear before his man quickly disappeared to one of the back rooms.

Sal and Snake sat and conversed. Twenty minutes later, Sal's men returned to the dining area with the kilos.

"Everything's there, boss," Hector said.

Sal nodded his head. "Hector, you know what to do with the money."

Hector nodded his head. "I'm on it, boss!" he said, disappearing out of the room.

Sal waved off his other two men, Miguel and Pedro, who were hanging around, then leaned forward. "While their getting everything together, how about me and you have a little lunch?" Sal asked, placing his handkerchief inside of his shirt.

Snake rubbed his stomach. "No, thank you. I just ate."

Sal eyed him. "Nonsense!" he yelled, slamming his heavy, hairy hands on the dining room table.

The loud thump from the table alerted Sal's men, who instantly stopped what they were doing and peeped around the corner to make sure everything was fine.

Sal waved them off. "I'm fine. We were just having a little fun," he said, simultaneously laughing and coughing at the same time.

Snake managed a fake smile.

"Relax. Sometimes you just gotta take it easy! Here, drink with me," Sal insisted, pouring Snake and himself a glass of overpriced wine, then handing Snake a glass. Sal lifted up his glass. "I'd like to propose a toast to the future. May the both of us die rich!"

The two cheerfully toasted, then tilted their glasses.

"Ahhh, that was good!" Sal said, as he wiped his mouth and slammed his empty wine glass on the table.

Snake sat his empty glass on the table and nodded in agreement.

"Not bad, huh?" Sal asked.

"Pretty good," Snake said, swallowing the last of his drink.

"Pretty good? At twenty-five hundred dollars a bottle, it better taste better than pretty good," Sal joked, playfully slapping him on the shoulder.

Snake almost choked, as the remainder of his drink went down his esophagus.

"Maria!" Sal yelled.

A teenage girl came out of the kitchen and trotted over to their table with a pen and pad in her hand. Snake was speechless. She was the most beautiful girl he had ever seen. Her skin was radiant, and she had the longest, silkiest hair. Her teeth were flawless, and her eyes were hypnotic.

"Maria, take my friend's order if you don't mind."

"May I take your order?" Maria asked in a Spanish accent.

Snake snapped out of his daze. "Ummm...yeah...let me get some empanadas."

Maria placed her pencil in her hair. "Okay, I'll be back in a couple of minutes," she said, then disappeared into the kitchen.

"That's my niece," he told Snake. She's gonna make somebody a helluva wife when she gets older. Her mother, my sister Eloisa, died when she was only six years old," Sal said, getting a little emotional and wiping his eyes with his handkerchief.

"I'm sorry to hear that," Snake replied.

Sal held up his hand. "It's okay." He took a couple of seconds to get him together. "Sorry, I get a little choked up when I think about Eloisa."

"It's alright. I get the same way whenever I think about my mother," Snake said.

"So, Snake...what are your plans after you retire?" Sal asked.

Snake smiled. "Well, first, I'm gonna..."

* * * * *

Back at the hotel, everybody was gathered in the girls' room and going over the plan.

"Okay, listen up, everybody," Andre said. "Monica, you and the girls are gonna follow us to the projects. There's this little restaurant that sits on the corner about a block away. That's where we'll wait while ya'll do your thing."

"The plan is simple. All ya'll gotta do is let the top down on the Mustang, drive through the projects, flirt with a couple of them niggas, and peep-out the whole set-up. I need to know how many niggas they got on each corner, if those niggas strapped, and where most of the action takes place. The rental got a Georgia tag on it, so naturally, them niggas gonna flirt with ya'll because ya'll from out of town. Ya'll follow me?" Andre asked.

"We listening," the girls replied, while nodding their head.

"Just make up a lie, like ya'll down here visiting an auntie or something. That should be easy for ya'll," Andre said, as he sarcastically eyed Monica, letting her know he still wasn't buying her story from earlier.

"And yeah, before I forget, one of ya'll look in the phone book and find a black woman's name with an address on the north side of town and memorize it, just in case one of them niggas asks where ya'll aunt stay. Ya'll gotta be on point because we don't want them niggas to get suspicious."

Andre looked at his watch. "It's 12:30 now. We'll pull out of here at around five o'clock. We finna go look at a couple of houses. So, go ahead and get yourselves all pretty and shit!"

"Yeah, make sure ya'll throw on some of that tight shit!" Robert said, playfully slapping Pam on the ass.

"Alright, boy!" Pam warned Robert.

Andre walked over, opened the door, and then stood in the doorway. "Five o'clock, ya'll," Andre repeated.

"We'll be ready," the girls said.

* * * * *

After eating a full-course meal and having three more glasses of overpriced wine, Snake was sitting behind the steering wheel of his Honda Accord, heading towards Mesha's apartment, with twenty kilos of cocaine in a duffle bag in the trunk of his car.

His pager had been blowing up nonstop. Ever since this morning, all of his workers had been paging him with 9-1-1 behind their numbers. The streets were drier than the Sahara Desert, and Snake was the only superficial witchdoctor who could make it snow.

Snake pulled into Mesha's apartment complex, conscientiously scanning the area as he parked. "Damn!" he said, spotting Mrs. Whitaker's nosey ass sitting on her front porch.

Mesha's apartment complex mostly housed a lot of the elderly. Snake had moved her out to this spot so he could feel comfortable leaving work at her house. The only negative thing about this complex was that nobody really left to go to work. So naturally, most of the neighbors were nosey.

Snake parked in the farthest parking space away from the unit that he could find. He turned off the car, reached into the glove compartment, and pulled out his headband, throwing it on. He then grabbed the bottle of spring water from out of the cup holder, and splashed water all over his shirt. Once he felt confident that it appeared he had been sweating in the gym for hours, he hopped out of the car, walked up the sidewalk towards the apartment, and climbed the stairs.

"Ahh...did you get you a good workout in, Sonny?" Mrs. Whitaker asked when he reached the top of the stairs.

Snake rotated his shoulders and smirked. "Yeah, I just ran me twenty blocks," he said sarcastically, then unlocked the door and disappeared inside of the apartment.

* * * * *

Andre and Robert were busy searching for an address they had found in the newspaper, which they were hoping to use as a hideout to hold Snake hostage.

Andre slowly drove down the street. "There it goes!" he said, as he located the house and pulled into the driveway.

"Damn, this muthafucka got a garage where we can drive straight in," Robert said.

Andre anxiously hopped out of the car. Robert followed.

Robert surveyed the area. "This is even a dead-end street."

"That's good," Andre said, as the two of them walked around the house, snooping and peeping inside of the windows.

After circling the house, Andre was pleased. "This is the spot," he told Robert, while nodding his head.

What really sealed the deal with Andre was the fact that the house had a wooden privacy fence.

Robert nodded his head in agreement.

Andre surveyed the block. Judging by all of the motorcycles parked in the front yard, he assumed the neighbors on the right were bikers. The house to the left was empty, and looked like it needed a little TLC. Judging by the trashy yards across the street, he assumed the tenants across the street were elderly or disabled.

Andre and Robert hopped back inside of the car, and then Andre headed to the nearest payphone to make the call.

CHAPTER THIRTY-TWO

"Good afternoon, everybody. I'm Agent Bradshaw," he cordially said, as he entered the precincts' conference room.

Agent Bradshaw went around the room placing folders in front of everyone. "In front of you is everything we know about "Operation Crackdown". If you'll open your pamphlets to page one, please."

Everyone did as instructed.

"This is a recent photo of Marcus Robinson, otherwise known as Snake. Mr. Robinson has terrorized the streets of St. Petersburg for a little over six years now. You guys had your chance, now he's in our hands."

Detective Ross did not like what he was hearing. He looked over at the chief, who just shrugged his shoulders.

Agent Bradshaw noticed that Detective Ross was uneasy. "Excuse me, Detective Ross, is there something you wanna share with us?" he asked sarcastically.

Detective Ross looked at the chief, then returned his attention back to Agent Bradshaw and dropped his head. "I'm sorry, sir," he said in a light mumble, like it killed him to apologize.

"As I was saying, Mr. Robinson has terrorized the streets of St. Petersburg for some time now. If you'll please turn to page three."

Everyone turned to page three.

"This is the organizational chart that we have arranged based on the information we gathered from some of our most reliable C.I.'s. If you'll look up under Mr. Robinson's picture, you'll see three other pictures. From left to right you have: Michael Roberts a.k.a Black Jesus, Rasheed Thomas a.k.a Peanut, and Marcus Jones a.k.a Mookie. These three are believed to be Mr. Robinson's lieutenants who orchestrate most of his transactions in the projects."

"Who are all these other people?" the chief asked.

"These are other known street-level dealers who we have seen Mr. Robinson conducting business with.

"So what are you guys' plans?" Detective Ross just had to know.

"Our plan is a sweep! We have a couple of known drug dealers on our team who have pending charges and are cooperating with us to make controlled buys off of members of Mr. Robinson's crew. Our plan is simple. I've done my research, and most of the members of Mr. Robinson's crew have lengthy priors, which would put them in the category for a lengthy sentence. If we pick up at least twenty members of Mr. Robinson's crew, five of them are bound to break," Bradshaw said.

"He must not know that his members would rather die than rat him out," Detective Ross leaned over and whispered into the chief's ear.

"This meeting is to let you know that Mr. Robinson is no longer a City of St. Petersburg problem." Agent Bradshaw held up a sheet of paper. "This here is a blank indictment. I don't plan on resting until I have Mr. Robinson's name on it!"

There was silence in the room.

"This meeting is adjourned!" Agent Bradshaw said, then quickly gathered his belongings and disappeared out of the conference room.

Everyone from the precinct sat in total silence, looking at each other dumbfounded.

"Chief, can he really just pull the plug on us like that?" Detective Ross asked.

"I'm afraid he can. They're FEDS, and they're over my head."

Detective Ross hopped up, frantically gathered his belongings, and charged towards the front door.

"Ross!" the chief yelled out.

"Yeah!" Detective Ross replied with an attitude.

The chief pointed his finger at him. "Don't go out there and do anything stupid! Let it go!"

"Yes, sir," Detective Ross said, in a tone that the chief knew was going to be trouble, then disappeared out of the front door.

CHAPTER THIRTY-THREE

Traffic in the projects was ridiculous. Everybody in the city had to be out of dope, the way business was booming.

"Boy, I love this shit!" Goldie said, joyfully counting a handful of bills, as he walked back toward the crew.

When a white couple in an abused Nissan Sentra pulled up, Mookie and Goldie competitively ambushed the car.

"Hell naw, lil' nigga. This one on me!" Mookie said, boxing Goldie out from the passenger's window, as if they were fighting for a rebound in a championship basketball game.

Mookie swiftly snatched the two twenties out of the passenger's hand, and then dropped two rocks in her hand. The driver sped off.

"Damn, lil' nigga, you can't make all the money," Mookie joked with Goldie, as he rubbed him on the head.

Peanut was growing agitated at just sitting back and watching them make money. The two were the only members in the crew who still had dope. Peanut impatiently looked at his nugget Seiko. It was six o'clock.

"Damn, this shit jumping today!" Mookie said, as he counted the remainder of the rocks left in the plastic bag.

"Man, I wonder where the fuck this nigga Snake at," Peanut said, agitated.

Monica and her girls were having a field day touring through the projects. Their access had been easily granted. The two armed lookouts at the front entrance were the first ones to flirt with them. The girls observantly cruised through the projects, peeping out the entire set-up. Every nigga in the projects was trying to wave them down and holla. The girls just giggled, and Monica kept on driving, searching for the big fish. She turned down the road that led to the park, the heart of the projects.

"Damn, who the fuck is that?" Peanut asked Mookie, as he patted him on the chest and removed his toothpick from his mouth.

"I don't know. I ain't never seen them before. They must be from out of town," Mookie said

The girls could feel a dozen eyes hawking them as they approached the park.

Peanut boldly stepped out into the road, and threw up his right hand like he was a crossing guard. Monica mashed on the brakes to avoid hitting him.

When the Mustang came to a halt, Peanut smiled, and then confidentially walked around to the driver's side of the car. Mookie, Goldie, and Jerome followed. Monica was blushing from head to toe when Peanut approached her door.

Peanut licked his lips like he was L.L. Cool J, then kneeled down and said, "Damn, I just had to stop this motherfucker and see who you was!"

Monica and her girls started giggling.

Peanut scanned the other two passengers. "Damn, what ya'll up to?" he asked.

"Nothing, we just riding," Monica replied.

Mookie was standing on the passenger side of the car licking his chops at the passenger. She had a high-yellow complexion, thick thighs, and some sexy-ass lips. "Damn, baby girl, what's your name?" Mookie asked.

"My name's Denise," she said, flirtatiously leaning towards Mookie and sticking her breasts in his face. "What's yours?" she asked, in a tone so sexy it made Mookie's dick harder than Chinese arithmetic.

Mookie was tongue-tied. Denise had him lost for words. She was fine as hell. At 5'6", most of Denise's 145-pound frame was precisely distributed between her butt and thighs. She had one of those distinctive looks that could have easily landed her a spot in one of New Edition's videos.

"So...what's your name?" Denise asked again, seductively running her fingers along Mookie's shirt.

Being that there was not a fourth party to entertain, Goldie excused himself.

Mookie could not believe his luck. He was so in shock that he was lost for words.

"So you not gonna tell me your name?" Denise asked, licking her lips.

"Moo-ooo-kie," he stuttered.

Denise smiled. She loved having that kind of effect on men.

Jerome made his way around to the backseat. "Damn, my black, beautiful, goddess, what's your name?" he probed.

"Pam," Pam said, blushing and fluttering her eyelashes.

At 6'2", Jerome was a tall man, so naturally, he preferred tall women. Pam was just that. At 5'10", she was what you called an Amazon. Her long, sexy legs were the first thing that caught Jerome's attention when he approached the car. She had long, natural, silky hair that perfectly complemented her dark complexion. Her perfectly healthy teeth looked like she had never eaten a piece of candy in her life. She was flawless from head to toe.

"So...what ya'll finna get into?" Peanut asked.

"We was just riding. It's getting late, though, so we gotta get back to our auntie's house," Monica said.

"Oh yeah? Where ya'll auntie stay?" Peanut asked.

"On 72nd Avenue and 15th Street North," Monica replied.

Peanut rubbed on his chin. "Damn, I don't know where that shit is at," he said, rubbing on his head. "Well, what ya'll doin' later on?"

Little did Peanut know, neither of the girls heard a single word he said. Their attention had been adverted to the cocaine-white Rolls Royce traveling up the street. The three were mesmerized, sitting in a trance with their mouths wide open.

Pam stood up on her long legs in the backseat to get a better view. "Damn, who the fuck is that?" she asked.

Peanut dropped his head and sucked his teeth, jealous at Snake's stature. Snake was cruising down the street with the top down, traveling at a turtle's pace, while he generously handed out money to all of the kids chasing behind his car.

After blessing all of the kids, Snake parked next to Peanut's Caddy.

"Hold up one minute, ya'll," Peanut said, as him and the fellas walked over to Snake's car. "Damn, nigga, why you ain't been answering your pager?" Peanut asked Snake, as he approached the car.

"Just chill, playboy. I got you!" Snake said, leaning in the car with a grin on his face.

Peanut's eyes lit up. "You took care of that?" he asked.

"Don't I always?" Snake replied.

Peanut and Mookie looked at each other, smiled, and then cheerfully gave each other high-fives. "Now that's what we talking about, playboy!" they both said simultaneously.

While Mookie and Peanut were busy celebrating, Snake curiously glanced around Peanut's body at the unfamiliar faces.

Pam excitedly slapped Monica on the back. "Girl, look. He looking over here," she said.

Snake smiled at the girls. "Damn, boy, what ya'll got over there?" he asked.

Peanut looked over at the girls. "Oh, them some hoes from out of town."

The girls started blushing and smiling when they saw the fellas eye-balling them.

"They fucking?" Snake asked.

"Shit...I don't know. That's what we tryna find out," Peanut said.

"Handle ya business then. I got a couple of corners I gotta go turn, but I'ma get at ya'll in the morning," Snake said, reaching his hand out of the car and giving everybody dap with his closed fist before pulling off.

"Mmm mmm mmm," the girls said, shaking their heads as they watched Snake pull off.

* * * * *

Agent Bradshaw and Agent Roberts watched Snake's Rolls Royce disappear down the street. The two were positioned on the rooftop of the John Knox building, conducting surveillance on the projects.

Agent Bradshaw lowered his high-powered binoculars away from his eyes. "This fucking kid thinks he's a fucking god!" Agent Bradshaw said, furious.

"When are we gonna move on him, sir?" Agent Roberts asked.

"Hold on one minute, Roberts. Bradshaw to Morris, do you copy?" Bradshaw said into his walkie-talkie.

"Copy, go ahead, sir," Agent Morris responded.

"Follow our little friend. I wanna know where he's parking that fancy car of his so we know where to confiscate it from."

"Copy, boss," Agent Morris said.

"Now what were you saying, Roberts?" Bradshaw asked.

"When are we gonna move on him?"

"Just be patient, Roberts. Timing is everything. I wanna catch him when he least expects it. Then we'll hit him where it hurts," Bradshaw said.

"Ohhhh, I get it! So your C.I. must have given you some valuable information today?" Roberts asked.

Bradshaw smiled. "Let's just say that the streets are all dried up, and our little friend is planning on making a major move in the next couple of days. Do you know that this egotistical son-of-a-bitch is planning on retiring? Like selling drugs is some kind of real profession."

Agent Roberts just shook his head. "Some guys!" he said, disgusted.

"Don't worry. I have surveillance as we speak on all of his crack houses. We will know the minute the drop-off goes down. And when it does...believe me...we'll hit him where it hurts," Bradshaw boasted.

"Cool!" Agent Roberts replied.

CHAPTER THIRTY-FOUR

The smell of homemade lasagna lingered in the air of Mesha's apartment, and wafted through the complex's hallway.

"Wheeee...wheee!" Lil' Marcus screamed, as Snake repeatedly tossed him into the air.

Mesha looked over at the two and smiled. She was glad Snake had taken time out of his busy day to spend a little quality time with her and their son.

"Dinner should be ready in a couple of minutes, you two!" Mesha yelled into the living room.

Snake tossed Lil' Marcus in the air once more, then sat him on the sofa.

"One more time, Daddy!" Lil' Marcus pleaded, grabbing on his shirt.

"One minute," Snake whispered to him, throwing his finger up to his mouth.

Mesha was in the kitchen stirring up a pot of corn, when Snake crept up behind her, threw his hands around her waist, and gave her an affectionate kiss on the neck.

"I missed you," he whispered into her ear.

"Ummm hmmm," Mesha replied, with her neck tilted to the side, gently rubbing on Snake's face.

Snake planted a couple of more kisses on the side of her neck.

Lil' Marcus darted into the kitchen and interrupted the two lovebirds. "Owwweee, ya'll kissin'," he said, pointing at them and laughing.

Snake smiled. "Daddy was just showing Mommy how much he loves her. You want Daddy to kiss Mommy again?" he asked Lil' Marcus.

When Lil' Marcus shook his head yes, Mesha turned around, looked at Snake, and smiled.

"You heard my boy. He wanna see his daddy kiss his mommy," Snake said, pulling her to him and throwing his hands around her waist.

Mesha threw her hands around Snake's neck. The two silently stared into each other's eyes.

"I love you," Snake whispered.

"I love you, too, baby," Mesha replied.

The two glanced over at Lil' Marcus, who stood with his hands covering his mouth and waiting on them to kiss.

Snake smiled. "My lil' man waiting on us."

"Then let's give him what he wants," Mesha said, initiating the kiss.

"Owwweee," Lil' Marcus said as the two kissed, then he ran into the living room and hopped on the sofa.

Their lips stayed glued together for about two minutes.

"Damn, I doubt if that lasagna gonna be able to top that," Snake said, tasting his lips as he pulled away.

Mesha playfully hit him on the shoulder with one of her cooking gloves. "Boy, you so crazy!"

Snake slapped her on the butt. "You better hurry up and feed me if you plan on me feeding you some of this tonight," he said, pointing at his manhood.

Mesha waved him off, and then went back to attending to the meal.

Snake walked back into the living room, grabbed Lil' Marcus off the sofa, threw him on the floor, and started tickling him.

"Stop, Daddy!" Lil' Marcus pleaded, as he kicked and squirmed.

A tear almost fell from Mesha's eye, as she watched them play like two kids. She wished everyday could be like today, just the three of them. It had been a couple of weeks since Snake spent the night.

Lil' Marcus was growing up, and fast. He thought the world of his daddy, and Mesha was growing tired of making up excuses to him about why his father was rarely around. Lil' Marcus was reaching the age when he really needed his father around. He was going to be seven next week. Mesha wiped her eyes. All she wanted was for the three of them to be a family.

When Snake looked up and glanced into the kitchen, Mesha had her hand covering her mouth, crying.

"Hold on one minute, lil' man," Snake said, standing up and storming into the kitchen to investigate. He placed his hand on Mesha's shoulder. "What's wrong with you, boo?"

"Nothing...I just got a little choked up watching the two of you play, that's all. I just wish I could come home from work every day and see that," Mesha said, dropping her head and nervously fidgeting with her hands.

Snake decided now would be the perfect time to break the good news. He lifted up her chin. "What if I told you that I wanted you and Lil' Marcus to move into my house with me?"

"Are you serious?" Mesha asked, ecstatic.

"As serious as a heart attack. I'm leaving the game, boo!" Snake said.

Mesha's eyes lit up like light bulbs. "Stop playing, Marcus!" she said in disbelief.

Snake grabbed her hands, entwining his fingers with hers, and stared into her eyes. "All I got left is twenty bricks, and I'm finished," he said softly, kissing her on the forehead.

"Oh baby!" Mesha screamed, joyfully throwing her hands around his neck and jumping on him.

Snake spun her around one time, then sat her down. "There's more," he added.

She nervously threw her hands up to her mouth, as he pulled a diamond ring out of his pocket.

"This is just a little token of my love. We'll see how things work out when we move in together. Then, we'll get you the real ring!"

Mesha was speechless, as he slid the ring on her finger. "It's beautiful!" Mesha said, admiring the sparkle.

"It's a karat solitaire."

"Baby, I love you!" Mesha cheered, jumping up and down and fanning herself.

"I love you, too!" Snake said, and then jokingly slapped her on the butt. "Now go on in there and get that food ready for big daddy!"

"Yes, Big Daddy," Mesha cooed.

The two of them had been through a lot over the years. Mesha had been by his side ever since his days of nickel and dime hustling. Truthfully, she was the one who had kept him grounded, and that is why he loved her so much. On numerous occasions, she had helped him come back up by handing over her entire nursing paycheck for him to flip. That was why he could never leave her. Unfortunately, his other two baby mommas, Janette and Lisa, were both mistakes. Still, he loved and cared for his other two children just as much as he did for Lil' Marcus.

After dinner, Snake promised to read Lil' Marcus a bedtime story after he bathed and dressed in his pajamas. Mesha put her hand on her chest, shocked by Snake's offer to their son. She could not believe what she had just heard.

Snake placed his hand on hers. "I told you, this is the new me," he said.

Mesha gave him a questioning look. "What else does this new you have to offer?"

"Let's just say…it's a long story," Snake joked.

Mesha playfully slapped him on the shoulder. "Alright, I'ma see," she replied, as she walked the dirty dishes over to the sink.

Snake eased up behind her and threw his arm around her hips. Mesha welcomed him. He kissed her on the neck.

"I'm finna go check on my lil' man, then take me a shower. See you on the battlefield," he said, then smacked her on the ass and walked off.

Lil' Marcus was just slipping into his pajamas, when Snake knocked on the door.

"Can I come in, lil' man?" he asked, peeping inside the door.

"Come in, Daddy," Lil' Marcus said, walking over to his bookshelf and retrieving a book.

As Snake sat down on the edge of the bed, Lil' Marcus walked over and handed him a book.

Snake read the cover of the book. "Charlotte's Web?"

Lil Marcus nodded his head, as he hopped into his bed and snuggled up under the covers.

Snake sighed, opened the book, and started reading. By the time he made it to the fifth page, Lil' Marcus was out cold. Snake closed the book, pulled the covers up over Lil' Marcus's body, and kissed him on the forehead. He felt something. For the first time in his life, he actually felt like a father.

"Don't worry, lil' man, Daddy's turning over a whole new leaf," he silently whispered, then walked over, flicked off the light, and disappeared out of the room.

* * * * *

Mesha was just hopping out of the shower, when he walked into the bedroom. Snake just stood and admired her flawless, 34-22-36, coca-cola bottle frame, as she dried off her long, silky hair. She was a 5'10", 145-pound stallion. She was the only baby momma who he truly loved. Truthfully, there was not even supposed to have been any others. Today's little family day had served Snake well. Today, he got a dose of reality. He had been ripping and running in the streets so much that he never realized that everything a man could ever want he already had. He had it all: money, a house, materialistic items, and a family that loved him.

"Listen, boo, I'm finna go hop in this shower...and when I come out, I wanna see you laying in the bed just the way you came into this world," Snake said.

Mesha smiled. "I'll see what I can do."

Snake winked at her, then disappeared into the bathroom.

Mesha freshened up by spraying on a couple sprays of Red perfume. Then, she walked into the kitchen and grabbed two wine glasses from off of the bar. She opened the freezer, grabbed a bottle of wine, popped the cork, then filled the glasses and returned to the bedroom. Snake was still in the shower. She sat the wine glasses on the coasters on top of the nightstand, then romantically dimmed the lights and walked over to the stereo to throw on a tape. Keith Sweat's "Make It Last Forever" came blasting through the speakers before she made it back to the bed. Mesha eased her naked body up under the covers and waited on Snake to return from the shower.

Five minutes later, Snake's naked body appeared back in the bedroom. Mesha was patiently sitting up in the bed, awaiting him.

"Waiting on somebody?" he asked, as he dried off.

"Stop playing and hurry up! You know I just got off my period, and I'm horny!"

Snake tossed his towel to the side. "Say no more," he said, as he walked over to the bed and pulled back the covers. Just as ordered, Mesha was wearing the same thing she was wearing on November 15, 1965...not a damn thing.

Snake flicked off the lights and hopped into bed. A couple seconds later, all you heard was, "Ummmmm, Dadddyyy!"

CHAPTER THIRTY-FIVE

Snake was awakened at six o'clock the next morning by the automatic "time to get money" alarm clock inside of his head. He looked down at his perfectly chiseled chest, where Mesha's gorgeous face was peacefully resting. Her beauty was flawless. He could sit and watch her sleep for hours. He felt like cutting off his pager and confining himself to the bedroom, just the two of them, but he had business to handle. He affectionately kissed her on the forehead, and then slowly eased her head from off his chest and onto one of the oversized, plush pillows. She squirmed for a couple of seconds, adjusting to the pillow, before drifting back to sleep. Snake eased out of the king-sized bed, admiring Mesha's natural beauty one last time.

It was nights like last night that made Snake feel apologetic for having ever cheated on Mesha. His only gripe was that she did not perform oral sex on him, but her toe-curling sex game compensated for that. Snake made a mental note to try to do right, as he walked up out of his boxers and disappeared into the bathroom to shower.

Twenty minutes later, a revitalized Snake was sitting on the edge of the bed, lotioning up. Afterwards, he threw on his khaki, heavily starched Dickie suit, then laced up his wheat-colored Timberlands. He tucked his Colt .45 in his waistband, stared into the bedroom mirror for a couple of seconds to get his game face

259

on, then reached into his pockets and left Mesha five-hundred-dollars worth of shopping money for the day on the dresser.

Next, he walked into the hallway, went into his hiding spot inside of the utility closet, and grabbed eight bricks. He took the bricks back into the bedroom, walked into the bedroom closet, and removed a laundry basket. He then walked into the kitchen and grabbed the two bricks he had cooked for Mookie and Peanut last night from under the sink, wrapped everything up in the sheets, and threw clothes on top of it.

He walked over to Mesha, and after giving her a "sleeping beauty" kiss on the forehead, he picked up the laundry basket and headed towards the front door. Realizing he hadn't kissed his lil' man goodbye, he sat the laundry basket down on the floor and headed down the hallway to Lil' Marcus's room

Lil' Marcus was balled up in the fetal position, peacefully resting, when Snake tiptoed inside of the room. He stood over Lil' Marcus for a minute and just watched him sleep. Realizing he was pressed for time, he kissed him on the forehead, left him a fifty-dollar bill on the dresser, and once more headed towards the front door.

As Snake pulled out of the parking lot of Mesha's apartment complex, he felt like a devoted family man heading to work. He had a long day ahead of him. The streets were all dried up, and he had just spoken with the meteorologist for the local news and told him to inform the city that there was a 100% chance of snow.

Traveling southbound on 34th Street, heading into town, Snake couldn't help but smile imagining what life was going to be like to come home every day to Mesha and Lil' Marcus. Getting back to business, Snake looked over his left shoulder, before hopping into the turning lane at the light on 38th Avenue North. He made a left turn, pulling into Burger King's parking lot and met Peanut and Mookie. He was surprised to see Mookie already parked in the lot. He pulled up next to him, hopped out of the car, and headed inside of the restaurant. Peanut and Mookie gave him a couple of minutes, and then headed inside. When the two entered, Snake was standing in line waiting to place his order. The two eased in line behind him.

"Ya'll left the doors unlocked, right?" Snake asked with his back turned to them.

"Yeah, they unlocked," Mookie said

"I'ma put three of 'em under the seat. I'll drop the rest of 'em off later on tonight," Snake said, next up to place his order

"What you want back off of 'em?" Mookie asked.

"Shit, what I paid for 'em...twenty!" Snake said, adding a little tax.

"Alright, that's straight!" Peanut replied in an excited voice.

Snake stepped up to the counter and placed his order. Five minutes later, he was walking out of the restaurant. When he reached the car, he sat his breakfast on the seat, reached into the laundry basket in the backseat, and grabbed the work for Peanut and Mookie. He wrapped it up in a jogging suit, then opened Mookie's door and slid the work up under the seat. He walked back over to his car, removed the laundry basket from out of the backseat, and threw it in the trunk. He observantly surveyed the area, before hopping back inside of the car.

Mookie and Peanut were just coming out of the restaurant when Snake was backing out. Snake gave them the nod, then blew the horn and pulled off.

"I hope these broads ready," he said to himself as he cruised down 38th Avenue North.

After traveling a couple of blocks, and making a couple of turns, he pulled into the driveway of the home that Nadine and Leslie shared. He honked his horn, and surprisingly, the girls were ready. Leslie was the first to come prancing out of the house, with her Gucci purse around her shoulder and a cute brown summer dress on. Nadine was standing on the front porch locking up the house.

"What's up, yo!" Leslie said in her heavy New York accent, as she hopped in the front seat.

Snake looked over and admired her well-toned, butter pecan legs. She was an explosive 50/50 combination of one shot of Puerto Rican rum and one shot of black coffee. She stood 5'9" whenever she wore those sexy ass heels. Snake loved hearing her talk dirty, especially whenever he fucked her.

Nadine rolled her eyes at Leslie, as she disturbingly walked over and hopped in the backseat. She was the forbidden fruit. She came from a wealthy California family, and never spent a day of her life in a public school. After graduation, she moved out on her own when her and her close-mind parents could not see eye to eye on her decision to pursue a career as an international model, instead of attending Harvard. Nadine had Brooke Shields in her prime beauty and stood six feet tall, which was rather tall for a woman. Not only was she drop-dead gorgeous, she had a banging body that said her career would be promising.

"What we smoking on?" Nadine asked, in a trying to be black tone, while leaning her head in the front seat. Snake and Leslie looked at each other and started laughing.

"What?" Nadine asked, not seeing what was so funny.

"It's too much shit in the trunk to be smoking!" Snake said, turning serious.

Nadine sat back in her seat and folded her arms, with a slight pout.

Leslie turned around and stuck her head in the backseat. "Just chill out, yo. We gonna smoke!"

Nadine fanned her off.

* * * * *

Thirty minutes later, Snake pulled into the garage of his new stash house in Tampa.

"Can we take these blindfolds off now?" the girls asked as they listened to the garage door descend.

"Yeah, ya'll straight!" Snake said, hopping out of the car and making his way to the trunk.

The girls took off their blindfolds. "Yo, B! I don't know why you don't trust us!" Leslie pouted, as she exited the car.

"Cause...I don't trust my muthafuckin' self!" Snake replied, slamming the trunk of his Honda and walking towards the garage door with the laundry basket in his hand. Once they were inside the house, Snake ordered, "Ya'll know what to do," then walked down the hallway to one of the bedrooms.

The minute he walked into the bedroom, he sat the laundry basket on the bed and unrolled the sheets that contained the bricks. He walked into the closet, grabbed his scale, then placed the bricks and the scale inside the laundry basket and headed back into the living room.

Just as ordered, the girls were standing over by the stereo system, thumbing through records, with nothing but their bra and panty sets on.

As Snake admired their backsides, he felt grateful he had attended that bourgeois Christmas party his financial advisor, Nick, had begged him to attend, which is where he met the two women.

That night, the girls vaguely left the party with Snake. They cruised the city, and after a couple of joints and drinks, the three found themselves waking up the next morning in a hotel suite at the Don Caesar on St. Pete Beach. That weekend, the three performed a demonstration that could have landed them roles in the porn business. To his surprise, the girls were not as square as he had anticipated. Both girls drank, smoked, and had sociable snorting habits. After a couple of weeks of tests, and feeling them out, Snake offered them a job, which they willingly accepted. He enjoyed their entertaining company, walking around the house in their bra and panty set, while bagging up dope. What he really loved was whenever he felt the urge neither girl had a problem continuing to work, while the other performed sexual tasks. For Snake, it was like killing two birds with one stone.

By noon, Snake was seated behind the dining room table dicing up rocks, with enough dope on the table to put a smile on every crackhead in the county's face. The table was like an assembly line. Snake diced, while the girls carefully counted off and bagged the ten kilos.

By one o'clock, the girls had the kitchen spotless, and everything was bagged up. While the girls were cleaning, Snake had made all of the necessary phone calls to line up his day. After he dropped the girls off, he had appointments to meet with Katrice, Candice, and Veronica. The three were girls he frequently used to drop off packages and pick up money. Five of the ten kilos were already accounted for. Two were for Mookie and Peanut, and the other three were for his workers.

"Here ya'll go!" Snake said, handing each girl a hundred and fifty dollars and their own personal eight ball.

"Appreciate it, yo!" Leslie said, thinking about the new pair of kicks she wanted.

Snake grabbed his oversized duffle bag, flicked off the lights, then the three of them headed towards the garage.

After dropping the girls off, Snake pulled into the parking lot of Winn Dixie and circled it in search of Katrice's Toyota Tercel. He found her. He shook his head when he pulled up next to her.

"This fat motherfucker knows she dead wrong! She knows she need to stop being cheap and buy a bigger car," he said.

Katrice wobbled her stout body out of the car and hopped in the car with Snake. Snake backed out of the parking space, and then circled the block.

Katrice reached under her dress and pulled out a bag of money. "Here!" she said.

"Damn, Katrice, I couldn't even tell you had that shit on you!" Snake joked, while placing the money in a Dillard's bag in the backseat.

"Funny," Katrice said, while rolling her eyes and reminding herself to go on a diet.

He loved cracking fat jokes at Katrice. At 5'7" and a whopping 260 pounds, Katrice was a big woman. Snake had been using her for pick up and deliveries for a little over three years. She was a hustler. When her petty-hustling boyfriend, Al, was hauled off to serve a five-year bid, all he left her and their four kids was a hundred dollars worth of food stamps, a hundred-dollar bill, and a pager. Katrice cursed him for days and thought that the pager was useless, until one day, it just kept vibrating and annoyingly sounding off back to back and she curiously called one of the numbers back. Turns out, Al had some decent, loyal customers. After Katrice explained who she was, she stepped right into Al's shoes. She took the hundred dollars, rushed to the projects, copped ten rocks, and started serving Al's clientele. One day after watching Katrice make six to seven trips back and forth to the projects, Snake pulled her to the side to see where her head was. Snake saw ambition in her eyes, and after hearing her story, he offered her a job. Now, Katrice lives in Lakewood Estates, buys a kilo a month, and grinds it out in between her full-time nursing job.

"How much is in the bag?" Snake asked.

"It's thirty thousand. I counted it myself," Katrice said.

"You know that I'm leaving the game, right?"

"Naw, I didn't know!" Katrice replied, surprised.

"Yeah, I'm finna do the family thang," Snake said with a warm smile.

Katrice dropped her head, nervously fiddling with her fingers. "You know, I should stop, too. These years have been good to me. I can't complain. It's just that the money be coming in so fast, you become addicted," Katrice said, shaking her head.

"Tell me about it!" Snake said, as the two of them shared a laugh. "Listen, I said that this was my last run, but I still got a couple of bricks left in case you wanna get one."

"Hold one for me. After this one, that's it!" Katrice declared.

"What's up with ole' Al?" Snake asked.

"Fuck him! He left my babies and me out here for dead! I sent him them lil' hundred dollars he left behind for us, some pictures of the new house, and told him don't call!" Katrice said, laughing.

"That's cold!" Snake said laughing. Then he reached into the backseat and handed Katrice a Ziploc bag full of rocks. "Tell them niggas I want thirty, but you just bring me back twenty-eight."

"Okay," Katrice said, then sucked in her stomach and made the bag disappear.

Snake shook his head. "I can't even see that shit on her," he mumbled to himself.

Snake pulled up behind Katrice's car and she hopped out.

"I'll holla at you when I got that!" Katrice said.

Snake honked the horn, then headed to meet Veronica.

* * * * *

Veronica was sitting in the parking lot of Maximo Plaza, impatiently tapping her fingers on the steering wheel, when Snake pulled up next to her smiling. He hopped out of the car with a duffle bag in his right hand, and Dillard and Champ's bags in his left. Veronica hopped out of the car and popped the trunk.

"Thank you, boo!" Snake said, dropping the duffle bag and Dillard's bag in the trunk, and keeping the Champ's bag.

The two kissed, then smoothly switched keys and changed cars.

Snake hopped inside of Veronica's Maxima, adjusted the seat, and let down the window. Veronica let down the window in Snake's Honda.

"It's under the seat. Tell them niggas I want thirty-six. Your two grand in the glove compartment," Snake yelled over to her.

"Look in that laundry basket in the trunk. It's thirty-six. I counted it myself!" Veronica said. "And no them clothes ain't dirty!" she yelled over to him, smiling.

"Alright, I'll be through there tonight," Snake said.

"Business or pleasure?" Veronica asked seductively.

Snake smiled. "We'll see when I get there," he replied, then pulled off.

* * * * *

Fifteen minutes later, Snake pulled into the parking lot of Tyrone Square Mall. After parking, he grabbed the Champ's bag from off the passenger seat, walked through the mall's doors, and headed straight towards Champ's.

Candice sarcastically looked at her watch when Snake walked inside the store. She was sitting on the bench, trying on a pair of all-white British Knights.

"Returning something, sir?" a nosey sales clerk asked.

"Naw, I just brought these shoes yesterday, and I'm tryna find an outfit to match," Snake said, trying to brush off the salesman.

"What color are you looking for, sir?" the persistent sales clerk asked.

Snake spun around. "Listen, man, I'm straight!" he yelled, agitated.

The salesman defensively threw up both hands. "Sorry!" he said, then nervously walked over and helped another customer.

Snake walked over and sat on the bench, with his back turned to Candice, then cunningly sat his bag on the ground.

Snake held up a pair of all-white Fila's from off the display. "Hey, yo!" he said, getting a different sales clerk's attention. "Let me get these in a size twelve!" he requested, while Candice switched bags with him. "Tell them niggas I want thirty!" Snake mumbled.

"Okay," Candice said. "It's fifteen in each of them boxes."

When the sales clerk returned with the tennis shoes, Snake stood up, grabbed his bag, and followed him to the counter to make his purchase.

* * * * *

Meanwhile, back in the city, Katrice was pulling up to one of Snake's traps on 9th Street.

"Sir, we have a visual on a black Toyota Tercel that just pulled up," Agent Walsh said into his mic, while sitting inside of an undercover van parked across the street.

"Hold tight," Agent Bradshaw responded into his mic.

When Katrice casually stepped out of the car, it seemed like the car let out a sigh of relief. She pulled her dress out of the crack of her butt, and then calmly headed up the sidewalk to the apartment.

"Sir," Agent Walsh said into his mic, as he watched Katrice disappear inside of the apartment.

"Copy," Agent Bradshaw replied.

"The lady doesn't seem to have anything in her possession, sir?" Walsh said.

"Maybe she's not who we're looking for. See if she comes out with anything. She may just be one of the guy's inside girl," Bradshaw said.

"Copy, sir," Walsh said, then sat tight.

Fifteen minutes later, Katrice re-appeared, wobbled down the sidewalk, hopped back into the car, and pulled off.

"Negative, sir," Walsh said into the mic, as he watched Katrice disappear down the road.

"Dammit!" Agent Bradshaw shouted, hitting his hand on the steering wheel, as he headed into town in his cruiser.

Veronica pulled in front of Snake's trap, across 34th Street, and parked. She threw her keys in her purse and opened her door. She reached over, grabbed the three McDonald's bags off the passenger seat and the cup holder with the drinks, and then exited the car. She pushed the door closed with her hip and headed up the sidewalk.

"Sir," Agent Watts said into his mic.

"Go ahead, Watts," Agent Bradshaw replied.

"A lady in a Honda Accord just pulled up."

"Does she have anything?" Bradshaw asked.

"10-4, sir?" Watts said.

Agent Bradshaw got excited. "What is it?"

"It looks like she's bringing somebody lunch or something."

"Shit!" Agent Bradshaw said to himself. "Watts, tell me if she come out with anything!"

"Copy, sir!"

As Agent Bradshaw cruised into town, he was beginning to grow agitated. He was en route to the John Knox building so he and Agent Roberts could conduct surveillance on the projects. He was beginning to wonder just how valid his informants' information was.

"All units just hold tight and keep your eyes open," Bradshaw said into his walkie-talkie, as he turned off the interstate on the 5th Avenue North exit.

After thirty minutes had passed, all of the agents were still in position. Agent Walsh sat up in his seat. He glanced over at the apartment and noticed a tremendous amount of activity. Crackheads were walking up the street, cheerfully whistling with their hands in their pockets. The black clouds over the city had disappeared, replaced with sunlight. The flowers started to bloom, bottles of champagne were being popped, women made hair appointments; dope was back on the streets.

"Walsh to Bradshaw," Walsh said into his mic.

"Go ahead, Walsh," Bradshaw replied.

"Sir, what's your 10-20?" Walsh asked.

"Conducting surveillance on the projects. What is it?"

"Sir, it seems like an enormous amount of traffic has picked up over here," Walsh stated nervously.

"What kind of traffic?" Bradshaw asked.

"Well, sir...I guess...crackheads."

"That's impossible!" Bradshaw screamed. "Haven't you guys been monitoring the block?"

"Yes, sir," Walsh retorted.

"Then how the hell could the drugs have gotten delivered?" Bradshaw asked, screaming at the top of his lungs.

"The only visitor was-"

"Who, Walsh?" Bradshaw screamed, his veins popping out of the side of his neck, while he restlessly paced the rooftop. "When did the traffic pick up?"

Walsh eased down in his seat. There was a lump in his throat. He swallowed. "After the heavyset lady left," he answered in a pitiful voice, knowing that his ass was grass.

"Son-of-a-bitch!" Bradshaw cursed. "Watts, come in," he said, sweeping his hand over his hair.

"This is Watts, sir. Go ahead."

"Watts, has traffic picked up over there?" Bradshaw asked.

"Matter of fact, sir, I was waiting for Walsh to finish so I could call you myself," Watts said.

"Answer my fucking question!" Bradshaw shouted, staring at the walkie-talkie.

"Yes, sir," he replied.

"Got dammit! When, Watts?"

"When the lady in the Honda left, sir."

"Shit!" Agent Bradshaw said, as his face turned fire engine red and steam evaporated off his head. "Code red! Code red! All systems move in. Move in, got dammit!" Bradshaw ordered.

CHAPTER THIRTY-SIX

After running a couple of errands, Snake pulled into the projects, parked at Goldie's bus stop, and waited on him. He scooted down in the seat, gathering his thoughts.

Five minutes later, the bus arrived and came to a screeching halt. Snake sat up his seat and smiled when Goldie exited, decked out in a pair of white Levi's, a white and green Polo, and a pair of matching white and green Fila's. Snake honked the horn a couple of times to get his attention.

Goldie kneeled down and tried to make out the driver of the Black Maxima. When Snake honked the horn again, he cautiously walked towards the unfamiliar car. It was not until he got a little closer when he realized Snake was the driver.

"What's up, nigga?"Goldie said, smiling as he threw his hands in the air.

Snake smiled, and then unlocked the door for him.

Goldie hopped in, threw his bookbag in the backseat, and scanned the interior. "Who shit you driving?" Goldie asked.

"This one of my lil' friends shit," Snake said, then started up the car and pulled off.

"Where we going?" Goldie anxiously asked as he turned around in his seat.

Snake smirked. "Nigga, just sit tight," he said, as he turned up the volume on the tape deck and headed towards his destination.

Fifteen minutes later, Snake pulled in front of Wilson's Carpentry Shop and parked.

"You want me to wait in the car?" Goldie asked.

"Naw, come in," Snake replied, as he exited the car.

When they entered the shop, Mr. Wilson was helping another customer.

"Hey! Snake, how are you?" Mr. Wilson asked.

"I'm doing alright," Snake said, making his way over to Mr. Wilson and shaking his hand. "Is it ready?"

Mr. Wilson gave him a warm smile. "Follow me," he instructed, and then led them down a long hallway to his workshop. "Here we go!" Mr. Wilson said, snatching the covers off the custom-made dresser.

Snake observantly walked around the dresser and nodded his head in approval. He looked over at Mr. Wilson and smiled. Mr. Wilson nodded.

Goldie was lost. He could not figure out why in the hell Snake was so excited about a damn dresser.

"Does it work just like mine?" Snake asked.

"Yes, but the compartment is a little bit smaller," Mr. Wilson retorted.

"Yo, Goldie! Come over here for a minute!" Snake said.

"What's up?" Goldie asked, walking over.

Snake threw his hand on his shoulder. "I had this dresser custom-made for you," he said.

Goldie managed a fake smile, and Snake noticed the boggled look on his face.

"Nigga, this ain't no ordinary dresser! This got a secret compartment!" Snake said.

Goldie's eyes lit up. "You mean like a safe?" he asked, ecstatic.

"Exactly!" Snake said. "Mr. Wilson, show him how it works."

Mr. Wilson graciously walked over to the dresser and worked his magic, opening the safe.

"Oh shit!" Goldie said, throwing his fist up to his mouth.

"Tight, huh?"Snake asked, nodding his head.

"Hell yeah! Tell him to do that shit again!" Goldie said.

Mr. Wilson threw up his index finger. "Watch very closely. I'm gonna walk you through it real slow." Goldie watched attentively as Mr. Wilson slowly preformed each step. "There," Mr. Wilson said, once the secret compartment popped open. "Think you got it?" he asked Goldie. Goldie nodded his head.

"Come on over and try it yourself," Mr. Wilson said, with a warm smile. He stepped back and motioned with his hand. "Go ahead. Try it!"

Goldie looked over at Snake and smiled, then kneeled down on his knees and went into action. "Now that's what I'm talking about!" He cheered a couple of seconds later, nodding his head in approval after successfully opening the secret compartment.

Snake nodded his head and smiled. "Put it on the dolly, Mr. Wilson. I'ma pull around to the back," Snake told him, as he headed towards the door. Snake paused. "Oh yeah, I almost forgot. What I owe you?" he asked Mr. Wilson, reaching into his pockets.

"The balance is four hundred and sixty dollars," Mr. Wilson replied.

Snake generously peeled off five hundred dollar bills and handed them to Mr. Wilson. "Appreciate it!" he said.

"No problem," Mr. Wilson said, stuffing the crisp hundred dollar bills in his pockets. "I'll meet you around back," he told Snake.

"Alright, Mr. Wilson. Come on, Goldie," Snake said.

Goldie stole one last look at his beauty, and then caught up with Snake.

The minute Snake hopped into the car, his pager sounded. He looked at the number. *Damn, I wonder why the fuck Katrina paging me with 9-1-1 behind her number,* he wondered as he started up the car.

His pager sounded again. "What the fuck? This shit is crazy as fuck!" Snake said, observing Veronica's number with 9-1-1 also behind it.

"What's wrong?" Goldie asked, hopping into the car and closing the door.

Snake was delusional. He was trying to figure out what the fuck was going on.

Mr. Wilson was standing at the back door with the dresser on the dolly when Snake pulled around. "Where you want it?" he asked Snake.

"Man, just throw that shit in the trunk!" Snake said with an attitude.

Goldie looked at him and sensed something was wrong.

Snake's pager sounded again, and again, then again. "Fuck!" Snake shouted, as he furiously hit his hand on the steering wheel. He stuck his head out of the window. "Mr. Wilson, just tie that shit up! I gotta go!"

After tying down the dresser in the trunk, Mr. Wilson slapped the car to let Snake know he was finished, and Snake sped off.

As Snake drove, searching for a payphone, his pager repeatedly sounded off. The minute he found a payphone, he recklessly pulled over and hopped out of the car like a madman. He rushed into the phone booth, inserted a quarter into the payphone, and dialed Katrice's number. He nervously tapped his fingers on the payphone while the phone rang.

Katrice answered on the fourth ring.

"Yeah, what's up?" Snake asked, already having a good idea of what was going on.

"They just hit the spot on 9th Street!" she said in a shaky voice.

"What? Who? The green team?" Snake asked.

"Unnhh Unnhh, the feds!" Katrice said.

"The feds?" Snake asked in disbelief.

"Yeah! Snake, they got the whole block roped off!"

Snake slapped himself on the forehead. "Who they got?"

"They got everybody! Tony and Rick ran, but they caught them over by Quickie's. I had just left, too!" Katrice said.

"Shit!" Snake cursed, as his pager sounded again. He looked at the number. It was Veronica paging him for the tenth time.

"Listen, Katrice, just find out everything that happened and call Scotty and see how much them niggas' bonds gonna be. I'm tryna get them niggas out by tonight, so call me when you know how much it's gonna cost."

"Alright, be safe," Katrice said.

"I'm cool," Snake said, then hung up the phone, pulled out another quarter, and dialed Veronica's number.

"Hello?" Veronica answered in an anxious voice.

"Let me guess...they hit the spot," Snake said in a pitiful voice.

"How you know?" Veronica asked.

"Because they hit the spot on 9th Street, too!" Snake said.

"Oh no!" Veronica said in a sympathetic voice. "What are you gonna do?"

Snake massaged his forehead. "Right now...I don't even know."

"What can I do to help?" she asked.

"Listen, I need you to go and grab me a rental car, nothing fancy. I'm finna dip out-of-town for a lil' minute until this shit blow over!"

"You alright?" Veronica asked.

"I'm straight," Snake lied.

"You know...I got some sick time I can use if you need some company," Veronica offered.

"I'ma be alright. Just call me when you got the rental," Snake said.

"Alright, be careful, baby," Veronica said sympathetically.

"Alright," Snake said, and then furiously hung up the phone.

He pulled out another quarter; then paged Peanut with the emergency code to meet him at the park.

Goldie observantly read Snake's body language as he headed towards the car. It was visible that the information he had received was bad news.

Snake drove all the way to the projects in total silence, gathering his thoughts. Goldie periodically glanced over at him while he drove. Snake nervously tapped his fingers on the steering wheel, wondering what had gone wrong in his operation.

"You alright?" Goldie sympathetically asked.

"Yeah...shit just real fucked up," Snake replied, as he pulled in front of Goldie's apartment.

The two hopped out of the car and made their way to the trunk.

"Did you lose a lot of money?" Goldie asked.

"Yeah, I lost a lot of money," Snake said, as he untied the string on the trunk.

"Damn," Goldie said compassionately, while shaking his head.

"Help me with this," Snake said, referring to the dresser.

The two lifted the dresser out of the trunk and sat it on the ground.

Snake closed the trunk. "Let's take it to your porch," he instructed, taking the bulk of the weight by lifting the bottom of the dresser.

When the two reached the porch, Snake dropped his end on the ground. "Hold up, I got something else for you," he said with a smile, as he shot back to the car.

Goldie pulled out his keys and unlocked the door. Snake returned with a Champ's bag, handing it to Goldie.

"What's this?" Goldie curiously asked.

"It's a half."

"A half of what?" Goldie asked.

"A half a brick."

Goldie's eyes lit up. This was some big-boy shit. "What I owe you?" he asked.

Snake smiled. "Just give me eight grand."

"It's already cooked?" Goldie asked.

Snake laughed. "Yeah, all you gotta do is just cut it up like we always do. You rollin' with the big boys now," Snake said, patting him on the back. "But, listen...shit real fucked up right now and I'm finna disappear for a minute. They hit two of my spots today," Snake said, biting his lip and shaking his head.

"Are you talking about the one on 9th Street and the one across 34th?" Snake nodded his head in response. "Damn! You think they gonna hit the projects?" Goldie asked, hitting Snake with a dose of reality.

"Shit!" Snake cursed. "Listen, let's hurry up and put this dresser inside of the house."

Once they managed to get the dresser up the stairs and into Goldie's room, Goldie snatched the linens off his bed, stuck his hand into the hole in his mattress, and grabbed eight thousand dollar stacks, handing them to Snake. "Here you go!" he said with a smile.

Snake took the money, shook his head, and laughed.

"I got a couple more grand if you need it," Goldie offered.

Snake was touched. He waved him off. "Naw, I'm straight, lil' man. Listen, I gotta run. Come let me out," Snake said, stuffing the money in his pocket.

Goldie escorted him downstairs, and the two paused at the front door.

"Listen, I gotta lay low for a minute, lil' man," Snake told Goldie, placing his hand on his shoulder.

"You mean I ain't gonna see you for a while?" Goldie asked in a pitiful voice.

Snake rubbed him on the head, and then smiled. "It's only until this shit blows over. Don't worry, I'ma be calling and checking on you."

Goldie smiled. "Alright, man, be safe," he said, giving Snake a warm hug.

Snake was touched. He fought to hold back his tears as they embraced. "I love you, lil' man," Snake said, squeezing him a little tighter.

"I love you, too!" Goldie added.

"Listen, I gotta go met Peanut and them," Snake said, quickly wiping a tear before it became visible. "Make sure you take that money out of that bootleg-ass hiding spot and put that dope in the stash spot," Snake joked.

"Alright," Goldie laughed.

Snake then disappeared out of the front door.

Goldie stood at the door, waving him goodbye before he pulled off. Then he closed the door and energetically shot upstairs.

CHAPTER THIRTY-SEVEN

Snake instantly caught an attitude when he pulled up to the projects and Mookie and Peanut were nowhere to be found. He checked his watch. It was 5:30 p.m.

"Damn, I can't depend on these niggas for shit!"Snake cursed, as he irritably stepped out of the car and scanned the area.

"There go our man!" Andre said, slipping his clip inside of his Tech-9.

"I'm ready, cuz!" Robert said, using his bandana to stick his clip into his Uzi.

The two were secretly parked up the street in a GTE van, staking out the projects. They had cleverly kidnapped a GTE worker, and were currently holding him hostage while they used his van.

The two watched as Snake nervously paced the sidewalk.

"I wonder what he's so jittery about," Andre said.

"Maybe that nigga knows he's about to die," Robert joked.

Andre pointed his finger at Robert. "Only if it's necessary! Remember, we're in it for the money!" Andre reminded him.

"Yeah...but if that nigga even look like he wanna buck, I ain't gonna hesitate to bust a cap in his ass!"Robert said.

Ironically, Andre and Robert were not the only ones watching Snake. Agent Bradshaw had a jovial smile on his face, as he stared through his high-powered binoculars from the rooftop of the John Knoxx building.

"I got you now, you egotistical son-of-a-bitch! Nervous, aren't you?" Agent Bradshaw said, as he observantly watched Snake nervously pacing the sidewalk. "Attention all units, stand by," Bradshaw said into his walkie-talkie.

A couple of minutes later, Mookie pulled up. Gritting his teeth, Snake gave Mookie and Peanut the look of death. It pissed him off even more when he saw the three girls from out of town sitting in Mookie's backseat.

"What's up?" Peanut said in a light mumble, as he and Mookie cautiously approached Snake.

"Nigga, I'm around here losing muthafuckin' money left and right while ya'll muthafuckin' niggas 'round here joyriding with some bitches!" Snake spat.

"We was just-" Peanut said.

"I don't give a fuck what ya'll was doing! I paged ya'll niggas thirty muthafuckin' minutes ago!" Snake shouted, his veins popping in his neck.

"Well, what's up?" Peanut asked.

"Nigga, they hit both of the muthafuckin' spots! That's what the fuck is up!" Snake shouted.

"What?" Mookie asked in disbelief.

"You heard me, nigga! They hit both spots! I'm outta 'bout eighty muthafuckin' grand, not to mention what it's gonna cost to bail all of them niggas out!"

"Damn!" Peanut said, nervously rubbing on his head.

"You think they gonna hit the projects?" Mookie asked.

"Shit...if they on to me, hell yeah!" Snake replied, nervously scanning the area.

"Them motherfuckers probably watching us now!" Peanut said.

"Shit! So what you want us to do?" Mookie asked.

"I want ya'll to lay low for a couple of days until this shit blows over. I'm flexing out of town for a lil' minute. I'ma send Mesha to grab that money from ya'll when ya'll finish. Get rid of those beepers. Give Mesha the new numbers, and I'll hit ya'll up with my new number."

"What about the other two bricks?" Peanut asked.

"I'ma get them to ya'll by tonight before I pull out," Snake said.

278

"Alright, playboy, be safe," Peanut said, as him and Mookie walked over and gave Snake farewell hugs.

* * * * *

Meanwhile, the girls were sitting in Mookie's backseat curiously scanning the area for Andre and Robert.

"Damn, Monica, where they at?" Pam asked.

"They said they were gonna be in a GTE van. There they go!" Monica said, spotting the GTE van parked up the street. Monica made eye contact with Andre.

Andre nodded his head, and then cranked up the van. "Show time, playboy!" he told Robert, as the two of them threw on their masks.

While Andre threw the van in drive and slowly crept up the street, the girls reached into their purses, pulled out their guns, and sat them on their laps.

Goldie was coming up the sidewalk, when he instinctively noticed a suspicious GTE van with two masked men slowly approaching the crew. The driver of the van stuck a Tech-9 out of the window, and took aim.

"Snake!" Goldie yelled.

Snake gave Goldie a dumbfounded look.

Peanut turned around. "Oh shit!" he yelled, as he took cover behind the church.

"Jack!" Mookie yelled, as he protectively pushed Snake out of the way and pulled out his .45.

Robert fired a couple of rounds, hitting Mookie in his upper torso.

"Ahhh!" Mookie yelled, as his body jerked with each bullet that entered his body.

"No!" Goldie yelled, running towards Snake and busting his 9mm, while Mookie's body fell to the ground.

Peanut let off five shots towards the van from behind the church building.

The girls hopped out of the car like Charlie's Angels. Monica carefully took aim, and then fired five shots towards Peanut.

"Ah shit! I'm hit!" Peanut yelled, as he grabbed his left shoulder and fell to the ground. "Fuck!" Peanut cursed.

Denise and Pam fired shots towards Snake and Goldie. Peanut could not figure out where all of the extra gunfire was coming from. It was not until he peeped around the side of the church and glanced over at Mookie's car when he realized the girls had set them up. Peanut gritted his teeth. "Dirty bitches!" he shouted with vengeance, while standing up and firing five shots, successfully hitting Monica and Pam in their upper torsos.

"Ahhh!" Denise frantically screamed, as she dropped her gun when she saw Monica and Pam's bodies hit the ground.

"Motherfuckers!" Snake yelled, charging from behind Veronica's Maxima and violently letting his Uzi rip.

Andre recklessly drove straight towards Snake, as the three men fearlessly exchanged gunfire.

Goldie took aim, and then skillfully shot out one of the van's tires.

"Jesus Christ! What's going on down there?" Agent Bradshaw blurted, observing all of the gunplay through his binoculars. Bradshaw frantically reached for his walkie-talkie. "All systems move in! Jesus Christ...all systems move in!"

"Oh shit!" Andre yelled, as he struggled to maintain control of the van and crashed into the church.

Fortunately, Peanut had managed to gather enough strength to move out of the way when he saw the out-of-control van coming towards him.

Snake anxiously rushed over to check on Mookie, who was lying in a puddle of blood and coughing up even more blood when Snake made it over to his body. Snake kneeled down. "No!" he yelled, shaking his head in disbelief as he lifted up Mookie's head. "Stay with me nigga!" Snake pleaded.

"Did...did...I get them niggas?" Mookie asked.

Snake bit his bottom lip. "You got 'em," he told him.

"Ughhhh! I told you I got your back," Mookie said.

Snake was touched. "Hold his head!" Snake instructed Goldie, as he furiously walked over to the van to finish off their assailants.

Denise was nervously hiding behind Mookie's car. She checked Monica and Pam's pulses. They both were gone. She panicked. Their plan had gone sour. Denise slowly peeped around the car. A young boy was holding Mookie's bloody body in his hands. Snake was nowhere in sight.

Denise knew she had to make it to Goodyear, where Richie was waiting with the getaway van. She slowly opened the passenger door. Today was her lucky day. The keys were still inside of the ignition. She quickly hopped behind the steering wheel, started up the car, and recklessly backed up.

The crowd that had just recently gathered moved out of the way.

"Where you think you going, bitch?" Goldie yelled, while resting Mookie's head on the concrete and firing five shots through the windshield.

"Ahh!" Denise yelled, as glass splattered in her eyes and she lost control of the car, crashing into a telephone pole.

"Shit!" Goldie yelled, tossing his gun down the drain when he heard sirens rapidly approaching. "Yo, Snake! Po-Po on the way!" Goldie yelled.

Snake ignored him, as he cautiously walked along the side of the van with his Uzi leading the way. He opened the driver's door, and then snatched Andre's body out of the van. He checked Andre's pulse. He was dead.

Robert was on the other side of the van, nervously hiding with his gun glued to his chest. After the crash, he had managed to drag his body out and escape with only a broken shoulder. Robert peeped under the van and saw Snake's feet coming around the side. He moved towards the front, and that is when he made himself visible.

"Snake! Watch out!" Goldie shouted.

Robert swiftly hopped up from behind the van with his gun drawn. He and Snake irritably circled each other in a standoff.

"I should have known it was you motherfuckers!" Snake said.

"You brought this on yourself!" Robert shouted.

"You know that you're dead, right?" Snake said.

"Both of us got guns," Robert taunted.

A dozen police cars pulled up on the scene. "Put your weapons down!" the officers yelled with their guns drawn.

Snake observed all of the police cars, smirked, and said, "Yeah, but I ain't scared to die!"

Then he pulled the trigger. Robert's body jerked with the impact of each bullet. Amazingly, he managed to get off a couple of shots before his body fell to the ground.

"No!" Goldie yelled, as he watched Snake's body fall to the concrete.

Goldie disturbingly charged towards Snake's body. He lifted up Snake's head. He was coughing up blood.

"Stay with me, Snake! Please don't go!" Goldie sobbed, rocking his body back and forth in his arms.

Two paramedics rushed out of the ambulance. One attended to Robert, while the other came over to assist Snake.

"Sir, I'm gonna need you to let me get there," the paramedic told Goldie.

"This is my big brother! I'm not leaving his side!" Goldie declared.

Snake produced a smile on his face. He grabbed Goldie's hand and squeezed it.

The paramedic ripped open Snake's shirt. "We have a gunshot wound to the chest!" the paramedic yelled.

Snake's entire life started playing before his eyes like a movie. He had flashbacks of his childhood years, the day lil' Marcus was born, and the day he bought his first kilo from Sal.

"Gotta...get up," Snake said weakly.

"Snake...Snake, keep your eyes open!" Goldie pleaded, as he sobbed.

"Gauges! We're losing a lot of blood here!" the frustrated paramedic yelled.

Snake found enough strength to slide the ring that Sal had given him off his finger and onto Goldie's. "This will always help you," he said, then smiled and started coughing up blood.

"Ahh!" Snake cried, as the pain became unbearable.

"You gonna make it, man! You gonna make it!" Goldie sobbed.

Snake squeezed his hand. "Never...under...estimate...your... enemies," he said, then closed his eyes.

Goldie got lightheaded. "Do something! Do something, motherfucker!" he said, violently hitting the paramedic in the chest. "Motherfucker, do something!" Goldie sobbed, as it took three police officers to restrain his 145-pound frame.

"We lost him!" the paramedic sympathetically said, after he did everything he could do.

"No!" Goldie screamed at the top of his lungs.

CHAPTER THIRTY-EIGHT

Over five hundred gloomy faces occupied every seat in Mt. Zion Progressive, while another hundred or so stood in the back of the church. Everyone had come to pay their last respects.

Snake's body was peacefully resting in a baby blue casket, with 24-karat gold trimming, which he had picked out six months prior. Snake must have sensed death. For some reason, he had popped up at Creal Funeral Home and made his funeral arrangements. The funeral home did such an exceptional job with Snake's body that it looked like he was napping. Snake was decked out in a white Armani suit, with a baby blue silk shirt, and a white fedora with a baby blue band. His wrists and neck were draped with every extravagant piece of jewelry he owned. Over two hundred beautiful flower arrangements decoratively surrounded his casket.

"Marcus Robinson died too young," the preacher preached.

"Amen," the congregation agreed.

The preacher gave a quick sermon directed towards the young folks, and then went into the reading of Snake's eulogy, while the pianist played the organ.

Mesha tried to be as strong as she could, but she broke down. "Oh lord! Why? Oh lord, why?" she sobbed, as she distressingly charged Snake's casket.

A couple of ushers rushed to her side to comfort her.

"Why? Why?" Mesha cried, as she clung onto Snake's casket.

"Momma! Momma!" Lil' Marcus cried, as he protectively rushed to her side and wrapped his arms around her leg.

"Momma's gonna be alright," Mesha said, as she hugged him affectionately, and then wiped her nose. "Momma's gonna be alright," she repeated, while staring up at the light shining through the stain-glassed windows.

Mesha got lightheaded and her legs buckled. Two ushers quickly caught her before she hit the ground, and then helped her back to her seat.

The preacher respectfully gave her a couple of seconds to get herself together, and then proceeded with his sermon. Ten minutes later, he called the choir director to the stage, who motioned for everyone to stand, and then orchestrated the choir as they sang, "Precious Lord".

As the choir sang, everyone prepared to say their last goodbyes. The ushers motioned for the front row to come up and view the casket first. Peanut caringly threw his arm around Mesha and escorted her up. Janette and Lisa, Snake's other two baby mommas, just rolled their eyes at him and fell in line.

Mesha took baby steps as she approached the casket. "Why...why...why?" she sobbed, as she just stood over Snake's body. "I love you...I love you, baby!" she cried, as she wrapped her arms around him and planted kisses all over his face.

The ushers attempted to intervene, but Peanut waved them off.

"Why...why...why did you have to leave me, baby? We were supposed to get married!" Mesha sobbed, as she caressed her engagement ring.

There was not a dry eye in the church. Even the toughest of the toughest wiped away a few tears before anyone could notice they had fallen. Everyone was on their feet, waving their hands in the air, and rocking their body back and forth to the choir's hymn. The louder the tambourines rattled, the more the tears poured off everyone's faces.

After holding up the line for about ten minutes, the funeral home director walked over to Mesha, sympathetically placed his hand on her shoulder, then escorted her down the aisle and out to the limo.

Peanut just stood over Snake's body, not knowing what to feel. Yesterday he had said farewell to Mookie, and now he was saying it to Snake.

"Damn, two funerals in two damn days," he said, massaging his temples.

Peanut studied Snake's face. Part of him missed Snake, yet another part of him was glad to see him out of the way so he could pursue his plan of taking over the streets.

He sarcastically smirked. *You don't look so muthafuckin' tough now, nigga,* he thought to himself.

Peanut looked behind him at the large crowd of mourners waving their fan, then went theatrical and broke down crying.

"I'ma miss you, man!" he sobbed, while staring up at the ceiling and biting his bottom lip. After feeling like he had put on a star-studded performance, he patted Snake on the chest, threw up a peace sign, and walked off. Mysteriously, when he got halfway down the aisle, he tripped and fell dead on his face.

Everyone looked over to see if he was all right.

Embarrassed, Peanut swiftly hopped back on his feet and searched the ground to see what he had tripped over. There was not a visible piece of evidence around. Peanut was not a believer of superstition, or at least not until he looked over at Snake's casket and swore he saw him smirk. Peanut's eyes got as big as quarters, and he terrifyingly shot out of the church.

The rest of Snake's funeral was your typical black funeral. Janette and Lisa looked like they were competing for Oscars, the way they theatrically cried over Snake's casket. Their performances were compelling, the way each of them approached Snake's casket and lifted up their sons, allowing them one last opportunity to remember the man who had shared the role of bringing them into this world.

Goldie just sat all alone on the front row in disbelief. He was hoping all of this was a bad dream. His chest felt like he had a 16-inch dagger stuck in his heart. He was in a daze.

Goldie watched a woman he had never seen before theatrically fall out. One by one, females from all across town came up, wept over Snake's casket, and claimed to be his mistress.

After the last person in line paid their respects, Goldie stood and approached Snake's casket. He stared up at the ceiling, and then sighed.

"What I'ma do without you, man?" Goldie asked. "Man...I feel like a part of me is missing now," Goldie sobbed, as he wiped his nose. The tears began to pour like a thunderstorm. "Damn, man, what I'ma do." He broke down and leaned on Snake's casket to maintain his balance when his legs buckled.

He looked down at the ring on his finger, which let off a spooky glare. He frantically stepped back from the casket, startled. He quickly looked over at Snake and thought he was going crazy. Snake winked at him.

Goldie stood motionless for a minute, then closed his eyes and reminisced on all of the good times they shared. As the memories played through Goldie's head like a movie, he could feel Snake's presence in the church. He just held out his hands, tilted back his head, and smiled. After Goldie's revelation, he opened his eyes and smiled.

"I love you, man," he said, then kissed Snake on the forehead and stepped back.

The funeral director walked up to him and placed his hand on his shoulder. "I know this is hard for you, but we gotta go, son," he whispered into his ear.

Goldie stepped back up to Snake's casket and placed his hand on his chest. "You'll always be in my heart, man. Be easy, big brother...be easy," he said, then threw on his dark shades and exited the church.

While Goldie stood next to Mesha as they loaded Snake's casket into the hearse, Peanut approached them.

"You alright?" Peanut asked Mesha.

"I'm okay," she replied.

Goldie just gritted his teeth, as he balled up his fist and felt his blood start to boil. He could not figure out what it was, but he knew that Peanut was up to no good.

"What's up, Goldie?" Peanut said, acknowledging Goldie.

Goldie gave him a disgusted look. He faulted Peanut for Snake's death. Peanut had gone out like a coward and abandoned them in the line of fire.

"Goldie, let it go!" Mesha said, observing the look on his face.

Peanut and Goldie engaged in a stare-off.

Rhonda pulled up to the church, honked her horn, then stepped out of the car and waved her hands in the air to get Goldie's attention.

"I'ma ride with Rhonda to the burial site," he said, while kissing Mesha on the cheek and eyeing Peanut out of the corner of his eye.

Peanut opened the limo's door for Mesha.

Mesha gave Goldie a concerned look. "Let it go," she whispered, pointing her finger at him, then her and Lil' Marcus eased into the limo.

Peanut and Goldie were left staring each other down.

"Look, Goldie…we the only ones left. We need to squash this shit! We don't need to be acting like this," Peanut said.

"Nigga, I don't do cowards," Goldie said, then gave Peanut a disgusted look and headed over to Rhonda's car, leaving him standing there alone.

Ten minutes later, they were at Snake's final resting place. Goldie looked over at Peanut standing next to Mesha and his blood boiled. He wished it were Peanut lying in that casket and not Snake.

"Ashes to ashes…and dust to dust. As Marcus Robinson came into this world, may he depart," the preacher said, as Snake's casket was lowered into the ground.

One by one, everyone came over and gave Mesha grieving hugs.

"Listen, Mesha, I gotta go. You alright?" he asked after making his way through the crowd to her.

"I need to be asking you if you alright?" Mesha said, playfully punching him in the stomach.

"You know that was my nigga, and I'ma miss the hell out of him!" Just then, Rhonda walked over and wrapped her arms around Goldie. "Oh, Mesha, this is my girlfriend Rhonda," Goldie said.

"You have my condolences," Rhonda compassionately said, giving Mesha a hug.

"She's a little older than you," Mesha whispered to Goldie during the hug.

Goldie smiled. "Listen, Mesha, I'ma call and check on you tomorrow, okay?"

"Okay," Mesha said.

"Alright then, I'll see you tomorrow. Watch that nigga Peanut. He's up to something," Goldie added, as he walked off.

There was total silence when Rhonda and Goldie hopped inside of the car. Goldie reached into his coat pocket, pulled out a joint, and lit it. Rhonda just looked at him. Goldie took a couple of pulls, and then slowly exhaled smoke.

"Where we going?" Rhonda asked, as she started up the car.

Goldie reclined his seat all the way back, then exhaled more smoke. "Go to the liquor store. Tonight I'm finna get fucked up!" he said.

CHAPTER THIRTY-NINE

After Snake's funeral, the projects were never the same. It seemed like a dark cloud came and settled over the projects and never disappeared. Traffic slowed down drastically because all of the crackheads were scared to come into the projects and cop. With Snake gone, nobody was around to put a package in the crews' hands and none of them had prepared themselves for a rainy day. Desperate, the crew started snatching crackheads' money, jewelry, and anything else valuable they had in their possession.

Peanut and Goldie were the only two members of the crew who had stayed afloat.

Peanut was living his dream. Not only had he inherited the two bricks that Snake had fronted him and Mookie, he had also cunningly convinced Mesha that she needed to get rid of whatever Snake had stashed inside of her apartment. Just as planned, Mesha panicked when Peanut told her the feds could charge her with whatever they found inside of the house, and she quickly turned over all ten kilos to him. Peanut gratefully accepted the bricks and tricked Mesha into believing the bricks were only worth $100,000. He agreed to sell all ten and split the profit with her. Well, the truth of the matter was that there was a dope shortage in the city at the time, and Peanut made well over $350,000 off all twelve bricks.

In only a matter of two weeks, Peanut stepped right into Snake's shoes and transformed into a baller. After moving all twelve bricks, and giving Mesha her $50,000, Peanut decided to give himself a total makeover. That weekend he grabbed himself a rental car, and him and a big-booty red-bone he met at the club shot down to Miami for a shopping spree.

Peanut hit USA Flea Market and draped his neck with oversized necklaces, then decorated his fingers with rings. He even toured South Beach and ate at the finest eateries. He stopped by a jewelry store downtown and picked up a Presidential Rolex, then bounced around to different clothing stores and bought himself an entire new wardrobe. He was in such a good mood from the performance his lady friend put on last night that he even spent a few dollars on bangles and a couple of necklaces for her.

Peanut did not stop there. That Monday, when he made it back into town, he sold his caddy, then went out and copped himself a brand new "Big Boy" Benz. He tried to set up shop in the projects, but nobody wanted to fuck with him.

"Alright, ya'll niggas gonna need me before I need you!" Peanut arrogantly told the crew one day when he sped off.

* * * * *

Goldie was also maintaining. He went solo when the crew started snatching all the crackheads' money and selling "Slap Heads." He cleverly started hanging out at the front entrance of the projects to shortstop traffic. He successfully managed to serve all of the "Big Spenders" before they reached the park, then slid them his pager number. Goldie's plan worked. In only a matter of a couple of days, business on his pager nearly tripled.

* * * * *

Detective Ross finally retired, feeling relieved that an animal like Snake was off the streets. Him and his wife moved to Milwaukee and vowed to spend the rest of their lives traveling and enjoying each other's company.

Agent Bradshaw ended up stuck in between a rock and a hard spot. With election time around the corner, his superiors were breathing down his neck and the case of the century had just run into a dead-end.

"Fuck!" Agent Bradshaw yelled, as he violently slammed his fist on his desk.

"Sir, are you busy?" Agent Green asked, as she peeped in the door.

"No, what is it?" Bradshaw asked.

"I think I may have a lead, sir," Green said.

"What is it?" Bradshaw asked, sitting up attentively.

At twenty-six years old, Agent Green was the youngest, and the only African-American woman in Agent Bradshaw's unit. Her beauty was captivating, and any man who dared to stare into her green eyes was sure to become hypnotized.

Agent Green stepped inside. "Well...you know that today I was out in the field, working undercover on the Sanchez case, right?"

"Yeah, yeah, yeah...what happened," Bradshaw asked, gesturing for her to get to the point.

"Well, I was dressed in this tight-fitting mini-skirt, using the pay phone, when this guy in a brand-new Mercedes pulls up blasting his stereo, then starts flirting with me."

"Yeah, I'm listening," Bradshaw said, now on the edge of his seat.

"Well, this guy shows me a wad of money, and then starts bragging about what he can do for me. I was gonna brush him off, but then I glanced into the backseat of the car and saw this bookbag and all of these cooking utensils used for cooking crack. My intuition told me to walk a little closer to the car, and when I did, guess who the driver up under the baseball cap was?"

"Who?" Agent Bradshaw asked.

"Rasheed Thomas a.k.a Peanut," Green replied.

"You mean Snake's lieutenant?" Bradshaw asked, raising his eyebrows.

"Yeah! And word on the street is that all of a sudden he's ran into a shit-load of money, and is running around town throwing away money like it grows on trees," Green said.

Agent Bradshaw's face lit up. "So what happened?"

Agent Green smiled. "Well, I decided to test the waters and flirt back. I told him that I dibbled and dabbled here and there, and he gave me his number," Green said, holding up a piece of paper.

Agent Bradshaw ran from behind his desk and started planting kisses all over her face. "You're a lifesaver, Green. Jesus Christ you're a lifesaver!" Agent Bradshaw placed his hand on her shoulders. "We can salvage the case, Green!" he excitedly chanted with newfound hope. "Listen, Green, this is what I want you to do. I need you to call this guy, flirt with him a little, and see if you can get him over to your place for dinner."

"Got you, sir," Agent Green said, then took a deep breath before dialing the number.

The phone rang a couple of times. "Who dis?" Peanut answered on the fifth ring.

"What's up? This Precious. What you doing?"

Peanut anxiously sat up and motioned for Cindy, a crackhead who lived in a complex that he fronted his work, to stop sucking on his dick. Then he stood up and walked into the kitchen with his cellular. "Damn, what's up, baby girl?"

"Well, the reason why I called is because I wanted to ask you what you were doing later on tonight."

Peanut laughed. "Shit, I'm tryna be with you tonight."

Cindy rolled her eyes at him, then mumbled, "Motherfucker!" as she lit herself a Newport.

"Well then, how about dinner?" Precious asked.

Peanut was tickled. "Oh, so you gonna cook dinner for me tonight?"

"Yeah, what's your favorite dish?"

"Shit...steak, baked potatoes, corn...shit like that," Peanut replied.

"Alright then, steak it is! How does seven sound?"

"Shit, it sounds like a date," Peanut said. "Where at?"

"My place," Precious said.

"Hold up one minute. Let me find a pen so I can write down the address," Peanut said, searching through the drawers of Cindy's messy kitchen for a pen. He found one, and then scribbled on a piece of paper to see if it worked. "Damn!" he said, frustrated.

"What's the matter?" Precious asked.

"I'm just tryna find a damn pen that works," Peanut said. Once he found one, he said, "Okay, give me the address."

"Okay, the address is…"

* * * * *

An hour later, the surveillance team had the entire house bugged, and had already set up shop from their surveillance van two houses down.

Seven o'clock, Peanut pulled into the driveway of the safe house. He surveyed the bourgeois neighborhood, and then nodded his head in approval. "Ole' girl got her shit together," he said to himself. As he walked up the sidewalk, the smell of good old-fashioned home cooking tickled his nose. "Damn, smell like ole' girl can burn, too," he said, as he stepped up on the porch and rang the doorbell.

"I'm coming!" a voice that Peanut could come home to for the rest of his life yelled from inside of the house, then the front door opened.

Peanut's mouth dropped to the ground. "Damn!" he said, while examining Precious' body.

Precious blushed. "Come in."

Peanut stepped inside. "Damn, you ballin', ain't you?" he asked, as he plopped down on the extremely comfortable, maroon leather sofa, overwhelmed by how spacious and laid-out the crib was.

"Dinner will be ready in a few minutes," Precious said, as she disappeared into the kitchen. "Make yourself at home!" she yelled.

"So what you do?" Peanut yelled into the kitchen, while observing the immaculate surroundings.

"Dang, ain't we being nosey!"

"What, you use to mess with a dude that hustled and got locked up?" Peanut asked, as he walked into the kitchen.

Things were going just as planned. Precious ignored Peanut's comment and continued setting the table. "I don't just talk about my business."

"That's it," Agent Bradshaw said to himself from the surveillance van. "Reel him in, Green. Reel him in."

Peanut did not give up. "I'm just saying, maybe we can help each other."

"Listen, I invited you over here because I like you, not to discuss what I do, and not to discuss what you do." Precious said. "What do you want to drink?"

"Shit, I'm from the hood. You got some Kool-Aid?" Peanut asked.

Precious placed Peanut's plate in front of him, and then joined him at the table.

The two spent the rest of the night getting acquainted with one another. Precious continued to play hardball, acting like how she made a living was a sensitive issue.

By the end of the night, Peanut had tried to impress Precious so much by bragging about how much money he was making and how much dope he was supplying that Agent Bradshaw went through two tapes.

The two agreed to go on another date, and Peanut was sent home with a kiss on the cheek.

CHAPTER FORTY

For the next couple of days, Precious and Peanut were like each other's shadow. Peanut was falling for Precious. He loved the fact that she was one of those women who played hard to get. He felt like she was worth the wait, and he was up for the challenge.

"Who we waiting on?" Peanut asked, as he surveyed the parking lot of the Webb City Shopping Plaza.

Precious looked over at him and rolled her eyes. "Didn't you say you just wanted to chill with me today?"

Peanut defensively threw his hands in the air. "My bad! Damn, a nigga was just asking."

When Precious spotted Agent Walsh pulling into the shopping plaza, she reached into the glove compartment and pulled out a bag of rocks.

Peanut's eyes got as big as quarters. He laughed. "I know you ain't finna do what I think you finna do?"

Precious smirked. "Watch me!"

Agent Walsh pulled into the parking space next to them.

"I'll be right back," Precious said, as she grabbed her purse and hopped out of the car.

"Damn, this bitch a true hustler," Peanut said to himself, as he nosily watched Precious hop into the car and drop a couple of rocks into some dude's hand.

Meanwhile, inside of the car, Walsh and Green were hoping Peanut was taking the bait.

"You think he's buying it?" Walsh whispered.

"Trust me, he's watching us as we speak," Green mumbled. "Okay now, Walsh, I'm getting ready to go Hollywood, so just follow my lead."

"Gotcha," Walsh said.

Agent Green pointed her finger in Walsh's face, and then started talking loud enough for Peanut to hear her. "You're twenty muthafuckin' dollars short! You playing games with my muthafuckin' money?" Green asked, as she reached into her purse and pulled out her revolver.

Agent Walsh frantically held up his hands.

"Woooo! This bitch crazy!" Peanut said, nervously surveying the area.

Walsh played right along with Green, then nervously reached into his pocket and handed her a twenty-dollar bill.

Peanut was sitting inside of the car tripping. He calmed down, and then smiled. "That's just what I need, a gangster bitch!"

Green put her revolver back inside of her purse and whispered, "Good job, Walsh," as she eased out of the car. She went back Hollywood. "And don't you ever play with my muthafuckin' money like that again!" she said, as she slammed the door.

When she hopped back into the car with Peanut, he just stared at her as if she was a mad woman.

While breathing heavily, Precious ignored him and threw the remainder of the rocks inside of the glove compartment.

"Let me see them," Peanut said, nosily opening the glove compartment and taking the bag out. Precious tried to snatch the bag out of his hands, but she was unsuccessful. Peanut twirled the bag in his hands. "Where you get these lil'-ass shots from?"

Precious rolled her eyes at him. "What, you the police or something?" she asked, snatching the bag out of his hand and stuffing it back in the glove compartment.

"I'm saying...them some lil'-ass shots," he laughed.

"Well, they workable and my people ain't complaining!"

Peanut grabbed her hands. "Listen, won't you let me help you?"

"I don't need your help! I told you, I can take care of myself!" Precious said, while snatching her hands back.

"Listen, I don't know what kind of niggas you've dealt with in the past, but if a female is with me, I take care of her."

"I don't need any man to take care of me! My daddy taught me how to hustle before he died, and that's how I've been getting by! Besides, you niggas don't wanna see a bitch come up anyways! Ya'll just wanna keep selling us rocks, but ya'll ain't tryna sell us no weight!"

"Wait a minute now! What's all of this 'you niggas' shit?" Peanut asked. "Just because you had bad experiences with other niggas, don't put me in that category."

"I ain't stupid! I use to watch my daddy when he use to cook up his dope, I know how much extra you make," Precious said. "But niggas think they got all of the sense. They wanna sell you rocks, but they ain't gonna sell you no weight. I need to just learn how to cook my own damn dope," she mumbled.

Peanut stared into her green, hypnotic eyes. The more she fumed, the more it aroused him. Her drive, determination, and ambition made his dick get hard. It was then that he became determined to make her his girl.

"I'ma be alright," Precious said, as she started up the car.

Peanut caringly placed his hand on her lap. "You really tryna learn how to cook?"

"Look, let's just forget we had this conversation," Precious said, and then attempted to throw the car in reverse.

Peanut threw his hand on the gearshift. "I said is you tryna learn how to cook?" he asked with a little bass in his voice.

Precious gave him a crazy look, then sucked her teeth. "Yeah, I'm tryna learn."

Peanut nodded his head. "Swing by my house."

* * * * *

On the way to Peanut's apartment, Peanut wanted to be a showoff, so he had Precious swing by the projects to pick up some money.

"Pull over by that green garbage can," Peanut instructed.

Precious did as told, and Peanut hopped out of the car.

"I'll be right back," he said.

Peanut walked over to a group of dudes and was greeted with daps. Then three different dudes reached into their pockets and pulled out a wad of money, handing it to Peanut. Peanut gave them dap, threw up a peace sign, then headed back to the car.

"Dang, Mr. High-Roller!" Precious joked.

"This lil' bit of money ain't shit!" Peanut arrogantly stated, while throwing the couple of grand in the armrest like it was nothing.

"Ain't this where that guy named Snake use to hustle at?" Precious asked, admiring the area like she was fascinated.

Peanut gave her a crazy look. "Yeah, why you ask that?"

Precious smiled. "Nothing...I just use to hear how all of them girls at the hairdresser use to be bragging about him. I heard that nigga had it going on," she said like a fan. "That's all you use to hear was Snake this, Snake that. You knew him?"

"Who do you think that nigga use to get all his dope from?" Peanut asked.

"Dang, you ballin' like that?" Precious asked.

"And then some!" Peanut boasted.

Precious sympathetically shook her head. "Man, it was fucked up how he died. I heard he went out like a soldier."

"I was right there with him!" Peanut confessed.

Agent Bradshaw sat up attentively in the van parked up the street. Little did Peanut know, Agent Green, a.k.a Precious, was wearing a wire.

"You were there?" Precious asked, raising her eyebrows. "I thought the paper said everybody involved died?"

"I got away. See, I got shot right here," he said, showing Precious his shoulder wound.

Precious massaged the wound. "Dang!"

Peanut had his chest poked out and was eating that shit up. "Yeah, that was my homeboy," he said, shaking his head. "But you know what they say; only the strong survive!"

"Well, at least Snake was able to take a couple of them with him," Precious threw out there.

Peanut took the bait. "That nigga only killed that nigga Robert. That other nigga died in the crash. I'm the one that killed them three hoes!" Peanut confessed.

"Why you kill them?"

"Shit, because those hoes were tryna kill me!" Peanut said defensively. "Don't worry, though. I ain't violent. I was just protecting myself."

Meanwhile, Agent Bradshaw and his men were inside of the van giving each other high-fives like they had just won the NBA Championship. Peanut was done. They had him on tape confessing to three murders. Agent Bradshaw had enough evidence to put him away for a lengthy sentence, but he wanted more. Instead of hopping out of the van and arresting him, he decided to follow them back to the house and let him dig a hole even deeper.

"Listen, baby, you did what you had to do," Precious said, patting Peanut on the lap.

Peanut playfully pinched her cheeks. "See, that's what a nigga dig about you. You as real as they come," he said, as he stared into her eyes and ran his fingers through her hair.

Precious bashfully dropped her head. "Listen, I'm sorry about the way I've been acting. I just don't wanna get hurt, Peanut."

"Don't worry, boo. As long as you're with me, you don't have anything to worry about."

Precious fluttered her eyelashes. "I'ma hold you to that!" she said, then headed to his apartment.

* * * * *

Thirty minutes later, after a brief pit stop to Peanut's apartment, Precious pulled up to the safe house.

"You sure you want me to show you here?" Peanut asked.

"Yeah, why not?" Precious replied nonchalantly, as she hopped out of the car.

Peanut grabbed his bookbag out of the backseat, and then followed behind her. Precious unlocked the front door and walked inside.

"Make yourself comfortable," she said, as she headed to her bedroom.

"I'ma go ahead and set this shit up!" Peanut said.

Precious walked into the bedroom, changed into a pair of sexy shorts, looked in the mirror, and let down her hair. She slid into a pair of fluffy bedroom slippers, and then returned to the living room.

When Agent Green returned to the living room, she could not believe her luck. Right before her very eyes, Peanut had a shitload of dope sitting on the kitchen counter.

"Ready to learn something?" Peanut asked.

"Man, this a lot of shit!" Precious said in a euphoric voice, as she entered the kitchen.

"I don't bullshit!" Peanut boasted.

Precious walked over to the counter, then flirtatiously rubbed up against his body. "How much is all of this, baby?" she asked.

"Oh, this ain't nothing but four kilos," Peanut said, like it was nothing.

"Damn! That's a lot of shit!"

"It's a lil' something," Peanut said, as he filled the cooking pot with water and set it on the stove.

"Dang, I didn't know you was finna show me with this much dope!" Precious said, like she was excited.

Peanut smiled. "If you gonna do it, you might as well do it big! Besides, I had to drop some dope today anyways, so I figured I might as well do everything at one time."

Not only did Agent Green have him confessing to three murders on tape, she also had him confessing to being Snake's supplier, and now was on camera manufacturing four kilos of crack. As Agent Green glanced over at the hidden camera, she dropped her head and felt a little sympathetic for playing Peanut, but then she realized it was her job.

"I'm hungry, baby," Precious said, easing behind him and massaging his shoulders. "I'ma order a pizza," she said, as she picked up the phone and dialed Agent Bradshaw's number.

"You did a good job, Green," Bradshaw replied when he answered.

"Yes, I would like to order a large pizza with all of the toppings," Precious said in code, acknowledging that her work was done. She gave her address, and then hung up.

Peanut was just pulling the last cookie out of the pot, when Precious eased behind him and wrapped her arms around his waist.

"So you think you got it?" Peanut asked.

Precious nodded. "I think I can handle it."

"Good, because I saved two ounces that I'ma let you drop yourself to get you some practice," Peanut said.

Precious massaged his chest. "I got a little surprise for you myself. I'ma go use the bathroom and freshen up," she said in a flirtatious tone, then disappeared down the hallway.

Peanut smiled and admired her backside as she walked down the hallway. He felt like today was his lucky day. He walked into the living room, plopped down on the sofa, and grabbed the remote off the coffee table, turning on the TV.

Approximately twenty minutes later, there was a knock at the door.

"Somebody's at your door!" Peanut yelled.

"See who it is. It's probably the pizza man!"

"I hope this ain't no nigga," Peanut mumbled to himself. When he arrived at the door, he peeped through the peephole, and then yelled, "It's the pizza man!"

"Will you take care of that for me, please, baby?" Precious yelled.

Peanut laughed, and then reached into his pockets. "This motherfucker thinks she got all of the senses."

When Peanut opened the door, what he saw outside made him piss on himself.

"Get down on the floor!" the masked officers yelled.

Peanut defensively threw his hands in the air, bit his bottom lip, and slowly got down on the ground. The agents rushed into the house, then aggressively rolled Peanut over on his stomach and placed their feet on his back.

"Clear!" Agent Bradshaw said through his earpiece, as he made his way into the kitchen to retrieve the tape that was gonna put Peanut away for life. "Well, well, well...whatta ya know... looka what we got here, boys," Bradshaw said, observing the enormous amount of dope scattered on the counter. Bradshaw walked over to Peanut, kneeled down in front of him, and antagonistically twirled the tape in his hands. "This here tape outta be enough to put you away for life," Bradshaw said.

When Agent Green walked into the room, Peanut looked up and made eye contact with her. Bradshaw threw his arm around her, then handed her his cuffs.

"Peanut, I'd like you to meet Agent Green a.k.a Precious. Cuff him!" Bradshaw ordered.

Green placed her knee on Peanut's back, then cuffed him.

Peanut spun his head around and spit in her face. "Stankin' bitch!" he yelled with an evil grin.

The agents rushed over and quickly commenced to beating the shit out of Peanut, while Agent Bradshaw handed Green his handkerchief.

Green wiped her face. "Thank you, sir," she said with a warm smile.

He placed his hand on Green's shoulder. "You did an excellent job!"

"Get this son-of-a-bitch up!" Walsh told the other agents. "Well, looka here. The tough guy pissed all over himself," he said, observing the piss stain in the front of Peanut's pants. "Get him outta here!" Walsh said.

"Hold up, you guys!" Green told them, as she furiously walked over to Peanut. She coldly stared into his eyes, and then issued him a brutal blow to the stomach with all that she had.

Peanut folded up like a lawn chair. "Ahh!" he cried. "Bitch, that's assault!"

The agents looked at each other and smiled.

"Anybody see anything?" Walsh asked everyone.

"Nope!" everyone said, while shaking their heads.

"Looks like that's gonna be hard to prove with no witnesses," Bradshaw told him. "Get this trash out of here!"

* * * * *

The newspaper's headline the next morning read: **BEAUTIFUL UNDERCOVER AGENT SEDUCES HORNY DRUG DEALER.**

Goldie picked up the newspaper and laughed when he saw the look on Peanut's face as the FEDS escorted him.

"This dumb motherfucker!" was all Goldie kept saying, as he shook his head while reading the article. "They gonna give that nigga four life sentences!" Goldie said, folding the newspaper and setting it on the dining room table.

Goldie looked over at the calendar. It was Saturday April 12th, and there were only a couple more weeks left in the school year. Goldie looked out of their living room window and saw a crackhead steal some flowers off their neighbor's porch. He just shook his head.

"I gotta move Momma and them outta this shit!" he said, as he grabbed his sack and hit the block

CHAPTER FORTY-ONE

Monday afternoon, Loretta pulled into the Downtown Barnett Bank parking lot. She parked, then removed her pocket mirror from out of her purse and inspected her hair. Pleased, she grabbed her purse and hopped out, locking the doors behind her. She checked her watch as she headed towards the front entrance of the bank. It was only 12:45 p.m., and her appointment with Mrs. Simpson was not until 1:00 p.m.

The bank was not as crowded as Loretta expected it to be for a Monday afternoon. She strolled into the lobby, located a seat in the waiting area, and took a seat. She patiently waited for Mrs. Simpson to call her name.

Ten minutes later, Mrs. Simpson walked into the waiting area, and then looked on her pad. "Is there a Mrs. Walker?" she asked, while surveying the room.

Loretta jumped up, adjusted her blouse, and threw up her hand. "I'm Mrs. Walker," she replied.

Mrs. Simpson gave her a warm smile and extended her hand. "Hi. How are you doing?" she asked, as she shook Loretta's hand.

"I'm fine," Loretta replied.

"If you don't mind following me," Mrs. Simpson said, as she led the way to her office.

Loretta followed her down a long, heavily waxed hallway.

This has to be where all of the money is at, Loretta thought, as she observed the immaculate area.

Mrs. Simpson veered off into the third door on the right. After walking into her office, she took a seat behind her desk.

Loretta took a seat. She was nervous. She needed this to work. She was able to relax a little when she looked on Mrs. Simpson's desk and saw a picture of her and her kids at Disney World. She was hoping that since Mrs. Simpson was also a mother that she would be a little sympathetic.

"Mrs. Walker, do you have all of the information I asked you to bring along with you?"

"Yes, I do," Loretta said, handing it over, with a warm smile on her face. "You have a beautiful family," she added, kissing up.

"Thank you," Mrs. Simpson said, then handed her a clipboard. "Please fill this out for me."

Loretta grabbed the clipboard and looked over the papers.

"If you'll excuse me," Mrs. Simpson said.

Two minutes later, Mrs. Simpson returned to her office. Loretta handed her the clipboard.

Mrs. Simpson looked over the application. "Give me a couple of minutes to process your application," she said, then stood up from behind her desk and disappeared.

For the next couple of minutes, Loretta sat in total suspense. She nervously fiddled with her nails, played with her hair, and squirmed in her seat. The waiting was killing her. She had prayed so much on the prayer line last night that she knew GOD would be screening her prayers today. Loretta attentively sat up in her seat when she heard the clicking of Mrs. Simpson's heels coming down the hallway. When Mrs. Simpson entered the office, Loretta tried to study her face to distinguish if she had been approved.

Mrs. Simpson took a seat behind her desk and got down to business. "I'm afraid I have some good news and I have some bad news."

"Just give it to me," Loretta said, sitting on the edge of her seat.

"The good news is that you've been approved."

"So what's the bad news?" Loretta asked.

"The bad news is that the maximum amount you have been approved for is only three thousand dollars," Mrs. Simpson replied.

"I don't understand! I've been on my job for twenty years! I need six thousand, not three thousand!" Loretta pleaded.

"I'm sorry, ma'am. Unfortunately, three thousand is the best I can do for you."

Loretta sighed and placed her hand on her forehead. "Okay, how long will it take for you to cut the check?" she asked.

"I can have it ready for you in seven working days," Mrs. Simpson replied.

Loretta went hysterical. "I don't have seven working days! I need this check by Thursday!" she screamed, slamming her hands on the desk.

The security guard protectively rushed into the office. "Is there a problem, Mrs. Simpson?" he asked, eyeing Loretta.

Mrs. Simpson raised her hand, indicating she was all right. "It's okay, Frank. I can handle this." She felt sorry for Loretta. She could see the pain in her eyes.

The security guard nodded his head, and then slowly walked off, looking back until he disappeared out of the door.

Mrs. Simpson compassionately patted Loretta's hand. "If it'll help, I'll see if I can pull a couple of strings to have the check ready for you by Friday morning."

"You don't understand!" Loretta cried.

Mrs. Simpson sympathetically handed her some tissue. "I'm sorry, Mrs. Walker. It's out of my hands," she replied.

THREE DAYS LATER

As Goldie walked up the sidewalk heading to his apartment, he was surprised not to see the family car parked in front of the apartment.

"I wonder where Momma at?" he said, as he opened the door.

He was starving. He closed the door behind him, then rushed straight into the kitchen and fixed himself a bologna and cheese sandwich. As he fixed his sandwich, he thought about how strange his mom had been acting. While he poured himself a glass of Kool-Aid, he glanced on the kitchen counter and saw that the answering machine was blinking. Snooping, he pressed play.

"Mrs. Walker, this is Randolph calling, regarding the 3-bedroom, 2-bath, stucco home you were interested in purchasing. I am afraid the deadline to come up with the additional six thousand dollars needed as your down payment expires tomorrow. Unfortunately, if you are unable to come up with the additional money needed, two hundred and fifty dollars of your three thousand dollar deposit will be forfeited, and a check containing the remainder of the balance will be mailed to you. I'm sorry, ma'am. I got you the longest extension my boss would allow me. I wish you the best of luck, and hopefully, I will see you tomorrow."

Goldie disturbingly cut off the answering machine. He did not want to hear any more messages. He violently slammed his fist on the kitchen counter.

"That's why she's been looking so stressed out lately and working all of them damn hours of overtime! Damn, six thousand dollars," he said, rubbing on his chin.

Goldie grabbed a bag of Doritos from off top of the refrigerator, and then furiously shot upstairs. After storming into his bedroom, he tossed his bookbag on his bed and started fumingly pacing his room. He hit his fist in his hand.

"Damn, why all of this crazy shit keep happening to me!" he said, then plopped down on his bed and buried his head in his hands. He started massaging his temples. "Why didn't she say she needed some money?"

He should have known something was wrong when all of a sudden she started working doubles, five days out of the week. She was literally killing herself. Some nights she would be so tired when she came home that she would dose off to sleep in her uniform in the recliner. Goldie could not afford to let her stress herself out and risk dying of a heart attack. Everyone he had ever been attached to was gone. His father, Tina, and Snake were all gone. His mother, sisters, little brother, and nephews were all he had left.

Goldie kept hearing Snake's face echoing inside of his head. *Remember, lil' man, whatever you do, always make sure you take care of your family before anything. They're all you got!*

Goldie hopped up off the bed, rushed over to his dresser, and opened the secret compartment. He started counting all of his money. "Twenty-two thousand, five -hundred!" he said.

He just smiled. He already knew what he had to do.

FRIDAY-THE DEADLINE
Rhonda impatiently honked her horn. "Gotdamn it!" she cursed, as she glanced at her watch, which showed a time of 3:05 p.m.

Rhonda glanced over her right shoulder, then maneuvered her way out of traffic and detoured off on a back road. Ten minutes later, she was pulling in front of Azalea Middle School.

Goldie was standing with an attitude on his face when she pulled into the car circle. After she unlocked the doors, he hopped in.

"Damn, if a nigga knew you were gonna be this late, I could have rode the bus!" Goldie said.

"I'm sorry. I got stuck in traffic, dang!" Rhonda wondered how Goldie could be so selfish not to appreciate her driving all the way across town, even if she was ten minutes late.

"I told you I had something to do!" he spat, throwing his bookbag in the backseat.

Rhonda stared into his eyes and then boldly reached over and grabbed his manhood. She gave him a mischievous grin. "I'll make it up to you."

"You better!" Goldie said arrogantly. "Swing by my house. I need to go grab something," Goldie instructed.

"Yes, daddy!" Rhonda said, as she drove off with her left hand on the steering wheel, while stroking Goldie's manhood with her right.

After making a quick pit stop to Goldie's apartment, Rhonda headed northbound down Central Avenue.

"Make a left right here," Goldie instructed, pointing over at the parking lot of the real estate office.

Rhonda obediently pulled into the lot and searched for a parking space.

"Wait right here!" Goldie hopped out of the car before Rhonda could throw the car in park.

Goldie strolled into the real estate office with his chest poked out and a confident swagger. He quickly noticed the real estate agent seated behind his desk and jabbering on the telephone. He looked at his watch. It was only 4:45; he had made it in time.

"Hold on one minute," Randolph said into the receiver, then covered the mouthpiece with his hand. "May I help you, sir?"

"Yeah, I'm here for Mrs. Walker," Goldie said.

"Where is she, if you don't mind me asking?" Randolph asked.

"She had to work a double, so she sent me," Goldie lied.

Randolph quickly put the receiver back up to his ear. "Mr. Moore, I'm gonna have to call you back," he said, and then rudely hung up. "So did she manage to come up with the other six thousand dollars she needed?" Randolph asked, entwining his fingers and leaning forward on his desk.

Goldie arrogantly threw the envelope, and a couple of hundred dollar bills fell out of the envelope when it landed on the agent's desk.

Randolph's eyes got as big as quarters. He looked up at Goldie in astonishment, then quickly grabbed the envelope and started counting. The more he counted, the more he selfishly smiled. As he counted, all he could think about was the long overdue vacation he needed. Randolph returned his attention to Goldie.

"There's sixty-one hundred here," he said.

"Yeah, I know," Goldie replied.

"Why the extra hundred?" Randolph asked, hoping it was a tip.

"I want you to make sure that a new mailbox is placed in front of the house, and it should say 'Walker Family' on it," Goldie said, making hand gestures in the sky as if he was a movie director.

"Will do!" Randolph said, then graciously reached out and shook Goldie's hand. "Let me grab your keys for you!" He walked over and grabbed the keys off the board. "Here are your receipt and keys," Randolph said, as he handed Goldie both.

"Thank you," Goldie said with a Colgate smile.

"Okay, you're all set, pal! You guys enjoy yourselves, and I'll have somebody over there first thing Monday morning to install that mailbox for you," Randolph said.

Goldie cheerfully tossed the house keys in the air, then snapped his fingers and caught them. He threw up a peace sign.

"Alright, Randolph, I'ma holla at ya," he said, before disappearing out of the front door.

* * * * *

The drive home was a bumpy one. When Loretta pulled in front of her apartment, she cut off the car and sat in total silence for a moment to gather her thoughts. She felt like a total failure. She had tried everything in her power to try to come up with the extra six thousand she needed, but it was bad timing for everybody.

She sighed as she observed her environment. "Well, looks like this is where I'm gonna be for a minute," she said, as she grabbed her purse and hopped out of the car.

Loretta instantly caught an attitude while walking up the sidewalk. "I told that damn boy about blasting that stereo," she said to herself, as she stood on the front porch and took her keys out of her purse.

She unlocked the front door and stormed inside of the house. When she charged into the living room, Goldie was standing with his back turned. Rhonda tried to alert him of his mother's presence, but he was too busy singing and dancing. Loretta stood there for a couple of seconds.

"Here's a little something 'bout a nigga like me...," he sang.

Loretta charged over to the stereo and turned it off.

"What the -?" Goldie said, as he turned around, and then threw his hand up to his mouth.

Loretta was irritably standing with her hands on her hips. "What did I tell you about all of that loud damn music? You gonna go deaf around here," she yelled at him.

"I thought you were at work."

"So you do what I tell you not to do when I'm at work?" she asked.

"I just-" Goldie said, searching for an excuse.

"Boy, just shut up!" Loretta said, waving him off. "Listen... I'm tired, and I got a headache. I don't feel like being bothered right now. I'm going into my room to lie down. Fix you and your brother something to eat."

"Alright," Goldie replied.

"Hi, Mrs. Walker!" Rhonda cheerfully said.

"Hey, child," Loretta said nonchalantly. "Goldie, did anybody call for me?"

"Nope," Goldie said.

Loretta took a deep breath. "Alright," she said, and then dragged her body into her bedroom.

Rhonda waited for Loretta to close her room door. "Did you do it, Goldie?"

"Yeah, I did it," Goldie said arrogantly.

"Where did you leave it?" Rhonda asked.

"On her dresser," Goldie replied.

Rhonda just smiled, as the two sat in the living room and waited for Loretta to come storming back into the living room like a bat out of hell.

Loretta sat her purse down on the bed, then plopped down next to it. She stared up at the ceiling

"Oh God, Albert! Why aren't you here to help me?" she asked aloud. She cried for a couple of minutes. It was not until she lifted up her head to wipe her nose when she noticed a present next to a card on her dresser. She stood up, and then curiously walked over to the dresser to investigate. She grabbed the two, and then plopped down on the edge of the bed. "This little boy," she said, shaking her head as she smiled.

She opened up the card, which read:

Dear Mom,
For fourteen years, you've provided a roof over my head, food, and clothing. You always put us first, and yourself last. Now I feel that it's time for me to return the favor and provide for you. Open the box.
I love you, Ma!
Your son, Goldie

Loretta was clueless. She immediately started removing the gift-wrap off the box. When she opened it, she placed her hands over her mouth. .

"Oh my GOD!"

Inside of the box was a key ring with the keys to Loretta's dream home.

"Oh my GOD!" was all Rhonda and Goldie kept hearing his mother repeating.

Goldie looked over at Rhonda and smiled. "Here she comes," he said.

Just as Goldie had predicted, his mother stormed into the living room. "Goldie...Goldie...come here, baby!" she energetically screamed, hyperventilating.

Goldie smiled, hopped off the sofa, and walked towards his mom. Loretta wrapped her arms around his waist, then euphorically lifted him up and spun him around.

"Dang, she strong," Rhonda mumbled to herself.

Loretta put Goldie down, then affectionately smothered him in her bosom and started planting wet kisses all over his face. Then reality hit her. She grabbed Goldie by the shoulders and looked him in the eyes.

"Boy, where did you come up with six thousand dollars?"

Goldie made up the quickest lie he could think of. "Didn't nobody know, but Snake didn't like using banks, so I use to hold some of the money we be done made from the carwash for him. The night before he got killed, he gave me six thousand when he dropped me off, and told me to hold it for him."

Loretta gave him one of those motherly serious looks.

"What? I ain't lying!"Goldie cried.

Loretta paused for a moment, and then studied him. The story seemed believable.

Goldie waited impatiently on his mother's reaction.

Loretta crossed her arms. "And there wasn't anybody else who you could've given the money to?" she asked.

"Naw, you know he ain't really have any family," Goldie said.

Loretta went back into action and started smothering him in kisses.

"Thank you, baby! Thank you!"

Goldie just stood there, smiled, and absorbed every kiss.

When Loretta finally ran out of kisses, she started fanning herself, trying to calm herself down.

"Oh my GOD! Oh my GOD! I gotta call everybody and let them know that my baby just bought me a house!" she said, as she stormed into her bedroom to hop on the phone.

Goldie looked over at Rhonda, and was shocked to see her crying. "Girl, what's wrong with you?" he asked her.

"That was just so beautiful," she struggled to get out, as she wiped away her tears.

Goldie paused for a moment, then threw his hand on his chin and stared up at the ceiling. "That was, wasn't it?" he said sarcastically.

He walked over to the sofa, and then sat next to Rhonda. He arrogantly threw his hands behind his head. He was the man of the house now. He had kept his word with everybody: his father, Snake, and his mother. He had fulfilled his mother's dream...and today was the happiest day of his life.

CHAPTER FORTY-TWO

JUNE 6, 1989 – THE LAST DAY OF SCHOOL

"Take care, Goldie!" all of his classmates yelled, waving him goodbye, as he eased into the front seat of their Cutlass.

"How'd your day go, baby?" his mother asked.

"It was alright," Goldie lied, knowing that today was an emotional day for him.

"You'll be alright," his mother said, as she pulled off.

That afternoon, while standing on the front porch of his castle, Goldie thought about how much he was going to miss being around his friends. Deep down inside, though, he knew he had made the right choice.

It was a beautiful day outside. Goldie just nodded his head as he admired his new neighborhood. Three girls coming up the street on beach cruisers caught his attention. He made his way to the sidewalk.

"Ah yo, let me holla at ya'll!" he yelled to the girls.

The girls obediently stopped, and Goldie made his way over to them. He had already chosen his victim, so he stood in front of the cutest of the three.

"What's up? I'm new in the neighborhood, and I was wondering if a beautiful young thang like you could show a brother around," he said.

"I don't even know your name," the girl replied.

Goldie smiled, and then seduced her by rubbing on his bare, masculine chest. "Please excuse my rudeness. I apologize. My name is Goldie," he said, extending his hand.

When the girl shook his hand, he raised her hand to his lips and kissed it.

"And may I ask your name?"

"Sheila," the girl said, blushing.

Goldie licked his lips. "Sheila and Goldie, that sounds good together, don't it?"

Sheila shrugged her shoulders. "I guess."

An ice cream truck turned on the street and Goldie waved the truck down.

"It's hot out here. I can't let ya'll leave without extending my hospitality and offering ya'll some ice cream," Goldie said. He walked up to the truck. "Yeah, let me get a nutty buddy, and give these beautiful young ladies whatever they can carry," he said.

The girls walked up to the truck and placed their orders. Goldie reached into his pockets, and then pulled out a wad of money that made the girls' mouths drop to the ground.

Goldie peeled off a twenty-dollar bill, handing it to the ice cream man. "Keep the change," he told him.

The driver tipped his hat, thanked Goldie, and drove off.

"If ya'll don't mind, we can go in my backyard and eat our ice cream," Goldie offered.

The girls looked at Sheila. "Okay," Sheila said, as they put their bikes on their kickstands and followed Goldie.

While Sheila's two friends, Jocelyn and Alice, sat at the picnic table and ate their ice cream, Goldie had Sheila off in the cut, putting his mack game down.

"You know, today was like the fifth time I saw ya'll riding down the street. I told myself the next time I saw you I was gonna stop you. So where you stay at?"

"On 44th and 17th," Sheila replied.

"Damn, that's only a couple of blocks away," Goldie said. "So listen, how about we exchange numbers and get acquainted? I got a little psychic in me, and I see a bright future with me and you," he joked.

"You so crazy!" Sheila said, slapping him on the shoulder.

Goldie grabbed her hands. "Fo' real, though, I'm on some grown man shit. I gotta warn you, I ain't nothing like these other lil' fourteen-year-old niggas around here."

"And I ain't nothing like these other lil' fourteen-year-old girls around here," Sheila said, throwing her hand on her hip.

Goldie nodded his head and rubbed his chin. "I'ma see...I'ma see," he said. "So this gonna be your first year at Boca Ciega High, too?"

"Yep!" Sheila said. "And I'm trying out for the captain of the cheerleading team!"

Goldie observed Sheila's thick legs and nodded his head. "Okay then, Ms. Sheila, do your thang," he joked.

"Listen, we gotta go. Walk us to the front," Sheila said.

Goldie threw his arm around Sheila and walked her to the front yard. "So, listen, I'ma call you at about eight o'clock tonight," he told her when they arrived in the front yard.

"Okay," Sheila said, as her and her girls hopped on their bikes and rode off, snickering.

Goldie watched them disappear down the street, then rubbed his hands together and went inside of the house.

* * * * *

Later on that night, Goldie called Sheila, and they talked until the next morning. The two scheduled their first date for the movies.

Sheila could not wait until Saturday rolled around. She had called around and got the scoop on Goldie, and was amazed at all of the compliments he received.

"Girl, that lil' nigga is stacking paper! He the one we saw at the mall that one Saturday with Snake with all of them bags. Girl, if you don't wanna holla at him, let me holla at him," Sheila's cousin Felicia told her.

"Girl, I was just calling to find out a little something about him. Bye, with your crazy butt," Sheila said, then hung up the phone.

Sheila laid on her back in the bed, stared up at the ceiling, and smiled, as she daydreamed about her future with Goldie.

CHAPTER FORTY-THREE

After a couple of weeks of getting to know everybody, Goldie's transition into his new neighborhood went smoothly. For the past couple of weeks, he and Sheila had been spending a lot of time together. Since school was out, the two had plenty of time to get acquainted with each other.

"Goldie, I'm leaving to go to work!" his mother yelled. "Make you and Jeff some breakfast, and make sure he's at camp by eight-thirty!" Loretta added, before leaving out the door.

"Alright," Goldie mumbled, as he turned over on his side and pulled the covers over his head.

Ten minutes later, Jeff walked into Goldie's room and shook him. "Goldie, I'm hungry!" Jeff cried.

Goldie pulled the covers off his head and stared at Jeff with a crazy look on his face. "Boy, you better go in there and make you some damn cereal."

Jeff stormed out of the room, pouting. "You make me sick. I'ma tell Momma you ain't fix me nothing."

Goldie glanced over at his clock as he stretched out his arms and yawned. It was 7:30 a.m. "Damn, let me get up and hop in this shower," he said, as he tugged on his manhood and walked into the bathroom.

For the next fifteen minutes, Goldie gathered his thoughts in the shower. After fogging up the bathroom, he stepped out of the shower, dried off, and then performed his early morning hygiene.

Jeff barged into the bathroom. "I'm finna go!" he yelled with an attitude, and then slammed the door behind him.

Goldie just laughed, as he continued washing the Noxzema off his face.

Today was Friday. Goldie had a couple of errands he needed to run, and a couple of moves he needed to make. He needed to find a steady connect. He was tired of buying rocks off whoever came through. He had been trying to hook up with Dred, but that nigga was like a ghost.

By nine o'clock, Goldie was sitting on the edge of his bed applying lotion to his body. His phone rang.

"Hello," Goldie answered.

"What 'cha doing?" Sheila asked.

"Nothing, just chillin'. Why, what's up?"

"Nothing, I just wanted to see if you wanted to come over here," Sheila said.

Goldie's eyes lit up. This was Sheila's first time inviting him over. "Where your momma and them at?"

"They at work, silly!" Sheila said.

"So what time do you want me to come through?" Goldie asked.

"Whenever," Sheila said.

"Alright, I'll be through there at about eleven o'clock," Goldie said, as he laced up his shoes.

"Bring a rubber," Sheila boldly requested.

Goldie thought he was hearing things.

"Why you ain't saying anything?" Sheila asked him.

Goldie was speechless. Those two dates to the movies and late-night phone conversations had paid off. He had misjudged Sheila. He was not planning to hit that for another three weeks, and here it was she was already ready.

"Listen, Sheila, scratch that eleven o'clock. I'ma be around there at ten-thirty," Goldie said.

"Alright, I'll be waiting," Sheila replied, and then hung up.

Goldie stared at the phone in disbelief, before hanging up. "Damn, I love this neighborhood!" he said.

Next, he dialed one of his crackheads.

"Hello?" Peggy answered on the third ring.

"You got a car?" Goldie asked.

"Yeah, you need me to run you somewhere?"

"Yeah, come scoop me from the corner store," Goldie said, then hung up.

Goldie grabbed a wad of money from out of his dresser, his sack of rocks, and bounced out of the door. As he headed to the corner store, all he could do is think about how much he missed having Rhonda around. He shook his head as he thought about how he had been caught slipping.

It was three Saturdays ago when Goldie met this fine-ass red-bone at McDonald's. Goldie was standing in line, when he heard two older women behind him snickering. Goldie was dressed in a Florida State basketball short set and wearing a pair of Nike slippers. When Goldie turned around to see what all of the snickering was about, he caught the two women staring at his flawless toes. Goldie just looked up at the women and smiled. He knew he had feet that could have gotten endorsements from any sandal company in America.

"Girl, I'll suck that nigga's toes!" Goldie heard one of the women say.

That was Goldie's cue. "Damn, do you mind if I know the name of the woman that's gonna be sucking my toes?"

"I'm Renee, and this is my friend Angel," the woman said.

After fifteen minutes of conversation and making both women laugh like he was a standup comic, Goldie had a phone number in his hand and a date set up for that night.

When Goldie showed up at Renee's house, he got the shock of his life. Turns out Renee and Angel were lesbians, and both had agreed that he was cute and decided to have a ménage á trios. That night, Goldie put it down and represented like a grown man. After Goldie's star-studded performance, the two decided he would be valuable to keep around as a sex toy. That was until Renee's niece Rhonda popped up at the family reunion with him on her arm. When Goldie saw Renee and Angel at the family reunion, he knew he and Rhonda was over. That afternoon, Goldie was called every curse word imaginable.

"You dog!" Renee said.

"Dirty dick motherfucker!" Rhonda yelled.

"Fuck all of ya'll!" Goldie remembered telling everybody, as he walked off from the cookout to a payphone to call a cab.

When Goldie reached the corner store, a couple of hustlers were already posted up. "What's up with you niggas?" Goldie asked, walking around and giving everybody hugs and daps.

"What's up, Goldie?" C-Baby asked.

"What's popping, C-Baby?" Goldie asked, as the two embraced.

C-Baby was Snake's younger cousin. When Goldie moved into the neighborhood, C-Baby welcomed him with open arms and introduced him to everybody on the block as a thorough nigga. Most of the niggas on the block already knew of Goldie from frequently seeing him at either the carwash or rolling through the city on the passenger seat with Snake. Word on the streets was that he had a mean knuckle game, was a true hustler, a smooth talker with the ladies, and known to bust his gun.

After five minutes of shooting the breeze, Peggy pulled up in a Bronco. Goldie just shook his head. With Peggy, you never knew what she was going to pull up in.

"Listen, C-Baby, I got a couple of moves I gotta go make. I'ma be back through around two. I got this lil' thang that I'm tryna put together, and if it comes through, it ain't gonna be nothing but love," Goldie said, as he gave C-Baby dap.

"Hey, handsome, where we going?" Peggy asked when Goldie hopped in the truck.

"Go to the cleaners so I can grab my clothes," Goldie ordered, as he adjusted the seat, leaning it all the way back.

After fifty minutes of running Goldie around town, and dropping his clothes off at his house, Peggy pulled in front of the Jamaican restaurant to drop him off.

When the truck came to a halt, Goldie reached in his pants, pulled out his sack, handed her two rocks, and then hopped out.

"Thank you, honey! Call me if you need me later on!" Peggy said, as she backed out of the parking space.

Goldie nodded his head, as he walked into the Jamaican restaurant and took his place in line to order. For six weeks straight, Goldie had been popping up at the restaurant and dining in the dining area, hoping to bump into Dred. Today was his lucky day. Dred was seated in a booth in the corner, buried in a plate of ox tails.

"May I take your order?" the cashier asked Goldie.

Goldie tried to keep his eye on Dred and order at the same time. "Yeah, let me get some curry goat, rice, and tropical punch."

"That'll be $12.50," the cashier said.

Goldie reached into his pocket and pulled out a twenty-dollar bill, then handed to the cashier.

Dred got up from the table, walked over to the trash can, and dumped his tray. When Goldie made eye contact with him, Dred nodded his head at Goldie.

"Me brethren!" a Jamaican came out of one of the back doors and yelled.

"What's happenin', star," Dred said, as he walked over to the other Jamaican and the two disappeared into one of the back rooms.

When Goldie's order came up, he grabbed a couple of napkins and a straw, then sat at a booth close to the door where Dred had disappeared in.

Thirty minutes passed and Dred still had not come out. Goldie had finished his meal over ten minutes ago, but had walked back up to the counter and ordered a patty just to stall.

Meanwhile, Dred and Rotti were staring at Goldie through the two-way mirror.

"Man, I tell ya, star, the lickle youth be here like every day," Rotti said.

Dred stared at Goldie and tried to make out where he remembered him.

"Me know the youth from somewhere," Dred said, rubbing on his goatee. Then it hit him. "Now me know where me know the lickle youth from," Dred said. "That's the lickle youth that use to run with that bad-boy named Snake."

"What you think him want?" Rotti asked.

"Me no know. Me go check him and see what's up," Dred said, then headed towards the door.

When Dred walked out of the door alone, Goldie's eyes lit up. Dred walked over to Goldie's table, then sat down and placed his hands in front of him.

"I here that ya come here a lot?" Dred asked.

Goldie nodded his head.

Dred observed Goldie's wardrobe, then stared into Goldie's eyes and tried to read them. "You the lickle youth that used to roll with Snake?" Dred asked.

"Yeah," Goldie said.

"Me have mad respect for the rude boy. Him go out like a soldier busting him gun," Dred said.

Goldie leaned forward and whispered, "I'm tryna get on. Snake use to be my connect, but he's gone now. Listen, I know you don't deal with just anybody, but when I heard that you owned the restaurant, I just felt like I'd keep popping up until I bumped into you."

Dred rubbed on his chin as he listened to Goldie.

"Listen, I ain't asking for no handout. I got my own money," Goldie said. He reached into his pocket, pulled out three grand, and sat it on the table. He then pulled a pen out of his pocket and wrote his pager number on a napkin. "I'm tryna cop a couple of ounces. Beep me if you wanna do business, or just leave my money with your cashier if you don't wanna," Goldie said as he stood up.

Dred looked up at him and smiled. "So you leaving your money with me?"

"You ain't hurting for nothing, so I know I ain't gotta worry about you taking it," Goldie said, then disappeared out of the restaurant.

* * * * *

Sheila was impatiently pacing her living room, waiting on Goldie to arrive.

"Here I am trying to give him some, and this nigga can't even be on time," Sheila said, as she plopped down on the sofa.

When the doorbell rang, Sheila hopped off the sofa and rushed to the door. She peeped through the peephole. It was Goldie. She opened the door.

"You're late," she told Goldie with a slight attitude, as she stood with her hands on her hips.

"Is you gonna let me come in or what?" Goldie asked.

Sheila stepped to the side.

"You got a nice-ass crib," Goldie said, admiring Sheila's living room, then plopped down on the sofa.

Sheila sat on the sofa next to him.

Noticing her slight attitude, he decided to cheer her up a bit. "Listen, I apologize for being late. My momma asked me to go and pay the cable bill for her at the last minute," Goldie lied.

Sheila fell for it. "That's alright. You brought some rubbers?"

Goldie looked at her, smirked, and then whipped out three gold wrappers.

"What kind are these?" Sheila asked, snatching the rubbers out of his hands. "Magnums?" she said with a puzzled look on her face. "Why you got these?"

Goldie raised his eyebrows. "You'll see!" he said with a devilish grin.

"Come on," Sheila said, grabbing Goldie by the arm.

As soon as she hit her bedroom, she came out of her clothes. Sheila had Goldie scared to death. She was so willing to give him some, he wondered if she had some kind of disease. Goldie just sat on the edge of the bed, as he admired Sheila's sexy, flawless body. Goldie removed his shoes, then came out of his clothes and slid under her sheets. Sheila smiled as she stood at the foot of the bed, then walked over to the left-hand side of the bed and hopped in.

Goldie initiated some foreplay by kissing her on the neck and then working his way down to her breasts.

"Mmmm," Sheila moaned, as she massaged his back.

After attending to Sheila's breast, Goldie licked the trail of hair that ran all the way down to her navel.

"Oh my God!" Sheila screamed, while arching her back the more Goldie descended.

Goldie sensually licked around her navel, and right when she thought he was going to go down further, he came back up.

"I'm finna put it in," Goldie whispered in her ear, then tore the rubber wrapper open with his teeth and slid it on.

Goldie maneuvered his way on top of Sheila, grabbed his manhood, and entered her.

"Unhhh!" was all Sheila said, as her eyes got as big as half dollars, and she clawed her nails into Goldie's back. Sheila looked at Goldie as if she was possessed.

Goldie smiled. "Now you see why I got them kind of rubbers."

For the next fifteen minutes, Goldie chased Sheila all around the bed until she scooted all the way back to the headboard and ran out of room. Goldie made Sheila throw in the towel when he flipped her over and started hitting her from the back.

"Umm umm, I don't want no more," she said, as she collapsed on the bed and Goldie pulled his third leg out of her.

"You finish?" Goldie asked.

Sheila rolled her eyes at him. "Don't worry. I just gotta get use to it."

Goldie smiled.

"Let me get a rag." Sheila hopped up and walked into the bathroom.

Goldie smiled as he admired his work. "Dang, I didn't know you were bowlegged!" Goldie yelled into the bathroom.

"You real funny," Sheila said, returning into the room, then handed Goldie a rag with soap.

As he wiped himself off, she plopped back down on the bed, looking like she needed a cigarette.

Goldie's pager sounded off. He grabbed it from off of his pants and looked at the number. "Damn, who the fuck is this?" he asked, not familiar with the number. "Let me use your phone."

Sheila threw him the phone, and Goldie dialed the number.

"Rude Boy," the other party answered.

"Who dis?" Goldie asked, puzzled.

"Come by the restaurant. Me got a couple of lickle things for you," Dred said.

"I'm on my way!" Goldie said, then hung up the phone and started getting dressed.

"Where you going?" Sheila asked.

"I got something I gotta go take care of," Goldie replied, sliding into his pants.

"But I'm ready to do it again!" Sheila said, hoping to get him to stay.

"Tomorrow," Goldie said, sliding his shirt over his head.

"I know you don't think you just gonna hump me and leave?" Sheila asked, with her arms folded.

Goldie walked over and kissed her on the forehead. "I'll call you."

"Oh...so you done caught your lil' nut...and you don't want no more right now?" Sheila asked.

"Business before pleasure," Goldie said, then let himself out.

* * * * *

That summer, Goldie bagged Sheila as his girl and Dred became his new connect. Dred liked the way he moved and started fronting him work, even coming down on his prices. Goldie began supplying many of the niggas in the hood with rocks, while continuing to work off his pager.

He and Sheila frequently made trips to the movies, and Goldie showered Sheila with extravagant gifts. By August, Goldie had Sheila wide-open and had turned her into a nympho. Sheila was like a dope fiend, addicted to Goldie.

School was due to start in a couple of weeks, so Goldie grinded extra hard. He was the new kid on the block, and on the first day of school, he wanted it to be all eyes on him.

CHAPTER FORTY-FOUR

On the first day of school, Goldie found his homeroom class just before the tardy bell rung. He had bumped into Sheila in the hallway and damn near made himself late walking her to her homeroom class.

"Good morning, everybody, my name is Ms. Drayton, and welcome to Boca Ciega High School," the homeroom teacher said, as she sat on her desk, crossed her legs, and gave everyone a warm smile. She clapped her hands together. "Okay, why don't we go around the room and introduce ourselves. Let's start with you," the teacher said, gesturing at a dark-skinned girl with braces.

After everyone was acquainted, Ms. Drayton called each of the students up to her desk, one by one, and handed them their schedules. When the bell rang, all of the energetic freshmen anxiously poured into the hallway with their schedules in their hands, searching for their first period class.

Goldie's first three classes, English, Algebra, and World History, were all conveniently located in the same vicinity of each other, on the west-wing of the school. Unfortunately, his fourth period class was located on the east-wing.

When the fourth period bell rang, Goldie put a little pep in his step to make it to the other side of the schoolyard. After dapping up a couple of the dudes out of the neighborhood and flirting with a couple of females in the hallway, he strolled into his fourth period Earth Science class right when the tardy bell rang. All of the other students were already seated. As Goldie searched the classroom for an empty seat, his attention was drawn to a beautiful red-bone sitting in a desk at the front of the classroom. Goldie wanted to walk over to the dude sitting next to her and tell him to get up.

"Damn, I've seen her somewhere before. Where do I know her from," Goldie mumbled, as he walked down the aisle and examined her from head to toe out of the corner of his eye.

Goldie sat at a desk at the back of the classroom.

"Good morning, boys and girls. I'm Coach Pooch, and welcome to Earth Science. Listen up for your names," Coach Pooch said, then started calling roll.

Goldie sat and waited patiently to find out the red-bone's name.

"Sandra Johnson!"

"Here!" the red-bone yelled.

"So that's her name," Goldie said, while rubbing on his chin and tapping his pencil on his desk, plotting on his new mission.

He and Sheila had only been dating for a couple of months, and already Sheila was starting to get on his nerves. Goldie did not know what it was, but the minute he walked into the classroom and laid eyes on the red-bone a chill ran up his spine. The feeling was spooky.

The rest of the day went smoothly for Goldie. After eating lunch with Sheila, he walked her to her fifth period class and crossed paths with Sandra in the hallway. When Sandra passed by, Goldie glanced over his shoulder to see which classroom she walked into.

Got it. Fifth period she got Home Economics, Goldie said to himself, as he walked Sheila down the hallway to her class.

By the third week of school, everybody in the school knew who Goldie was. Day by day, he accumulated more and more phone numbers. A lot of girls knew that he and Sheila were an item, but they hated Sheila's guts so bad that they messed around with Goldie just out of spite.

Just as he had done in middle school, Goldie was secretly knocking down freshman girls like they were dominoes. He fed all of them the same lines, promising them that they were going to be his girl. Even though Goldie got a little sidetracked, he reminded himself that bagging Sandra was his ultimate goal. He did his homework, finding out all he could about Sandra, because when the timing was right, he planned to make her his girl.

* * * * *

Today marked the beginning of the second grading period of the first semester. Today was also the day Goldie decided he was going to push up on Sandra and say something. There was just something special about her. He had already thoroughly conducted his research on her and everything had checked out. Basically, she was a bookworm. Besides her only friend Lisa, she was pretty much anti-social. I guess you can say opposites attract.

Sheila turned out to be a stuck-up, spoiled brat. She was beautiful, but her arrogant ways took away from her beauty. On top of that, Sheila was too controlling for him. That is why he had his eyes set on Sandra.

During class, Goldie glanced over at her and smiled. Sandra acknowledged him and bashfully dropped her head.

After Coach Pooch finished roll call, he came from behind his desk and stood in front of the class. "Okay, boys and girls, today we're pairing up into groups of two. Find you a partner and pair up," he said.

Everyone stood and searched for a partner. Goldie stood and looked over at Sandra. He knew that now was the ideal time for him to make his move. He grabbed his textbook, and then confidently strutted over towards her.

Sandra got nervous when she looked up and saw him coming her way.

"Mind if I be your partner?" Goldie asked.

"I don't care," Sandra said, shrugging her shoulders.

Goldie sat down next to her, and then attentively listened to Coach Pooch's directions.

Sandra glanced over at him and quickly stereotyped him as a thug. *He probably just wants to be my partner so he can copy off my paper,* she thought to herself.

After Coach Pooch finished giving the instructions, Goldie went into action. He opened up his textbook and quickly started answering each question on the group worksheet. Sandra stared at him in shock. To her surprise, he turned out to be more intelligent than she had thought. She watched as he worked with such precision, confidently answering each question carefully. She rubbed on the side of her neck, as she smiled and watched him work. She began looking at him from a different perspective.

There was not any doubt in her mind that he was fine. His hairy, sexy, bowlegs were definitely the enhancer of his athletic frame. Little did he know, Sandra also had her eye on him. Even though she was not into boys, Goldie's candor mysteriously did something to her hormones.

I don't even know why I'm thinking like this and he mess with Sheila, she thought, as she shook her head.

For the next couple of minutes, they both worked diligently together. When the bell sounded, Sandra wrote their names at the top of the worksheet, then gathered her belongings and walked up to Coach Pooch's desk to turn in their paper. Goldie was standing in the hallway and waiting on her when she walked out of the classroom. Sandra dropped her head in nervousness when she saw him.

Goldie walked up to her. "Hey, Sandra, let me holla at you for a minute," he said in a sexy tone that just made her melt.

"Whatta you wanna talk about?" Sandra asked him, as she stood holding her books up against her chest.

Goldie grabbed her arm, pulling her to the side by the lockers. She did not resist.

"Look, Sandra, I know you look at a nigga like I'm a thug. I mean...it's true that a nigga be thuggin' and shit, but a nigga got a decent head on they shoulders. Look, I paired up with you today for a reason."

"And why was that?" Sandra asked.

"See...me and you, we're on the same level. We got something in common; we both got a decent head on our shoulders. Listen, I've been watching you for a minute now. I dig you! You the type of girl a nigga will settle down with and marry someday."

"But don't you mess with Sheila?" Sandra asked, with an inquisitive look on her face.

"Man, that's just to be doing something," he shot back, waving off her question.

"Then why you mess with her?"

"I mean...it ain't like I don't like her or nothing. It's just that I really don't see no future with me and her. Now, with you, I see things differently. You got a future ahead of you. You got class, and a nigga like the way you carry yourself. You ain't like these other hoochie mommas around here throwing themselves at me, and that tells me that you got morals. All I'm asking for is a friendship," Goldie said, holding his hands out in sincerity.

There was silence, as the two stared into each other's eyes.

Goldie came a little closer. "All I want you to do is to get to know the real me," he said in a soft, irresistible voice.

Sandra felt light as a feather. How could she ever resist someone as fine as Goldie?

Goldie gently grabbed her chin. "And besides, I think you're beautiful," he added.

Sandra bashfully dropped her head and started blushing from ear to ear. Being that she was a late-bloomer, she rarely received compliments. She was beautiful, but all it seemed like boys in school cared about at the time was rather a girl had a big booty or big tits. Unfortunately for Sandra, good ole' Mother Nature had not blessed her with either yet.

"So whatta you say?" Goldie asked after a couple of seconds had passed.

Sandra knew she had to come up with an answer. She did not know a thing about boys. She had never been on a date, kissed, or even talked to a boy on the phone before. She courageously decided to try something different. *Besides, what can just talking on the phone do?* she thought to herself.

"So what about Sheila?" she asked.

Goldie shrugged his shoulders. "What about her?" he replied sarcastically.

"I'm saying, I don't want her to be all up in my face about you," Sandra said.

"Listen, Sheila don't run me! Besides, we ain't gonna be doing nothing but talking on the phone anyways. For starters at least," Goldie said, with a grin on his face that Sandra really did not want to trust.

Sandra gave him an inquisitive look, while she thought about his offer. Her mischievous side, which she did not know she had until now, told her to go for it.

"Alright, let me write down my number," she said, then opened up one of her folders, tore off a piece of paper, and wrote down her number.

Goldie stood with a smile on his face, waiting for her to finish. He had big plans for Sandra. He knew she was still a virgin, but he was not sweating that. She was going to be his little project. Besides, based on his popularity alone, he was seeing more high school pussy than a gynecologist. First, he was going to build a friendship with Sandra. Then when things progressed, he was going to make his move and drop Sheila like a bad habit and make Sandra his girl. Sheila was too stuck-up for him. He needed someone down to earth, like Sandra. He felt comfortable around her. She was not caught up like all of the other girls: wearing tight clothes, putting on excessive makeup, and having sex with athletes to be accepted. There was not a doubt in his mind that one day she would make the perfect wife.

Sandra handed him her number. "I guess you can call whenever you get a chance," she said, new to the whole boy thing.

"Alright, I'ma call at around seven then," he told her.

"Okay. Look, my class is on the other side. I'll talk to you tonight," she said, then waved goodbye and headed to her fifth period class.

"I'ma holla at you tonight!" Goldie yelled down the hallway, as he watched her disappear out of sight. He looked down at the piece of paper with Sandra's number on it, and then smiled. He nodded his head in approval. "I'ma make that girl my wife," he said to himself.

* * * * *

That night the two talked for hours. Goldie opened up to her, telling her all about his life struggles and touching on the impact of losing his father. Goldie always felt like the situation concerning his father was a sensitive issue, but he felt comfortable expressing his feelings to Sandra. Goldie got a little choked up when he talked about Snake and how much he missed him.

As their conversation progressed, Sandra was surprised at how much she and Goldie had in common. Her father had also passed when she was only eight years old. Goldie had her speechless. Not only was he intelligent, he was athletic, multi-talented, and the breadwinner of his family. Just by listening to his story, Sandra could tell he had been through a lot.

"And you say that you put down the down payment on your momma's house?" Sandra asked in disbelief.

"Yeah, I'm the man of the house now, so I gotta hold shit down," Goldie boasted.

Little did Goldie know, being a provider for his family earned him major points with Sandra. Now she understood why he did what he did. That night, Sandra went to bed seeing Goldie from a very different angle.

For the next couple of weeks, their conversations continued. They ended up becoming good friends, and everyday like clockwork Sandra's phone rang at four o'clock. Sometimes the two would talk four times a day, with some calls lasting up to three hours. Sandra had convinced her mom to install her own line in her room. She knew how much her sisters hogged up the line, and now, she did not have to worry about missing Goldie's call.

Goldie and Sandra became so caught up in each other that neither of them noticed the changes in how they were acting.

Sheila was the first one to notice. Lately, she wondered why Goldie did not want to talk to her on the phone as much as they use to. She had seen Goldie and Sandra in the hallway, laughing and giggling as if they were a couple.

"Man, you trippin'. We just good friends!" Goldie told Sheila when she popped the question on what was going on between the two.

Sandra's mom had even noticed the change in her behavior. Her mother knew it was only a matter of time before she became interested in boys. Being that Sandra had made it all the way through middle school without having one single crush on a boy, her mother was beginning to wonder if her daughter was destined to become a nun. Unlike her sisters, Sandra always stayed confined to her room, either reading or doing her homework.

That was the old Sandra, though. The new Sandra stayed in the mirror longer than she use to, wore perfume, and pranced around with a newfound attitude. Not only that, her body started to fill out.

The way Sandra made a total 360, her mother knew there had to be something special about the boy who her daughter was interested in.

One day, when Sandra and her mother was in the living room alone, her mother said, "Baby, tell me a little bit about this little boy that you're dating."

"Aw, Ma, we just friends," Sandra said, glowing and grinning from ear to ear.

Her mother patted her leg. "I know, baby, but that's how it starts out. Believe me, I know. Your daddy and I were friends once. Baby, I want you to feel like you can come and talk to me about anything. You're still a virgin, aren't you?" her mother asked, suspiciously eyeing her.

Sandra sucked her teeth. "Aw, Ma, I ain't even ever kissed a boy before!"

Her mother felt relieved. "I still wanna meet this boy," she insisted.

"But, Ma, we just friends!" Sandra told her for the second time.

"I know, and your momma wants to know what kind of friends you got. Ya'll may be friends now, but it can always escalate into something later. I wanna meet this boy! Invite him over for dinner Saturday," her mother said, then stood up and headed into the kitchen.

"But, Ma!" Sandra pouted as she followed behind her.

"My decision is final," her mother said, as she pointed her finger at Sandra.

Sandra just stood with her mouth poked out for a minute, then stormed into her room, slammed the door behind her, and dove onto her bed. What was she going to do? She knew her mother stereotyped all boys with gold in their mouths as thugs. Not only did Goldie have gold in his mouth, he also dressed like a thug. Sandra could see him now, knocking on the door with a creased up Dickie suit on. She knew that after taking one look at Goldie, her mother would ban him from ever coming over again. She wanted to tell him not to wear his gold plate in his mouth, and how to dress, but instead, just thought, "Whatever happens, happens."

Sandra picked up the phone and called Goldie to give him the news.

"Damn, so ya momma wanna meet a nigga? That's tight!" Goldie said, excited.

"Just make sure you're here on time at seven o'clock. My momma real funny about people being late," she said.

"Alright, tomorrow at 6:59 it is then," he joked.

"Boy, you so crazy! Bye," Sandra said, then hung up the phone with a glow on her face.

CHAPTER FORTY-FIVE

The smell of beef stew, collard greens, and homemade cornbread lingered in the air. Sandra nervously glanced over at the clock. It was 6:45 p.m. She could not sit still. Her future with Goldie depended on tonight.

"Sandra, I hope this boy doesn't make a bad impression with me by showing up late!" her mother yelled from the kitchen. "You know, whether a person is punctual or not tells a lot about their character. It lets you know how dependable they are."

Sandra just shook her head and rolled her eyes.

"You listen to your momma. Your momma knows!" her mother continued.

Sandra glanced back over at the clock. It was 6:50 p.m. "Come on, Goldie, where are you at?" she quietly said to herself. Sandra's mind started racing a hundred miles per hour. She really was into Goldie, and already had decided that even if things did not work out today, she was still going to sneak around and see him. She had learned firsthand never to stereotype someone based on their appearance alone.

When the doorbell rang, Sandra's face lit up. "I got it!" she yelled, as she hopped off the sofa and headed to the door. She smoothed out the wrinkles in her dress, and then asked, "Who is it?"

"It's me," Goldie arrogantly answered.

Sandra took a deep breath and opened the door. She instantly threw both of her hands up to her mouth, like the people from

Publisher's Clearinghouse was on her front porch with a gigantic check with her name on it.

"So you gonna let me in?" Goldie asked with a devilish grin.

Sandra was flabbergasted. Goldie was standing on her front porch in a pair of Eastland boots, some khaki Polo pants, and a plaid Polo shirt neatly tucked in his pants. He had taken his gold plate out of his mouth, displaying his pearly whites, and held two long stem roses in his hand.

"Come in!" Sandra said with a smile.

Goldie handed her one of the roses, then whispered, "I got this!" into her ear as he brushed by her.

When Goldie walked through the front door, Sandra's mother was standing in the kitchen nodding her head, impressed. Goldie casually walked into the kitchen and handed her the remaining rose.

"Why, thank you!" Sandra's mom said, blushing.

Goldie took her by the hand. "No, thank you for bringing someone as beautiful as Sandra into this world," he charmed.

Sandra's mother looked over at her and was flattered. Sandra smiled. Goldie released her hand, and then said, "Mmmm, it smells good in here. Is there anything I can pitch in and help you with?"

"I'm fine, honey. Dinner should be ready in about twenty minutes. In the meantime, sit down and tell me a little bit about yourself," her mother said, as she walked into the living room and sat down in the recliner.

"Ma!" Sandra yelled, embarrassed.

Goldie waved Sandra off. "It's cool! I'm open to whatever she wants to ask me."

"Sandra, won't you give us a couple of minutes together," her mother said.

Sandra eyed her mother, and then pouted to her room.

"As I was saying, Goldie, tell me a little bit about you," Sandra's mother said.

"Well, first of all, my real name is…"

* * * * *

Meanwhile, Sandra was lying in her bed, staring up at the ceiling and wondering what kind of questions her mother was asking Goldie. Goldie had impressed her. With each day, she learned something new about him. She smelled her rose, and then sighed. "I hope my momma don't mess things up," she said to herself.

Back inside of the living room, Sandra's mother was busy reading Goldie's body language. "So what are your intentions with my daughter?"

Goldie looked her directly in the eyes. "Listen, ma'am, Sandra is gonna be somebody when she grows up. She's different from all of the other girls. She's special. Just judging by the way that she carries herself, I can tell you raised her right. She has morals and values. Unlike all of these other wild girls, I can actually carry a civilized conversation on the phone with Sandra."

"And what about sex?" Sandra's mother asked.

"I ain't sweating that!"

Sandra's mother gave him a serious look. "Come on now, I was once young myself. I know how you young boys think."

"Listen, ma'am, I'm not your typical fifteen-year-old," Goldie replied.

Sandra's mother gave him a baffled look.

"What I'm trying to say, ma'am, is that I don't wanna sound conceited or nothing, but I'm the most popular guy in school. I can have sex with any girl I want. With Sandra, sex isn't even on my agenda."

Sandra's mother studied his face.

"I'm serious!" Goldie told her, pleading his case. "When I'm around Sandra, I feel comfortable because I can be myself. We sharpen each other's minds when we are on the phone by playing educational games. When it comes to education, these other girls got their priorities mixed up. All they seem to ever wanna talk about is music and fashion."

Sandra's mother was quiet for a moment. Although she thought Goldie had a lot of shit with him, she still had to admit she was impressed with how well mannered he was.

"Listen, DeQuan, all I ask is that you don't hurt my baby."

"I'll never hurt Sandra, ma'am, and I'll never let anybody else hurt her either," Goldie said.

"I have to admit, you impressed me tonight," Sandra's mother said with a partial smile.

Goldie smiled.

"I can tell you really must care about Sandra the way you went out of your way to dress appropriate to make yourself look presentable to me."

Goldie raised his eyebrows, giving her mother a puzzled look.

"Son, I ain't no fool," she said, walking over to the sofa and taking a seat on the arm, then crossing her legs. "Son, I know you're one of them boys who be up there on that corner. I didn't recognize you at first without that stuff in your mouth."

Goldie was speechless.

"First of all, let me tell you that I don't approve of what you're doing! However, after sitting here tonight, and listening to your story, I have to say I respect you for stepping up to the plate and being a provider for your family. That shows me strength, and I like that," Sandra's mother added.

Goldie smiled.

"Here's the deal," her mother said, standing up in front of Goldie. "Being that I've never seen my daughter as happy as she has been these last couple of weeks that the two of you have been socializing, I've decided to bend the rules."

"Yes!" Sandra said, gesturing with her hand, with her ear glued to the bedroom door.

"I've decided to allow you to continue seeing my daughter based on three circumstances. One, you keep that stuff out of your mouth whenever you come over here. Two, since the two of you stimulate each other's mind so much, I want both of you to maintain at least a 3.0 GPA, and three, if you should ever happen to step one foot in any jail, the minute you do, your future with my daughter is over," Sandra's mother said, laying down the law. "Deal?" she said, reaching out her hand for Goldie to shake on it.

Goldie stood up with a smile on his face. "Deal," he said, as the two of them shook hands.

"Sandra! You can come out now," her mother said, then walked into the kitchen to prepare the plates.

Sandra walked into the living room and sat on the sofa next to Goldie. Goldie threw his arm around her and she started blushing.

Sandra patted Goldie on the leg. "What did she ask you?"

Goldie eyed Sandra's mom, then returned his attention back to Sandra. He smiled.

"We just talked, that's all," he replied, with a smirk.

"Ummm hmmm, I bet ya'll did," Sandra said, suspiciously eyeing her mother.

* * * * *

After dinner, Goldie offered to help with the dishes, but Sandra's mother said she was all right.

While Sandra's mother cleaned up the kitchen, Sandra and Goldie watched a little TV.

After tidying up the kitchen, Sandra's mother stared at the two lovebirds for a moment and had a flashback of her high school fling with a thug, Sandra's father. "I'm gonna leave you two alone," she yelled from the kitchen as she took off her apron. "Thanks for the rose, and nice meeting you, Dequan."

Goldie stood up, then walked over and held out his hand for Sandra's mother. She attempted to shake his hand, but he charmingly took her hand and kissed it.

"Thank you for dinner, ma'am, but most of all, thank you for allowing me the chance to continue seeing your daughter. I won't disappoint you," he said.

Sandra's mother looked over at Sandra and shook her head. "You just make sure you take care of my baby," she said.

"Don't worry, Mrs. Johnson. I'm like Allstate Insurance; she's in good hands," Goldie replied.

His last comment made Sandra's mother walk off and wave her right hand in the air. "That boy too much," she mumbled to herself.

When Sandra and Goldie were alone, the two sat in total silence, staring into each other's eyes. They both attempted to talk at the same time. They started laughing.

"You go first," Goldie insisted, patting her on the thigh.

"I really enjoyed myself tonight."

"Me, too," Goldie replied.

"You really impressed my mom," Sandra said, laughing. "I'm just glad all of this is over. I really didn't want her to stand in the way of us getting to know each other. Now that you're welcomed, when are you coming back?"

"That's on you. When you want me to come back?" Goldie shot back.

"How about tomorrow afternoon at around four?" Sandra asked.

"That's cool," Goldie said as he stood up.

"What's wrong? Why are you leaving?" Sandra asked.

"Listen, boo, I would love to stay a little longer, but I gotta get back on the block. The first of the month is right around the corner, and I gotta get that bill money up. Walk me to the door," Goldie told her.

Sandra stood and walked him to the door. The two stepped out onto the porch. When Sandra closed the door behind her, Goldie grabbed her by the chin. He stepped forward, and then planted a soft, intimate kiss on her lips. Sandra just closed her eyes and enjoyed the kiss. The kiss felt so good that she thought her legs were going to buckle. After the kiss was over, Sandra opened her eyes and felt like she was in another world. Standing before her, she no longer saw Goldie as Goldie; he was now her knight in shining armor.

Sandra's mom was peeping through the curtains of her bedroom window and had seen everything. She smiled.

"Ahh, my baby got her first kiss," she said, as she closed the curtains.

CHAPTER FORTY-SIX

Today marked the first day of the 1990 school year.

"I'll see ya'll later," Sheila told her girls as Goldie escorted her to her first period class.

"So Goldie, we're going to the Valentine's Day dance, right?" Sheila asked, as she walked down the hallway with her arms folded and books up against her chest.

Goldie nervously rubbed on his head. He was caught up in a love triangle. The more time he spent with Sandra, the least interested he became with Sheila. To make matters worse, Sandra was starting to become bothered by Goldie and Sheila's relationship and showed signs of jealousy.

Sheila disturbingly stopped dead in her tracks. "How hard is it for you to give me an answer?" she asked with an attitude.

A couple of girls standing at their lockers stopped what they were doing to eavesdrop on Sheila and Goldie's conversation.

"I'll let you know," Goldie mumbled.

Sheila tooted up her nose. "You know, ever since I came back from visiting my family in New York during the Christmas break you've been acting funny. You don't even wanna hold my hand like we use to when we walk down the hallway. We don't talk on the phone anymore like we use to. I mean...what is it, Goldie? You don't wanna be with me no more?"

Goldie shook his head and massaged his temples. "Listen, man, I just got a lot on my mind."

"Like what?" Sheila asked, shifting her weight and throwing her hand on her hip with an attitude.

Goldie looked down the hallway and spotted Sandra at her locker. The two made eye contact.

"Listen, Sheila, we'll talk about this later," he said, then quickly kissed her on the cheek and disappeared down the hallway.

Sheila sucked her teeth, shook her head, and walked inside of her classroom.

When Sandra went to lock her locker, Goldie was leaning up against the one right next to hers.

"Whatta you want? I saw you down there talking with your little girlfriend," Sandra said, locking her locker and walking off.

"Wait a minute!" Goldie said, grabbing her arm.

"What?" Sandra asked, tapping her foot while staring up at the ceiling.

"Listen, Sandra...I promise, just give me another week to handle my business," Goldie pleaded.

"Humph!" Sandra said. "So you mean to tell me that she didn't ask you to take her to the dance?"

"Yeah, she asked, but I ain't going. Why, you going?" Goldie asked.

"For what?" Sandra asked.

"I don't know," Goldie said, shrugging his shoulders. "I thought you might be going with somebody."

Sandra gave him a stupid look. "Look, I gotta get to class," she said, then sashayed off.

"I'ma call you later on!" Goldie yelled.

"Whatever!" Sandra said, throwing her hand in the air as she disappeared down the hallway.

* * * * *

Later on that afternoon, Sandra rushed straight home from the bus stop and stayed cooped up in her room, staring up at the ceiling while trying to understand love. She affectionately caressed her teddy bear as she tried to figure Goldie out.

"Knock...knock. Can I come in?" her mother asked, peeping around the door.

"Yeah, come in," Sandra mumbled.

"Sandra," her mother said, eyeing her, "tell Momma what's wrong."

"It ain't nothing," Sandra said, dropping her head.

Sandra's mother lifted up her chin. "Sandra," she said.

"Okay...there's this dance..."

* * * * *

Meanwhile, Goldie was also engaged in conference himself.

"So, Youngblood, what's on your mind?" Dollar asked.

Goldie sat up on the edge of his chair, and then licked his lips. "Okay, it's like this. Man, Dollar, I'm trapped in a love triangle."

"Whatta you mean?" Dollar asked, curious.

"Okay, there's this one girl...she fine as hell, the captain of the cheerleading team, and the most popular girl in school. We been going together for a couple of months now, and at first, she was cool, but now I just don't dig her the same way," Goldie said.

"And what about this other girl?" Dollar asked.

Goldie's face lit up, and then he sat back in his chair and just smiled. He entwined his fingers. "Man...the way I feel when I'm around her...man, it's scary!"

Dollar studied his face and motioned with his hands. "Explain it to me," he said.

Goldie sat on the edge of his seat again. "Man, Dollar...she fine, smart as hell, and got some long-ass silky hair that reaches down to her back." Goldie stared up at the sky, and then shook his head. "Man, everything about her is right."

"So what's the problem then?" Dollar asked, raising his eyebrows.

Goldie dropped his head. "Man, she ain't doing nothing," he said.

Dollar looked at him with a puzzled expression.

"In other words, she ain't putting out...ya know...sex," Goldie clarified.

Dollar sat forward and looked Goldie in the eyes. "Let me get this straight, you really digging this other girl, but you ain't really trying to be with her because she ain't doing nothing?"

"Exactly!" Goldie said, nodding his head.

"Nigga, you a damn fool!" Dollar said, sitting back in his chair.

"Man, what you mean?" Goldie asked, confused.

"Youngblood, you think you know so much, but you don't know a damn thing about women! From what I'm hearing, and correct me if I'm wrong, this girl that you're with now she's controlling, isn't she?" Dollar asked.

"Yeah," Goldie said, smiling and shaking his head.

Dollar sucked his teeth and looked at his fingernails. "I give ya'll another month and ya'll gonna break up. Once she sees that she can't control you anymore, she gonna bounce right on to the next dude who's weak and who she can control. Right now, you just a trophy she walks around and shows off."

Goldie rubbed on his chin. He had never looked at it like that.

"Now, this other girl," Dollar said, pointing and shaking his finger at Goldie. "This other girl is gonna be something when she gets older. And you call yourself a player," Dollar said, sucking his teeth.

"I am!" Goldie said.

"Nigga you ain't a muthafuckin' thing! If you want my opinion, I think you need to drop your lil' girlfriend and get with this other girl. See, son, this other girl is wifey material. Regardless of how popular your lil' ass think you are, if this girl is keeping her legs closed, it says she was raised right and she has morals. That's the kind of girl that you want!" Dollar said, pointing his finger at Goldie.

Goldie shook his head and rubbed on his chin. "You know… you right," he mumbled.

Dollar placed his hand on his shoulder. "Every time I look at you I see an image of your father when he was your age. It's funny how history repeats itself," Dollar said, massaging his shoulders. "This good girl that you're telling me about kind of reminds me of your momma," Dollar said, smiling as he stared off into nowhere.

Goldie gave him a serious look.

Dollar defensively threw up his hands. "I don't want any trouble, Youngblood," Dollar joked.

"Man, you trippin'!" Goldie said.

"Naw, but seriously, this girl reminds me of your momma. Your momma was a bookworm in school. It's strange how opposites attract. Your daddy was the class clown and ran with a local gang called the Maniacs. Everything you've just told me about this girl describes exactly how your mother carried herself in high school," Dollar said. He laughed. "Hell, your daddy stayed with your momma for two years and didn't get any until their senior prom." Dollar laughed again, and then said, "Hell, that's how your oldest sister got here."

"You crazy!" Goldie said, slapping him on the shoulder.

"Listen, Youngblood, I gotta make a run," Dollar said, then stood up and gave Goldie dap.

"Alright, I got a couple of things I need to take care of myself. Good looking out, Dollar!" Goldie said, as the two embraced.

"Anytime, Youngblood," Dollar said, then pointed his finger at Goldie. "Don't let that good girl get away!"

Goldie smiled. "I won't. I'ma holla at you tomorrow," he said, then threw up a peace sign and headed to the house.

* * * * *

That night, Goldie called Sheila with every intention on breaking things off.

"Hello," Sheila answered on the third ring.

"What's up?" Goldie asked.

"Oh, hey, baby!" she said, twirling the phone cord. "I was just sitting here looking at this catalog with all of these cute dresses, and trying to pick out one to wear to the dance. You got fitted for your tux yet?" she asked, as she flipped through the pages of the catalog.

"Naw, I ain't got fitted yet," Goldie mumbled.

Sheila attentively sat up in the bed. "Why?"

"Listen, man, that's what I called to tell you. I ain't going to the dance."

"What? Whatta you mean you ain't going?" Sheila asked with an attitude.

"I just ain't going," Goldie said.

"Unhh Unhh, you taking me to the dance!" she demanded.

Goldie shook his head. "That's the controlling shit that Dollar was talking about," he mumbled to himself.

"Listen, Goldie, I don't know what's going on with you right now, but I'm gonna give you a little time to think about this. Everybody else's boyfriends are taking them!"

"Listen, man, I just need a little time to myself," Goldie said.

"Some time? For what? You cheating on me, Goldie?" Sheila asked.

"Ain't nobody cheating on you!" Goldie spat. Truthfully, he was not, because he and Sandra had only kissed.

"Well, I'm just letting you know that I'm going to that dance, with or without you!" Sheila stated.

"Alright," Goldie said, and then hung up.

"Goldie...Goldie," Sheila said, then frowned up her face when she heard the dial tone.

She stared at the phone in disbelief. "Unhh Unhh, I know he didn't just hang up on me."

CHAPTER FORTY-SEVEN

The student council had done an excellent job on the decorations inside of the gym. Cupids with arrows and various size hearts decoratively hung from the ceiling. Carnations were throughout the gym.

The walkway to the picture booth was set up with red carpet, and had an elegant chair sitting in the middle, with red silk drapes that served as the backdrop.

All of the guys were decked out in their tuxedos and shiny pointed-toe shoes, while the girls pranced around like queens in their elegant dresses and fresh hairdo's.

Principal Reeves walked over to the D.J. booth and grabbed the microphone. "Good evening, everyone. First of all, I'd like to welcome everyone to the 40th annual Student Council Valentine's Day Dance," she said.

Everyone started clapping.

"Let's give another round of applause to our student council for the beautiful decorations," Principal Reeves said.

Once again, the crowd clapped.

"And now, I turn it over to D.J. Easy T," Principal Reeves said, handing over the mic.

"Ya'll ready to party up in here?" D.J. Easy T asked.

"Yeah!" the crowd yelled.

"Well let's get this party started!"D.J. Easy T shouted.

"Set It Off" came blasting through the speakers, and everybody rushed to the dance floor and started doing the electric slide.

While everyone was on the dance floor, two knuckleheads, Willie and Billy, reached into their coat jackets, pulled out two bottles of Vodka, spiked the punch, and then vanished.

"Sheila, you look so cute!" Jenny Myers told her.

"Thanks!" she said.

* * * * *

Meanwhile, Goldie was still at home standing in front of the bathroom mirror.

"Goldie! This limo is outside. Boy, you had better hurry up. You're already thirty minutes late!" his mother yelled.

"I'm coming!" Goldie yelled, as he adjusted his tie.

He looked down at his Gucci watch and saw that it was ten o'clock. He felt like now was the perfect time to make his grand entrance.

Goldie blew a kiss at the mirror. "Damn, you a fine motherfucker."

"Ahh! Don't my baby look handsome!" Loretta said when he walked out of the bathroom, and then took a couple of pictures with her camera.

Goldie arrogantly posed, as if he was in a photo shoot. After taking five different pictures in five different poses, Goldie kissed his mother on the cheek and headed out to the limo.

"Enjoy yourself!" his mother yelled.

"I will!" Goldie yelled back, as he eased into the backseat of the limo. He let down the window and yelled, "I should be home around two!"

"Just enjoy yourself!" his mother said.

Goldie waved his mother goodbye, and then let up the window as the limo driver pulled off.

* * * * *

Back at the dance, Sheila and her two sidekicks, Jocelyn and Alice, were picking at all of the other girls' dresses and hair dos.

"Unnhhh unhhh, what was she thinking to think she could wear that dress without a girdle to hold everything in place," Alice commented about a fat girl.

"Unnhh unhhh, Tina Bell know damn well her black ass can't wear no red lipstick," Jocelyn said.

The girls went on and on picking on everybody that walked through the door.

Meanwhile, Goldie was just arriving at the dance. The limo driver parked, hopped out of the car, and opened the backdoor. Goldie eased out of the backseat, then stood up and adjusted his jacket.

"Enjoy yourself tonight, sir?" the driver told Goldie.

Goldie nodded his head, and handed the driver a twenty-dollar tip. "The dance is over at one o'clock. Make sure you're parked out front at 12:30."

"I'll be right here, sir," the driver said, tipping his hat.

Goldie vainly inspected his appearance in the limo's window, and then ran his hand across his waves. He smiled, spun around, and headed up the sidewalk. The sound system was pumping inside of the gym. Goldie anxiously rubbed his hands together as he listened to the sounds of "It Takes Two" by Rob Base when he entered.

"Ticket, please," Mrs. Hampton said. Goldie handed her his ticket. "Thank you. Enjoy!" she said.

When Goldie walked through the gym doors, it was all eyes on him. All of the girls savagely looked at him as if they were deserted on an island with no food and he was a 16-ounce steak. Goldie was decked out from head to toe in an all-white Sacino & Son's tuxedo and a pair of white pointed-toe dress shoes.

"Heeeyyy, Goldie!" a group of girls said, as they stood in a daze and waved as he walked by them.

Goldie just grinned, nodded his head, and said, "What's up?"

"Damnnnnn! Goldie looks good!" Jocelyn said when she spotted him.

"Where?" Sheila said, breaking her neck to look for Goldie. When Sheila spotted him, she rushed over to where he was standing. "Hey, you!" she said, jumping in front of Goldie.

Goldie acknowledged her with a head nod.

Sheila grabbed him by the arm and led him over by the bleachers.

"Man, what the fuck is wrong with you?" Goldie asked Sheila with a grimace on his face.

"Look, I know that it seems like I've been tripping a lot lately, but I'm use to getting my way. I guess you can say I'm spoiled. But anyways, why don't we just put all that has happened in the past couple of weeks behind us and just enjoy ourselves tonight," Sheila suggested.

"Listen, man, like I told you, I just need a little space!" Goldie said bluntly.

Sheila's blood got hotter than fish grease. She folded her arms. "Fine!" she said, and took off with an attitude.

Goldie just shook his head as he watched her walk off, and then headed over to the buffet table to grab a bite to eat.

* * * * *

Twenty minutes passed and Goldie was becoming bored. He was ready to leave, but right when he prepared to, his plans changed.

When Sandra walked into the gym, it seemed like everyone paused for a second and stood frozen. She looked like a contestant for Mrs. America.

"Damnnn! Sandra?" a group of boys asked in disbelief.

"Oh my God!" Alice and Jocelyn said, as they threw their hands up to their mouths.

When Sheila turned around to see what all of the commotion was about, she distastefully tooted up her nose. As much as she hated to admit, Sandra looked stunning.

"Woooow!" a group of boys yelled, and then started whistling at Sandra.

Goldie was busy talking to a couple of the fellas, when he inquisitively turned around to seeing why they were all whistling. His eyes got as big as quarters, and his mouth dropped down to the ground.

"Excuse me. Excuse me," Goldie said, as he made his way through the crowd.

Little did Goldie know Sandra was searching through the crowd for him. She smiled, then dropped her head and started blushing when she saw him heading her way.

Goldie greeted her with a warm smile when he made it over to her. He shook his head as he admired her beauty, examining her from head to toe. "I thought you said you weren't coming?"

Sandra smiled, and then shrugged her shoulders. "My momma and sisters talked me into coming."

"Wow!" Goldie said, taking her by the hand and spinning her around.

"You like?" Sandra asked.

"Hell yeah!" Goldie replied, foaming from the mouth.

Sandra looked beautiful. Her long, silky hair was let down, her lipstick was popping, she smelled edible, and she was wearing just the right amount of makeup. She was wearing an elegant satin dress with spaghetti straps, while exposing her French pedicure in a pair of sexy open-toe heels.

Goldie grabbed Sandra by the hand, and they stepped off to the side.

"Gurl, looks like you may lose your man tonight, Sheila!" Alice said, as she sipped on her third cup of punch.

Sheila gave Alice a look that said, "Say it again."

"You gotta be honest though, Sheila. Sandra does look cute tonight," Jocelyn said.

"Humph!" Sheila said. She fumingly folded her arms and frowned, while watching Goldie and Sandra laughing and giggling as though they were newlyweds. "Okay, two can play this game," she said, as she stormed towards the varsity basketball team.

"Look who's coming our way," Stan Rogers said.

Ronnie White smiled when he saw Sheila heading in his direction. He was the captain of the varsity basketball team, an honor student, and came from a wealthy family. Since the first day of school, Ronnie had his eyes on Sheila and vowed to make her his girl. He was crushed when he found out Sheila was Goldie's girl.

Sheila boldly walked over to Ronnie and grabbed his hand. "Let's dance."

Ronnie took a sip from his cup, and then handed it to one of his teammates as he willingly followed Sheila to the dance floor. The entire team cheered him on.

"Oh, I see you've finally come to your senses," Ronnie yelled over the music.

"Just shut up and dance," Sheila told him, then turned around and started dancing.

Meanwhile, Goldie and Sandra were in their own little world.

Sheila kept glancing over at Goldie to see if he was paying her any attention, but he wasn't. Therefore, she decided to turn things up a notch. When "Move Something" came on, Sheila grabbed Ronnie's hands, placed them on her waist, and started dancing dirty. Everyone on the dance floor stepped back and made room for the two. Sheila lifted up her dress and started dropping like it was hot. Ronnie tried his best to keep up with her, but holding on to Sheila's waist while she danced was like riding a bull. The crowd cheered Sheila and Ronnie on.

Ricky Barber came over and nudged Goldie, then pointed out on the dance floor and said, "Isn't that ya girl?"

Goldie and Sheila made eye contact. Goldie just smirked at her and nodded his head.

"I gotta go to the bathroom," Sandra said, then stood up and disappeared.

"I'll be over by the bleachers," Goldie told her, as he headed over towards the bleachers.

For the next ten minutes, Goldie just mingled with everybody and waited for Sandra to return from the bathroom.

"Alright, everybody, it's midnight, and I think it's about time we slow it down. So, fellas, grab that special someone and make your way to the dance floor," D.J. Easy T said.

As everyone paired up with their dates, Sheila pulled away from Ronnie and searched the gym for Goldie.

"Aren't we gonna slow drag?" Ronnie asked.

Sheila gave him the hand, then left him standing on the dance floor looking stupid as she headed over to her girls.

"Hey, Ronnie, wanna dance?" Pam Moore asked him.

Ronnie shrugged his shoulders, and then took Pam up on her offer.

* * * * *

Goldie had made his rounds around the gym and was searching for Sandra. "Damn!" he said when he spotted her sitting behind Sheila and her girls. Goldie headed over to her.

When Alice spotted Goldie walking towards them, she nudged Sheila. "Girl, here comes Goldie!"

Sheila just smiled. "Watch this, ya'll. I'ma play hard to get at first and make him beg a little bit, and then I'ma give in. I knew that I'd make him jealous."

"What up?" Goldie asked when he walked over to the three.

Sheila confidently stared up in the air, as if she was waiting on an apology.

Goldie walked over to Sheila. "You know, I was wrong thinking that maybe we needed to spend a little time apart."

"Ummm hmmm," Sheila said, looking at her nails and waiting on Goldie's apology.

When Sandra looked up and saw Goldie talking to Sheila, she was ready to go.

"Listen, Sheila, what we really need to do is break up," Goldie said.

Sheila's eyes got big as quarters. "Huh?" she said.

Goldie smiled. "You heard me. It's over," he said, and then walked off to get his girl.

Sheila was left looking like a fool. Her plan had backfired.

While everyone were mingling and enjoying themselves, Sandra was sitting alone with her head in her lap. She knew she should have never come. The only reason why she had come was that her mother and sisters had convinced her not to give up on Goldie.

Roger Troutman and Zapp's "I Wanna Be Your Man" came on.

"Excuse me, mind if I have this dance?" Goldie asked Sandra, reaching out his hand.

Sandra thought she was dreaming. When she lifted up her head, she was surprised to see Goldie standing over her with a glow that looked like he was her guardian angel. Sandra willingly took his hand and stood up, as he led her to the center of the dance floor.

"Unnhh unhhh! I know he didn't!" Alice said, as she watched Goldie place Sandra's hands around his neck, and then wrap his arms around her waist.

"But I-," Sandra tried to get out, but Goldie placed his hands on her lips.

"Shhhh…just listen to the song," Goldie told her.

Sandra stared into Goldie's hazel eyes and was mesmerized. The two moved together like professional dancers.

"Why are you doing this?" Sandra asked.

"I'm just listening to my heart," he charmed. "I wanna be your man," he told Sandra, then softly planted an intimate kiss on her lips.

Sheila's mouth dropped to the ground when she saw Goldie and Sandra tongue kissing out on the dance floor.

"Don't worry, gurl, you can get any man in here you want. Except for Goldie," Alice said.

"Shut up, Alice!" Sheila said, and then stormed to the bathroom.

* * * * *

While Goldie and Sandra danced, Goldie popped the question. "So...do you wanna be my girl or what?"

Sandra nodded her head.

Goldie jokingly put his ear by her mouth. "I can't hear you."

"Yes," Sandra said over the music.

Goldie smiled. "Then it's official now. You're my girl."

After two slow songs, Goldie and Sandra worked their way over to the picture booth and waited in line. Goldie admired her natural beauty while they waited.

"Next," the photographer said when it was Goldie and Sandra's turn.

The two stepped into the booth, then Goldie took a seat in the chair and Sandra sat on his lap. After their mini-photo shoot, the two mingled through the crowd as a couple. Sandra bashfully blushed as Goldie held her hand and introduced her to everyone as his new girl.

A while later, Goldie looked at his watch. It was 12:45 a.m.

"Listen, my limo's outside. Let's blow this place," Goldie said, and then lead Sandra out of the door.

When Goldie and Sandra arrived at the limo, the driver graciously opened the back door for them.

"Ahhh...I see you have company," the driver said.

Sandra blushed as she hopped into the backseat, with Goldie right behind her.

When the driver got behind the steering wheel, he let down the privacy window, and asked, "Where do you want me to go?"

"Just drive!" Goldie told him, then let up the privacy window, grabbed Sandra's hand, and stared into her eyes. He ran his hand through her long, silky hair. "You need to wear your hair like this all the time," he suggested.

Sandra giggled. "It was my mother and sisters' idea."

"Well, I need to thank them," Goldie said, as he stretched his body out across the backseat and laid his head in her lap.

Sandra massaged his chest, while the two stared into each other's eyes. Sandra initiated a kiss.

"Mmmm, that taste good," he said, licking his lips after the kiss. An idea came to mind. Goldie sat up. "Why don't you stay the night with me tonight?"

"Where?" Sandra asked.

"We'll get a room."

"I don't know," Sandra said, dropping her head and nervously fiddling with her nails.

Goldie lifted up her chin, and then grabbed her hand. "Let's make tonight special," he whispered softly, while staring into her eyes.

Sandra bit her bottom lip.

"Come on, boo, let's not ruin the night. Besides, what better night than tonight," Goldie said.

"I'm not ready," Sandra replied.

"You are ready. You just think I'm gonna look at you differently if we do it," Goldie said, like he was reading Sandra's mind.

"How I know that ain't all you want?"

"Listen, I'm crazy about you, boo! Whether we do it or not, I'm still gonna feel the same way that I feel about you," Goldie charmed.

Sandra smiled. "Fo' real?"

"Fo' sho! But I really would like for us to take things to another level," Goldie replied honestly.

Sandra stared into Goldie's eyes and lost the battle. She sighed, and then said, "Okay, I'll do it." She pointed her finger at Goldie. "But you gotta promise you ain't gonna hurt me."

"I promise," Goldie said, then let down the privacy window and yelled, "Peter, swing by my house so I can grab my boom box."

CHAPTER FORTY-NINE

Goldie and Sandra were so busy in the backseat kissing that they did not notice they had been parked in front of Goldie's house for five minutes.

The limo driver lowered the privacy window. "We're here, sir."

Sandra placed her hand up to her mouth and started giggling.

Goldie adjusted his jacket, then told Sandra, "I'll be right back," and hopped out of the car.

Goldie walked up the sidewalk in a cheerful mood. However, that mood instantly changed when he reached the front door. He thought his mind was playing tricks on him. It sounded like he heard his mother screaming inside of the house. Deliriously, he quickly stuck his key into the lock and opened the door.

"Stop it, Leroy! Stop! You're drunk!" Loretta screamed.

Goldie ran down the hallway to his room, lifted up his mattress, grabbed his 9mm, and stormed towards his mother's bedroom. He threw the clip in and cocked one in the chamber.

"Shut up, bitch!" Goldie heard Leroy say, and then heard him slap his mother.

"Oh Lord," Loretta cried.

Goldie furiously kicked down his mother's bedroom door like the S.W.A.T team. He went delusional when he saw Leroy, who his mother had been dating recently, naked on top of his mother's body, raping her. The bed was bare, and his mother was lying in a puddle of blood. Loretta looked exhausted.

Goldie snapped. "Motherfucker, get off of my momma!" he yelled, pointing his gun at Leroy.

Leroy smiled, then threw his hands up in the air and eased out of the bed. "Oh, what you gonna do, shoot me you lil' punk muthafucka?"

"Move over by the wall," Goldie told Leroy, as he made his way over to the bed to check on his mother. "Momma, you alright?"Goldie asked sympathetically.

Loretta moved her hair out of her eyes. "I'm finna call the police on this bastard!" she said, picking up the phone.

"I told you this motherfucker wasn't shit!" Goldie said with a grimace on his face.

As the two men stared into each other's eyes, Goldie had a flashback to that night when he could not pull the trigger on Rufus.

"Bitch, hang up that damn phone!" Leroy yelled.

"Call my momma a bitch again and I'ma peel your muthafuckin' cap!" Goldie yelled, as he gripped his gun a little tighter and stepped a little closer.

Leroy smirked. "Lil' nigga, you ain't got the heart to pull that trigger."

Goldie bit his bottom lip. "Try me!" he replied with a poker face.

"Yes, I would like to report a raping," Loretta told the dispatcher.

"Bitch, I told you to hang up that phone!" Leroy yelled.

Goldie came a little closer. "Call her a bitch one more time!"

Leroy just smiled. "You right...she ain't no bitch. She a bloody bitch!"

Goldie fired five shots to Leroy's face, and his brains came out of the side of his head. Blood splattered everywhere.

Sandra and the limo driver jumped when they heard the gunshots from inside of the house.

Leroy's lifeless body fell to the ground. Loretta nervously dropped the phone.

"Ma'am, ma'am, is everything alright?" the operator yelled through the phone.

Goldie dropped his smoking gun to his side, and then rushed over to assist his mother. He took Loretta into his arms and kept repeating, "It's okay now," as he rocked her back and forth in his arms.

"I'm going in to see what happened," Sandra told the limo driver, then courageously ran inside of the house to check on Goldie. Sandra pushed the cracked door open and yelled, "Goldie, are you alright?"

"I'm in my momma's room!" Goldie yelled.

Sandra rushed to the bedroom, and cautiously entered when she observed blood splattered all over the walls. "What happened?" she asked.

"That motherfucker was raping my momma!" Goldie said, while still protectively rocking Loretta.

Sandra went into convulsions when she looked down on the floor and saw Leroy lying with his brains hanging out of his head. She got lightheaded, and then passed out by the walk-in closet.

In less than five minutes, the entire house was squirming with police officers. Five police officers entered the house and identified themselves.

"Police, we have reports of gunshots," the lead officer yelled.

"In here!" Loretta yelled from the bedroom.

One by one, the officers cautiously entered the room with their guns drawn.

"Ma'am, are you the one who reported a raping?" the lead officer asked.

Loretta shook her head.

"Ma'am, I'm Officer Lewis. What happened?" the officer asked, putting away his gun.

"He was raping me and my son came in and tried to stop him."

Officer Lewis scribbled a couple of things on his pad. "Then what happened?"

"He charged towards my son, and my son shot him in self-defense," Loretta said.

"Is this true?" Officer Lewis asked Goldie.

"Yep," Goldie replied, without the slightest bit of emotion.

"What about the little girl?" Officer Lewis questioned.

"She's my son's girlfriend. She passed out when she saw all of the blood," Loretta told him.

Just then, two homicide detectives walked into the room.

"What we got here, Lewis? Jesus Christ! Who did him in?" Detective Woodson asked, observing Leroy's body lying on the floor.

"Well, the guy was raping the kid's mother, and the kid grabs a gun and blows the guy's head off."

The detectives and Officer Lewis looked over at Goldie.

"Jesus, the kid isn't the slightest bit shook up," Detective Woodson said, before walking over to view the body. "Jesus Christ, he did blow his whole fucking head off!"

"It looks like self-defense to me," Lewis said.

"Where did the kid say he got the gun from?" Woodson asked.

Lewis shrugged his shoulders. "I didn't ask him."

"Well, we'll let a court of law decide if it was self-defense," Woodson said.

"But what are we gonna charge him with?" Lewis asked.

"Second-degree murder for now," Woodson replied.

When Goldie saw Officer Lewis walking their way with the long face, he already knew what time it was.

"Ma'am, I'm gonna have to take your son into custody," Officer Lewis told Loretta.

Goldie patted his mother's hand, kissed her on the forehead, and then courageously held out his hands to be cuffed.

"For what?" Loretta asked.

"I'm sorry," Officer Lewis said sympathetically, as he cuffed Goldie.

A crew of paramedics entered the room. One gave Sandra some smelling salt, while the other came over to attend to Loretta.

Loretta pushed the paramedic out of the way. "Where are ya'll taking my baby?"

"Ma'am, you're in no condition to be getting yourself worked up," the paramedic told her, while sitting her down in the bed.

"What's going on?" Adriana, Ciera, and Melissa asked as they entered the bedroom.

"We're gonna have to ask you guys to leave," one of the officers told the three, and then tried to escort them out of the room.

The three maneuvered away from the officer. "This is our momma!" they said, as they rushed to Loretta's side.

"Don't worry. I'ma be alright," Goldie looked back and told his mother.

"No!" Loretta yelled, reaching out her hand as she watched two officers escort Goldie out of the room.

"Okay, everybody, make room!" the officers outside of the house said.

Goldie could not believe his eyes when he stopped outside of the house. Dozens of cameras were flashing in his face, news reporters were asking him a million questions, and hundreds of nosey neighbors had gathered outside of the house. Although it was two o'clock in the morning, the street was lit up like a football stadium. Goldie was ushered through the crowd and placed in the backseat of a police cruiser. He just stared in awe and smiled as the photographers snapped picture after picture of him. He looked down at his tuxedo, and saw that in the midst of everything he had not accumulated one stain. When the cruiser escorting Goldie drove off, he turned around, took one last glance at what he called home, and wondered when he would ever return.

CHAPTER FIFTY

Goldie was booked at the county jail and arraigned the next day on charges of second-degree murder, and scheduled a speedy trail. His case was the talk of the jail. Everyone looked at him like he was a cold-hearted killer.

Leroy ended up having a closed casket funeral. Loretta refused to attend the funeral, and was still in shock from the whole ordeal.

For the next couple of months, Goldie stayed confined to his cell, with a t-shirt wrapped around his head, doing push-ups and sit-ups, getting his weight up. He knew he was going to have to do some time, but he did not know how much.

Sandra religiously wrote Goldie every day, and called the radio station on Sunday nights to make dedications to him during the Quiet Storm. Reading Sandra's mail was what kept Goldie's sanity, along with the visits from his mom.

When his day in court rolled around, Goldie was ready to get everything over with. He was tired of the unknown, and was just ready to get his time, start on his bid, and get back home.

"Walker, they're ready for you," the bailiff said, as he released Goldie from the holding cell and escorted him to the courtroom.

The courtroom was packed. Goldie located his mother and Sandra, and then gave them both a warm smile as he took his seat next to his lawyer.

"I love you, baby," his mother whispered, as she gripped her handkerchief.

Goldie winked at her, and then blew her a kiss. After smiling at Sandra, he turned and faced forward.

For the next twenty minutes, the prosecution drilled the jury with her opening statements, and then it was Goldie's lawyer's turn.

"Self-defense. This case says nothing else but self-defense," Ira Bernstein said, as he re-capped what happened on that night. "What would you have done?" Mr. Bernstein asked the jury, as he made eye contact with each one of them. "Your mother is being raped...the woman who brought you into this world is standing in front of your very eyes and being raped! You try to stop her assailant, but he charges towards you. You have a gun, you're young, and you're scared. What would you do?" Bernstein asked, and then sat down.

For the rest of the trial, Bernstein drilled self-defense into the jury's head. As he proceeded with his case, he read the faces on the jury, and knew he had the bulk of them eating out of his hand.

As the trail progressed, Judge Stoudemeire saw that the trial was going one way. He quickly intervened, to save both parties time and the government money. He distressfully took off his glasses and rubbed on his forehead.

"Will both counsels approach the bench," he said.

Mrs. Wilcox and Mr. Bernstein both looked at each other baffled.

"I'll be right back," Bernstein leaned over and whispered to Goldie, then approached the bench, joining Mrs. Wilcox.

Whispers could be heard throughout the courtroom.

"What is it, Your Honor?" Bernstein asked when he approached the bench.

Judge Stoudemeire eyed the two, then leaned forward and whispered, "You two are pissing away government money." He directed his attention to Mrs. Wilcox. "Your case is going nowhere."

Mrs. Wilcox dropped her head.

"I'm gonna call recess, and what I suggest you two do is put your egos to the side for a moment," the judge said.

"But-" Mrs. Wilcox tried to get out.

Judge Stoudemeire pointed his finger at her. "Mrs. Wilcox, I suggest you come up with a sensible plea, and Mr. Bernstein, I suggest you willingly accept."

"I have no problem if the plea is fair," Bernstein added.

Judge Stoudemeire eyed him, and then told the two, "Return back to your tables."

"What was all of that about?" Goldie leaned over and whispered to Bernstein when he returned to the table.

"The judge told the prosecutor that her case is going nowhere, and he suggests that we reach a plea agreement," Bernstein said.

Goldie smiled. "So that means we have them by the balls?"

"Not exactly. Even if we beat the murder, since you're charged as an adult, you still could be looking at three years at least for the gun," Bernstein informed him.

Judge Stoudemeire directed his attention to the jury. "Members of the jury, I'm afraid we have some aggravating factors that need to be addressed. We're gonna take a quick recess, and we'll return at one o'clock. Court is adjourned!" the judge said, then hit his gavel and departed from the bench.

Everyone in the courtroom was left with puzzled looks on their faces. Leroy's family could not figure out what was going on. Goldie looked over at them and smirked, then nodded his head.

"Okay, Walker, let's go," the bailiff came over to Goldie and said.

Goldie rose to his feet, blew his mother and Sandra a kiss, then the bailiff escorted him back to his holding cell.

* * * * *

Mrs. Wilcox and Mr. Bernstein were in the judge's chambers slugging it out. They went on and on for two hours, debating and quoting cases back and forth. The two were stubborn workaholic classmates, who had graduated in the top of their class from Stetson. After two hours of debating, the two reached a mutual agreement. Mrs. Wilcox agreed to drop Goldie's second-degree murder charges down to manslaughter in exchange for a guilty plea. Bernstein agreed to enter a guilty plea to manslaughter, with the stipulation that adjudication be withheld after the completion of a level-10 youthful offenders program. The two put everything in black and white, looked over the documents, shook hands, and then headed to Subway to grab a bite to eat and reminisce on old college days.

When one o'clock rolled around, everyone gathered back inside the courtroom, waiting to hear the verdict.

"Okay, welcome back, everybody," the judge joked.

Everyone laughed.

"Mrs. Wilcox, Mr. Bernstein, have we reached an agreement?" the judge asked.

Mrs. Wilcox and Mr. Bernstein looked at each other, and then shook their heads.

"Yes, we have, Your Honor," Mrs. Wilcox said.

"Mr. Bernstein, is your client willingly ready to enter a guilty plea?" the judge asked.

"Yes, Your Honor," Bernstein said.

Mumbles and whispers filled the courtroom. Leroy's family was fumingly sitting with their arms folded, wondering what in the hell was going on.

Judge Stoudemeire directed his attention to the jury, and then smiled. "I apologize, but at this time, I'm gonna have to ask the members of the jury to leave the courtroom."

Judge Stoudemeire waited until the jury was ushered out, before continuing. "Mr. Walker, are you knowingly and willingly entering this guilty plea and waving your rights to a trial?" the judge asked Goldie.

"Yes, Your Honor," Goldie said. He looked over the plea agreement, and then signed it.

The judge looked over Goldie's guilty plea, accepted it, and then called the jury back in.

"Once again, I apologize," the judge told the jury members. "I'd like to thank you all for taking today off from your jobs and sitting in on the jury. This case has reached a plea agreement. So, at this time, everyone is dismissed."

After the jury left the courtroom for the second time, the judge set Goldie's sentencing date thirty days from that day's date, hit his gavel, and dismissed court.

EPILOGUE

Thirty days later, Goldie was sentenced to a level-10 youthful offenders program for sixty months on charges of manslaughter and possession of a firearm. Leroy's family was pissed. They felt the judge was too lenient on Goldie.

"Walker, roll it up!" Goldie heard an officer come to his cell and yell.

"Damn, what time is it?"Goldie mumbled, as he looked over at the clock in the pod. "Damn, it's two-thirty in the muthafuckin' morning," he said, as he sat up in his bunk.

"Damn, celly, you out of here," Bullet said, while sitting up in his bunk, also.

"Yeah, I'm outta here," Goldie replied, making his way over to the sink to wash his face.

Bullet swung his feet around to the edge of the bunk. "They taking you to OCI today to get classified."

"I'm just ready to start on the bid, you feel me?" Goldie said, as he brushed his teeth.

"I feel you, playboy!"

After brushing his teeth, Goldie walked over to his box, grabbed his commissary, and handed it to Bullet. "Here, my nigga, this outta hold you down for a couple of weeks."

Bullet's face lit up. "Good looking out, dawg. You a real ass nigga!"

He and Bullet had been cellmates for six months, and the two had gotten close. Bullet was still waiting to go to trial on five armed robberies. Bullet had an extensive record, and knew he was looking at doing at least a dime.

"Here go my ole' girl's address and number," Goldie said, handing Bullet a piece of paper.

"Alright, pretty boy, let's go," the officer told Goldie. "Slide lower two," the officer said into his walkie-talkie.

The cell opened.

Bullet hopped down off the top bunk, then gave Goldie a farewell hug. "Be easy, my nigga. We gonna hook up when I touch," Bullet said, as the two embraced.

"Fo' sho'," Goldie replied.

"Alright, enough of the mushy shit," the officer joked.

Bullet released Goldie. "Fuck you, Jones. This my nigga!"

Goldie grabbed all of his legal work and personal belongings, gave Bullet dap, and then stepped out of the cell.

"Close lower two," the officer said into his walkie-talkie, and the cell closed.

Goldie patted his chest a couple of times at Bullet.

"Be easy, my nigga!" Bullet told him.

"Alright, you niggas, I'm outta this motherfucker!" Goldie yelled to the tier.

Everyone rushed to their gates, and yelled out various farewell words.

Goldie was placed in a holding cell with about fifty other dudes. Almost two hours later, they were all shackled and marching down the hallway in a single file line to a bus. One by one, the inmates were called up to state their name and date of birth, then loaded onto the bus.

"Walker!" the officer yelled.

Goldie wobbled his way up the bus stairs, stated his name and date of birth, then found him a window seat in the back of the bus.

By 4:30 a.m., the bus pulled out of the Pinellas County Jail and headed to Orlando Reception Institution. Goldie just stared out of the window at the city and smiled, as he already started making plans for his return.

The End...or is it?

ORDER FORM

Mail to: BURGSTYLE PUBLISHING, LLC
P.O. BOX 13047
ST. PETERSBURG, FLORIDA 33733-3047

Name: _____

Address: _____

_____

Email: _____

TITLE	PRICE	QUANTITY
Ghetto Résumé	$14.95	

**SHIPPING/HANDLING: ADD $3.00 per book
(Shipped via U.S. Media Mail)
TOTAL: $_____**

FORMS OF ACCEPTED PAYMENTS:

Personal checks (additional delays may incur pending bank clearance), institutional checks & money orders are preferred methods of payment. Burgstyle Publishing, LLC does NOT recommend sending cash through the postal system. All mail-in orders take 5-7 business days to be delivered.

Contact Publisher directly about discounting availability for special bulk orders (ten-book minimum).

FREDDIE SIMMONS